The Boxcar Children Mysteries

The Boxcar Children Mysteries

THE BOARDWALK MYSTERY

created by
GERTRUDE CHANDLER WARNER

ALBERT WHITMAN & Company
Chicago, Illinois

Library of Congress Cataloging-in-Publication Data

Warner, Gertrude Chandler
The boardwalk mystery / by Gertrude Chandler Warner ;
[interior illustrations by Robert Dunn].
p. cm. — (The Boxcar children mysteries ; 131)
Summary: "The Aldens visit the shore in New Jersey and help out at an
amusement pier that is rumored to be unsafe"—Provided by publisher.
ISBN 978-0-8075-0802-2 (hardcover)—ISBN 978-0-8075-0803-9 (pbk.)
[1. Mystery and detective stories 2. Brothers and sisters—Fiction. 3. Orphans—
Fiction. 4. Beaches—Fiction. 5. Amusement parks—Fiction. 6. New Jersey—Fiction.]
I. Dunn, Robert, ill. II. Title.
PZ7.W244Bnm 2013
[Fic]—dc23
2012020161

10 9 8 7 6 5 4 3 2 1 LB 17 16 15 14 13

Cover illustration © 2013 by Tim Jessell.
Interior illustrations by Robert Dunn.

For information about Albert Whitman & Company,
visit our web site at www.albertwhitman.com.

Contents

THE BOARDWALK MYSTERY

CHAPTER 1

Grandfather's Surprise

Henry shut down the lawn mower and suddenly everything was very quiet in Grandfather's front yard. It was so hot that the birds were not chirping. Henry looked up at the blazing sun. He wiped his brow. Then he looked around the yard. Something was missing.

"Benny!" Henry called out to his little brother. "Where are you?"

Just then, ten-year-old Violet came out onto the front porch.

"Have you seen Benny?" Henry asked.

"No, I haven't," Violet said. "I thought he was helping you to cut the lawn."

Only six years old, Benny was the youngest of the four Alden children. Henry, Violet, and their sister Jessie took very good care of their little brother. The Aldens were orphans. When their parents died, they ran away from home and lived for a while in an abandoned boxcar in the woods. Their grandfather found them and brought them to live with him in his big house in Greenfield.

The screen door opened and twelve-year-old Jessie stepped outside. She was carrying a pitcher of lemonade and a plate of cookies.

"Benny is missing," Violet said.

Jessie looked around the yard. For a minute, she was concerned. Then she smiled. She saw something that Henry and Violet had not seen. "Watch this," Jessie said to Violet.

Jessie leaned over the porch rail. "Who wants chocolate chip cookies and lemonade?" she shouted.

Henry, Jessie, and Violet soon saw two

little white sneakers dangling from within the tree on Grandfather's front lawn.

"I do!" came a small voice from behind the leaves. "But I can't get down!"

Henry rushed to the tree and caught Benny just as his brother slid from the bottom branch.

"Thanks, Henry!" Benny rushed straight to the porch. "Are there any cookies left? I'm starved!"

Benny was small, but he was famous for his big appetite.

"What were you doing in the tree?" Henry asked. "I thought you were raking up the grass for me."

"I'm sorry, Henry," Benny said. His shoulders slumped. "It's just that it is so hot. I was melting. The tree looked like the coolest place to be. But I was sweating even in the tree. It is hot everywhere!"

Mrs. McGregor, the Aldens' housekeeper, appeared in the doorway. "Benny Alden!" she cried. "Look at all that dirt on your clothes! What happened? Are you okay?"

Benny looked down at his shirt. He tried to brush the dirt off. "I climbed the tree, Mrs. McGregor! I'm tall enough to reach the bottom branch!"

Mrs. McGregor smiled. "I hope you are tall enough to reach the sink. You need to wash up before you have any cookies."

"I'll take him inside," Henry said. "I need to wash up, too."

"Be quick," Mrs. McGregor said. "I was just coming out to tell you that your grandfather called. He will be home soon and he has some exciting news for you children."

Henry and Benny cleaned up and quickly joined their sisters on the front porch.

Jessie took a long drink of lemonade. She was wearing a light summer dress and fanning herself with a magazine. "What do you think the news could be?" she asked.

Violet patted her face with a cool cloth. Her cheeks were bright red from the heat. Even the purple ribbon in her hair seemed to droop. Purple was Violet's favorite color. "I don't know, Jessie. But I can't wait to find out!"

"We'll soon know," Henry said. "Here comes Grandfather now."

A big car drove up the long driveway. Grandfather waved at the children.

"Grandfather!" Benny jumped up. "What is the exciting news? Did you bring ice cream?"

Grandfather laughed. "That would have been a good idea, Benny, but I do not have ice cream. I wanted to tell you that I have to go out of town for a business meeting. Would you like to come with me?"

"We'd be happy to come, Grandfather," Jessie said. "Where is the meeting?"

"It is in a town called Oceanside in New Jersey. I have an old friend who recently moved to Oceanside. He has a big house right on the beach and he invited all of us to be his guests."

Benny dropped his cookie and ran into the house.

"Benny!" Jessie called. "Wait! Where are you going?"

"To pack my suitcase!" Benny called.

Everyone laughed and followed Benny inside.

It wasn't long until their bags were packed and everyone was settled comfortably into Grandfather's car for the long ride.

Violet was the first to guess when they got close to Oceanside. She saw seagulls flying above. Some were perched on the top rails of a bridge that the car was approaching. The bridge crossed over a lot of water.

"The bay is beautiful," Violet said.

"I like it here already," Benny said. "And it smells good."

Grandfather lowered all the windows in the car. He took a deep breath. "I also like that smell, Benny. It is the salt air."

All at once, Benny cried out. He pointed out the car window. "Look! Is that the top of a Ferris wheel?"

Violet looked off into the distance. "I think you are right, Benny. Is there an amusement park in Oceanside, Grandfather?"

Grandfather smiled. "In Oceanside, it is called an amusement pier. And there are several of them."

Benny bounced in his seat. "There is more than one? Cool!"

"Why is it called an amusement pier?" Jessie asked.

"I will show you." Grandfather turned the car onto Ocean Avenue. "See the boardwalk over there?"

Henry, Jessie, Violet, and Benny stared. They had never seen anything like the boardwalk. It was made out of wood planks. It was like a street, but it was raised above the ground, and there were no cars. People were strolling along it. It seemed to go on for miles.

"Does it go on forever?" Benny asked.

Grandfather laughed. "The boardwalk is several miles long, but it does not go on forever. You cannot see from here, but on the other side of the boardwalk are the beach and the ocean."

Just as Grandfather finished speaking, he pulled the car up beside a large, old house on Ocean Avenue. A pretty porch with wooden rails circled the house. Potted flowers hung from the top of the porch and swayed in the cool ocean breeze.

"Hello!" called a friendly voice. "Welcome!" A tall man with short brown hair hurried down the wooden steps. He shook Grandfather's hand. "It's so good to see you, James," he said.

Grandfather introduced his friend to the children. The man's name was Carl Hanson.

"We're very pleased to meet you, Mr. Hanson," Jessie said.

Violet was still gazing at the old house. "And your home is very lovely," she said.

Benny looked past the house. He started to jump up and down. "I see it! I see it!" he cried. "There's the ocean! It's right in your front yard, Mr. Hanson! Right over those dunes. This is way cooler than sitting in Grandfather's tree."

After everyone had unpacked and was settled into their rooms, Mr. Hanson invited his guests outside onto the porch. The porch sat up high on the second story of the house and looked out over the dunes, the boardwalk, and the beach.

Benny was too excited to sit. He hung over the rail and stared out at the waves crashing onto the beach. People strolled past on the boardwalk. Some pushed babies in coaches or licked dripping ice cream cones. There were lots of shops and arcades. And Benny could now see the big Ferris wheel slowly turning against the sky.

Violet came and stood beside Benny to see all the sights. They noticed one girl walking very slowly across the beach. She was staring at her phone. She was wearing shorts and a T-shirt and there was an odd spray of red dots on her shoes. Violet and Benny watched the girl walk all the way up to the Hanson's porch.

"Wendy!" Mr. Hanson cried. "What are you doing here?

The girl looked up. She seemed surprised to see the Aldens. She had long blond hair and her green T-shirt said "Hanson's Amusements" on the front.

"The roller coaster is broken again," the girl said. "I hurried here to tell you."

Benny looked at Violet. He was confused. Wendy had not been hurrying at all.

Mr. Hanson sighed. "How could that be? I just had it fixed yesterday! Did Will look at it? Is anyone stuck on the ride? Who is working in the ticket booth while you are gone?"

Wendy shrugged. "I don't know." She went back to looking at her phone.

Mr. Hanson introduced Wendy as his daughter. Then he jumped up. He ran his hand through his hair and walked back

and forth on the porch. "I'm sorry to be so distracted," he said to the Aldens. "But I am a little worried. I recently bought one of the amusement piers on the boardwalk."

Benny's eyes grew wide. He pointed toward the Ferris wheel. "Do you mean the amusement park down there? That is so cool!"

Mr. Hanson nodded. "That's the one, Benny. But it hasn't been as much fun as I thought. I used to work there during the summers back when I was a teenager and visiting with my grandparents. Those were some of the best summers of my life. So when I heard that the amusement pier was up for sale, I bought it and moved my family here from Colorado."

"But why isn't it fun?" Benny asked.

Mr. Hanson ran his hand across his forehead. "Nothing is going right. The rides keep breaking down. The tickets have gone missing. One day there was a nest of bees in the cotton candy machine! Last week someone even painted smiley faces on the walls of the haunted house. It took me hours to clean it up."

"How terrible!" Jessie said.

"And now the roller coaster is broken again. And it is my most popular ride. Two of my employees have already called in sick. It's going to be such a busy night. I don't know what I am going to do."

"We could help," Jessie said.

"Yes," Henry agreed. "I'd be happy to do any small repairs you might need."

"Henry is really good at fixing things," Benny said.

Mr. Hanson looked very surprised. "But you children are on a holiday. I could not ask you to do all that work."

"My grandchildren are very helpful," Grandfather said. "They don't mind hard work."

Wendy glared at the Aldens.

"Well," Mr. Hanson said. "If you are sure you don't mind, I really could use the help."

"I guess you don't need me anymore," she said to her father. "I'm going to go take a nap." Wendy turned to the Aldens. "Have fun, kids. But you better watch out for old Mrs. Reddy. She's prowling around again." Wendy stomped into the house and slammed the screen door.

Mr. Hanson sighed again. "Don't pay attention to that, kids. Mrs. Reddy is the lady who used to own the amusement pier. Even though she sold the pier to me, she can't seem to stay away."

"Then why did she sell it to you?" asked Benny.

"She told me she was ready to retire," Mr.

Hanson said. "Running an amusement pier is a lot of work. But now I think she misses it. She does not like any of the changes that I have made to the pier. She complains that I am doing everything wrong. And she gets into arguments with Bob Cooke."

"Does he work for you, too?" Benny asked.

"Oh, no, Benny. Bob does not work for me. He owns the amusement pier next to mine. It's a long story." Mr. Hanson rubbed his hands together. "I better get going. Why don't you kids have a snack and relax for a little bit after your trip? I'll see you later on tonight." Mr. Hanson hurried away

"What a shame," Grandfather said. "Owning the amusement pier has always been Carl's dream."

Jessie stared toward the tall Ferris wheel. "It sounds like his dream is turning into a nightmare."

CHAPTER 2

Lost in the House of Mirrors

After Grandfather left for his meeting, Henry, Jessie, Violet, and Benny cleaned up the snack plates from the porch.

The children could hear Wendy walking back and forth in a room upstairs. The old floorboards creaked. She was talking to someone on her phone. Soon she began to shout angrily.

"We should probably leave now," Jessie said. "It is not right for us to eavesdrop."

Henry agreed. The children quietly left the

house and began walking on the boardwalk toward the amusement pier. The sun was warm, but a fresh ocean breeze blew through their hair.

"Why was Wendy shouting?" Benny asked. "Who was she was talking to?"

"I don't know, Benny," Jessie said. "Something must have upset her."

"I hope she is all right," Violet said.

Benny began running ahead. "Wow! Look at all these shops!" he cried, pointing to the long rows of stores along the boardwalk. There was an ice cream shop with thirty different flavors. Next to it was a candy store. In the window a machine moved back and forth, pulling saltwater taffy. A souvenir store displayed colorful shells, beach balls, postcards, and paddleball games.

"Can I buy a souvenir?" Benny cried. He darted toward the store.

"Benny, watch out!" Jessie cried.

Violet dashed toward her brother.

"Watch the tramcar, please! Watch the tramcar, please!"

Violet grabbed Benny's shoulders and pulled him back just in time. Benny turned, wide-eyed. A long yellow vehicle, like a train on rubber wheels, came to a slow stop right where Benny had just been standing!

Henry and Jessie rushed to their brother. "Are you all right, Benny?" Jessie asked.

Benny was shaken. He looked like he might cry.

A girl with dark hair jumped from behind the wheel. "Is everyone all right?" she asked.

"Yes. We're sorry for holding you up," Henry said.

"Oh, that's okay," said the girl. "It happens all the time. People are looking at the ocean or the shops and they do not see me coming. But I drive very slowly. I have never hit anyone!"

"But why are you driving a train on the boardwalk?" Benny asked.

The girl laughed. "It does look like a train. But this is the tramcar. The boardwalk is very long. Sometimes people get tired of walking. The tramcar takes them on a nice ride so they can rest. Why don't you hop aboard?"

"Really?" Benny turned toward Jessie. "Can we?" he asked.

Jessie smiled. "I don't see why not," she said.

The tramcar driver introduced herself. Her name was Leslie. She showed Benny a button next to the steering wheel. Every time she pushed the button, a tape played over a loudspeaker. "Watch the tramcar, please! Watch the tramcar, please!"

"So, you see, it wasn't just you, Benny," Leslie explained. "Plenty of people do not notice the tramcar coming. They are too busy having fun on the boardwalk! That is why I have this recording. It saves my voice!"

Suddenly, the children heard a loud banging. An older lady seated in the last car of the tram was banging her cane against the side. "Let's get a move on!" she shouted. "What is going on up there, Leslie?"

"We'll be starting in a minute, Mrs. Reddy," Leslie called. "Just picking up a few passengers."

"Tell them to stop standing around and get into a seat!" Mrs. Reddy called.

"We're very sorry," Jessie said.

Henry, Jessie, Violet, and Benny quickly climbed aboard. Benny leaned from his seat so that he would not miss a thing. Suddenly, he felt a tap on his shoulder. The old woman

was poking him with her cane.

"Better not lean too far out, boy," she said. "Do you want to fall out?"

Jessie had her arm around Benny's shoulder. She knew Benny would not fall out. "He is safe, thank you," she said.

Benny turned to face the old woman. "We're going to Hanson's Amusement Pier!" he said. "They have rides there!"

The old woman folded her hands over her cane. "Well, maybe it is called Hanson's now. But it used to be called Reddy's. It was called Reddy's for fifty years. Stupid to change the name, if you ask me."

"Watch the tramcar, please! Watch the tramcar, please!" Leslie turned on the recording to warn a lady who was walking too close to the tramcar. The lady had a large camera and she was taking pictures of the boardwalk.

"Who built the amusement pier? The Reddy family, that's who! Who made it a big success? The Reddy family! Carl Hanson will ruin the place. He doesn't know what he is doing." The old woman scowled.

Just then, Leslie stopped the tramcar. "This is Hanson's Amusement Pier, kids. Do you need to get off?"

"Yes, thank you," Jessie said.

The children jumped down from the tramcar and thanked Leslie for the ride.

"Any time," Leslie said. Then she lowered her voice. "Don't mind old Mrs. Reddy," she whispered. "She is still upset about why she had to sell her amusement pier." Leslie waved good-bye, and the tramcar began to roll off down the boardwalk.

Jessie held Benny's hand. She wondered what had happened that made Mrs. Reddy sell her pier. The old woman seemed very unhappy about her decision.

Benny waited for the tramcar to safely pass, then let go of Jessie's hand and ran across the boardwalk to the pier. "Look!" he cried. "This is it!"

The name "Hanson's Amusement Pier" flashed in red letters high over Benny's head. There was a log flume that splashed water on the passengers. A tall roller coaster with lots of twists and turns made the boards under Benny's feet rumble. A scary monster with green eyes looked out from the top floor of the haunted house. There was even a giant slide and swings that flew round and round out over the beach below.

"I'll go ask where we can find Mr. Hanson," Henry said. He walked toward the ticket booth. For a moment, he was confused. He thought he saw Wendy's face in the booth window. But she could not have been there. Then he realized that it was a boy in the booth. The boy had the same blond hair and blue eyes as Wendy. He also had the same unhappy look on his face.

"Excuse me," Henry said to the boy. "But would you please tell me where I can find Mr. Hanson?"

The boy opened a door and walked out of the booth. He was a little taller than Henry and he looked a few years older. "Are you those Alden kids?" he asked.

"Yes," Henry replied. He introduced his sisters and brother.

"I'm Will Hanson," the boy said.

"You look just like Wendy!" Benny said.

"We do look alike," Will said. "Wendy and I are twins. My father is in the shed at the back of the pier."

"Thanks," Henry said. "We promised we would stop by."

Will shrugged. "Suit yourself. If I were you kids, I wouldn't hang around this pier. I would go relax on the beach. I'm sure it is much more fun." Will went back into the booth and closed the door behind him.

Henry, Jessie, Violet, and Benny walked back toward the shed at the end of the pier. There, Mr. Hanson was painting something on a white cloth. He smiled when he saw the Aldens.

"Hello! Welcome to my workshop." Mr. Hanson had a big smile on his face. He held up the white cloth. "What do think?" he asked.

Benny cocked his head. "What is it?" he asked.

Mr. Hanson's shoulders slumped. "It is supposed to be a ghost. Someone stole the family of ghosts from my haunted house. I need to replace them. But I guess I am not doing a very good job."

"Violet is a terrific artist!" Benny said. "She can draw anything!"

Violet blushed. "I do like to draw, Mr. Hanson," she said. "If you would like, I could make a family of ghosts for you."

Mr. Hanson jumped up. "That would be great!" he said. He showed Violet all the materials that he had bought for the job. "Now I can go fix the motorcycles."

"You fix motorcycles?" Benny asked.

"Not real ones," Mr. Hanson said. "I have a motorcycle ride for children. They can sit on small motorcycles and pretend that they are riding them. But two nights ago, someone took all the handles off the motorcycles. I had to order new handles. Now I have to screw all the new handles back on to the motorcycles."

"I can do that for you," Henry offered.

"Thank you so much," Mr. Hanson said. "Now I just have to fix up the house of mirrors and the boat ride."

"What's a house of mirrors?" Benny asked.

Mr. Hanson smiled. "Have you never been in one? It is a lot of fun. It is a maze where all of the walls are made of glass. It is fun to try to find your way out. But first I need to clean it up. Someone has written all over the walls."

"That's terrible!" Jessie said. "Who would do such a thing?"

Mr. Hanson shrugged. "Probably one of my customers. It is a big amusement pier. I cannot watch every ride at the same time. Some customers are not very respectful. They break things when I am not looking. I don't know why they do that."

"You should fix the boat ride, Mr. Hanson," Jessie said. "Benny and I will clean the house of mirrors."

Benny and Jessie grabbed some sponges and a bucket of soapy water and headed to the house of mirrors. Just before they got there, a man rudely bumped into Jessie and she almost spilled the bucket of soapy water.

"Watch where you are going!" the man shouted.

"Excuse me," Jessie said. "But I believe you bumped into me."

The man was tall with dark, curly hair. He looked down at Jessie. "Maybe I did. I don't know. Do you kids work here?"

"We are helping out," Jessie said. "Is there something that you need?"

Just then, Mrs. Reddy walked toward them, shaking her cane. "Get off this pier, Bob Cooke!" she shouted.

The man rolled his eyes, but he did not move. "You don't own the pier anymore, Mrs. Reddy. You can't order me off."

Mrs. Reddy banged her cane into the boardwalk. "You don't belong here!"

"You don't, either," he said. Mr. Cooke pointed to Jessie and Benny. "Do you see that Carl is making little children work for him now? He is desperate."

Jessie's face flushed with anger. Before she could answer, Mrs. Reddy did. "These are just kids helping out. But Carl Hanson is ruining this amusement pier."

Mr. Cooke smiled. "I know," he answered.

"He will be out of business by the end of the summer. And then I will buy the amusement pier. I will own more amusements than anyone on this boardwalk."

"You will never own this pier!" Mrs. Reddy said.

"Come on, Benny," Jessie said. She felt uncomfortable listening to the two adults arguing. Jessie and Benny walked into the house of mirrors.

"Wow!" Benny cried. "Look at it!"

There were walls of glass as far as Jessie and Benny could see. Every time they turned one corner, another wall of glass was in front of them. It was hard to know which way to go. Jessie set her bucket down. She was about to ask Benny for a sponge when she noticed that he was gone!

"Benny!" Jessie cried. "Where are you?" But there was no answer. Jessie began to run through the maze of mirrors. Several times she banged hard into a glass wall that she did not see. She could not find her way out!

CHAPTER 3

A List of Clues

Jessie stood very still for a moment and listened. She could hear footsteps from somewhere inside the maze. She tried calling to Benny again, but he did not answer. She put her hands in front of her face and felt her way around the glass walls. Then, suddenly, it became easier. Someone had splashed a red liquid on the glass. Now Jessie could see where she was going. Soon, she saw black scribbles on the glass walls, too. And she saw words. "This way out" was written on one wall. Arrows pointed the way. "This is a stupid ride," read another wall. Finally, Jessie saw "Go to Cooke's Amusement Pier. It is much more fu—" The sentence was not finished.

Jessie looked down. A black marker was laying on the ground. She picked it up and put it in her pocket. She felt a tap on her back and she jumped!

"Benny!" Jessie cried. "Where were you?"

Benny rubbed his forehead. "I was just trying out the maze, Jessie. It is hard. I ran right into the glass walls two times. But then I saw the red paint. I was going to come back to you."

"Didn't you hear me calling to you?" Jessie asked.

"No," Benny said. "I got too far away. There was someone else in the maze with us. I thought it was you. But it wasn't. The person was writing on the walls. The person saw me coming and ran away."

Jessie pulled the marker out of her pocket. "I found this," she said. "Did you see who was writing on the walls?"

"No," Benny said. "I could not see the person. There were too many glass walls in the way. But the person was wearing blue pants. I could see that."

Jessie and Benny carefully retraced their steps. They found the bucket with the soapy water. They worked hard and rubbed off all the red splashes and all the black words from the maze walls. When they finished, they walked back toward the shed.

They passed Henry. He was just screwing on the last handle on a motorcycle. "That should do it," he said. Then he joined Jessie and Benny.

"Wow! Look at what Violet has done!" Benny cried as they arrived at the shed.

A family of scary-looking ghosts stood on the table.

"Listen to this," Violet said. She pushed the button on a recorder. Benny jumped and grabbed Jessie's hand. The frightening wail of ghosts filled the shed.

"It's just pretend, Benny," Violet said. "Mr. Hanson recorded it. The ghost sounds will play when customers ride through the haunted house. We are going to set up the ghosts soon."

"You kids have been working very hard," Mr. Hanson said. "Why don't you go get some dinner on the boardwalk? We can set up the ghosts in the haunted house when you get back. There is a wonderful pizza place called Mack's. I will write down the directions for you."

Mr. Hanson walked toward the ticket booth.

Will was there. He looked bored. There were no customers buying tickets yet.

"Will, where is the black marker? I need to write something down for the Aldens," Mr. Hanson said.

Will stood up. He patted the counter. "I don't know. It was here earlier. I guess someone took it."

Jessie suddenly remembered something. She pulled the marker from her pocket that she had found in the house of mirrors. "I have a marker," she said. "You may have this one if you like."

Will narrowed his eyes at Jessie. "That looks just like our marker." He turned toward his father. "You better watch these kids, Dad. You don't know very much about them."

Jessie's face flushed. "I found that marker in the house of mirrors," she said.

Mr. Hanson held up his hands. "Will, please don't say such things. I trust the Aldens."

"Maybe you shouldn't." Will walked out of the ticket booth. He pointed to Jessie and Benny. "I saw those two talking to Bob Cooke and Mrs. Reddy earlier today. Who knows what they were plotting?" Then Will stomped off down the boardwalk. Benny noticed something odd about Will's sneakers as Will walked away. They had the same red splatters on them as Wendy's shoes.

"Don't mind Will," Mr. Hanson said. "He and Wendy have had a hard time moving here to Oceanside. They miss their friends in Colorado. They haven't been themselves lately."

Henry, Jessie, Violet, and Benny headed

down the boardwalk toward Mack's. Jessie was still upset at Will's accusation. The children found Mack's without any problem. The smell of baking pizza wafted over the boardwalk.

"Hello!" called a friendly man in a white apron. "Are you the Aldens? Carl Hanson just called to tell me how hard you have worked today. I saved the best booth for you."

"Thank you so much," Jessie said.

The children slid into a booth. On the side of the restaurant that faced the ocean, there was no wall. A fresh ocean breeze blew through the restaurant.

"I'm sorry that Will accused you," Henry said to Jessie and Benny. "That was wrong of him."

Jessie explained how she and Benny had run into Mr. Cooke. She told Henry and Violet about the argument between Mr. Cooke and Mrs. Reddy.

"Do you think Mr. Cooke or Mrs. Reddy could be causing the problems at Hanson's Amusement Pier?" Violet asked.

"It is possible," Jessie said. "Mr. Cooke wants Mr. Hanson to fail. Mr. Cooke wants to buy Hanson's Amusement Pier so that he can own the most amusements on the boardwalk."

Jessie pulled out a notepad. When the Aldens were faced with a mystery, Jessie liked to keep notes. Many times her notes helped solve the mystery. Jessie wrote Mr. Cooke's name in her notepad. She wrote down the things he had said.

"What about Mrs. Reddy?" asked Benny. "She seems angry at Mr. Hanson."

"That's true, Benny," Jessie said. She added Mrs. Reddy's name to her list. "Mrs. Reddy thinks that Mr. Hanson is ruining the amusement pier. The amusement pier was owned by her family for a long time. She seems to want it back."

"I don't understand why she sold it," Violet said.

"She told Mr. Hanson that she wanted to retire," Henry said.

Jessie continued to write. She looked thoughtful. "But Leslie, the lady from the tramcar, said that Mrs. Reddy was upset about *why* she had to sell the amusement pier."

"That's true," Henry agreed. "I wonder what she meant by that."

Just then Mack delivered a large, hot pizza with bubbling cheese to their table. A boy followed him with four glasses of ice-cold lemonade.

"Wow!" Benny cried. "This pizza looks great! I think I could eat the whole thing by myself."

Mack introduced the boy with the lemonade as his son, Hunter. Hunter had soft brown hair and a dark tan. He looked like he was a few years older than Henry.

"Pleased to meet you," Hunter said. "Are you kids here on vacation?"

"Yes," Henry answered. "And we're helping out at Hanson's Amusement Pier, as well."

"That's very nice of you," Hunter said. "Mr. Hanson can use all the help he can get. His kids, Will and Wendy, don't seem to like to work. And they're not very friendly."

Mack shook his head. "They're just having

a hard time. They moved here from far away and left all their friends behind."

"Then they should make new friends here," Hunter said. "There are lots of great kids in Oceanside."

"Maybe you should invite them surfing with you," Mack suggested.

"Surfing? Are you a surfer?" Benny asked. "I would like to surf too!"

Hunter smiled. "I do like to surf. You might be a little small to surf, Benny. But I could teach you how to boogie board."

Benny hopped out of his seat. He turned to Jessie. "Can I boogie board? Please? Can I go now?"

Hunter laughed. "I'm sorry, Benny, but I have to work right now. But maybe I can take you another day."

"Thanks!" Benny said.

The children began eating the delicious pizza. Benny was so excited about boogie boarding that he almost dropped his slice of pizza. Some of the red sauce squirted onto his T-shirt. Violet tried to clean it off with her napkin.

"It won't come off, Benny," Violet said. "We'll have to wash it when we get home."

Benny looked down at the red stains on his shirt. It reminded him of something. "Now my shirt looks like Will's and Wendy's shoes," he said.

Jessie thought for a minute. Benny was right. She did remember seeing red stains on the twins' shoes. She pulled out her notepad. She added Will's and Wendy's names to her list. She told Henry and Violet about the red liquid that was spilled on the walls of the house of mirrors. Benny explained about the words written in black marker. He also told how he had seen someone in blue pants running away through the maze.

"Jessie," Henry said. "Is that the marker you found in the house of mirrors?"

Jessie looked down at the marker in her hand. "Yes, it is. I suppose that I was so upset at Will's accusation, I forgot to put it back on the counter."

"Look at what is printed on the side of the

marker," Henry said.

Jessie turned the marker on its side. She read out loud, "Captain Cooke's Amazing Amusement Pier."

The children were surprised.

"I have another clue for your notepad, Jessie," Benny said. "Mr. Cooke was wearing blue pants."

"You are a good detective, Benny," Violet said. "But I think that Will was also wearing blue pants today."

Jessie wrote all the information down in the notepad.

"It's getting late," Henry said. "We promised Mr. Hanson that we would come back to help set up Violet's ghosts in the haunted house."

"Yes," Jessie agreed. "But perhaps we should take a look around Captain Cooke's pier first."

CHAPTER 4

Benny Disappears

Captain Cooke's pier was smaller than Hanson's, but there were many exciting rides there.

"Look!" Benny cried. He pointed to a very large pirate ship. The ship rocked high into the air, back and forth.

There were also games where people could win prizes. One booth had a big wall filled with balloons. People threw darts and tried to pop the balloons.

"Can I try that?" asked Benny. "It won't take long. Please?"

Henry laughed. "Sure, Benny," he said. "Let's see if you can win a prize."

Henry paid the man in the booth. The man handed Benny three darts.

Benny rubbed his hands together. He was excited. He reached back and threw his first dart very hard, but he missed. The dart stuck into the corkboard wall.

"Almost, Benny!" Violet said. "You'll get the next one."

Benny took aim again. He threw his second dart and it hit a small yellow balloon. But the balloon did not pop!

The man in the booth whispered to Benny. Benny looked confused, then he nodded. He aimed for a big red balloon down in the corner. He let the dart fly. It hit the red balloon and there was a loud pop!

"You did it, Benny!" Violet cried.

A green ticket fluttered to the ground. The man in the booth picked it up and handed it to Benny. "Looks like you are a winner!" he said. The man smiled and gave Benny a long rubber snake.

"Cool!" Benny showed his snake to his brother and sisters. "It looks so real! Do you think I can scare Grandfather with it?"

Henry laughed. "Maybe you can."

The children were so busy looking at Benny's prize that they did not see Mr. Cooke walk toward them. He was carrying a folder and some papers. He stopped at the dart-throwing booth.

"I see you have come to the better amusement pier," Mr. Cooke said. "Did you get tired of all the broken rides at Hanson's?" Mr. Cooke spoke very loudly. He spoke like he was an actor on a stage. People on the boardwalk turned and looked at him.

"Not at all," Jessie said. "And the rides at Hanson's are not broken. We are just on our way there right now."

The man in the dart booth was counting money. He handed the bills to Mr. Cooke. Mr. Cooke took a paper out of his folder.

"Be careful over at Hanson's," Mr. Cooke said. "They have been having so much trouble with their rides, it might not be very safe over there."

"We are sure that it is perfectly safe," Henry said.

The man in the dart booth held out his hand. "I need a receipt for the money, Mr. Cooke," he said.

Mr. Cooke put his hand into each of his pockets. "I know," he said. "But I can't find my marker."

"Is this your marker?" Jessie asked.

Mr. Cooke took the marker from Jessie's hand. He started to nod, but then he stopped, as if he was remembering something. He looked at the marker, then stared at Jessie. "There are a hundred markers with my name on them on this boardwalk," he said. "I give them out for free. They are a good advertisement. You can find them everywhere."

"Well, I found your marker at Hanson's pier," Jessie said.

Mr. Cooke signed the receipt for the man in the dart booth. "I'm not surprised you found it at Hanson's. Like I said, those markers are everywhere."

Mr. Cooke handed the marker back to Jessie. "You can keep this as a souvenir," he said. "It is probably not the one I lost." Then he quickly walked away.

The Aldens were running late. They hurried toward Hanson's pier. But very soon they heard a familiar recording. "Watch the tramcar, please! Watch the tramcar, please!"

"Hello, kids!" Leslie waved from behind the wheel of the bright yellow tram. "Why don't you jump aboard? Are you headed to Hanson's?"

"Yes," Jessie said. "Thank you so much!"

Henry, Jessie, Violet, and Benny took the front seat right behind Leslie.

"So how do you like Hanson's pier?" Leslie asked.

"It's wonderful," Jessie answered.

Leslie nodded her head. "I knew you would enjoy it. The Reddy family added many great rides over the years. They built it up into the best pier on the boardwalk."

"Do you mean Mrs. Reddy's family?" asked Violet.

Leslie slowed the tramcar. She picked up two families with small children. "That's right, Violet," she said. "Mr. and Mrs. Reddy and their son, Paul, ran the pier for many years."

Violet hesitated. "Do you mind if we ask why the Reddy family sold the pier?"

"Not at all. It is not a secret." Leslie started up the tram again. "Mr. Reddy was a wonderful man. But he died five years ago. Paul helped Mrs. Reddy run the pier. He is a good son and he helped for several years. But Paul did not like working at the amusement pier. He is an engineer. He got an offer for a very good job in California. He moved away and he lives in California with his family."

"It is a shame that he lives so far away," Violet said.

"Mrs. Reddy tried to run the pier by

herself," Leslie said. "But it is a big job and she has a very sore leg. Paul and all of her friends encouraged Mrs. Reddy to sell the pier and to retire. She was very sad that her son did not carry on the family business."

The tramcar slowed to a stop in front of Hanson's pier. "Here we are, kids!" Leslie said. "Have fun tonight!"

The children thanked Leslie and climbed down from the tramcar.

"It must have been very hard for Mrs. Reddy to sell the pier," Violet said.

"Yes," agreed Jessie. "And she must be lonely with her son living so far away."

Benny looked up at all the lights and the spinning rides. "If it were my pier, I would not want to sell it, either!"

The children hurried off to find Mr. Hanson. He was in his workshop carefully placing Violet's ghosts into a large box.

"There you are!" Mr. Hanson said. "How was dinner?"

"It was great!" Benny said. "I ate five pieces of pizza all by myself."

Mr. Hanson's eyes grew wide. He patted Benny's stomach. "Where do you put it all?"

Henry laughed. "That is one mystery we have never been able to solve."

The children followed Mr. Hanson to the haunted house. No one was in line yet. Mr. Hanson placed a sign outside that said "Ride temporarily closed." Then he pushed open a side door and the children followed him into the haunted house. It was very dark.

Benny clutched Jessie's shirt. This was the darkest room he had ever been in! He couldn't even see his own hand!

The children could hear Mr. Hanson struggling with the box. "I can't reach it," he said. "There is a switch on the wall on the left. Can someone turn on the lights?"

Henry felt around in the darkness until his hand felt a switch. He flicked it up. Suddenly, the room was flooded with light. All four Aldens jumped back in fear.

"I'm sorry," Mr. Hanson said. "I should have warned you that we were standing in the zombie room before you turned on the lights."

Jessie was holding her hand over her heart. "Whoever made those zombies did a very good job."

Everyone stared at the rows of tall zombies. They had white faces and red eyes. Their clothes were shabby and their arms were outstretched.

Mr. Hanson set his box on the floor. "It is a good display, isn't it? I made it myself. Watch this." He flipped another switch. The zombies' legs began to move back and forth and the room was filled with a moaning sound. It looked like the zombies were marching straight at the Aldens!

Benny held on to Jessie's hand. "I don't like it in here," he whispered. "It's all pretend," Jessie said. "Don't worry."

Benny stayed very close to Jessie as Mr. Hanson led the children through the haunted house. There was a room with a huge green-faced Frankenstein and a room with a cackling witch on a broom. In the last room, scary jack-o'-lanterns blinked orange. But the rest of the room was empty.

"The ghosts used to be right here." Mr. Hanson pointed to an empty side of the room. There were dark posts lined up next to the wall. But there was nothing else. Mr. Hanson opened the box and everyone carefully removed the ghosts. Mr. Hanson showed the children how to fit the ghosts onto the posts. After the ghosts were screwed on, Violet fluffed out the long white material.

Mr. Hanson turned to Violet. "You did a wonderful job. These ghosts are even better than the ones that were stolen. Why don't you turn on this switch and I will show you what your ghosts can do?"

Violet hit the switch. The posts moved up and down and so did the ghosts! A hidden fan blew air across the ghosts and they seemed to be floating and shimmering in the air.

"Oh my!" Violet cried. "That is very clever! Your machine makes my ghosts move. It really looks like they are flying!"

"Thank you, Violet," said Mr. Hanson.

Suddenly, a loud banging came from the zombie room.

"What could that be?" Mr. Hanson hurried toward the sound. The children followed.

They found Will. He was kicking the wall with his shoe.

"Will! What are you doing?" asked Mr. Hanson.

"I called you, but you didn't answer," Will said. "Linda and Jake are not showing up for work tonight. Mr. Cooke hired them for his pier and he promised to pay them more money. I can't do everything by myself. And I am hungry. I'm leaving to go get some food." Will kicked the wall again.

"Will, can't you just wait until later? I need your help."

Will shrugged. "Sorry, Dad. This whole amusement pier thing is your dream, not mine. It's not my fault that you can't make it work." Will turned and left.

Mr. Hanson sighed. He put his hands deep into his pockets. "Maybe Will is right," he said. "Maybe I just can't make it work. I've worked so hard, but nothing seems to be turning out right. Maybe I should sell the pier and go back to my old job in Colorado."

"But it's not your fault that everything is going wrong," Benny said.

Mr. Hanson looked up, surprised. "What do you mean?"

"Benny is right, Mr. Hanson," Henry said. "You have a wonderful amusement pier. But someone wants you to fail. Someone is trying to ruin you."

Mr. Hanson rubbed his forehead. "Ruin me? But who would do such a thing?" he asked.

"We're not sure yet," Jessie said.

"But whoever it is, is playing a lot of very mean tricks on you," Henry said.

"And you have a truly wonderful amusement pier," Violet added. "You have created some amazing rides."

Mr. Hanson smiled. "Thanks, kids. You are very kind. I guess I shouldn't give up just yet."

He sighed. "Looks like I will be short on help again tonight, though."

"What jobs did Linda and Jake have?" Henry asked.

"Jake runs this haunted house ride," Mr. Hanson said. "And Linda is in charge of the Big Slide. I'll have to close a few of the rides tonight. It's always so hard to choose."

"You don't need to close anything," Henry said. "Benny and I can run the haunted house ride."

"And I would be happy to help out with the Big Slide," Violet said.

"I'll go straight to the ticket booth," Jessie added.

Mr. Hanson smiled. "You are sure that you don't mind?"

"We don't mind at all," Henry said. "It will be fun."

It was late when the amusement pier finally closed. Mr. Hanson, Henry, and Jessie checked that all the rides were safely turned off and locked. Violet and Benny picked up stray wrappers and put them in the trash. When they were done, they climbed onto the dark merry-go-round and each picked a horse. Benny climbed onto a large black horse that looked as though it were galloping.

Violet sat on a white horse that had purple ribbons hanging from its mane.

Benny held the reins of his horse. "Do you think we will get to ride the rides sometime when they are on?"

Violet patted the side of her horse. "I hope so," she said. "I want to try the Big Slide and the roller coaster. I am sure that once Mr. Hanson gets all his problems settled, we can ride the rides."

"And play games, too," Benny said.

"Yes," Violet replied. "That would be fun, too."

Suddenly, Benny slid off his horse. "I'll be right back!" he cried. "I just remembered something!"

"Benny, wait!" Violet called. But it was too late. Benny had disappeared!

CHAPTER 5

Benny Gets Hurt

Violet ran across the amusement pier, but she did not see Benny. A few lights were on here and there, but all the rides and food stands were dark.

"Violet! Is something wrong?" Jessie asked. Jessie, Henry, and Mr. Hanson were locking the gate to the Ferris wheel.

"Have you seen Benny?" Violet asked.

"No," Jessie replied.

Violet explained how Benny had slid from his horse and run away.

Mr. Hanson looked concerned. "Let's split up," he said. "Henry and Jessie, you search the ocean side of the pier. Violet and I will look on the other side. We'll meet up at the ticket booth."

Violet climbed all the way up to the very top of the Big Slide. From the top, she could look down on the whole amusement pier. She could see Henry and Jessie running from ride to ride. She could see Mr. Hanson checking under benches and behind the game booths. But she did not see Benny. Clouds covered the moon, and the beach and the ocean were very dark. Violet worried. What if Benny had run down to the beach and could not find his way?

Out of the corner of her eye, Violet saw something move at the back of the pier. Someone, or something, had just run down the steps and into the blackness of the beach. It looked like the person was carrying something very big.

"Stop!" Violet called. But she was too far. She sat and quickly flew down the Big Slide to the very bottom. She called for Henry, Jessie, and Mr. Hanson. They came running.

Just as Violet was about to tell them what she had seen, loud screaming came from the haunted house! All the lights in the front of the haunted house went on. The cars began to run on the track and bump through the doors. But there were no riders! Everyone rushed toward the ride.

"Was that Benny who screamed?" asked Jessie. "I hope he is all right."

"Don't worry," Mr. Hanson said. "It was not Benny. The screams are part of the ride. Someone has turned it on."

Mr. Hanson quickly found the off switch and shut down the ride. He pushed open the door and Henry, Jessie, and Violet followed him inside.

"Benny!" Jessie cried. "Are you all right?"

Benny sat on the floor in the zombie room. His head was in his hands.

"The zombie hit me," he said. "Then it ran away."

Everyone looked at the platform next to

where Benny sat. The tallest zombie was missing from its stand!

* * *

Back at Mr. Hanson's house, everyone sat out on the deck overlooking the ocean. Mr. Hanson scooped ice cream into bowls.

"Extra chocolate sauce and rainbow sprinkles for Benny," Mr. Hanson said. "How do you feel?"

"I'm fine," Benny said. He lifted an ice pack from his cheek. "It is just a small bump. It hardly hurts at all."

"Can you tell us what happened?" Grandfather asked.

"I won a snake today when I threw darts at a balloon. But when we helped Mr. Hanson set up the ghosts in the haunted house, I left my snake there. I remembered it when I was sitting on the horse on the merry-go-round. I told Violet that I would be right back. I ran to the haunted house to get my snake."

"Wasn't it too dark to find the snake?" Jessie asked.

Benny nodded. "At first it was too dark. But I knew where the light switch was. I turned on the lights and ran to the ghost room. I found my snake. It was sitting right next to the smallest ghost. I picked it up, but just then all the lights went out. I couldn't see anything."

Violet drew in her breath. "You must have been so frightened!"

"I was a little scared," Benny admitted. "But I felt along the walls. I walked into the zombie room. There was a light in there."

"But I don't have any lights just in the zombie room," Mr. Hanson said. "The switch you used turns on all the lights in the haunted house."

"It wasn't that light, Mr. Hanson. It was a small light, like from a cell phone or a little flashlight. Then the giant zombie started to move. He came right off the machine that you built. His arms swung around. One of them hit me in the side of the face. I fell down."

"Where did the zombie go?" asked Henry. "It can't walk. It's not real. And it was not there when we found you."

"I don't know," Benny said. "It was too dark. The little light went off. And then all of a sudden the ride started up and you came and found me."

Just then, everyone heard giggling coming from the beach. But it was too dark to see anyone.

As everyone was finishing their ice cream, Will and Wendy came in the front door. When their father called to them, they walked back toward the deck.

"Where were you tonight?" Mr. Hanson asked. "I sure could have used your help."

Will looked down at his feet.

"We're sorry, Dad," Wendy said. "We went for a long walk after dinner and we lost track of the time."

Wendy played with a string hanging from the bottom of her shirt. Her eyes quickly glanced toward Benny. "Are you okay, little guy?" she asked. "How about I get you some more ice cream?" Wendy asked.

Grandfather smiled. "Benny never says no to ice cream."

Wendy carried Benny's bowl into the kitchen.

"Hello up there, Aldens!" A shout came from the boardwalk below.

Mr. Hanson leaned over the rail. "Come on up, Hunter," he said. "We are just having some ice cream. I hope you can join us."

"Sounds great!" Hunter ran up the stairs. "I'm glad I saw the candles flickering on your deck," he said. "I wanted to stop by to see if anyone is up for hitting the beach tomorrow morning."

Benny jumped out of his chair. "Are you going to teach me how to boogie board?"

Hunter laughed. "That's the first thing I am going to do. But it won't take long. You'll figure it out quick."

"You children have been an enormous help. You should go and enjoy the beach tomorrow," Mr. Hanson said.

Benny clapped his hands. Wendy came back out onto the deck and handed Benny another heaping bowl of ice cream. "Wow!" Benny said. "This is the best night ever!"

Will and Wendy turned to leave the deck. Hunter called to them.

"Do you want to come tomorrow, too?" Hunter asked. "There will be lots of kids there. We always have a good time. Do you like to surf?"

Will hesitated. He folded his arms and leaned against the door frame.

"Thanks, but we don't surf," Wendy said. Then she sighed. "But we used to ski when we lived in Colorado."

"That's cool," Hunter said. "I've never been skiing. If I teach you to surf this summer, maybe you can teach me how to ski in the winter. I've heard the Pocono Mountains in Pennsylvania have some great slopes. And they are not too far from here."

Wendy smiled. She looked over at Will. Will shrugged his shoulders. "It's a deal," Wendy said. "We'll see you in the morning!"

When Benny awoke, it was early morning. He rushed downstairs and out onto the deck. He wanted to see how big the waves were. He could not wait to swim in the ocean and try out the boogie board that Hunter promised to bring. But when Benny looked toward the beach, he saw something that made his heart beat fast. He stumbled back into the house.

"Henry! Jessie! Violet!" Benny called. "Come quick!"

CHAPTER 6

Zombie on the Beach

Henry, Jessie, and Violet heard Benny's shouting and rushed out onto the deck to find him. Even Grandfather and Mr. Hanson had jumped from their beds. They all stood looking out at the beach. At first, no one knew what to say. The tall zombie, the one that had hit Benny in the face, was standing on the beach, its arms outstretched as though it was marching toward the Hanson's beach house. The sun was rising behind it on the ocean, and the zombie cast a huge shadow across the sand.

some fun. This is my problem. I have been asking you and Will to do too much."

"No, Dad," Wendy said. "Will and I can put the zombie in the haunted house. We will go right now. We'll be back in plenty of time for the beach."

"Thanks," Mr. Hanson said. "The key to the haunted house is on my key ring. It is hanging on the hook by the door."

"Will and I have a spare key," Wendy said. "We don't need it."

Will looked down at the zombie. "You have to admit," he said. "It does look kind of funny down there, doesn't it?"

Grandfather smiled. "It certainly gets your attention."

There were a few early morning joggers and walkers on the beach. Some of them were stopping to look at the zombie. They were admiring it.

Violet looked thoughtful. "Mr. Hanson, maybe you could leave the zombie on the beach for a while. We could put a sign on it advertising the amusement pier."

Wendy smiled. "I hope you like it. It is the least we can do after . . ."

Will poked Wendy in the arm. "You are our guests," Will said. "What Wendy means is that it is the least we can do for our guests. We are going to go find the sunglasses for the zombie. We'll be back soon. Enjoy your breakfast."

The children sat on the deck and ate the delicious breakfast. Soon there was only one waffle left on the big platter that Wendy and Will had set on the table.

"May I have the last waffle?" Benny asked.

"I think you have eaten more waffles than me, Benny," Henry said. "I don't know where you put it all." Henry slid the waffle onto Benny's plate.

"Me either," Benny said. "But my stomach sure does like this breakfast!"

"Does it hurt to eat?" Jessie asked.

Benny touched the side of his face. He had a purple bruise on his right cheek. It was swollen, too. "It hurts a little when I chew," Benny said. "But if I didn't eat, my stomach would hurt more!"

"Who do you think could have done such a thing to Benny?" asked Violet. "It certainly was very mean. He could have been hurt very bad."

Henry poured himself a glass of milk. "I don't know," he said. "And I was quite sure that Mr. Hanson had locked up the haunted house. How did the person get inside? And who turned the ride on?"

Benny wiped a drip of syrup from his chin. "It wasn't locked when I went in," he said. "But I did not turn the ride on. It went on all by itself."

"Someone turned it on," Henry said. "Whoever it was must have sat at the control panel and turned the switches that make the ride start."

"But why would someone do that?" Jessie asked. "Turning the ride on only got our attention. It made us run to the haunted house. The person could have been caught if we were closer and had gotten there quicker."

"That is true," Violet said. She suddenly remembered something. "When I was on the top of the Big Slide, I saw someone or something running down the steps from the pier onto the beach. It was very dark. But it might have been someone carrying the zombie."

"But the ride did not turn on until you were already at the bottom of the Big Slide," Jessie said. "The person could not have run onto the beach, and then snuck back to turn on the ride. We would have seen something."

"That is true," Violet said. "And a person cannot be in two places at the same time. That is a hard mystery to figure out."

While the children discussed the mystery, Violet had finally finished her sign. She turned it around for her sister and brothers to see. "What do you think?" she asked.

"Oh, Violet! It's perfect," Jessie exclaimed.

Henry read the sign aloud. " 'I love the beach. But I can't wait till dark. I am going to go to Hanson's. It is the best amusement pier on the boardwalk!' "

As the children were washing the breakfast dishes, Wendy and Will returned. They had a giant pair of sunglasses, a big yellow duck float, and a colorful beach towel.

"Are you ready to dress up our zombie?" Wendy asked. She handed the float to Benny.

"I'm ready!" Benny ran down the steps and out into the sand. Everyone followed him. Benny gazed up at the giant zombie. "He doesn't look so scary when he is not in the haunted house," he said.

Will agreed. "He looks pretty silly on the beach."

Henry placed the silly sunglasses on the zombie's nose. Benny hung the duck float from the zombie's right arm. Jessie draped the colorful towel over the other arm. A group of people on the beach came over to watch. Many were laughing and calling to their friends.

Violet took her sign and hung it from the zombie's neck.

Two little boys with buckets and shovels ran up to the zombie. "Mommy!" they called. "Come look!"

A woman in a pink bathing suit hurried

to stand behind her boys. "Can we go to Hanson's pier tonight? Pleeeease?" the boys asked.

The mother laughed. "I think we should," she said. "It looks like a fun place!"

Violet noticed a woman taking photographs of the zombie. "This is so great!" the woman said. "Would anyone like a picture taken with this zombie?"

Benny raised his hand. "I would!" he said.

Benny stood beside the zombie with a great big smile on his face. He looked very small next to the big zombie.

The photographer snapped several pictures. When she was done, she handed Jessie her card. "My name is Donna Mancini," she said. "I work for the local paper taking shots for stories. But I also have my own shop.

Jessie looked down at the card. "Thank you very much," she said.

A man wearing a red baseball cap came to admire the zombie with his children. "Is it safe at Hanson's pier?" he asked. "I have heard rumors that they are having lots of trouble with their amusements."

"It is perfectly safe!" Jessie said. "Those rumors are false."

"Mr. Hanson is my dad," Wendy said. "He is a great mechanic and he loves the amusement pier. He would never let anyone get on one of his rides unless it was perfectly safe."

The man folded his arms across his chest. "That is good to know," he said. "But I heard that the roller coaster was broken twice this week."

"It wasn't really broken." Will looked down at his feet before continuing. His face was very red. "Someone accidentally turned off the power. That is all. It is a very fun ride and a great amusement pier. You should come and see for yourself."

"Can we, Dad?" asked the man's children.

The man smiled. "I suppose we can. We'll stop by tonight after dinner."

The children clapped their hands and ran away toward the ocean.

Violet looked up just in time to see Benny racing toward the water as well.

"Benny! Wait!" she called. "Where are you going?"

CHAPTER 7

A Mysterious Find in the Ocean

Hunter waved at the Aldens and at Will and Wendy with his one free hand. He was walking at the edge of the ocean. He had a surfboard and a boogie board under his right arm.

Hunter set his things down in the sand. When Benny reached him, he gave Benny a high five. "Ready to ride the waves?" he asked.

"I sure am!" Benny said.

Henry, Jessie, Violet, and Benny waded

into the ocean. The water was cold, but it was refreshing on such a hot day.

Hunter held the boogie board still. He showed Benny how to grip the front of the board with his hands and wait for a good wave.

"How about this one?" Benny called over the roar as a big whitecap came crashing toward him.

"Go for it!" Hunter yelled.

The wave pushed under Benny's boogie board and shot him toward the beach. He had a very long ride. When it was over, he jumped up and splashed back to Hunter.

"Great job, Benny!" Henry said.

After a long swim, everyone rested in the sand. Wendy had brought a blanket and a cooler full of sandwiches and cold drinks. Hunter's friends joined them.

"Will and Wendy surfed for the first time today," Hunter told his friends. "And they already can catch waves."

Wendy smiled. "We had a good teacher," she said.

"You two should hang out with us," said a boy named Zach. "We come to the beach a lot. And tonight, I am having friends over to my house. Would you like to join us?"

"That sounds like fun," said Will. "But we may have to work. We help out at Hanson's Amusement Pier."

"You work there?" Zach looked down the beach toward the amusement pier. "I heard that place isn't safe. They have been having lots of problems since the new owner took over."

"Who told you that?" asked Jessie.

Zach shrugged. "I don't know. Just people talking. I suppose they are only rumors."

"They are only rumors!" Wendy said. "Hanson's is a great amusement pier. It is very safe."

"I agree with Wendy and Will," said Hunter. The pier is safe. And they should know. Their dad is the owner."

Zach's face turned red. "I'm sorry," he said to Wendy and Will. "I didn't know that your dad was the owner. I didn't mean to say anything against him."

"It's not your fault," Wendy said. "We know that there are false rumors going around."

"Someone is trying to ruin Hanson's," Jessie said.

"Why would someone do that?" asked Tori.

Just then, the lifeguards stood up in their stands and began to blow their whistles. They began to wave at all the swimmers to get out of the ocean. Everyone jumped up and ran to the water's edge to see what was going on.

"There's something in the water!" a woman cried, picking up her toddler.

"Maybe it is a whale!" Benny said.

"It's big, whatever it is," said a man. "There are three strong lifeguards dragging it out of the water."

Suddenly, there were gasps from the crowd. The lifeguards came out of the water and the people all moved out of their way. They were carrying the zombie from the haunted house!

"It's our zombie!" Benny cried.

"This is yours?" asked a dark-haired lifeguard.

Wendy stepped forward. "It is from Hanson's amusement pier," she said. "It belongs to my father."

"How did it get into the water?" asked the lifeguard. "You cannot dump things you do not want in the ocean. That man over there hurt his ankle banging into your zombie. He could not see it beneath the waves."

An older man sat on a blanket in the sand.

He rubbed his ankle as he talked with one of the lifeguards. "I'm fine," the man said. "It's just a little bruise. No need to make a fuss."

"We're so sorry that anyone got hurt," Wendy said. "But we did not dump the zombie in the ocean."

"Someone stole the zombie from the haunted house!" Benny said. "The thief must have put the zombie in the ocean."

The lifeguard looked concerned. "A thief? You should call the police," he said. "They should investigate this."

"No!" Will said quickly. "We do not need the police." He looked at Wendy. "I'm sure it was just a prank."

Wendy nodded. "We'll get to the bottom of it," she said. "We will take the zombie back to the haunted house right now. No one else will get hurt."

Henry, Will, Zach, and Hunter lifted the zombie. Saltwater ran out of holes in his metal shoes and from his eyes.

"It looks like the zombie is crying," Benny said.

"Yes, it does," Wendy agreed. "I feel like crying, too. I feel so bad."

Hunter put his arm around Wendy. "You don't have anything to feel bad about," he said. "This is not your fault."

Wendy looked down at her feet. "In some ways . . ." she began.

"Let's go!" Will said. "Let's get this zombie back right away!"

After the older kids had left with the zombie, Henry, Jessie, Violet, and Benny cleaned up the sandwich wrappers and napkins from their picnic and folded the towels.

"I sure could go for some ice cream," Violet said.

"That's a great idea, Violet," Jessie said.

The children headed up toward the boardwalk.

"Where shall we go?" asked Benny. "There are so many different places!"

Just then, someone called out to them. "Hey, kids!"

Henry, Jessie, Violet, and Benny turned.

Mrs. Reddy was hurrying toward them.

"I heard that Carl Hanson is so upset with the things going on at his amusement pier that he threw his own zombie into the ocean! Isn't that terrible?"

Violet's lips were pressed tightly together while Mrs. Reddy spoke. "Mrs. Reddy," Violet said. "I am sure that Mr. Hanson would not have thrown his own zombie into the ocean."

"Well then, how did it get there?" she asked. "When I ran the amusement pier, none of the ghosts or zombies from my haunted house ever went missing. And none of my property ever ended up in the ocean! And did you hear that some poor man got hurt by the zombie in the ocean? I heard that a wave threw the zombie on top of the man and he got knocked out. He almost drowned!"

"We were there on the beach," Henry replied. "The man only banged his ankle into the zombie under the water."

Mrs. Reddy clicked her tongue. "I don't know," she said. "But that is what I heard. Things are getting bad on that amusement pier. Carl Hanson needs my help. You should tell him that."

Violet looked thoughtful. Mrs. Reddy seemed like a person who liked to be busy and useful.

"Maybe you can help us," Violet said. "We are looking for some ice cream. Do you have a favorite ice cream stand on the boardwalk? Would you have the time to take us there?"

Mrs. Reddy smiled. "Of course!" She linked her arm through Violet's. "Come with me!"

The children walked a half block to Kohr's frozen custard stand. Mrs. Reddy waved to the man behind the counter. "Noah!" she said. "Here are some special guests. These are the Alden children. They have never been to our boardwalk before. I told them that you serve the best ice cream on the whole coast!"

Noah smiled at the compliment. He introduced himself and welcomed the children. While he made their cones, Mrs. Reddy talked nonstop.

"Noah, did you hear that Hanson's zombie

knocked out an old man in the ocean? Poor man almost drowned!"

"I did hear that," Noah said. "Your friend Karen stopped by earlier. She told me. As a matter of fact, there she is now." Noah pointed across the boardwalk.

"Oh yes," Mrs. Reddy said. "I see her. I promised to help her out in her souvenir shop today. Take care, kids. Enjoy your ice cream. And make sure you tell Carl Hanson that he can call me any time he needs advice." Mrs. Reddy hurried off to join her friend.

The children walked toward a bench to eat their ice cream. Benny's cone was vanilla dipped in a hard chocolate shell. Violet got a twist of orange crème and vanilla with rainbow sprinkles. Jessie chose strawberry with chocolate sprinkles and Henry had a thick milkshake.

"This is delicious!" Violet said. She watched the people stroll along the board-walk while she ate her cone. "Look," she said. "There is the photographer."

Donna Mancini was snapping photos of a

small sandwich shop with a "Grand Opening" banner hanging over the front door. A man in an apron stood under the banner.

"I wonder if that man will get his picture in the paper," Benny said.

"The picture might be for the paper Benny. But it might be for an advertisement for the new store as well." Violet was very interested in photography and she enjoyed watching Ms. Mancini work.

As she watched, Violet saw someone familiar pass by. "Isn't that Bob Cooke?"

Henry, Jessie, and Benny looked across the boardwalk. Mr. Cooke was alone. He was walking quickly. Suddenly, Mrs. Reddy and her friend approached Mr. Cooke. He stopped to talk with them. The children were too far away to hear what he was saying. But Mr. Cooke was smiling.

"What is wrong with Mr. Cooke's pants?" Benny asked.

"I noticed it, too, Benny," Violet said.

Mr. Cooke was wearing a pair of long tan pants. But from the knees down, the pants were very dark. The children also noticed that Mr. Cooke's sneakers left footprints on the boardwalk. It looked as though he had gotten wet somehow.

Mr. Cooke looked up from his conversation with Mrs. Reddy. He saw the Aldens. He looked down at his pants, then quickly hurried away.

CHAPTER 8

A Castle on the Beach

After their ice cream, the children headed back down to the beach. They arrived just in time.

"Hurry!" Jessie called.

The tide had come in. Their blanket and towels were just about to get drenched by the ocean! The children grabbed their things and moved them back out of the way of the water.

"That was close," Jessie said.

"Hunter told me about the tides," Benny

said. "He said that when the tide goes out, I might be able to find some cool seashells to take home as souvenirs."

"It will be fun to look for them," Violet said. "But would you like to help me build a sand castle right now?"

"Sure!" Benny said.

When the castle was finished, the children sat in the sand and waited for the tide to come in.

Violet watched the waves breaking. "Do you think that Mrs. Reddy made up the story about the zombie hitting the man in the head? Or do you think she heard it from someone else?"

"I don't know," Jessie said, tracing her finger through the sand. "It is always hard to tell where rumors start."

"One thing we do know," Henry said, "is that Mrs. Reddy certainly enjoys spreading rumors."

"I think she is just lonely and bored," Violet said. "I think she is sorry that she sold the amusement pier."

"I wonder what was she talking to Mr. Cooke about," Jessie said. "Do you think that Mr. Cooke and Mrs. Reddy could be working together to ruin Hanson's Amusement Pier?"

"Last time Benny and I saw Mr. Cooke and Mrs. Reddy together, they were fighting," Jessie said. "But today they were not. Mr. Cooke was smiling."

"I'm not sure if they are working together or not," Henry said. "But if Mr. Hanson cannot stop these rumors soon, his amusement pier will fail. No one will go there."

"We have to think of something to stop all these rumors," Violet said.

"Watch out!" Jessie cried.

A big wave came. It hit the castle and the walls fell away. Big chunks of sand slid into the ocean. Only the very top of the tower with the sea grass flag still stood.

"That was so cool," Benny said. "I love playing in the sand. Can we build another castle?"

"We can, but not right now," Jessie said. "I think we should go back to the house and get cleaned up. It is getting late."

The children splashed into the ocean and rinsed the sand from their arms and legs. They collected their things and walked back to the Hanson's beach house. Wendy waved to them from the porch.

"I was just going to come to look for you," she said. "How was the beach?"

"It was great!" Benny said. He told Wendy all about their sand castle and how the tide had come in and knocked it down.

"That does sound like fun," Wendy said. "Do you kids have any plans for tonight?"

"No," Jessie said. "We have not planned anything."

"I hate to ask this," Wendy said. "You have already done so much to help. But my father has lost two more employees today. There are so many rumors. People think that the amusement pier is unsafe. They think it is going to close soon. My father could really use your help tonight."

"Of course we'll help," Jessie said.

"We'll be glad to," Violet added.

The children showered and dressed. They rinsed their bathing suits and hung them to dry out on the line in the sun. Benny had a small collection of seashells that he had found. He set them in a pile by the steps.

Benny sat beside the shells. "Jessie, do you think I could buy a big bucket to put my shells in?" he asked.

"I think that is a good idea," Jessie said.

"We should get some shovels, too, Benny," Henry said. "We can build an even bigger castle with shovels."

"I would like to stop in the souvenir shop as well," Violet said. "I want to buy something to remember our trip."

"We should leave right away," Jessie said. "That way we will have time to go into the stores before we are needed at the amusement pier."

"I'll be right out," Violet said. Violet went back into the house. She wanted to get her money from her bedroom. She had just opened her drawer and was looking through her things when she heard Wendy and Will talking in the hallway.

"Did the kids leave yet?" Will asked in a quiet voice.

"Yes," Wendy said. "Did you get the zombie back in place in the haunted house?"

"Dad was working on it," Will said. "But there is a bolt missing. I don't know if the zombie will be working by tonight if we can't find that bolt."

"Where could it be?" Wendy asked. "Are you sure that you don't have it?"

"I don't have it, Wendy," Will said.

"Okay. I'm just checking," Wendy said. "Because we agreed that our plan was . . ."

Violet felt uncomfortable listening to a private conversation. She grabbed her money and closed the drawer very loudly.

Wendy and Will stopped talking. Wendy peeked around the corner and into Violet's room. "Violet!" she said. "I thought you had gone to the boardwalk."

"I forgot my money," Violet said. "I want to buy a souvenir in one of the shops. I am leaving now."

Violet joined Henry, Jessie, and Benny

outside, and the children headed down the boardwalk. On the way, Violet told her sister and brothers what she had overheard.

"What kind of plan do you think Wendy meant?" Jessie asked.

"I don't know," Violet said. "And why would Wendy think that Will had the missing bolt?"

"It could be that Will misplaced the bolt when he was putting the zombie back," Henry said. "Sometimes, when I am fixing things, I misplace a bolt or a screw. It can happen very easily."

"Look!" Benny cried. "Here is the store! Can we go in?"

At the Beach Stop Shop, Benny picked out a blue bucket and a large red shovel. Violet found a small jewelry box decorated from top to bottom with very tiny seashells.

Then the children paid for their purchases and left the store. They soon passed a woman in a white apron and a tall chef's hat. She stood outside Laura's Fudge Shop with a tray. "Would you like to try some of our fudge for free?" she asked the children.

"Free fudge! I would like some," Benny cried. He tried the chocolate peanut butter flavor. "It's so good!" he said.

"I'm glad you like it," the woman said. "We also have delicious saltwater taffy."

Benny shivered. He remembered when he accidentally got saltwater in his mouth when he was boogie boarding with Hunter. It did not taste good. "You put saltwater in your taffy?" he asked.

The woman laughed. "No. There is no saltwater in our saltwater taffy."

"Then why is it called that?" Benny asked.

"A very long time ago, a man had a taffy stand on the boardwalk in Atlantic City," the woman explained. "One night a big wave came and hit his stand. It ruined all his taffy. He was upset. He had nothing to sell the next day. When a customer asked for taffy, the man said that all he had to sell was saltwater taffy. He had to throw all the taffy away. The man worked hard and made more taffy. But he thought the name saltwater taffy was catchy. And he was right! We still call it saltwater taffy more than one hundred years later!"

The woman reached into her apron pocket. She pulled out some saltwater taffy. She gave one to each of the Aldens. "Try some," she said.

Benny took a bite of the soft candy. "This one tastes like peppermint!" he said. The soft and chewy candy seemed to melt in his mouth.

"Mine is butterscotch," Violet said. She laughed after she took a bite.

"Thank you very much," Jessie said, swallowing a chocolate-flavored taffy. "It is delicious. We will stop back later to buy some more! We don't have time right now."

"You kids are in a hurry?" the woman asked.

"Yes," Jessie said. "We are on our way to Hanson's Amusement Pier."

The woman looked concerned. "Be careful, kids," she said. "I've heard that it might not be safe at the pier."

"Someone is spreading false rumors," Jessie

said. "Please do not believe them. The pier is very safe."

The children thanked the woman and left.

"It was nice of that lady to give us free samples," Benny said.

"Yes, and smart, too," Violet said. "It makes us want to go back and buy more candy. And it has given me a very good idea for Hanson's Amusement Pier."

"Free candy?" Benny asked.

"No," Violet said. "Something even better. Something that will help stop all of the false rumors."

CHAPTER 9

Violet Has an Idea

The children found Mr. Hanson sitting in his shed at the back of the pier. There were tools all around him on his workbench, but he was not working.

"Hi, kids," Mr. Hanson said. "Thanks for coming. But I'm not sure that I will need your help tonight."

"Is something wrong?" asked Jessie.

Mr. Hanson pointed toward the door. "Did you see how few customers there are out there? Everyone thinks my pier is unsafe.

Even the local safety inspector heard the rumors. He stopped by today for a surprise inspection."

"Were there any problems?" Jessie asked.

"No, not at all," Mr. Hanson said. He showed Jessie the copy of the inspector's report. "The inspector congratulated me on my pier. He said it was very safe. I could post the report outside, but no one will see it. I do not know how to fight these false rumors."

"We have heard the rumors, too," Henry said "But Violet has come up with a wonderful idea."

Violet stood in front of the workbench. "Mr. Hanson," she said, "if we could only get people to come visit your pier, they would see how much fun it is and how it is safe. They would want to come back and visit many times."

Mr. Hanson held up his hand. "Thank you, Violet. I agree with you. But I cannot get people to come here. Did you see Bob Cooke's pier? There are long lines for all the rides. My rides are empty."

"But what if you had a special night where all the rides on Hanson's pier were free? I think many people would come for free rides. Then they would see how wonderful your pier is. The rumors would die because people would see the truth, that you have a safe and fun amusement pier."

Mr. Hanson sat up straight in his chair. He looked at Violet. "Violet," he said, "may I shake your hand?"

Violet's face was flushed. Mr. Hanson grabbed her hand and shook it up and down. There was a big smile on his face. "You are a genius!" he said. "I think it is a great plan. We should have the free night as soon as possible! I think we should do it tomorrow!"

The children looked at each other. "We would have to let everyone know first," Henry said.

"I'll put an ad in the paper," Mr. Hanson said, clapping his hands together.

"I can make flyers," Violet said. "We can put them up all around the boardwalk so that everyone will know about the special night."

"There is a T-shirt shop on the boardwalk," Jessie added. "We could have special shirts made that advertise the free night. We could wear them all day tomorrow."

Just then Will and Wendy walked into the shed. "Dad," Will said, "I found the bolt that you were looking for. I want to apologize. The bolt was in my . . ."

"Listen to this, Will!" Mr. Hanson said. "The Aldens have come up with a plan to save the pier." Mr. Hanson explained the plan to Will and Wendy.

"It sounds great!" Will said. "Wendy and I will help, of course."

There was no time to spare. Mr. Hanson headed straight to the *Oceanside Times* newspaper office to place a big ad for the next day's edition. Will and Henry went to the haunted house to put the bolt back on the zombie. Jessie, Violet, and Benny walked to the T-shirt shop and Wendy stayed to run the pier while everyone was gone.

The Oceanside Shirt Shop was a small store crowded with many racks of T-shirts.

"May I help you?" asked a young man behind the counter.

"Yes," Violet answered. "We would like to purchase some T-shirts, but can we make our own design to put on them?"

"Of course," the man answered.

Violet worked on the T-shirt design with the man while Jessie and Benny picked out a pile of plain green T-shirts in different sizes.

The man's name was Dennis. He was impressed with Violet's design. "You are a very

good artist," he said. "Is Hanson's pier really going to let people ride for free tomorrow?"

"Yes," Violet said.

"But is it safe? I have heard some bad rumors about Hanson's," Dennis said.

"They are false rumors that someone has been spreading," Violet explained. "The safety inspector checked out the whole pier today and he said it was very safe."

"That is good to hear," Dennis said. "I have a little boy. I will bring him over tomorrow to ride the rides. And I will tell my customers all about it, too."

Dennis finished pressing Violet's design onto the T-shirts and handed them to the children.

"Look at me!" Benny cried. Benny had put his small T-shirt on. "If I run up and down the boardwalk, everyone will know about the free night at Hanson's! I am a walking flyer!"

Jessie and Violet changed into their shirts as well. Then the children headed back toward the amusement pier. They noticed that people were staring at their shirts.

"Free rides!" The children heard a woman shout, and they turned. It was Mrs. Reddy. She was hurrying toward them.

"Hanson is giving out free rides?" she asked. "He must be crazy. He cannot make money if he gives the rides for free. He will be ruined." Mrs. Reddy looked toward the pier. "I know I could run it again," she said. "I do know a lot about running that pier. And my pier was always safe. I could be very helpful there."

"Hanson's pier is safe, Mrs. Reddy," Jessie said. "The safety inspector declared today that the pier is very safe. Someone has been spreading false rumors. The free rides are just for one night so that everyone can see how fun Hanson's pier is."

Violet turned toward the old woman. "I am sure that the pier was wonderful when you ran it, Mrs. Reddy," she said. "And I am sure that you must miss being in charge there. But it is still a very fun and very safe place."

"Would you like a T-shirt?" Benny asked. "It is free!"

Mrs. Reddy looked startled. "You are giving me a free T-shirt?"

"Sure," Benny said. "Why not?"

Mrs. Reddy took the T-shirt. "Thank you," she said. "I must admit, this is a very good idea. I never had T-shirts made when I owned the pier. I never thought of it! And maybe I will stop by tomorrow night to see how everything is going. If it gets very busy, maybe Carl will ask me to help."

When Jessie, Violet, and Benny got back to the pier, they went straight to the workshop. Mr. Hanson, Henry, Will, Wendy, and Hunter were sitting around the large wooden table. They were very impressed with the T-shirts. They each took one.

Mr. Hanson told them about the ad he had placed in the paper. "And Donna Mancini, the photographer, has been taking lots of pictures of the boardwalk. I am going use some of her pictures of the pier and put more ads in newspapers and magazines."

"What a wonderful idea," Violet said.

"My dad is donating pizza from his

shop," Hunter said. "The first one hundred customers tomorrow night will get a coupon for a free slice of pizza."

At the mention of the word pizza, there was a strange growling noise in the shed. "What was that?" Hunter asked.

"I'm sorry!" Benny's face turned very red. "But my stomach heard you say 'free pizza.'"

Everyone laughed.

"Why don't you go get something to eat? And then head back to the house and rest. Tomorrow will be a very busy day and we will need everyone's help."

The children stopped at Mack's and ordered take-out. They carried their dinners back to the Hansons' home and sat outside on the deck overlooking the ocean.

Jessie poured four glasses of cold milk. "Mr. Hanson has said that he will have to move back to Colorado if the amusement pier fails."

"That would be terrible!" Violet said. "Owning the amusement pier and living in this house on the beach was always Mr. Hanson's dream."

Henry took a bite of his cheesesteak. He looked thoughtful. "That is true, Violet. This is Mr. Hanson's dream. But I don't think that Wendy and Will had the same dream. I think they liked Colorado."

"Do you suspect them of trying to ruin the amusement pier?" Violet asked.

Henry took a long drink of milk. "I don't know," he said. "But remember that they both had red stains on their shoes, just like the red paint from the house of mirrors. And if the amusement pier fails, they would get to go back to Colorado to their old school and all their old friends."

"And remember that I accidently overheard them talking in the hallway the other day." Violet sprinkled cheese on her pasta. "Wendy said that they had a 'plan.' I wonder what that meant."

Jessie had her notebook on the table and was looking through the clues she had written down. "And didn't Will say that he had the bolt to the zombie in his pocket? How did he get it?"

"He could have found it on the floor in the haunted house," Violet said.

Jessie tapped a pencil on her notebook. "What about Mrs. Reddy?"

"She spreads bad rumors," Benny said.

"That's right, Benny," Henry said. "Mrs. Reddy seems like she would be happy if the amusement pier failed. I think she is sorry that she sold it. She wants to run it again. She does not like being retired."

"But she did like the T-shirt we gave her. She said she would wear it." Benny said.

"Don't forget about Mr. Cooke," Violet said. "He also would like to run the amusement pier."

"That's true," Jessie said. "When he was arguing with Mrs. Reddy, he said that he wanted Mr. Hanson to fail. And someone with a black marker wrote on the walls of the house of mirrors. We found a marker with 'Captain Cooke's Amazing Amusement Pier' written on the side."

"But Mr. Cooke is right," Violet said. "There are many markers like that on the boardwalk. Anyone could have used it. But I agree that he acts suspicious sometimes. Remember the other day when we saw him on the boardwalk? His pants and shoes looked very wet. And it was not raining. He hurried away when he saw us looking at him."

"He might have been fixing a ride on his pier," Henry said. "He does have a log flume and a boat ride."

The children finished their meals and cleaned up the little table on the deck. Violet leaned on the rail. She stared out at the moonlight glinting off of the ocean. She wished she could take a photograph of the view and save it. She thought of Mrs. Mancini, the photographer who took so many pictures of Oceanside.

Suddenly, Violet stood up straight. She turned to her sister and brothers. "I have an idea," she said. "I think I know how we might catch the people who are trying to ruin the pier."

CHAPTER 10

An Accidental Confession

Early the next morning, the children started their day at Dottie's Pancake House. They wore the T-shirts that Violet had designed. Everyone in the small restaurant asked them about the free rides. The people seemed excited and made plans to visit Hanson's Amusement Pier.

Dottie, the woman who owned the restaurant, stopped at the children's table. "How is everything?" she asked.

Benny tried to answer, but his mouth was stuffed with pancakes.

Jessie was cutting up her French toast. She laughed. "I think you can see that our brother loves your pancakes. Everything here is wonderful."

Dottie smiled. "Thank you. I noticed your T-shirts," she said. "Everyone is talking about them. Are the rides really free tonight?"

"Yes, they are," Jessie answered.

Dottie smiled. "Maybe I will stop by and check it out tonight."

After breakfast the children visited a copy store. The night before, Violet had designed the flyer that would advertise the free night. It looked a lot like the design on the T-shirts. The man made the copies for the children right away.

Next to the copy store was the photographer's shop. Violet gazed in the window at all the beautiful photographs. Ms. Mancini had many colorful pictures of sunsets over the bay, shore birds, and happy families posing on the beach. A sign on the door said, "Out taking photographs. Be back soon!"

As the children walked farther down the

street, they saw a shop that rented bicycles. Bikes in every size lined the sidewalk.

"Look!" Violet cried. "They even rent surreys!"

"What is a surrey?" Benny asked.

Violet walked up to the surrey and showed Benny. The surrey had four wheels and four sets of pedals. It had two seats in front and two in the back. There was a steering wheel, just like a car, and there was a yellow and blue striped cloth roof over the top.

A woman in a blue apron walked up to the children. "Would you like to rent the surrey?" she asked. "They are lots of fun."

The children agreed. They paid the woman and climbed in. Henry and Jessie sat up front. Violet and Benny were in the back. With all four children pedaling, the surrey could go quite fast. They took turns driving. Even Benny had a turn! As they rode back down the boardwalk, they made many stops and posted the flyers in stores and on announcement boards.

Henry looked at his watch. "It is almost

ten o'clock," he said. "We should return the surrey now to the rental store."

The children pedaled back the way they had come. "Look," Benny said. "Isn't that Mr. Cooke?"

"It is," Jessie said. "What is he carrying?"

"I don't know," Henry said. "It looks like big poster boards. Maybe he is making signs for his pier, too."

After the children returned the surrey, they got right to work. Henry and Benny took half of the remaining flyers and Jessie and Violet took the other half.

"Benny and I will give these out on the beach," Henry said.

"And we will hand them out on the boardwalk," Jessie said.

But before the children could start, they

saw Mr. Hanson hurrying toward them. He had a worried look on his face.

"What's wrong?" the children asked.

Mr. Hanson wrung his hands together. "I don't know exactly. I just got a call from Ms. Mancini, the photographer, that she saw something wrong at the pier. We don't open for a few more hours. I hope it is something I can fix."

Everyone hurried toward the pier. They saw the problem right away.

"Oh no!" Violet said. "Who could have done such a thing?"

The top six cars on the giant Ferris wheel each had a very large letter pasted to its side. All together, the cars spelled out the word "UNSAFE." It was so big, everyone on the boardwalk could see what it said. Ms. Mancini was standing nearby taking photographs.

They all hurried to the Ferris wheel. Mr. Hanson pulled his keys from his pocket. He turned the Ferris wheel on so that the cars at the top moved to the bottom. Ms. Mancini and the children helped him remove the letters. It was not hard. The letters had been printed on white poster board and taped to the sides of the car.

"Who else has keys to the Ferris wheel?" Henry asked.

Mr. Hanson was ripping the cardboard letters into pieces. "Only Wendy, Will, and I have keys," he said. "And I suppose Mrs. Reddy might. She was supposed to turn over all the keys to me when I bought the pier. But I suppose that it is possible that she kept some."

"What about Mr. Cooke?" asked Jessie.

Mr. Hanson shook his head. "Mr. Cooke would not have any keys to my pier."

"Is there any other way to get the letters up on those cars?" Henry asked.

Mr. Hanson looked up at the Ferris wheel. "I suppose you could climb up," he said. "It's not too hard. But most people would be afraid to do such a thing."

"I took a lot of pictures of your pier over the last week," Ms. Mancini said. "I will develop them and leave them in your workshop. I don't know if they will help. But maybe they will show something that will help you to figure out who is doing these things. I will drop them off around four o'clock."

The Alden children looked at one another and smiled. This would help their plan.

Mr. Hanson thanked Ms. Mancini. He asked the Aldens if they could help him to look through the pictures. Everyone agreed to meet in the workshop at about five o'clock. Henry and Benny then headed toward the beach to distribute their flyers.

Jessie and Violet walked up and down the boardwalk to hand out their flyers. Just as they had hoped, they saw Mrs. Reddy. She was wearing the T-shirt that they had given her yesterday.

"Hello!" Mrs. Reddy waved to Jessie and Violet. "I am wearing my T-shirt," she said. "How does it look?"

"It looks very nice on you," Violet said. "Green is a good shade for you. It matches your eyes."

Mrs. Reddy smiled. "Thank you, Violet.

You are very sweet. Do you think anyone will come to Hanson's pier tonight?"

"Yes," Jessie said. "Many people will come."

"But what about that sign on the Ferris wheel?" Mrs. Reddy asked.

"We saw it," Jessie replied. "But Mr. Hanson has taken it down. And we hope to figure out who put it there. A photographer has been taking pictures of the pier. She is dropping them off in the work shed at four o'clock. We will look through them later for clues."

Mrs. Reddy put her hand up to her mouth. "Oh my," she said. "I wonder what those pictures will show. I better go. But I will stop by the pier later." Mrs. Reddy hurried away.

When Jessie and Violet got to Captain Cooke's amusement pier, they stood outside handing out the flyers until Mr. Cooke noticed and came rushing toward them.

"Get out of here with those flyers!" he said.

"You are wasting your time anyway. Hanson's pier is not safe and it will close before the summer is over."

"It is safe," Violet insisted.

"Didn't you see that sign on the Ferris wheel?" Mr. Cooke said.

"Yes," Violet answered. "We saw it. But it is nothing more than a mean trick. It does not mean that the pier is unsafe."

"Then why would someone go to all the trouble to put that sign up?" Mr. Cooke asked.

"We don't know," Jessie answered. "But we may have a clue."

Mr. Cooke's eyebrows went up. "Really? What kind of clue?"

Jessie explained about Ms. Mancini's photographs. "She has been taking photographs all over the boardwalk. She has many of Hanson's pier. No one really noticed that she was there. We are going to the work shed at five o'clock to look through the photographs. They might show who has been trying to ruin Mr. Hanson."

Mr. Cooke's face turned red. "Those photographs probably won't show a thing!"

he said. "What time did you say that Mrs. Mancini is dropping off the photos?"

"At four o'clock in the work shed," Violet answered.

Mr. Cooke turned away. "I have a busy night ahead of me," he said. "I have to get back to work. And keep those flyers away from my pier!"

After Henry and Benny were finished on the beach, they met Jessie and Violet at a lemonade stand on the boardwalk.

The children bought lemonades and walked out over the ocean.

"I sure hope everything works out tonight," Benny said. "Some people on the beach said that they saw the 'unsafe' sign on the Ferris wheel."

"I think people will be curious about the free rides," Henry said. "They will come and see how safe the amusements are. I just hope that there are no more pranks tonight. I hope our plan works."

Jessie took a long sip from her cool drink. "Violet and I saw Mrs. Reddy and Mr. Cooke on the boardwalk this morning," she said. "We told them that Mrs. Mancini had some photographs that might contain clues as to who has been trying to ruin Mr. Hanson's pier."

Violet nodded. "We told them that the photographs would be dropped off at the work shed at four o'clock."

"Mrs. Reddy loves to spread news on the boardwalk. I am sure she will tell many people," Jessie said.

"Now I get it!" Benny said. "The person who has been playing all the mean tricks will want to steal the photos in case he or she is in them!"

"Exactly!" Jessie said.

The children agreed that they would arrive early at the work shed to see who might show up after Mrs. Mancini dropped off the photos. In the meantime, they relaxed on the beach. They talked about all the things they had seen and all the clues they had gathered. Jessie wrote everything down in her notebook.

When the Aldens returned to Hanson's pier later in the afternoon, they went straight to the work shed as planned. They were surprised to find Wendy and Will sitting with their father on a bench. He had his arms around them.

"We're sorry," Jessie said. "We did not mean to intrude. We will come back later. We thought we would come a little early."

"Please stay," Mr. Hanson said. "Wendy, Will, and I were just having a long talk. I now realize that we should have talked a long time ago. I didn't take their feelings into account when we moved to Oceanside."

"Dad, it's okay," Wendy said. "Everything is fine now."

"Yes," Will said. "We weren't fair to you either, Dad. In the beginning, we did not give Oceanside a chance. We thought that if you had a lot of problems with the pier, you would not like it here. We wanted you to hate running the amusement pier. We thought you would let us move back to Colorado."

"You were the ones who splashed the red

paint in the house of mirrors," Jessie said. "You were careful, but some of the paint splattered onto your shoes."

Wendy and Will looked down at their feet. "Yes," Will said. "You're right, Jessie. A house of mirrors is not fun if you can see where you are going. We're very sorry, Dad."

"We want to apologize to Benny, too," Wendy said.

Mr. Hanson looked confused. "Benny? What did you do to Benny?"

Wendy rubbed the top of Benny's head, but she was too embarrassed to speak.

"Will and Wendy took the zombie from the haunted house," Henry explained. "I am sure that they did not know that Benny would be there. The zombie is very heavy, and Will must have accidentally hit Benny in the face when he was moving it. It was very dark."

Mr. Hanson turned to Henry. "You knew that Will took the zombie?"

"Not right away," Henry said. "We could not accuse him. But there were clues. Today on the beach, we put all the clues together."

"I was on top of the Big Slide," Violet explained. "I saw someone going down the steps toward the beach carrying the zombie."

"And at the same time," Jessie added, "the haunted house ride was turned on. So it had to be two people working together."

"And they had to have had a key to turn the ride on," Henry said.

"Will and Wendy had a spare key," Jessie said. "We heard Wendy say so the next day."

"It was very dark in the haunted house that night. I'm sorry, Benny," Will said. "It was an accident. Wendy turned on the ride so that the lights would come on. She knew that your brother and sisters would come and help you."

Mr. Hanson listened in amazement. "You should have stayed and helped Benny yourselves!" he said. "You should not have left him there."

"We know," Wendy said. "We're so sorry."

"We feel terrible about what we have done," Will said. "But now we know that Oceanside is a wonderful place. We understand why you wanted to move here. And we have met some very nice friends."

Just then Ms. Mancini stepped inside the shed. She handed a stack of photographs to Mr. Hanson. "I took a quick look through the photos. They don't really show anything that would help you catch the person who has been playing the tricks," she said. "I'm sorry. But there are some nice shots that we can use for advertisements."

Mr. Hanson glanced through the photos. He held up the one of the Ferris wheel with the word *unsafe* on the cars. "Did you do this, too?" he asked Wendy and Will.

Suddenly, the doorknob of the small work shed began to rattle. Everyone grew quiet. The door slowly creaked open. A head peered around the side of the door.

"Bob!" Mr. Hanson cried. "What are you doing here?"

Mr. Cooke looked startled to see the room so full of people. He looked down at his watch. "It is not five o'clock yet. I . . . I just came to see if . . . I mean, to say good luck tonight."

Jessie pointed to the stack of photographs in Mr. Hanson's hands. "Are you sure you did not come for the photographs, Mr. Cooke?" she asked.

"But how did Bob know we had the photographs?" Mr. Hanson asked. "I don't understand."

"Those kids told me," Mr. Cooke said. "So you have looked through the photographs already?" he asked.

"Yes, we have," Mr. Hanson answered.

Mr. Cooke shoved his hands deep into his pockets. "Then you know that I am the one who put the word *unsafe* on the Ferris wheel. But it was just a joke, Carl."

"Actually, Bob," Mr. Hanson said, "the photographs don't show you at all."

"What?!" Mr. Cooke turned toward the Aldens. "Those kids told me that the photos had clues in them."

"We did not," Violet responded. "We said that we hoped that there were clues in them. But you have just admitted that you put the word *unsafe* on the Ferris wheel."

"But how did you get up there?" Benny asked. "It is so high!"

"I fix rides all the time. I know how to go up and down them. I have my own Ferris wheel on my pier, remember?" Mr. Cooke turned toward Mr. Hanson. "And my Ferris wheel has always been better than yours! I was just trying to protect the public from this unsafe pier."

"You were not protecting the public when you put the zombie in the ocean," Henry said.

Mr. Cooke looked startled.

"It was you," Jessie said. "We saw you later walking down the boardwalk and your pants and shoes were quite wet. You did not seem to care that a swimmer banged his ankle against the zombie in the water."

"You wanted Mr. Hanson to be blamed for it," Violet said.

"And Mr. Cooke wrote with black marker in the house of mirrors," Benny added.

Mr. Hanson looked upset. "Did you really do all these things, Bob?" he asked.

Mr. Cooke looked around the room.

Everyone was staring at him. "I . . . I . . . All right, I admit it! I did those things. But so what? It is just a little friendly competition."

"There is nothing friendly about it," Mr. Hanson said. "I want you to leave my amusement pier right now. And don't ever set foot here again or I will call the police. You are lucky I am not calling the police right now!"

Mr. Cooke's face turned very red. Then he hurried out of the shed.

A few moments later, there was knock on the door. "Carl? Are you in there?"

Mr. Hanson opened the door. "Mrs. Reddy! Come in. What are you doing here?"

Mrs. Reddy cleared her throat. "I um . . . I want to apologize."

"More apologies!" Mr. Hanson exclaimed. "What could you have done, Mrs. Reddy?"

"Mrs. Reddy wanted your pier to fail also," Jessie said. "She misses being the owner and running the pier. She thinks that she made a mistake to retire. She would like to run the pier again."

Mrs. Reddy nodded. "Jessie is right. So many things were going wrong here, I thought that you would ruin the pier. And I was bored at home with not much to do. I love this pier. I want to keep it great. It is the best pier on the boardwalk."

Mr. Hanson nodded. "I know how you feel. And I sure could use your help," he said. "You have so much experience. Would you be willing to help out here?"

Mrs. Reddy smiled. "Really? You would let me help? I would love to!"

There was another knock at the door.

Mr. Hanson scratched his head. "Now what?" he said.

It was Madison, one of the pier workers. "Mr. Hanson!" she cried. "We need your help out here!"

"What is the problem?" Mr. Hanson asked.

Madison's face was flushed. "There are so many customers, we need help running the rides! I think the whole town of Oceanside has come to your pier tonight!"

"How wonderful!" Violet said.

Everyone rushed out to help run the pier. Jessie sold tickets. Henry and Benny ran the haunted house ride. Violet helped children on the Big Slide. Mrs. Reddy went from ride to ride, helping wherever she was needed, and smiling happily at all the customers. She told everyone what a safe and wonderful pier Carl Hanson was running. Wendy ran the motorcycle ride and Will took care of the Ferris wheel.

When the pier finally closed, all of the customers went away talking about how much fun they had had.

"We will be back!" many people called as they walked away. "Thank you so much for a great night."

Mr. Hanson, Will, Wendy, Mrs. Reddy, and the Aldens sat at a picnic table at the end of the pier overlooking the ocean. They were very tired.

"The free ride night was a big success," Jessie said. "Now everyone knows that Hanson's is a terrific and safe amusement pier."

"Yes." Mr. Hanson smiled. "Thanks to you children."

Suddenly, there was a loud growling sound. Mrs. Reddy looked startled. She put her hand over her heart. "What was that?" she asked.

Everyone turned to look at Benny. Benny held his stomach. "I can't help it!" he said. "My stomach always does that when I am hungry."

"And Benny is always hungry," Henry explained.

"Then I am just in time!" Hunter walked up to the picnic table. His arms were full of boxes of pizza from Mack's.

"Oh boy!" Benny cried. "Mack's has the best pizza in the world. It smells so good!"

"Congratulations, Mr. Hanson," Hunter said. "Everyone on the boardwalk has been talking about your amusement pier. The free ride night must have been a great success."

"It was," Mr. Hanson said. "And it is not over yet."

Benny swallowed a big mouthful of pepperoni pizza. "It's not over yet?" He looked around. "But all the customers are gone. I thought the pier was closed."

Mr. Hanson smiled. "The pier is closed, but we are still here. And now that the crowds are gone, I think you children should try all the rides."

Benny jumped up from the table. "Really? Can I ride the motorcycles? And the roller coaster? And the Ferris wheel, too?"

"Of course you can," Will said. "And you can ride them as many times as you like."

"I'm going to ride everything!" Benny said. Then he paused. "Except maybe not the haunted house. The zombies still scare me a little bit. I know they are not real but . . ."

Just then another long, loud growl came from Benny's stomach.

Mrs. Reddy laughed. "Benny, I think the zombies should be afraid of your stomach! It sounds much scarier than they do."

"You're right, Mrs. Reddy!" Benny grabbed another piece of pizza and headed toward the haunted house. "Okay, zombies, here I come," he called. "I am not afraid of you!"

Everyone laughed. Henry, Jessie, Violet, Benny, Will, Wendy, Hunter, Mr. Hanson, and even Mrs. Reddy spent a fun night riding on all the rides, playing games, and eating the pizza that Hunter had brought.

"Mr. Hanson," Benny said at the end of the night, holding his very full stomach, "I hope that you own this amusement pier forever and ever!"

"We all do," Violet said.

Mr. Hanson smiled. He put one arm around Will and one around Wendy. He gazed up at the big Ferris wheel. "This has always been my dream," he said. "And now, because of all of you, my dream has come true! Thank you!"

DARK RIDERS
OF DOOM

DARK RIDERS
OF DOOM

Peter Dawson

Thorndike Press • Chivers Press
Thorndike, Maine USA   Bath, England

This Large Print edition is published by Thorndike Press, USA and by Chivers Press, England.

Published in 1997 in the U.S. by arrangement with Golden West Literary Agency.

Published in 1997 in the U.K. by arrangement with Golden West Literary Agency.

U.S. Hardcover   0-7862-0628-4   (Western Series Edition)
U.K. Hardcover   0-7540-3083-0   (Chivers Large Print)

Thorndike Large Print ® Western Series.

The text of this Large Print edition is unabridged. Other aspects of the book may vary from the original edition.

Set in 16 pt. Plantin by Rick Gundberg.

Printed in the United States on permanent paper.

British Library Cataloguing in Publication Data available

Library of Congress Cataloging in Publication Data

Dawson, Peter, 1907–
        Dark riders of doom / Peter Dawson.
            p.   cm.
        Contents: Vengeance in Shadow Cañon — The Hangtree rebellion — Long gone — Dark riders of doom — Lost homestead.
        ISBN 0-7862-0628-4 (lg. print : hc : alk. paper)
        1. Large type books. I. Title.
    [PS3507.A848A6 1997]
        813′.54—dc20   95-47318

Table of Contents

Jonathan Hurff Glidden's first Western story was written and rewritten according to suggestions from his younger brother, Frederick Dilley Glidden, who had established himself in the Western pulp magazines by 1935 under the byline Luke Short. When Fred thought the story publishable, he sent it off to his agent, Marguerite E. Harper, who sold it on March 3, 1936 to Street & Smith's *Complete Stories*. It appeared in that magazine as "Gunsmoke Pledge" in the May, 1936 issue. Harper informed Jon that henceforth his byline would be Peter Dawson (after a brand of Scotch whiskey she drank) and that would be the case for well over one hundred stories of varying lengths, his serials for *The Saturday Evening Post*, and all of his novels.

"Vengeance in Shadow Cañon" was the thirty-third Peter Dawson story to be published and the seventh in Street & Smith's *Western Story Magazine*. It was originally titled "Bullets Bury a Back-Trail" by the author and was sold on April 11, 1938 for $135.00 — a sum computed at the rate of 1½¢ a word. It was published in the issue dated October 8, 1938. Along with Fiction House's *Lariat Story Magazine*, Street & Smith's *Western Story Magazine* was at the top of the ladder among pulp magazines

that published Western fiction exclusively. In the 1920s, *Western Story Magazine* customarily paid its top three authors — Max Brand, Robert J. Horton, and Robert Ormond Case — 5¢ a word and the magazine cost 15¢ a copy. The Depression changed that. The cover price fell to 10¢, and after 1934 the top rate paid for most stories was 2¢ a word, but that was more than most of the competition paid, ever. By the time the Peter Dawson story "Lost Homestead," also included in this quintet, appeared in this magazine, the author was customarily paid 2¢ a word for every story or serial he wrote featured in its pages.

VENGEANCE IN SHADOW CAÑON

I

"BUSHWACKER IN THE CAÑON"

Tim Gilpin counted six riders coming across the pasture. As they started to climb up the slope toward his cabin, he recognized one of the horses. That sent him into the cabin quietly — so his daughter, busy with the breakfast dishes in the kitchen, wouldn't hear — to get his shotgun. He met the six riders down by the corral, well out of hearing of the cabin.

It was Gilpin who spoke first, giving no greeting and receiving none: "Turn around and ride down out of here, Rudd. You aren't wanted."

Mike Rudd, owner of the Whip, was a somber, squat man sitting a silver-mounted saddle atop the finest horse of the lot. His outfit was a black Stetson, broadcloth coat, and fawn-colored trousers stuffed into expensive soft boots. His slate-gray eyes took in the shotgun in the crook of Gilpin's arm,

finally came to rest on Tim's blunt Irish face.

"You've got the wrong idea, Gilpin," he said suavely. "It wasn't me that did it nor any of my men. Ask the sheriff here."

Gilpin flashed a look at Bob Scholl, sheriff of Roco Verde County. He had a hearty respect for this lawman, and it was this that made him say, "Bob, you aren't particular who you travel with."

"Now don't go off half-cocked," Bob Scholl warned. His grizzled face was set in a frown, and he was plainly ill at ease. "I came up here to tell you folks that Rudd and ten of his riders was in town all last night. They unloaded two trains of short-horns yesterday afternoon, spent most of last night at the saloon. Now, Tim. . . ."

"I said to get out of here," Tim Gilpin intoned.

"We'll get," the sheriff said. "Only I want to know . . . have you seen Ed Soule?"

"No. If I do, I'll tell him you're lookin' for him."

"You tell him to see me before he. . . ." Scholl abruptly checked his words as though realizing the futility of talk. He nodded to Mike Rudd and wheeled his horse about. Rudd, after one glance at Gilpin, did the same. His riders followed, and in ten min-

utes the group had disappeared into the timber two miles below.

That was at eight in the morning. At ten a lone rider crossed the pasture and came on rapidly toward the cabin. This time Tim Gilpin didn't go for his shotgun. He sat on the slab step at the door and called back over his shoulder, "Hope, here comes Ed."

A girl appeared in the doorway, untying her apron and laying it on a chair inside. She took a long look at the approaching rider. "Dad, I'm afraid!" she said abruptly.

"Of Ed Soule?"

"No. Of what'll happen to him . . . to all of us, but mostly to him."

Her father got up without comment and walked out to the hitch rail. He waited there until Ed Soule had come up past the corral and reined in his bay horse twenty feet away.

"Mornin', Ed," Tim greeted. " 'Light, won't you?"

"Haven't time, Tim." Ed Soule was a lanky, tall shape in the saddle, his lean sun-blackened face set bleakly. Eyes that were more gray than green did not lose their hard glitter even when he looked across at Hope Gilpin and touched the brim of his Stetson in greeting. Twin horn-handled guns rested in holsters at his thighs. Tim Gilpin had never before seen him wearing those .45s.

11

It was this last that worried Gilpin most, for Ed usually called here to see Hope, and Tim had never thought of him in any other way than as a prospective son-in-law. Here was a different Ed Soule. Tim decided to come straight to the point.

"How many critters did you lose, Ed?"

"All I had, and every horse but this one. It cleans me, Tim. I'm through in this country."

"How about the rest?"

"The same. Baker, Knee, Hollister, and Baggins so far. They cleaned you, too?"

Tim Gilpin nodded. "Mike Rudd was up here an hour or two ago, the sheriff with him," he said.

"Which way did they head out? Above, to see Crippen?"

"No. They headed back toward town. Scholl said you were to see him before you did anything."

"I'll find Rudd when I want him," Ed Soule said flatly. "Why I stopped was to ask you. . . ."

"If I'd side you in a play against Rudd?" Tim Gilpin shook his head soberly. "No, Ed. It'd be suicide. Besides, we haven't proof. We never have had proof against him."

He went on to tell Ed that Rudd and

12

most of his Whip riders had been in town all last night, that the sheriff would back Rudd in that alibi. Ed Soule took this in with little change in expression.

"That about leaves it up to me . . . and to Fred Crippen, if he wants to come along," he said finally.

Hope Gilpin spoke for the first time: "Please, Ed! Don't do it."

There was a tenderness and a pleading in the girl's brown eyes that at any other time would have quickened Ed Soule's pulse. Now he purposely ignored it, for there was no place for softness in him this morning.

"You'll sell to Rudd?" he said to Gilpin.

"What else can I do?" Tim Gilpin shrugged. "We're licked. I'll take Rudd's offer, which is fair, and pull out of here."

Ed understood what lay behind Gilpin's words. Tim had responsibilities that made caution and reason come before all else. Tim had Hope to think of. It had been the same with the others whose herds had completely vanished in the roar of the storm's downpour last night. Knee had a wife. Baker was crippled. Hollister and Baggins weren't the kind who would readily take to guns.

"There's two sections in my layout, Tim," Ed declared. "Rudd offers five hundred for

13

them. What good is five hundred dollars to a man?"

"Better than losin' everything, maybe your life too, Ed."

There wasn't any point in arguing that. Ed said abruptly, "Be seein' you," and reined his bay around and started away. Hope called after him, but by that time his pony's shoes were racketing across the gravel out by the barn and her call went unanswered.

Ed Soule heard Hope's voice. But he couldn't let it stop him, for he knew that the things he would say and the look in her eyes would dull the sharp edge of his anger. And more than anything else he wanted to strike back at the man who had ruined him.

It had been nothing but trouble these past three years, trouble with Mike Rudd. The Whip was the biggest outfit in the country, its brand sprawled over fifty sections of good grass range. It was Ed's hard luck, along with the rest, that he'd put all his savings into a land company five years ago — the same land company that had thrown a dam across a steep-walled gorge high in the hills and turned dry and barren Alkali Valley into a rancher's paradise. It was hard luck because Mike Rudd was an ambitious man and resented these small outfits mushroom-

ing out of the waste of what he considered his own private domain. Whip range almost entirely encircled Alkali Valley.

Rudd had made it hard for these small ranchers from the beginning. His hardware store, the only one within two hundred miles, had its own price on any merchandise sold to an Alkali Valley man. Paying twice over for barb wire, nails, tools, and implements meant hardship to the small ranchers. They had patiently put up with it, buying only the necessities and sometimes going without. And they had stoically repaired the damage to their fences and ditches resulting from mysterious night raids made by unknown riders. They had always suspected Mike Rudd, but they had always lacked proof, just as they lacked it now.

Ed Soule was broke, the hope of owning his own brand wiped out in the thunder and wind squalls of a single night's storm. But his pride wasn't broken, and in those early hours before dawn this morning, after he'd discovered his loss, he had come to the only decision his pride could make. He would meet Mike Rudd face to face with a gun, and one of them would go down.

Tim Gilpin and the others had failed him and now Ed was headed above to the last outfit in the valley, old Fred Crippen's.

Fred, who worked alone on his place, had a temper as thin as the edge of his razor, and he hated Mike Rudd. Ed knew that Crippen would side him, with his shrewdness, his guns, or his fists. Together, they could wreak enough damage on Whip so that the price Mike Rudd finally paid for Alkali Valley would be high. After that Ed would choose Rudd and have it out with him.

This upper-valley trail climbed the side of an abrupt steep wall at the Narrows, hanging eighty feet above the churning bed of the stream that now ran a torrent of water. It was along this precipitous trail that Ed Soule suddenly reined in on the bay and stared ahead in mild wonder. Forty feet beyond here the ledge of the trail suddenly broke off in a jagged opening. Last night's storm had washed out its foundations, and the rotten rock below had given way to let down a good thirty yards of the ledge.

Ed reined close to the edge, and his glance traveled downward along the scarred path of the landslide. What he saw below brought him swinging quickly out of the saddle and made him run to the drop-off. It took five minutes of careful going before he had climbed below to stand alongside the up-legged carcass of a saddled horse that lay

half buried in the loose conical pile of earth and rock on the valley floor. But he paid the dead horse scant attention. Farther out lay a man's broken, twisted body. Ed hated what he was to find, and he had to force himself to walk over there.

It was Fred Crippen, his bearded face twisted in a grimace of pain that made Ed give him one quick look and then take his eyes away. Old Crippen had been a good friend, and Ed didn't like the task he faced of burying him. A rotten rock overhang lay directly above the horse's carcass. He'd bury Crippen and the horse together, probably the way the oldster would have wanted it had he been able to choose.

Lifting Fred's broken body, Ed found the underside of his shirt and vest still damp from last night's rain, and in that sign read his own meaning into this tragedy. Crippen had been riding down this trail during the storm, probably coming for help after hearing or seeing his herd driven off. For Ed had no doubt now that Crippen's herd, like his own, would be missing.

"We'd have made it a good fight, Fred," he murmured regretfully as he lifted the body and started to carry it up under the overhang.

Half way up he thought of something that

made him ease the body to the ground once more. He knelt there a long while, thinking, and during the interval he built and smoked a cigarette. As he at last flicked it from his fingers, rising to his feet once more, he looked down at Fred Crippen and drawled: "You'd have done the same for me, Fred."

Half an hour later, after he'd gone up for his bay and led him back along the trail until he could walk the horse into the water of the creek, Ed Soule threw his rope over a cedar that grew high above the spot where the dead horse lay. He snubbed the rope on his saddlehorn and eased the bay into the pull. Then, striking the bay's flanks gently with his spurs, he sat the saddle until suddenly the cedar above tore loose, and tree and overhang thundered down in a slide of earth and rotten sandstone that completely buried the remains of Fred Crippen's horse.

Five minutes later Ed Soule headed up the creek, walking his horse in the stream so he would leave no sign that could be read later. Across his nervous bay's withers hung Fred Crippen's body.

II

"BUSHWHACKER IN THE CAÑON"

It rained again that night and it wasn't until well into the next morning that Tim Gilpin rode into Roco Verde and brought the sheriff the news. Fred Crippen's cabin had been burned. Tim couldn't say when — probably the first night of the rain — but he'd found Fred inside. "He wasn't a pretty sight either, Sheriff," he ended soberly.

Bob Scholl was an honest, if a harassed, lawman. Just now something akin to fear showed in his blue-eyed glance, although Tim Gilpin doubted that Roco Verde's sheriff had ever feared a living thing. "Tim, you don't suppose . . . ?" Scholl broke off.

Gilpin waited a moment for the sheriff to finish. When he didn't, Gilpin supplied the words for him. "That Whip riders killed Fred and started that blaze? You're damned right that's what I think. This makes things different."

"Easy, Tim, easy!"

"Easy, hell!" Gilpin exploded. "This time we've got what we wanted . . . proof. It's there, Bob, and it's up to you to hang this on the right man."

"Does Ed Soule know about this yet?"

"No. I steered clear of his place on the way in here. I wanted to give you your chance first."

"Thanks," the lawman said dryly. "Otherwise we'd have a one-man war against Rudd on our hands. Ed liked old Crippen."

"It won't be a one-man war, not now, Bob. This thing'll bring every man in Alkali against Mike Rudd. The safest place for that sidewinder's in your jail here. Mark my words, you get him in here and lock him up. Otherwise, I'm not answerin' for what'll happen. I'll give you an hour's start on me. There's some things I have to get at the store." Gilpin turned to go out the sheriff's office door.

"Wait, Tim. What's this hour you're givin' me?"

"Before I start back to tell Ed Soule about it."

"That puts me in a tight hole, Tim."

Gilpin laughed harshly, his broad face unsmiling. "Then you'll get a sample of how we've felt for three years now. I thought at

first, after what happened to my herd the other night, that I might sell out to Rudd like the others. Now I'm damned if I will! They won't either. We can't sit by and see murder done!"

"This'll take some thinkin', Tim. I wouldn't be too hasty. For instance, like I told you the other mornin', Mike and ten of his men were here in town two nights ago. He left only four of the crew at Whip. Four men couldn't have made that raid on your layouts."

"And what was Rudd doin' in town all night?" Gilpin demanded.

"He had three hundred shorthorns shipped in that afternoon. They unloaded and bedded 'em down out beyond town. Now don't say they could have gone back and driven off your stuff. All but two of those eight were in the saloon until three the next mornin', Rudd with 'em. I know because I had to lock up Fiddle Horn for gettin' drunk and bustin' the front hotel window. I was up all night."

Tim Gilpin was frowning. A moment ago he had been certain of things. Now he wasn't.

"You're askin' yourself who else could have done it," Bob Scholl said. "I don't know yet. But I do know this. Three nights

21

ago Jim Crawford was ridin' home from town when he saw something damned strange. You know his place is out west beyond Whip at the edge of the badlands. Jim says he saw at least half a dozen men ridin' up Shadow Cañon that night."

Tim's look sharpened. "What would take men up there? There's nothin' in that *malpais*."

"I know that. And while you're tellin' Ed Soule about Fred Crippen, tell him about that, too. If your crew is really aimin' to settle this thing, my idea would be to start by havin' a look at Shadow Cañon. I intend to go up there myself."

Ed Soule was that minute having his own look at Shadow Cañon. The night before, a bare half hour after he'd dumped the five-gallon can of coal oil onto the floor of Fred Crippen's cabin and thrown the match that started the blaze, he had been waiting in the timber above the cabin, looking down to make sure he'd done a thorough job. It was while he sat there motionless in his saddle that the bay had lifted his head, ears up in attention. Ed had come down out of the saddle in a hurry and barely managed to clamp his hand over the animal's nostrils in time to stop him from nickering. Then,

sounding softly but unmistakably, he had heard the muted plodding hoof pound of a walking horse above him, near the crest of the wooded hill.

No horse could have strayed up there without a rider. And Ed Soule didn't want anyone to witness this thing he was doing. He had planned it carefully as the only way of getting the other small ranchers to come in with him against Whip. He knew that Fred Crippen's place was so isolated and so well hidden that no neighbor would see the blaze. And to make things even better, dark storm clouds now hid the stars. There would be rain before morning, and no man would be able to tell when the fire had started.

Ed's instinct was to go up through the timber and identify that rider. He made a wide circle, walking his horse as soundlessly as he could until he finally came to the spot where he calculated the sound had originated. He was bent over in the saddle studying the ground as best he could in the dark, looking for sign, when suddenly a gun thundered close at hand.

The bullet clipped a one-inch strip of felt neatly off Ed's Stetson. He jerked straight in the saddle in time to see a shadowy figure cut out of the trees ahead. His right hand dipped to holster and came up swinging one

of his Colt .45s into line. He thumbed three quick shots at that fading blur of shadow until the flash of his gun blinded him and he couldn't make it out any longer.

Then he recklessly put spurs to his bay and followed the hoofbeats of that other pony. They faded out before he had gone a half mile. Then, knowing that in burning Fred Crippen's body he had neatly framed himself with murder, he waited there on the hill above the layout all that night, his poncho held tightly about him during the brief hard rain. At the first hint of dawn he had picked up the now partly washed-out sign of the other rider and was following it west, down out of the hills.

That sign had held strong all morning. It had swung wide of Whip's north fence, past Jim Crawford's place at the edge of the badlands, and angled down off open range to lead Ed directly into the mouth of Shadow Cañon and across the mile-long punishment of the jagged *malpais* bed that shaped the opening.

Now, he was seeing other sign along with the one he had followed. Interesting sign, too. A mile above the cañon mouth, where the rain hadn't been so heavy two nights ago and where the rock gave way to a thin top soil, the ground was churned by hun-

dreds of hoofs, the sign that a large herd of cattle had passed by.

Ed was beginning to understand the meaning of all this when suddenly from ahead and above him a voice called down, "Jerk 'em up, stranger! Reach!"

Ed's instinct prompted him to roll out of the saddle before that voice had stopped speaking. A shot blasted out, sending its racket up the long corridor of the cañon. Ed hit hard on one shoulder, the sand kicked up by a second bullet which cut his face. He rolled onto his feet an instant later, palming up both of his guns.

Whipping his glance upward, he saw the pale, wicked face of the killer twenty feet above. The man was perched awkwardly on a ledge of rock. There was blood on his shirt, on the hand that held the gun. For a moment Ed Soule hesitated. But, as the wounded man's weapon swung down in line with him again, Ed thumbed three quick shots that cut loose an inferno of sound. Up there the bushwhacker's body jerked spasmodically three distinct times, doubling forward at the waist. It took two long seconds for the man to lose his balance and topple down off his high perch. He hit hard and rolled loosely down the less abrupt slope until he lay spread-eagled and unmoving.

When Ed stepped over there, he needed only one glance to see that the man was dead.

A bend of the cañon lay ahead. It was that abrupt angling of the high walls that cut off all sound until it was too late. Hearing the thundering of oncoming horses shuttle down suddenly and loudly, Ed ran for his bay horse thirty feet away. While he was yet ten feet short of the bay, three riders suddenly swung around the bend.

The leader saw him and threw himself out of the saddle, jerking a rifle from its boot. He knelt in the sand and whipped a shot that caught Ed Soule in mid-stride and knocked his feet from under him. Ed tried to get up but a white-hot pain coursed the length of his right leg, leaving it numb and, for the moment at least, helpless.

By that time three guns were on him. He dropped both his weapons and slowly lifted his hands.

"Take a look at Feeney," called the first rider out of his saddle, the one that stepped in and picked up Ed's two guns.

"Four slugs in him," said the man who went over to look at the dead man. "Dead as he'll ever be, and he's come a long ways since he started bleedin'."

"Maybe you ought to tell us about it."

This from the last of the trio who now stood in front of Ed, looking down at him.

"I was ridin' up the cañon here when he tried to cut down on me," Ed said. "It had to be one of us."

The obvious leader of this trio was the man who had spoken last, the one who had taken that first shot at Ed and so neatly brought him down. He was a tall man, almost as tall as Ed, lean and with a thin face that was almost handsome. "Suppose you tell us what brought you up here," he now drawled.

Ed nodded toward the body lying a few feet away. "Him."

"And what did Feeney do to you?"

"Stole seventy-odd head of my beef night before last," Ed said, deciding on a bluff.

"Let's get it over with, Stretch!" one of the others growled impatiently.

Stretch waved a hand carelessly to command the speaker to silence. "Be quiet, Tonto. We're paid to steal cattle, not to gun every stranger we meet." He turned and called to the man kneeling beside the dead Feeney: "Joe, come over here and patch this gent's leg so he can ride with us." Then, to Ed: "You won't be able to fork a hull far the shape you're in."

"Because of the leg?" Ed asked.

Stretch grinned significantly. "We'll call it that."

Stretch Dooley rode down to Whip an hour after dark more worried than he admitted even to himself. He was a rustler and not ashamed of it. The stranger's arrival in Shadow Cañon complicated things. As he passed beneath the branches of the tall cottonwood midway the length of the lane, a rider suddenly appeared out of the shadows and called brusquely, "Hold on! Where you goin'?"

"In to buy my girl a hair ribbon," Stretch drawled, pulling his chestnut to a halt. "What's the matter, Pete, you boys spooky tonight?"

"You can get it from the boss," Pete answered. "Go on in. I ain't got any time for talk." His tone was surly.

So Stretch Dooley had a slight forewarning of what was to come. But it was nothing to the explosion that cut loose the instant he stepped into Mike Rudd's office. The rancher was sitting at his desk. When the door opened, he raised his glance and saw who it was. His square, loosely-jowled face took on a quick grimace of anger, and he lunged up out of his chair, planted his fists on the desk top, and glared at Stretch as

he said, "You've got guts to come in here! You. . . ." But then the slow hardening of Stretch's face warned him. That, and the lazy gesture of the man's hand that put it within reach of the tied-down holster at his thigh. Stretch wasn't a handsome man now; there was a live anger imprinted on his aquiline face.

Mike sat down heavily, and his voice intoned flatly, "You had your orders! We'd have made this play stick if you hadn't done it. Stretch, I trusted you."

"Suppose you get it off your chest, Boss. After you're through, maybe you can tell me what's makin' you so proddy."

"Proddy!" Rudd blazed. But his anger died out before a mounting shrewdness. "Who did it, Stretch? Name the man that did it, and I'll have him gunned."

"Did what?"

"Burned Fred Crippen's layout, the one at the head of the valley."

"I was up there myself. No one burned it. The old jasper came hellin' down into his pasture after us, but we'd already driven most of the stuff out. We parted his hair with a few slugs and let it go at that. He high-tailed."

"And who went back and cut him down and burned his place? Stretch, this is seri-

ous. The law's looking for the man who did that."

Stretch was frowning now, the momentary anger gone from his glance. "Mike, you'll have to take my word for this, but no one of us did it. We made that a clean job. Crippen was the only one that saw us. And he didn't get a close look. If his place was fired, he did it himself."

"And went in there and lay on his floor and let the blaze cook him to a cinder!" Rudd scoffed. But then he understood that Dooley was telling the truth. "All right, Stretch, it didn't happen while you were along. One of your bunch went back later, we'll say. But I've got to know who that man was. I've got to have him dead, to turn over to the sheriff . . . dead, so he can't talk."

"That's another wrong guess. There wasn't a man in the crew left the herd all the way to the cañon hide-out. We hit the breaks about sunup, and it was an all day drive in across that *malpais*. No one of my bunch did it, Mike."

"Then who did?" Rudd queried, plainly baffled.

"I couldn't say, but here's what I came to tell you. A man followed Feeney in today." And Stretch went on to tell of the

man who was now a prisoner in the cabin at the hide-out.

During Stretch's brief account of the fight up in Shadow Cañon, Mike Rudd's glance narrowed in deep deliberation. Suddenly he slammed a fist onto his desk. "That's Soule! Tall, a face that doesn't tell much, man crowdin' thirty?"

"That's him. He did say Feeney'd run off with about seventy head of his beef. He made a mess of Feeney."

"Stretch," Rudd breathed, "we've got the man we can turn over to the sheriff for burnin' out Fred Crippen!"

"How'll you make that stick? If this Soule was one of them, he'd be a friend of Crippen's."

"Exactly. I happen to know that yesterday morning Soule called on all his friends and tried to make them come in with him against me. They wouldn't. If we bring this Soule, or his body, in to the sheriff, Bob Scholl can think what he likes. Maybe I can help him decide that Soule and Crippen had it out because Crippen wouldn't help him make his fight against Whip."

Stretch Dooley shook his head dubiously. "It's pretty thin, Mike."

"We'll fix it so something of Soule's will be found up there in the ruins of Crippen's

cabin. A spur, maybe, or a. . . ."

"He's got a pocket match case, different from any I've seen around here. It's metal, and he carries it in his shirt pocket. He'd need matches to start a fire!"

"Stretch, you've got a head on your shoulders. I've seen him use that match case." Rudd got up from his desk. "We'll go back and get it from him. This may be the one thing that'll make those ranchers pull out. Soule was the only man of the lot that hated me enough to bring this into the open. Without him, the rest won't fight."

III

"VENGEANCE BOUND"

Rudd and Stretch started west from Whip less than ten minutes later. It took them an hour and a quarter to raise the far-off winking lights of Jim Crawford's place on the edge of the badlands.

"Crawford's up late," Rudd commented as they left the lights behind. "He usually turns in when the sun does."

There was a reason for that light of Crawford's being on. This bachelor oldster wasn't in any way involved in what was happening between Rudd and the Alkali Valley ranchers. Yet a lonely life and an instinctive dislike of Mike Rudd's high-handedness had drawn Jim Crawford's sympathies toward Ed Soule, Tim Gilpin, and the rest. That morning, having gotten a quick look at Soule's bay horse and recognizing it, as Ed struck a straight line for Shadow Cañon on Feeney's sign, Jim Craw-

ford's curiosity had quickened.

Off and on all day, Crawford had watched the north, toward the badlands. Shortly before sundown he had seen a rider come out of the breaks from the direction of Shadow Cañon and head east, toward Whip. Any activity in that direction was odd, for no man ever went into those badlands unless he had to. Two riders, one going in, the other coming out, all in one day, was a little too much for Crawford's peace of mind.

He had eaten his evening meal and had already taken off his boots, ready to turn in, when he suddenly decided that he couldn't sleep unless he had something settled in his mind. That something made him saddle his one pony and ride north toward Shadow Cañon a few minutes later. Two miles from the layout he looked back and saw that he'd left the lamp in his adobe house burning. He cursed mildly at the waste of coal oil that would result but kept on going.

Deep in the cañon a half hour later he had enough warning of Mike Rudd's and Stretch Dooley's approach to cross the cañon floor and put himself and his pony well into the shadow of one wall, his gnarled old fingers clamped about the animal's nostrils. He recognized the Whip owner, and

heard the other rider say as he passed, "Mike, you're leavin' me out of this. I'll steal this whole range empty of beef, but I won't be saddled with a killin'." Mike laughed and the echo of that laugh was the last Jim Crawford heard of the pair.

A stroke of intuition told Crawford the meaning of those words. He went up into the saddle, and it took him a full two hours to ride out and make the circle to Alkali Valley. When he pulled in on his pony in Tim Gilpin's yard, the animal was ready to drop from sheer exhaustion.

Crawford was barely out of the saddle before Gilpin's voice sounded from the far corner of the cabin. "Stand where you are! You've got a shotgun lined at your middle, stranger!"

"It's me, Jim Crawford, Tim!"

"It's all right, Hope," Gilpin called. "Light the lamp."

Even before Gilpin walked down into sight a light shone in the cabin's single front window. Crawford didn't wait to get his breath before beginning his story. As a result, it came out in spasmodic, broken sentences that time and time again made Tim Gilpin want to take the oldster by the shoulders and shake the words loose. Hope came out, a quilted robe wrapped about her, to

hear the last of Crawford's story. And once she interrupted him to say quietly to her father, "I'll go in and get your guns."

Gilpin threw Crawford's saddle onto a fresh horse, and the two of them rode at a hard run across the pasture below. Back at the cabin, Hope finished dressing and went to the corral to saddle her own chestnut mare. Her father wouldn't have liked what she was doing, but she was thinking only of Ed Soule now. Thinking of Ed Soule was what made her bring along her father's old Sharps rifle and a handful of shells for it, even though she wasn't certain that the twenty-year-old ammunition would fire.

Gilpin gathered his eight men in a little under an hour. All eight had learned earlier that day of Fred Crippen's death and of Ed Soule's mysterious absence. All of them had undergone a change of heart at these new, ominous developments. Even Baker, who was so crippled that he could keep only one foot in the stirrup, was along tonight. And there was Hollister and his two men, Knee with his fourteen-year-old-son, and Sam Baggins and his brother.

"Crawford, you lead the way," Tim Gilpin said, as Baggins, at the lower end of the valley, rode out to join the rest. "We'll have to take our luck as it comes," he went on.

"From what Crawford saw and heard to-night, it's a fair bet that Ed Soule's up in Shadow Cañon somewhere and in trouble. And it's also a fair bet that our missin' herds are in there with him. Gents, tonight'll either see this thing finished, or it'll finish us. If any one of you wants to pull out now, do it, and no one of us will hold it against you."

He paused, and the silence that followed his words was freighted with tension. Yet not a man made a move to swing his pony out of that closely knit group of riders. Finally, Gilpin said, "Then we'll be ridin'," and he followed after Jim Crawford who set the pace at a stiff, mile-eating trot.

Ed Soule doubted that any man in Roco Verde County knew what lay at the head of Shadow Cañon. There was, as Jim Crawford had often put it, nothing to bring a man in here. A mile-long stretch of *malpais* choked the cañon's mouth, the crystalline edges of the lava rock so sharp that they could cut a horse's hoofs to the flesh in five minutes' time unless a man was overly cautious, as cautious as Ed himself had been this morning coming in. Once a man was across the *malpais,* there was nothing beyond, nothing for five tortuous miles of bad up and down going across rock and sand. Even at the end

of that five miles there was nothing to arouse a man's interest, unless by chance he took that narrow off-shoot that was no more than a broad crevice in what appeared to be the blank end wall of the cañon.

That narrow off-shoot twisted for another quarter mile between towering walls until suddenly it rounded a sharp bend and opened into a mile-wide basin where fair grass offered temporary feed for six hundred head of cattle now hidden there, Ed Soule's small herd along with the rest. At the basin's far end was a shack built of poles dragged down from one of the low hills three miles away. The shack squatted near the basin's one scant source of water, a weak spring that year after year watered the grass until well into the summer when it finally dried up under the sun's fierce glare.

Ed hadn't been told, but he knew that there was a way out of the back of this basin back, leading into the hills. Once today he'd heard one of Stretch Dooley's men mention Horse Creek, which was the name of both a town and a stream seventy miles across the hills in the next county. If Stretch and the others were from Horse Creek, it was a dead certainty that these cattle would eventually be driven there, their brands changed so that they could be mixed with Horse

Creek herds, and forever lose their identity.

"Take it easy on him, boys," Stretch had said on leaving the cabin before dusk. Stretch was an easy-going man Ed Soule somehow liked despite the fact that he was a rustler. And Stretch's men were typical 'punchers, all but one.

Tonto Keene was the one who had that morning suggested "getting it over with." He was plainly of the killer breed, both in looks and actions. He wore two guns, and they were tied low on his bowed legs. His face was an inscrutable mask of hardly concealed viciousness. He had evidently been the dead Feeney's friend, for after Stretch left the shack at sundown he made several pointed remarks.

"Stretch always was soft," he complained once. "We could gun down this stranger and tell Stretch he made a break for it." He spoke to one of the others loud enough so that Ed could hear.

"Lay off, Tonto. You want to buy some trouble with Stretch?"

Tonto evidently didn't want trouble with Stretch, for he said nothing more about Ed Soule but kept a surly silence and ignored the others. Acting on Stretch's orders, they gave Ed all he could eat for supper that evening and didn't tie him where he lay in

his bunk, his leg throbbing with pain from the rifle bullet that had put a hole through the flesh of his thigh. They had taken his guns away from him but not his belts.

"How much is Mike Rudd payin' your crew to drive this herd out of the country?" Ed asked one of Stretch's men.

"Plenty," the man replied, and from there on Ed Soule had at least one slim doubt erased from his mind. Mike Rudd was admittedly behind the rustling.

After they had eaten, four of Stretch's men pulled the slab table out from the wall of the shack's single room and settled down to a game of stud. One man stayed out of the game for two hands to go and gather wood and build a fire in the sheet-iron stove. After that Ed watched the game from where he lay, uncomfortable because of his leg and the stiff bulky shell-belts at his waist. The belts became so bothersome that he finally sat up in the bunk and started unbuckling them. All at once something stopped him, and he fastened the first belt again.

"How's chances on gettin' in the game?" he said to the men at the table. "Or isn't my money any good?"

One of the four, a man called Summers, nodded. "Sure, stranger. Only won't that leg bother you?"

"Did you ever try lyin' down with a tooth-ache?"

Summers grinned. "Once, for about half a minute. It hurt so bad I had to get up."

"This leg's like a whole mouthful of bad teeth," Ed declared, rising from the bunk and stepping across to the table to take the one remaining chair.

He had a little money in his pockets and made it a point to lose consistently. The game reminded him of many others in the bunkhouses of the Colorado outfits he'd worked for years ago. These four were ordinary 'punchers, no different from half a hundred others he had known; they made the same jokes, played the game the same way.

He made it a point to get up out of his chair occasionally and walk the length of the room and back again, "to get the stiffness out of this bum pin," he said the first time. After that they didn't pay him much attention, at least no one but Tonto who sat in a chair in one remote shadowed corner. And Ed realized from their indifference that there was at least one man standing guard outside the shack.

Finally, after more than an hour's play, he saw his chance. He got lazily up out of his chair, hunched his shoulders, and

drawled: "That fire could stand some more wood." He limped across and lifted the lid off the stove and dropped some wood in. Then, as he laid the lid back, his free hand shucked two .45 shells from his belt, and he threw them down onto the coals.

His back crawled as he limped slowly back to the table. He noted three things instinctively — that the lamp on the table was within his reach, that the room's single window was set in the wall ten feet in back of his chair, and that Tonto was eyeing him in that cold, inscrutable way that made him the man to watch most carefully.

Ed had barely let himself down in the chair when the blast of the first exploding shell cut loose. Summers, directly across the table, stiffened and stabbed for his gun. A split-second later Ed was lunging up out of his chair and knocking the lamp from the table with a wide sweep of his arm.

The second shell exploded before the lamp hit the floor. Summers yelled stridently, "Watch him! Someone's out there!" and in that brief interval of time Ed Soule had covered the ten feet to the window, dragging a chair along after him.

He threw all his weight into the swing of his two arms that lifted the chair from the floor and hurled it through the window. The

glass and frame crashed outward, and with the sound Ed stepped back close against the near wall. Tonto's guns blazed a sudden inferno of sound from the corner, the flashes of the weapons lancing straight for the window. Under cover of the sound, Ed crossed the room and stood to one side of the door. A sudden lull followed.

"Did he make it?" Summers's voice asked harshly.

There was the hurried tread of boots outside, and abruptly the door swung open. The man standing there with a six-gun in his hand had barely time enough to ask, "What's comin' off up . . . ?" before Ed Soule's smashing fist caught him full in the mouth.

Ed lunged through the door, reaching for the six-gun as the man sprawled backward. A gun blasted out behind him, the bullet whipping past his head as he wrenched the gun loose from the guard's grasp. Armed now, he stepped quickly out of line with the door and ran obliquely from the cabin.

From close ahead someone shouted loudly, "That you, Summers?" Ed could just make out the shapes of two riders in the darkness. He brought up his weapon, thumbed two quick shots and saw one horse lunge and fall to his knees. He heard Mike

Rudd's voice calling sharp oaths, and then the two were out of sight, wheeling frantically back into the darkness.

The next hour was sheer torture to Ed Soule. His leg bandage loosened and the wound started to bleed so that he had to waste precious minutes binding it up again. He had crossed the floor of the draw and was now on one cedar-dotted upslope, heading in the general direction of the entrance from Shadow Cañon. Time and again riders approached almost close enough for him to see them, only to swing away again and go back down into the draw. Twice he heard Stretch Dooley's voice down there, once Mike Rudd's as the rancher directed the search.

After that first hour, Ed Soule moved carefully, knowing that a single sound might give him away. He was relieved when he found that the weapon he had taken from the guard in the doorway was a .45, and one of the first things he did was to shuck the empties from the gun and reload it with shells from his belts.

IV

"GUNFIRE RECKONING"

It was Stretch Dooley's hunch that took him, his six men, and Mike Rudd to the head of the draw. "He can't get far with that leg," Stretch told Mike. "And the only way out he knows is Shadow. Let's get over there, spread out, and stop him as he tries to get through."

Rudd agreed with this reasoning and went along. Stretch had his men get out of their saddles and leave the horses with one lone guard. Then he placed his men so that either side of the off-shoot entrance was closely watched.

"We may have a long wait. But we want this Ed Soule and we want him alive," he said.

"Dead'll do," Mike Rudd remarked.

"Mike, you'll play along with me on this. Your bargain was for us to get away with anything up to a thousand head of beef. But

you didn't hire us as a gun crew. We'll get this Ed Soule and turn him over to you alive. What you do with him's none of our business."

"You can get hung for rustlin' as quick as for killin'," Tonto put in pointedly.

"But if you don't get hung for either, I'd a damn' sight rather think back on alterin' a steer's brand with my runnin' iron than on alterin' the looks of a man's face with a bullet," Stretch drawled. In those few words he summed up his philosophy.

Tonto was a troublemaker. For that reason, Stretch stationed him close in to the opening of the off-shoot and took up his own place nearby. Rudd was across on the other slope with Summers and two others.

They waited there for more than an hour, until Stretch himself began to think that he'd made a wrong guess and that Ed Soule wouldn't try this way out. He was about to rise from where he was hunkered down behind a stunted cedar when he caught the hint of an unmistakable sound slurring out of the opening between the high walls of the off-shoot that led up from Shadow Cañon. Two seconds later he had identified the sound as the muffled hoofbeat of several ponies. Then, before he could shout a warning to the others, that sound suddenly in-

creased in volume as Tim Gilpin led his small posse of ranchers out of the opening and into the draw.

Tonto's gun spoke sharply, its explosion slapping back off the high walls with a flat detonation. Jim Crawford, close behind Gilpin, lurched in his saddle and fell stiffly to the ground. Someone behind Gilpin answered Tonto's gun with a quick shot from a Winchester and, opposite Stretch, Mike Rudd's six-gun suddenly blasted three times in a staccato burst of sound.

Gilpin spurred his horse down out of the way, giving those behind him room to fan out on either side of the narrow opening. He wheeled and headed for the spot where the gun had a moment before sounded. Suddenly a shape rose from behind a low-growing *chamiza* bush close in front of him, to be outlined a moment later by a burst of gun flame. A bullet caught Gilpin high on his left shoulder, yet he lifted his Winchester, took cool aim, and brought the man down as his horse plunged by.

A hundred yards short of Stretch's position Ed Soule was startled by this sudden burst of sound across a silence that had a moment ago been complete and ominous, a silence that had taken him to his knees to crawl warily toward the off-shoot opening

47

in the full knowledge that a trap might lie ahead. Now he rose to his feet, stood there a moment undecided, catching an occasional glimpse of an unmounted rider, twice seeing men on foot running down from the shelter of the clump of cedars footing the opening.

Far across to the other side came Tim Gilpin's shout, "Ride 'em down!" and with the sudden knowledge that these mounted riders were his friends, Ed Soule swung up his six-gun and fired once at the shadowy figure of a man running back from the shelter of the trees.

His bullet grazed Tonto's left arm. The rustler stopped, arced both his guns upward to line at that wink of powder flame that had for a split-second spotted Ed's gun. The weapons bucked in Tonto's hands, his bullets whipping with deadly accuracy at that now blacked-out target. But Ed Soule had instinctively stepped aside as he shot, so that Tonto's bullets whipped the air close to one side of him.

By the flashes of those twin guns, Ed recognized Tonto and, as those bullets cut closer toward him, he threw one more blasting shot with the .45. The explosion of his weapon sounded at the exact instant a bullet caught Ed in his wounded leg and knocked

him off his feet. Abruptly the rustler's guns ended their staccato rhythm. Tonto dropped both six-guns, his hands clawed his shirt open at the chest, suddenly his knees buckled, and he fell hard on his face, his hands still clenching his shirt with the stiff grip of death.

Below, Gilpin and the others had fanned out and now came sweeping back toward the off-shoot's entrance. Ed, unable to move his leg, saw three empty-saddled broncs go plunging wildly off into the darkness before Gilpin's riders opened their fire again at two men on foot who made a wild break from the cover of the cedars and tried to run down to the spot where they'd left their ponies. Seeing that they couldn't make it, these two abruptly stopped, and their guns blasted at Gilpin and the others. One rider melted out of the saddle, another dropped his rifle and clutched his side before the pair on foot were finally cut down.

The sound of the guns faded for a moment and was then taken up again two hundred yards below. Two rifles down there were throwing shots at a rider who suddenly cut out from the knot of horses that had an hour ago brought Stretch Dooley's men up here. In another ten seconds those rifles were quiet, and Gilpin's two riders came up

from below. A voice Ed recognized as Charlie Knee's called, "That's the last of 'em, Gilpin. He got away. Now we'll try and find Ed Soule."

"Up here!" Ed Soule called faintly.

Gilpin, identifying the voice, reined his pony up the slope. Ed called once again, and in half a minute Gilpin was alongside him and coming out of his saddle.

"You hurt?" Tim said as he knelt beside Ed.

"Don't know, Tim. I can't feel much down there."

Ed tried to lift himself up onto his knees, but Gilpin reached out and pushed him down again. "Easy, Ed. You're bleedin' like a stuck pig." Gilpin took out his knife, slit the leg of Ed's Levi's and took a quick look at the wound. Then he came onto his feet and called down to the others. "A couple of you get up here and build a fire so we can see what we're doin'. The rest take a look for Jim and Hollister."

"You go along and help, Tim," Ed said. "I saw Jim Crawford leave his hull close in near the off-shoot. He may need doctorin' a damn' sight worse than I do."

It took twenty minutes after the fire of dead cedar branches started blazing to account for the last of Tim Gilpin's posse. A

bullet had broken Baker's forearm. One of Hollister's men had a flesh-wound in the calf of his right leg. John Baggins was missing the lobe of one ear, and Gilpin himself had a bullet-grazed shoulder. And after a long search they found Jim Crawford's lifeless body wedged between two jagged rocks near the mouth of the off-shoot.

Tim Gilpin helped carry Crawford's limp form down to the fire. "Never knew what hit him," he said quietly, his voice edged with bitterness. "I counted four others up there that make it up a little for losin' him. The rest are gone."

"Anyone see the gent that took off on that pony?" Ed Soule asked from where he sat alongside the fire, his right hand holding the tourniquet Hollister had wrapped about his leg. He was thinking of Mike Rudd and of Stretch Dooley.

"I did," Knee spoke up. "Had a good look at him. He was about your size, big and leggy. Funny thing about that. He had a clean chance at me and didn't take it."

Ed Soule smiled, knowing at once that it was Stretch Dooley who had ridden down the draw. He was somehow relieved to think that Stretch wasn't one of the four dead men. Then he had another thought that

51

made him ask quickly, "And how about Mike Rudd?"

"How about Mike Rudd?" a deep-noted voice spoke out from beyond the fire. There was a quality of harshness in that voice that brought the eyes of all these men swinging there to identify it. An instant later a wide, low-built shape came into the range of the firelight.

It was Mike Rudd. He had a six-gun in each hand, weapons that swung slowly in tight arcs that menaced them all, made them lift their hands above their heads. Rudd's square ugly face was gray-looking and twisted with pain. His black broadcloth coat was unbuttoned to reveal a smear of red on his white shirt front, high up and to one side. That was the damage done by the first shot Tim Gilpin had thrown in the fight.

Rudd came on a step or two until he stood directly opposite Ed Soule. And it was on Ed Soule that his bleak, gray-eyed glance finally rested. Now that he was closer they could all hear his breathing, a rattle that was the unmistakable sign of a lung wound.

"You nearly got away with it, Soule," he said bleakly. "Before I shoot your guts out, tell 'em about Crippen! Tell 'em who burned his place."

Ed Soule told them soberly, explaining

the reasons for what he'd done as briefly as he could. He hadn't raised his hands as the others did at the threat of Rudd's guns. And as he talked, he edged his right hand in toward the holster at his thigh. When he finished speaking, the thumb of his hand was touching the walnut handle of the weapon.

Mike Rudd saw that, smiled twistedly. "Go ahead, Soule. Make your play!" And, to emphasize his words, he thumbed back both hammers of his guns.

Ed felt his forehead bead with perspiration. He was staring across at Rudd, not at the man's eyes but into the black holes of those twin gun muzzles. He knew he didn't have a chance, but he knew, too, that in another second those guns would blast flame at him and that he'd have to make this one futile try.

His right hand lifted, his forefinger snapped out the gun. Suddenly from far behind Rudd the darkness was spotted with a purple burst of flame and a low-throated explosion blasted the silence. Ed, staring at the two six-guns, saw them jerk to one side as Mike Rudd's body jumped. Then the guns exploded, Ed's own .45 swung up, and he emptied it with a prolonged burst of sound that slapped out across the draw in

a series of repeated echoes. It was over then, Mike Rudd down off his feet, his shirt front torn ragged by Ed's bullets, and now more red than white.

Ed struggled to his feet. "See who's out there, Tim," he said, peering into the darkness behind the spot where Mike Rudd had a moment ago stood.

"Dad! Dad, are you all right?"

It was Hope Gilpin's voice. The sound of it brought Tim wheeling around, running away from the fire.

Ed Soule, remembering the jerk of Mike Rudd's guns a split-second before they had fired, hobbled to the other side of the fire, and threw a blanket across Rudd's still body.

Tim and Hope came into the firelight, the father's arm about the girl's shoulders. Tim held the old Sharps rifle in his other hand.

Abruptly Hope Gilpin stopped, her horrified gaze riveted to the blanket and the shape that lay beneath it. "I . . . I killed him!" Her voice was barely above a whisper, a hint of hysteria touching it. She buried her face in her hands and turned to put her head on her father's shoulder. "He was . . . he would have shot Ed, Dad. I had to do it."

"But you didn't," Ed Soule said. "You missed. Your bullet kicked up the dust off

there beyond the fire."

Hope raised her head, wonder and relief in her eyes. "You're sure?"

"Sure as I'll ever be of anything," Ed told her soberly. "Rudd must have felt how close that bullet came. He waited just long enough to let me get my gun onto him. He was dead right when he pulled his triggers."

He flashed a glance at the rest, a glance that was at once understood, for John Baggins spoke up: "That's right, Miss Hope. Either the sights on that old smokepole are twisted, or you're a poorer shot than your old man."

Ed Soule had only a hazy recollection of what happened from then on. He knew that they put him on a horse and that Hope rode close beside him on the way back to the shack, once or twice putting an arm about him to keep him in the saddle. And he had a dim, fevered memory of climbing out of his saddle and walking a few steps and falling onto something that was softer than the ground and that immediately invited sleep.

It was nearly noon of the next day before he opened his eyes. Hope had just stepped in through the shack's doorway and was looking toward the bunk where he lay. She met his glance and smiled.

"Better?" she asked softly, coming over to him.

Instead of answering, he reached out and took one of her hands. Her face took on that tinge of color and the smile that made her beautiful. "Dad's gone to town for a doctor," she said.

"I don't need a doctor. Hope, that mornin' I rode up to your place so riled I couldn't see. . . ."

"Yes, Ed?"

"Well, I remember the way you looked. It was . . . it was a little like the way you look now." His grip tightened on her hand.

"How do I look now, Ed?" She bent down under the pull of his arm.

"Good enough to. . . ." But probably Ed realized the futility of words at that moment, for suddenly he was finishing what he had to say without speaking.

"The Hang-tree Rebellion" was the thirty-fourth Western story that Jon Glidden published. He completed it on March 30, 1938 and his agent sold it to .44 Western, one of the Popular Publications group, for $108.00 on July 5, 1938. Jon's original title for this story was "Hangman's Helper," but Ralph Perry, who edited .44 Western, changed it to the title that has been retained for its first appearance here since it was showcased in first position on the cover and in the table of contents of the issue dated 11-12/38. Fred Glidden had continued to exert some influence on the kinds of stories Jon wrote when he was starting out, but by 1937 Jon had already found the direction his own unique talent would take him.

THE HANG-TREE
REBELLION

I

"ONE LESS FOR BOOTHILL"

The cottonwood towered better than sixty feet skyward, its out-flung branches casting a shadow broad enough so that not a man of the twenty-seven riders had to stand his horse in the full glare of the beating sun that slanted into the cañon. There was even enough room in the tree's shade so that on horseback Bill Peace, the prisoner, felt pretty much alone as he twisted his neck against the prickly rub of the hemp rope and looked fully at Judge White.

"You're the last man I'd expect to catch at a lynchin', Judge," he remarked bitterly.

White's grizzled face lost its hard set for an instant. "I hate it as bad as anything I ever did, Bill," he said softly. Then, seeming to feel the uncompromising glances of the others, a subtle change rode through him. He stiffened and added, louder this time: "Damned if I do! I hope you take a long

time chokin' your life away at the end of that rope!"

Peace smiled thinly, his gray eyes unafraid, his lean, weather-burned face set stonily against the searching glances of these men who hoped to see some hint of fear there. "Get on with it," he said at last.

Sheriff Ralph Fowler, a wide, heavy shape alongside his prisoner, reached across to draw the knot tighter so that it cut a hard line past Bill Peace's right ear. The others shifted restlessly, stirred by an impatience to get this done with.

Peace's smile broadened as his neck-muscles took up the savage pull of the tightened rope. "Sheriff, I've got one regret," he said. "It's that I didn't take the trouble to beat your brains out with a gun butt long ago! I'd try it now . . . only you've got my hands tied."

Fowler clenched a fist and raised it. But before he could strike, Judge White said sharply: "None of that, Ralph!" The lawman relaxed once more and glared in cold, silent anger.

"There's one thing missin'," Peace went on tauntingly. "Where's the rest of your friends, Sheriff? Miles Root, for instance? He'd glory in seein' this."

Judge White intoned: "Neither Miles

Root nor anyone else had anything to do with this, Peace. You built your own noose around your neck. We're responsible citizens savin' the county and state the expense of a trial. Maybe we're stoppin' a war that would cost a dozen lives. We'll know that later." He squared his shoulders, thrust out his white-bearded chin in a stubborn gesture. "Is there anything you have to say before . . . before we . . . ?"

"Before you walk my horse out from under me?" Peace put in. "No, not even good bye to Joyce. She wouldn't care."

The judge's face lost color. "It's a shame I'll never live down, but she will care. It makes me wonder if she's really my own flesh and blood."

For a fleeing instant Bill Peace's features softened to betray an inner emotion. Then, as though something deeply within him was taking too strong a hold, he breathed shortly: "I said to get on with it!"

Sheriff Fowler grinned wickedly. He reined closer and raised his hand, about to slap Peace's horse over the hindquarters. There was a mixture of brutality and cunning in his glance. It was plain he was enjoying this. So were the rest, for a lesser measure of the sheriff's feeling held them all.

As the lawman's hand ended its upward arc, paused, and started downward in a stiff-armed blow, a voice from directly above sounded down sharply: "Hold it, Fowler! I've go my sights lined on you."

The sheriff's square-built body went abruptly rigid. He rocked back his head so that he looked up into the leafy mass overhead, toward the sound of that voice. It took him, and most of the others, a good five seconds to see the speaker. There, thirty feet overhead, sitting easily in a branch-crotch near the solid trunk of the huge tree, was a man who hugged the stock of a Winchester .30-.30 to his cheek. The blunt snout of the barrel was lined directly down at the lawman.

Fowler choked, "Al Sisson!" Involuntarily, he ducked his head to one side.

The rifle-barrel swung a fraction of an inch to cover this move, and the stranger above said: "You'll all shuck out your hardware, gents. Fowler, reach over and loosen that hemp necktie. Peace, see that they shed their irons."

As Bill Peace's glance swung upward to take in this outlaw whom he had never before seen but had heard much about, Judge White said sharply: "Don't move, Fowler! One of you others make a try at Sisson."

From above Sisson's voice sounded in a low chuckle. "Sure, make a try at me! Make a try and one of my hands will cut you down. They're up above on the rim, lookin' down at you over their rifle sights!"

Twenty-seven pairs of eyes jerked their glances from the leafy mass overhead and swung far out and up to the cañon rim. Bill Peace saw no sign of life up there nor did the rest. But when Sisson called down again, "How about that rope, Sheriff?" Fowler moved with a frightened quickness that made him look a little ridiculous.

In ten seconds the lawman's shaking hands had flipped the noose from Peace's neck and untied the rawhide thong that bound his wrists. Once his hands were free, Bill Peace reached across to lift one of Fowler's heavy Colt .45s from its holster. He swung the weapon into line with the nearest man.

"Unbuckle your belts, friend," he drawled, and the threat of his gun seemed to bring the others out of their inaction. One by one, a little hurriedly, they loosened their belts and dropped their weapons to the ground.

It was then that Bill Peace had his first good look at Al Sisson. The outlaw came down off his high perch and swung lithely

to earth. He moved quickly among the riders, gathering their weapons and threading them by the trigger guards on the belt he took from his own waist. Al Sisson had already become a legend in this country. Bill Peace was satisfied as he studied the man's unhasty but efficient moves.

At length, approaching Fowler, Sisson said: "Climb down, Tin Star! I'll fork your horse out of here."

The lawman obeyed with surprising swiftness, and in five seconds Sisson was astride the bay. Judge White suddenly reined in closer alongside Bill Peace and struck him an open-handed blow in the face. Peace drew away, the color draining from his lean visage. He let the hand that held the six-gun fall to his side.

"You're the only man who could do that and live, Judge," he said tonelessly.

"We'll hunt you down like a killer wolf," White breathed.

Sisson laughed softly and put in, "A couple years ago you made the same talk about me, Judge. For a man with brains, it's takin' you a long time to see the straight of things. Peace didn't kill Wes Stanley."

White ignored the outlaw, his glance fixed on Bill Peace. "You may live a month, maybe two, Peace. Sooner or later we'll

finish what we started today."

Peace abruptly wheeled his black and rode beyond the margin of the encircling riders. One man made a stealthy move, and Peace swung up his weapon and thumbed a shot that sent blasting echoes along the corridors of the cañon. On the heels of that sound the rider jerked spasmodically in the saddle, and his right arm fell to his side. His gun spun out of his grasp to, fall into the dust. A splotch of red showed at his shoulder. He brought up his other hand to clutch at it, rasping: "Damn you for a sidewinder, Peace!"

Sisson swung wide of the group, rode in, and picked up the fallen weapon. "You're lucky to be alive, stranger," he remarked dryly. He came back and handed the weapon to Peace. It was then that Peace spoke once more to Judge White.

"If you'll ride herd on your temper long enough, you might like to take a closer look and find out who really killed Wes Stanley. Sooner or later you'll know I was framed."

"We'll have a reward of two thousand on your head before sundown!"

Bill Peace considered that, certain now that nothing would ever change the hot hatred these men felt for him. Fate had fed the flames of that hatred so that not even

this group, honest, respectable, the pick of this wide range, could temper its hostility with reason. He was all at once impatient to ride out of here, to put behind him once and for all the misery of these past eight months.

Al Sisson must have sensed his feeling, for he said crisply: "We'll ride upcañon and pick up my bronc."

He looped his belt of weapons over his saddlehorn, drove his spurs into the flanks of Fowler's bay, and sent the animal into a leaping run. Peace whirled his black about and followed. As the outlaw rode diagonally out across the cañon floor, putting distance between him and the cottonwood, he reined his bay from side to side, cutting a zigzag course. Peace, close behind, read the reason for this and dogged the outlaw's tracks. He was none too soon, for shortly a hollow, muted blast cut loose behind and a plume of dust spurted up ten feet to one side of them. Someone in the posse had hidden a gun and was now using it.

Once Peace turned in his saddle and emptied his six-gun in a staccato burst that turned back four pursuing riders who suddenly streaked out from the cottonwood's shadow. Seconds later he and Sisson swung around a turn in this high-walled cañon and

for five minutes held their horses to a steady hard run. Abruptly, Sisson reined to one side, slowed the bay to a walk, and swung into a narrow off-shoot, calling, "Wait here for me."

In a quarter-minute he was back again, mounted on a rangy dun gelding. The belt-load of guns was no longer slung from his saddle.

"Dropped 'em in the spring up there," he explained as he reined up in front of Peace. He cocked his head and held it that way for a long moment, finally smiling as no sound of pursuit broke the afternoon's utter silence. "They'll come along slow, expectin' us to fort up and hold 'em back. It'll take half an hour to find their guns, and by that time we'll have covered plenty of ground."

Peace said: "What about the others . . . your men up on the rim?"

Sisson laughed softly, shrugged: "I've never traveled in any company but my own. It's safest that way."

Bill Peace's gray eyes widened. "Then what's this talk about your wild bunch?"

"Just that, talk!"

Sisson's smile broadened at the expression of surprise that came to Peace's face. The outlaw wheeled away and lifted the dun into a fast walk that soon became an easy mile-

eating trot as Peace fell in alongside. They rode steadily, saying little for two full hours. Alternately trotting and walking their horses, they put distance behind them without tiring their animals. They neither saw nor heard sign of the posse behind.

II

"A DANGEROUS DECISION"

It was Sisson who chose their direction once they gained the upper reaches of the cañon. They cut west into the broken hilly country that was the north boundary of Steeple range. It flanked the high spire of snow-capped Steeple Peak that rose three thousand feet above the lesser mountains.

During those two hours Bill Peace reached a decision he fought against making. He was through with this country. He didn't want to be, but a man with a price on his head had little choice. His regret wasn't for the ten-section ranch that had been his home for the past eight months since he had come onto this range. The bank still owned all but a small part of that land, and there would be more and better land in a new country. Rather, he was losing a thing he would never find in his life again when he rode away from Twin Rivers — Joyce White.

He told himself that he had been a fool ever to think of her seriously. From the first he had seen that fate would line him against her father. He had had the misfortune to stake out his ten sections along the banks of a dry wash, known for years as Snake River. That was two months before a government dam, high in the hills, had broken through its foundations, washed out the side of a cañon, and sent the waters off those snowy peaks spilling down the mountainside to make a green, fertile land of the Snake River bottoms.

His ten sections suddenly increased in value to a hundred times their former worth. So had the value of other small outfits along Snake River, that of the dead Wes Stanley among them. Overnight, this land was priceless for the raising of alfalfa, for the pasturage of yearlings, and for the remudas of the bigger outfits. Some of the big brands bought out a half dozen of the smaller spreads, paying a fair price. But Miles Root, owner of the Quarter-Circle R, didn't do things that way. He made a low offer for Peace's ten sections, then for others, and had been refused. It caused hard feelings between Root's high-riding crew and Peace and the others. Two men were killed from ambush — both Quarter-Circle R riders —

and several hundred head of Root's steers vanished into thin air. It looked as if a small war was shaping up between the big and the small ranchers, with the Snake River outfits forcing Root's hand. Root had the law on his side. He was Judge White's friend and apparently in the right. Yes, Peace had made a mistake in ever thinking of Joyce White.

"We'll circle back to Wes Stanley's layout," Sisson said at sundown.

By then they were high in a rocky country, long ago having lost their sign below where the thin soil gave out in an uptilted, barren stretch that ran for a hundred miles at the foot of the high peaks.

Bill Peace was fast developing a respect for this outlaw. It had taken guts to make that play at the cottonwood, foresight even to be on hand for the attempted hanging. Peace was intrigued with the mystery of the outlaw's presence there but decided to wait until later to put his questions. Just now he thought he saw a method in Sisson's wide circle back onto home range. The last place the law would look for them would be at Wes Stanley's — within five miles of Twin Rivers.

They rode by the light of the stars for a full three hours. Finally, Sisson led the way to a rocky, high-walled gulch a mile behind

Stanley's place. There they made camp, even had a fire, for this country was wild, and the towering steep walls of the gulch hid the light of their blaze. Sisson's saddlebags yielded jerky, beans, flour, salt, and coffee — enough for two.

After they had hungrily wolfed their meal in silence, Peace lit his pipe and hunkered down with his back to the stump of a lightning-blasted cedar, well out of the circle of light. He studied Sisson for many long minutes. Then, abruptly, he mentioned what was on his mind.

"I want to know all about it," he said. "How it comes you're in this country, how you know I didn't kill Wes and burn his place, how you came to be there at the cottonwood this afternoon?"

Sisson was busy with the making of a cigarette. He didn't reply immediately but studied his hands as they shaped his quirly. When he had lit it, flicking the match into the hot coals of the fire, he looked across at Peace. He smiled thinly.

"By rights I should have let you hang. Wes Stanley brought me in to bushwhack you."

For an instant Peace was confused. At length he queried: "Did Wes hate me that bad?"

"He did," Sisson nodded solemnly. "And

he had good reason, from what I can learn. You were against Wes and the others along the river, thought you ought to make your choice between them and the big outfits. They thought you were double-crossin' 'em. Wes spoke of one of your neighbors bein' burned out two weeks ago. They figured you were the only one who could have told Miles Root that neighbor would be gone from his layout that particular night. It was Root's crew they blamed for that fire . . . Root and you."

Peace shook his head, meeting the outlaw's level glance squarely: "And what do you think?"

"I don't think you did it . . . or killed Wes, either."

"Thanks for that. But how come you don't agree with Wes about me?"

Sisson chuckled softly, looking at his cigarette once more. "Wes was a good man in many ways, a bad one in a few. The way I figure it, he was in the wrong. Most of the men he chose as his friends were these small ranchers. Maybe it wasn't his fault, for a man has to have friends, and the way things are he couldn't be too particular. But his friends are a mangy crew, mostly squatters who've never had a dollar and don't know what to do with their

73

money now that they have it."

"That's puttin' it a bit strong," Peace said cautiously.

"But it's the truth, nevertheless . . . and just about the way you've sized 'em up." Sisson eyed Peace shrewdly. "The pack of 'em wants to fight Root openly. You're smart enough to know they'd be licked. Wes Stanley wasn't. That's why you wouldn't throw in with 'em."

"But I didn't side with Miles Root."

"I know," Sisson nodded. "And I'll tell you how I know. Two years ago Root 'gulched his foreman and framed me with the killin'. I can't prove it, but I'm sure that's the way it was. Root's always swung a sticky loop, although not many people know it. He made the mistake of hirin' an honest man to rod his outfit. The ramrod discovered his crookedness, and so Root had to get rid of him. He framed me for killing that man. Only I broke jail, and they've never found me. Wes was my friend. A week ago, when he saw things shaping up this way, he sent for me, knowin' I'd side with him. I don't think you're the kind that'd trust a man like Root."

"You still haven't said why Wes hired you to get me."

"Because he and the rest didn't think they

74

could make a play against Root without your comin' in with 'em. And so long as you wouldn't . . . so long as Wes was sure you'd double-crossed them . . . he wanted you out of the way."

Sisson paused, and Peace waited. He wanted him to tell his story in his own way. At length, the outlaw went on: "Wes primed me into thinkin' you were ten kinds of a coyote. Late yesterday afternoon I was forted up in that grove of cottonwoods behind your place, with a rifle, waitin' a chance at you, but I couldn't get a sure shot. When you went into your cabin about dark, I went back to Wes's place, decidin' to wait for another try. That's how I know you didn't kill Wes. You were at home when Wes was murdered, and his house fired. I even saw the tobacco tin."

Peace couldn't hide his amazement. "You mean you understood what it meant, why it was put there?"

"Not at first. You see, I rode down to Stanley's place shortly after the fire started. Whoever did it must have ridden away only a few minutes before I got there. I had a look at Wes, lyin' on the floor, but I couldn't get to him because of the blaze. But I did see the empty tobacco tin in front of the door."

"You might have seen it, but you couldn't have guessed what it meant . . . that it was put there to frame me."

"I partly guessed it. I know Wes, and I know he's a neat man, one who wouldn't let trash lie around square in front of his door. Wes didn't smoke. And another thing that gave it away was that the brand of tobacco is one you almost never see in this country. So last night I rode to town and talked to a stranger or two. It didn't take much talk to learn that you're the only one man around here that smokes that brand . . . you have it mailed in from Kentucky."

Peace was frowning. He had pieced together all but the last fragments of this puzzle: "But how come you were up the cottonwood?"

Sisson smiled tolerantly. "Since it looked to be a frame-up, I went back to Wes's place to make sure it was you they were framin'. The sheriff rode out with a posse late this mornin' and picked up that tobacco tin and headed for your place. I hung along the posse's back trail. They got you and started back to town, and I saw Fowler arguin' with Judge White."

Peace nodded: "I heard most of that argument. White wanted to jail me . . . Fowler won the argument."

76

"When they swung to the south of the trail, I figured it that way. It's a treeless country and, when Fowler took his rope off his saddle, it looked like they were headed for the big cottonwood. So I rode on ahead, hid my horse, and climbed the tree."

For a long moment Bill Peace was silent, too full of emotion to put his thoughts into words. Finally he drawled: "Sayin' thanks is a poor way of payin' off this kind of a debt."

"You can do it another way," was Sisson's answer. "Stay here and help me fight Miles Root . . . instead of headin' out of the country." Sisson paused, watching Peace carefully. Then he added: "It won't be easy. Wes's bein' gone knocks the props out from under this fight his friends were buildin'. We'll be alone. Those squatters will stick close to home and keep out of this. Root has 'em buffaloed."

It was five seconds before Peace made his answer. What he said was: "Those squatters wouldn't have been much help. I think we can win anyway. They'll think we headed out of the country." He looked squarely at the outlaw. . . . "I'll stay here as long as you do."

III

"MONEY BUYS DEATH"

Judge White stabled his horse at about the same hour Peace and Sisson were making camp near the Stanley place. The judge had ridden into town alone.

Late that afternoon the posse had lost the sign of the men they followed. After that Sheriff Fowler had split his twenty-five riders into three groups, sending them in different directions to search for sign. These groups, in turn, had divided into pairs to cover more ground. They hadn't met after dark but headed directly for town. White's companion had left him two miles from town, heading south to his small ranch.

The judge was a man who prided himself on his honesty and fairness, not openly of course but merely as a way of answering to his conscience. Just now, as he crossed his back yard and walked up the steps of the rear porch, his conscience was troubling

him. Although Peace was a comparative stranger in this country, the judge had grown to like him. This afternoon a subtle mob feeling had gripped the whole posse, fed by Fowler's arguments after they had taken Bill Peace. It was that mob feeling that had finally made White give in to the lawman and agree to the verdict of a cottonwood jury. This was a rugged country; a man was either right or wrong; and Bill Peace had been obviously guilty. Once convinced of that, a hanging seemed no stranger to White than it did to those others. But now that fatigue had sobered him, he wasn't so sure. Bill Peace hadn't fought, hadn't had a chance. Yet his nerve hadn't broken, and time and again he had proclaimed himself innocent. Then, too, White was remembering Al Sisson's words, *Peace didn't kill Wes Stanley.*

Since Sisson had broken jail and made himself an outlaw, White's original respect for the man hadn't diminished. He told himself that there was no need for Sisson to have said that this afternoon — no need, unless what he said was the truth.

The judge hoped he wouldn't have to face Joyce tonight. His daughter loved Bill Peace, although they'd never openly discussed her feeling for him. So, when he went in the

back door of his house, he sprung the latch softly and swung the door open gingerly. He was glad he had made it a habit to keep the hinges oiled.

As he stepped into the kitchen, he heard voices from the front of the house. One was Joyce's voice, and his disappointment was keen. He had ridden up the back alley and hadn't been able to see the lights in front. Now he'd have to talk with her, explain what had happened, why he'd made himself a member of a lynch mob.

But two seconds after he had softly closed the door, his regrets vanished before a sudden curiosity. From the living room up front he made out a voice he recognized as Miles Root's. The rancher was saying: ". . . may be too soon to mention a thing like this, but I mean it, Joyce. I want you to marry me."

Joyce's answer came to her father, low-throated and filled with an emotion he couldn't identify. "Miles, I'll never marry you. But I do thank you. I feel honored."

"Is it Bill Peace?" Root asked.

There was the scrape of a chair. Then Joyce's voice sounded more vibrant this time as she said: "That's a question I needn't answer!"

"Remember, Joyce, I wasn't a part of what

happened today. For all I know, Peace may have been innocent."

"He was innocent!" she flared. "He's too good a man, too much of a man, to commit murder."

For a long moment a strained silence hung on. At length the sound of Root's steps crossing the room shuttled back through the house.

The judge heard the rancher pause at the front door, saying clearly: "I'm a clumsy fool, Joyce. I won't mention this again, not for a long time. But someday, when you've forgotten what's happened today, I'll ask you this same question. I think I could make you happy."

"Perhaps you could, Miles." Joyce's tone held a measure of tenderness. "But I can't think of it now . . . I can't think of anything. Please understand."

Shortly there was the soft closing of the front door, Joyce's light step as she crossed the room. Before the judge could rid himself of the amazement that held him at what he had heard, Joyce came into the kitchen, holding a lighted lamp in her hand. She stopped abruptly, just inside the door, her eyes wide in surprise.

"Dad!" she breathed. "Dad, you heard!"

He nodded guiltily. "I didn't mean to. I

just came in, thought I'd get a bite, and go to bed without wakening you. I thought you'd turned in for the night."

The girl shrugged lifelessly. "Of course you didn't mean to overhear." She stepped across to the table to place the lamp on it then went on lifelessly: "There's some cold chicken you can eat. You must have had a hard day."

White, for the moment, was wordless, held by an emotion of tenderness toward his daughter. She stood there — tall, erect, with none of her pent-up emotion showing in the set of her strong aquiline face. But it did show in her deep brown eyes. There was a hurt look in them that somehow carried to him the fact that she was suffering deeply. With a sudden impulsive gesture he stepped over to her and took her in his arms. She let her head sink against his chest, her chestnut hair softly caressing his face, turned coppery at the edges as it caught the glow from the lamp.

"I'll get over it, Dad," she whispered, her voice steady and low.

Somehow he knew that she wouldn't give way to her grief, that it was too deep to be relieved by tears. He admired her for that stubborn check to her emotion, strangely enough convinced in his own mind that she

couldn't be entirely wrong about Bill Peace.

He pushed her gently from him: "I'm hungry, Joyce. How about that chicken?"

There was a fire in the range, and she warmed his meal and set it before him. Her silence was a relief, for his thoughts were still too confused to try and frame into words. But when she had taken the chair opposite, and after his first few mouthfuls of food had dulled the sharp pangs of his hunger, he said, looking at his plate: "You're sure you don't want Miles, honey? He's a good man."

"No, Dad, I don't want Miles." Then, after a long awkward silence: "Bill Peace will be back."

The conviction in her voice startled him. He looked at her squarely. Her head was held proudly, a tenderness mirrored in her eyes that made him proud she was his.

"You heard about it?" he queried. "About Bill . . . escaping?"

She nodded.

"Maybe we all lost our heads today," he said, feeling the need of explaining his actions to her. "Fowler talked me into it. The evidence against Peace was so convincing . . . and then we all thought a lot of Wes."

"You thought a lot of Bill, too, Dad," Joyce reminded him, her tone lacking the

bitterness of a moment ago.

"I know, but there was a lot against him. Tonight I've been thinkin' . . . thinkin' over a few things Bill and Al Sisson said. I think I'll go down and have a talk with Ralph Fowler. There might be a thing or two we'd find out at Wes's place if we looked a bit closer."

The happiness that shone in Joyce's eyes somehow tempered the feeling of self-loathing that had been like a cancerous growth deep within Judge White during these past few hours — since his knowing that he had been in the wrong on the long ride today. He wasn't a man who often made mistakes, and he was too old to admit an error readily. This helped, for in trying to satisfy his own doubts of Bill Peace's guilt, he was bringing happiness to the one person in the world he loved.

He finished his meal quickly, even forgot to take out his pipe and light it as he put on his Stetson and went out the front door. He headed down the street for the jail and Ralph Fowler's office. He wasn't sure what he'd say to the sheriff, how he'd convince him there was a reasonable doubt — but he would try. Joyce's parting — "Good luck, Dad!" — made him realize even more strongly that this was a serious thing.

Miles Root was lighthearted as he left Judge White's house and walked up the street. Soon he was striding beneath the awnings in front of the stores along the plank walk. After the heat of the day the cool night air was bracing, and the fragrant richness of the expensive cigar he smoked tasted good. Tonight was only the beginning with Joyce White. She cared a little for him — it was easy to see that. And sooner or later she would forget Peace.

He was startled out of his thoughts as a figure loomed out of a narrow passageway between two stores a few feet ahead of him. Instinctively his right hand streaked up and slid under the lapel of his broadcloth coat. It settled on the butt of the .38 at his armpit.

A familiar voice drawled softly, "It's me, Trank!"

Miles Root's tense muscles relaxed, and he brought his hand down empty. But an instant later hidden relief gave way before a rising of cold anger. He stepped closer to that lone figure.

"I thought I told you to leave the county!" he said, barely audible.

He was close enough now so that he could make out the expression on Ed Trank's

gaunt face. It bothered him a little to have to look up at this high-built man. Trank was well over six feet, a full head the taller, and his height subtly robbed Root of a certain dignity.

Trank said: "Wait'll I tell you why I didn't go. Can we talk here?"

Root's glance swiveled up the walk. Then he turned and scanned the shadows behind, seeing that the street was deserted. "We can if you make it quick. What do you want?"

"Money," Trank said and smiled wickedly, his thin lips parting over yellowed teeth.

Miles Root's square-built frame went taut once more. He knew how to deal with this breed of man, and his glance settled on Trank's hands. He watched for a hint of a move there as he intoned: "No understrapper ever blackmailed me and got away with it, Ed!"

"This isn't blackmail, Boss! It's somethin' I seen last night."

Root's curiosity came alive. "Something you saw? What?"

"I'd want my pay first."

The rancher waved a hand in a quick gesture of irritation. "You've always been well paid, haven't you? What was it you saw?"

"Someone was there last night right after I got the blaze goin'."

"Who?" Root snapped the word, his black eyes beady. His jaw muscles corded, giving his rugged face an ugly expression.

Trank lifted his thin shoulders in a shrug. "How would I know? I'm a stranger here. But he was there and tried to get in and pull Stanley out. The flames was too strong. And he saw that tobacco tin, picked it up, and looked at it."

"And you let him get away?"

"I was on that slope above the place and only happened to look back. It was too far to make sure of a shot with a plow handle. By the time I'd got out of my hull and worked closer, he was gone. So I stayed on today, thinkin' you'd want to know."

On the way to town, late that afternoon, Root had talked with a member of the posse, heard the details of what had happened. Now he was fairly certain that the man Trank had seen was Al Sisson. His confidence of a few minutes ago gave way to a troubled feeling of irritation and uncertainty.

"The money, Boss," Trank all at once reminded him.

Grudgingly, Root reached to his hip pocket and took out a wallet. He handed Trank two crisp new twenty dollar bills.

"Here's forty dollars," he said. "You'd better put plenty of distance behind you tonight. Tomorrow mornin' there'll be a hundred men on the hunt for Peace and. . . ." Abruptly he broke off, toying with an idea. Then he added hastily: "No, you're not to leave. Maybe I can use you. Ride up to Stanley's place and hole up there and wait. I'll send for you when I want you."

"For how much?" Trank queried, grinning mirthlessly.

Root took two more banknotes from his wallet. "We'll talk about that when the time comes. This ought to make it interesting enough for you to stay. Wait at Stanley's a week. If I haven't sent for you by that time, slope out of the country. Now get goin'."

Trank took the money, touched the brim of his Stetson in a gesture that might have been one of courtesy but wasn't, and stepped back into the shadows of the alleyway. Then he was gone.

IV

"RUNAWAY LAWMAN"

When Root went on down the street, his lighthearted confidence of minutes ago had vanished. He was sure it was Al Sisson that Trank had seen, and he was very disturbed over how much the outlaw knew. He had planned the events of this day for weeks, and it was his habit to make sure that anything like this went off smoothly. Today it hadn't. First there was Peace's escape. Now the unknown quantity of Al Sisson's being in the country and against him. Root was remembering Sisson and knew that it wasn't in the man's nature to be forgiving. And he knew too that he had given Sisson enough reason to hate him.

He was walking leisurely toward the livery stable when he saw the light in Fowler's office — a low-built adobe behind the jail across the way. Being in the frame of mind he was, he decided to have a talk with

Fowler. His entrance into the sheriff's office was abrupt. It brought Ralph Fowler out of his chair in a lunge, hands swiveling up to the twin holsters at his thighs. When the lawman saw who it was, he eased back down into his chair with a sigh of relief.

"Guess I'm jumpy tonight, Miles," he muttered. "I've had a hard. . . ." He caught the expression on the rancher's bleakly set face and stopped his talk.

After a brief interval that seemed interminable to the lawman, Root said: "You made a mess of things today, Ralph."

"A mess?" The sheriff bridled. "What I did was the same as you'd have done . . . or anyone else!"

"You could have rammed a cutter into Peace's middle and had both of them cold! They outbluffed you."

"The hell they did!" Fowler exploded. "Sisson had half a dozen guns on the cañon rim. You think I'd be damned fool enough . . . ?"

"Jerry Bates rode up there and claimed he couldn't find any sign. Sisson outbluffed you. He was alone."

Root's tone was so positive, the expression in his black eyes so like granite, that all at once the lawman sighed gustily. All the fight was gone out of him. "All right, they bluffed

me. But you're rid of Peace, and in two weeks' time you can buy both outfits from the bank. That's what you wanted in the first place . . . what you're payin' me for."

"I'd forgotten that," Root drawled pointedly, taking the wallet from his pocket for the second time that night. This time he counted out ten of the twenty-dollar notes. He stepped across to lay them on Fowler's desk. "There it is, two hundred. It was to be for hangin' Peace, but I'll never have a man sayin' I'm close with money."

Fowler was undecided. He looked greedily at the money, not the first he'd taken from Root. But a deep inner conviction made him hesitate to take it. "Pay me what you think it's worth," he said. "Hell, I don't take money for somethin' I don't do!"

Root shook his head slowly, his smile full of meaning. "It's yours, Ralph. All I ask is that you make a big play tomorrow of huntin' down those two. And you'd better give out orders for the posse to kill them on sight. Peace could talk, and I've a hunch that Sisson knows enough to blow this whole thing sky high. Have 'em brought in dead, if they're brought in at all."

Root stood there only a second, letting his glance add weight to his meaning. Then, before the sheriff could reply, he abruptly

turned and went out the door. His leaving was so sudden that Judge White had barely time enough to step back out of the light before the window outside. He hugged the wall's shadow, not daring to breathe until Root had rounded the corner of the jail and gone on down the street.

For the second time that night Judge White had stumbled upon a scene he wasn't supposed to be witnessing. Only this time he had seen, not heard, Miles Root. Five minutes ago, coming down the alleyway beside the jail and intending to go directly to Fowler's office, he had chanced to glance into the single window of the sheriff's office on his way to the door. He had seen Root in there. It was the look on Root's face that had stopped him. He hadn't heard anything but the muted undertone of their voices, but he had seen that Root had paid the sheriff money, for what he couldn't even make a guess. A growing curiosity held White rooted to the spot, watching the lawman.

Inside, Ralph Fowler was mopping his perspiring forehead with a trembling hand. These past few minutes had left him more shaken than the rifle Al Sisson had trained on him this afternoon. It was not because of what Root had said, but because of what he hadn't. Ralph Fowler had the average

measure of brains, but it had been his misfortune to use them in the wrong way. He still squirmed at remembrance of the first time he had taken money from Miles Root, years ago. On that occasion Root had paid him handsomely to be at the other end of town at a certain hour one night when a killer was broken out of jail. Since then, Root's money had been wisely spent on taking the sting out of the law. Fowler could remember a dozen times when he'd been paid a flat hundred dollars to overlook freshly altered brands in making a shipping count for Root at the railroad's loading corrals.

Tonight Fowler stripped aside his pretense and took a good look at himself. Beneath the floorboards of his back room at the hotel, nicely wrapped in a strip of oil cloth, was close onto three thousand dollars he hadn't dared deposit in the bank for fear of arousing suspicion. That three thousand had come to him over a period of eight years, too small a sum to make up for the risk involved in collecting it. Now he was Root's man, cleverly bought and at little expense. Letting his thoughts run on, unhaltered by his usual weak self-assurances, the sheriff had a clear look into the future — down the trail his greed was leading him.

What he saw made him afraid. Miles Root would use him just as long as he had need for him. And then?

No man ever lets an understrapper live too long or know too much, Root had once said over a bottle on the evening of a particularly large and successful shipment of stolen beef. Fowler remembered the rancher's words now, attached a grim significance to them. The thought made his palms moist with a clammy sweat, made the small of his back tingle. It would take only one bullet, a hired bullet perhaps, to rid Root of a man who knew too much about the secret of his sudden rise to wealth and power on Steeple range.

The full realization of how deeply he had involved himself sent a flood of momentary panic through Fowler. That emotion gave way to speculation and, after a half-minute's deliberate consideration of the fate that was in store for him, he knew what he must do. The border lay seventy miles south. His three thousand wasn't much but would be enough to take him far beyond Root's reach. By sunup he could be fifty miles on his way. He was through here, and a wise man would leave while his skin was whole. No sooner had the idea come to him than he got up out of his chair and began clearing out his

desk, sorting through his few personal belongings and dropping them in an empty saddlebag that he found in a pile of gear in one corner of the room.

Outside, his gaze held fascinated and his conscience eased by the knowledge that he was witnessing something unique here, Judge White watched Fowler through the window. As yet he was not quite able to grasp all that he was seeing. But when the lawman had finished rummaging through his desk and was filling the saddlebag, when he went to the gun rack on the rear wall of the room and took down an extra pair of Colt .45s and a saddle gun, the judge knew: *He's headin' out of here . . . for a long stay!*

By the time Fowler had blown out the lamp, the judge was hidden better than he had been five minutes ago when Root had left. He let Fowler get clear of the alley and far down the street before he moved from his hiding place in the deep shadows underneath a barred window of the jail. From the mouth of the passageway onto the street, he watched Fowler drop his saddlebag in the darkened doorway of a store and cross to the hotel. Waiting there, sensing that the lawman would be back, ten minutes later White saw the sheriff come out of the hotel, cross to pick up the saddlebag, and then

walk quickly down the street to the livery barn. But he was only half way guessing the truth when Fowler left town, turning south at the intersection of Twin Rivers' two streets.

V

"IN THE LOFT"

After breakfast the next morning, Bill Peace said: "We'll need grub. You'd better ride over to my place and pick up what we need. There's enough there to last us a week. And while you're there, turn the stock out of the corral."

Sisson nodded. "And what'll you do?"

"Take a *pasear* down to Stanley's place. I want to look around. Did they bury him?"

Sisson nodded. "The posse took care of that. But if you expect to find anything to steer you onto who did the job, you won't get far. I had a look myself, yesterday."

"It'll be spendin' time," Peace said. "Another thing. While you're at my place, go to the barn and dig down into the bottom of the feed bin and bring back that box I cached there. It's money. Tonight I'll take it into Twin Rivers. Someone I know there'll go to the bank tomorrow and pay up the

interest on my note."

"Then you're stayin' for good?" Sisson queried. Peace's answering nod brought a broad smile to the outlaw's face. "I've heard about the girl and, from what they tell me, she's worth stayin' around for."

Peace's lean face took on a shade more color. He hadn't consciously been thinking of Joyce this morning, but he knew now that she had been at the back of his mind ever since he'd crawled out of his blankets.

Later, riding down the gulch toward Stanley's place — after Sisson had left — he told himself once again that it was foolishness to be thinking of Joyce. But something deeply within him kept that hope alive. Tonight he would see her, and he would know then whether or not she thought him guilty like the rest. Remembering the sober hatred of those twenty-seven men in the posse, he was filled with a momentary dread of seeing her. But he put it down, hating to recognize the possibility that he might be losing the one real thing in his life.

As the walls of the gulch fell away into the gradual down slope behind Stanley's place, he came within sight of the layout and drew rein, warily studying what lay below before he went on. To all appearances, the place was deserted. The spot where

Stanley's cabin had stood was a black scar against the clay-colored yard — a few timbers thrusting up their gaunt, scorched outlines to mark the shape of the foundations.

His glance traveled onto the corral. It was empty, doubtless thrown open by a member of the posse. Two horses, both Stanley's, grazed below the corral in the small two-acre pasture. The weathered frame barn stood open, its loft doors swinging slowly in the breeze.

Certain that he was alone, he rode on. And, as he swung around a far corner of the barn, scanning the ground for sign, he sat relaxed in the saddle. Suddenly a gruff voice spoke to one side of him, from the barn door. It brought him all at once rigid.

"Lookin' for something, stranger?"

When he slowly turned his head to look at the speaker, it was to see Ed Trank leaning idly against the frame of the door, a whittled stick in one hand, an open clasp knife in the other.

Peace was too surprised for a moment to speak. His silence was what saved him, for the next moment Trank said: "Don't tell me the boss sent you after me already."

"No. He sent me to take a look around," was Peace's quick, noncommittal answer.

Trank's glance narrowed as he regarded

Peace, a faint suspicion edging it. "Maybe I spoke out of turn," he drawled. His gray eyes shuttled to take in the black's jaw brand. On sight of it he suddenly stiffened. His right hand opened, let go the knife, and dropped toward his holster.

Bill Peace drove his spurs into the black's flanks, tugging at the reins with his left hand as his right swept upward, palming out his gun. The black took a quick, nervous step that moved Peace out of line, so that Trank's whipping shot went wide. Peace's weapon swung down and into line and echoed the explosion of Trank's gun.

The gunman all at once dropped the gun and made a hurried stab at his chest. He tottered weakly back against the boards of the barn siding. His knees gave way, and he slid down to a sitting position. By that time Peace had thrown himself out of the saddle and was standing ten feet away, his Colt lined at the gunman's chest. His shot had been a lucky one, for it was thrown quickly with his arm unsteadied by the lunge of the black.

Sitting there, Ed Trank coughed pulpily, and blood flecked his lips. His hand came away from his chest to show a red smear centering his shirt, one that spread outward slowly. He cursed viciously time and again,

pausing only to gasp for breath. At length, he eyed Bill Peace coldly. Then, faintly smiling at some inner thought, he drawled: "Damned if this isn't luck! You're Peace, ain't you? That brand gave you away. The first time I ever had a chance to collect a reward that wasn't on my own head, and I fumble it!"

Peace said: "Your mistake was in goin' for your iron."

Trank laughed softly, and even that effort brought on a spasm of coughing. He shook his head. "No, my mistake was in ever staying in this country. It was the money that did it."

"Whose money?"

After a moment in which lines of pain robbed Trank's twisted smile of its mirth, the gunman said: "I never yet double-crossed a man. You go to hell!"

"You're Miles Root's man?" Peace queried, voicing his only logical guess.

"Who's Root?" Trank asked blandly. Then, again: "You go to hell!" As he spoke, his right hand edged slowly outward to take a hold on the handle of his fallen gun.

Peace saw that gesture and warned: "Don't make me throw down on you again."

But Trank said: "Why not? I'm cashin' in anyway." He raised the weapon.

It was sheer suicide, Trank's last gesture in defiance of having been beaten by a better man. Awed, hating what he must do, yet knowing that it was either his life or the gunman's, Bill Peace thumbed back the hammer of his .45, his gaze riveted to that upswinging gun of Trank's. Suddenly its feeble upswing ended, and the hand that held the weapon went limp and loosed its grasp. Ed Trank's chin rested on his chest. He was dead.

It took Peace two hours to dig the grave in the brick-hard clay down by the corral. When he had finished lugging rocks from the cabin foundation, rocks he put over the grave, the sun had topped its slow arc to the south and was lowering toward the uneven horizon to the west. He was hungry, sobered by this quirk of fate that had forced him to kill to defend his own life, so that he rode away from the layout without giving a thought to his purpose in going there.

Twenty minutes later he had unsaddled and hobbled the black and was gathering dry wood for a fire. He opened Sisson's one remaining can of beans, heated them in a pan, and hungrily devoured them. Then he settled down to wait, vaguely troubled by the outlaw's prolonged absence. It was only

six miles north to Peace's layout. Sisson should have returned long ago.

The reason the outlaw didn't return was that two members of the posse that spread out in all directions from Twin Rivers that morning had been sent to keep a watch at Peace's place. Sisson had left his horse in the grove of cottonwoods nearly a half mile away, walking the remaining distance, keeping to cover as best he could and wanting to make sure that no one was around. He found the place deserted and set about his first task, turning loose the three broncs in the corral. Once done with that, he went to the barn and thrust his hand deeply into the oats in the feed bin and found the box containing Bill Peace's money. Next, he went to the slab-sided cabin and had half filled a flour sack with provisions when he heard riders approaching. A quick look outside showed him two men had ridden directly into the yard. When they dismounted, they were close enough so that he heard one of them say: "This'll be better than ridin' all day."

One rider stayed in the yard, blocking the outlaw's chance of escape. The other took their horses to the corral. By the time he was back once more, Sisson had climbed

into the low-roofed loft above the beamed ceiling of the cabin's single room.

The loft was dark, the air close and hot from the beating sun on the roof. Al Sisson endured his discomforts with a time-trained patience as the two riders below made themselves comfortable.

At first there was little talk. One of the pair found a pack of cards and for two hours they played pinochle, sitting at a table directly below the spot where the outlaw lay. Through a space between the crude sheathing of the ceiling he could look down onto the table and watch their game. In a way it relieved the slow torture of the heat and his consequent thirst.

It wasn't until the two below gave up their game and started cooking their noon meal on Bill Peace's sheet-iron stove that either of them said anything interesting. Sisson, his senses dulled by the heat, had closed his eyes and was nearly asleep when he heard one of them say: "You got any more ideas on what happened to Ralph Fowler?"

The second man grunted his disgust. "Your guess is as good as mine." He didn't appear particularly interested.

But the first was in the mood for talk. "It ain't like Ralph to skip out and leave a job like this to a deputy."

"It ain't!" the other snorted. "You ought to have been along yesterday. Fowler had his chance to take them two and missed it. Slim, I'm beginnin' to think this county needs a new sheriff!"

That was all — until the middle of the afternoon. Al Sisson had been dozing, his mind utterly weary yet not relaxing completely due to a long-trained wariness. Because of this half alertness he heard the hoof pound of the running horse while it was still a good distance below the cabin. The sound jerked him into complete wakefulness, his first thought being that this might be Bill Peace riding into a trap. He reached down and took his pair of Colt .45s from their holsters and crawled to the loft opening. He'd jump down into the room and help Peace if the two down there made any move to threaten the approaching rider.

VI

"OVERTAKEN"

An instant later the gruff voice of one of
the pair below brought an immediate relief.
The man was standing at the door, looking
out, and he called to his companion: "Looks
like Jerry Bates. He's in an all-fired hurry,
too!"

After a brief pause his voice sounded from
outside the cabin, muted by the distance as
he greeted the newcomer who had ridden
into the yard in front.

Sisson holstered his guns once more, irritably deciding that he would be cooped
up for several more hours. But five seconds
later he heard the quick pound of boots in
the hard-packed yard outside, and the
man who had spoken a moment ago
called: "Slim! Goddlemighty, Slim, listen to
this!"

Slim's chair scraped across the floor. He
went to the door. The three of them stood

there talking, their voices plainly heard by the outlaw.

"Slim, it's about Ralph Fowler! He's been kidnapped!"

"The hell you say!"

"Tell him about it, Jerry."

"It didn't happen until after Brady'd sent the posse out this mornin'," came a new voice. "Brady was in the office when Miles Root came in, about noon. Miles listened to what Brady had to say then went over to the hotel. Later it come out he'd got suspicious and thought he ought to take a look at Fowler's room. The sheriff's bed hadn't been slept in, and Root found a sheet of paper lyin' on it. It was printed so as to disguise the handwriting of the man that left it there. But what it said was plain enough. We're takin' your sheriff along just in case someone tries to collect the reward."

In the brief interval of awed silence that followed Jerry Bates's words, Al Sisson lay there, taking in the full significance of this news. For the first time here was clear proof of Miles Root's cunning.

"It means Sisson and Bill Peace. . . ."

"It means they've got Ralph Fowler and that his hide ain't worth a plug nickel!" Bates put in. "You gents climb into your hulls and get on back to town. I'm roundin'

up as many of the boys as I can find. Root's takin' charge."

"What does he aim to do?"

"He hasn't said. But there's a meetin' in town at five. If you ride hard, you can make it."

In five more minutes Slim and his partner were pounding away from the corrals below. Jerry Bates had three minutes ago ridden in the opposite direction, north, obviously in a hurry to locate as many members of the far-flung posse as he could.

Al Sisson was in the saddle in twenty minutes. He had left the provisions and Bill Peace's money in the cabin. He was in too much of a hurry to bring them with him now. They could wait until later — until after he'd found Peace and told him the news.

He rode hard, cutting back through the hills directly for the gulch instead of using the winding, roundabout trail that flanked the course of Snake River. Had he taken the easier way, the trail that followed the river for four miles before cutting in toward Stanley's place, he would have met Bill Peace. For Peace, anxious because of the outlaw's absence, had decided to ride to his layout and find him.

When Al Sisson arrived at the gulch

camp, he saw that Peace had already been there and left. He tried to follow his friend's sign, but the rocky floor of the gulch made that impossible. So he came back to camp, knowing that Peace would eventually return.

Peace approached his cabin cautiously. The signs in the trampled yard meant only one thing. At least three riders had been here today. Al Sisson had undoubtedly been taken prisoner. Although at first unwilling to believe that, he was convinced when he found lying inside the doorway on the plank flooring the sack of provisions the outlaw had gathered. The money-box was in the bottom of the sack, the evidence plain. Al Sisson had been surprised and caught helpless as he went about his errand. That was the only explanation Peace could give for what he found.

"If he's alive, he's in Twin Rivers' jail," was his logical reasoning.

Persuaded of this, he took the three sheaves of paper money from the box he had cached in the feed-bin, stuffed them in his pockets, and headed down the trail. Six miles put him on the Twin Rivers road. He kept the black to a steady, mile-eating run, forgetting all caution, intent only on his sin-

gle purpose of helping Al Sisson if it wasn't too late.

Had he tempered his haste with wariness, he wouldn't have been surprised. As it was, he sighted the group of riders better than a mile ahead before they had seen him. He swung immediately off the trail, intending to take to the broken tree-protected country two miles to the north before he made his swing in toward town. But far to the north, Jerry Bates had found five more members of the posse and had sent them riding hard for town. Now they rode out of those trees two miles to the north — just as Peace headed toward them.

One of the five saw Peace as he right-angled from the trail and came toward them. At first this rider's curiosity was mild, held vaguely by the sight of the distant horseman whose black horse streaked across the sweep of range below at a hard run.

"Someone's in a hurry," he stated to the man in the saddle alongside him. "This meetin' of Root's will have every jasper on Steeple range rarin' up on his hind legs, headin' in toward Twin Rivers. I wouldn't give a peso Mex for Al Sisson's scalp right now. Peace's either!"

His neighbor smiled mirthlessly, eyeing the rider on the black far ahead. But sud-

denly his gaze hardened. He looked at the black horse intently, then breathed: "That black has four white stockings. Bill Peace owns a horse like that!"

The first rider's glance narrowed suspiciously. He muttered softly, "It couldn't be!" Then, louder: "Damned if it isn't!"

He rammed blunt spurs to his pony's flanks and sent the animal into a fast lope. He swung diagonally off to intercept Peace, who was now nearer. The rest, urged on by the shouts of the second rider, strung out behind.

Bill Peace had been too interested in the group of horsemen on the trail far ahead. He saw these others too late as they streaked down out of the dark shadows of the tree-margins to the north. He wheeled the black around and drove his spurs cruelly in an effort to outrun this remnant of the posse.

At first the black responded, keeping his distance, making the run of his life. But these last six miles at such a killing pace had robbed the animal of his wind. Gradually, the distance between Peace and the others lessened. From behind came the brittle, distance-muffled crack of a gun. Then another.

The second bullet was thrown from a rider who had stopped and taken careful

aim. Luck was against Peace. He felt the black's high frame shudder as the bullet took him. He had barely time to kick his feet clear of the stirrups before the black's forelegs buckled.

Peace was thrown clear. He lighted on one shoulder in a practiced roll. But as the force of his fall carried him over onto his back, his head struck hard against the ground. He fought to keep that curtain of blackness from blotting out his senses; but it hung on, dimming his sight, making his thoughts a hazy jumble. Then his body relaxed into unconsciousness.

VII

"THE KILLER'S TRAIL"

Judge White was in the most enviable position of his life. Mystified by Root's call on the sheriff and by Fowler's consequent disappearance, he had gotten out of bed that morning and carefully watched the shaping of events. He saw Stud Brady, Fowler's deputy, reassemble the posse and give the riders their directions and send them out on the hunt for Bill Peace. He speculated idly with the loungers along the awninged walk as to the reason for the sheriff's disappearance.

Later, when Miles Root rode into town, the judge inconspicuously dogged the rancher's every move. When Root turned up at the sheriff's office with the note he claimed he'd found on Fowler's bed in the hotel, White was an eager listener in the crowd that quickly gathered at the jail to hear Root publicly read the kidnapper's message and then send Jerry Bates and two others out to

call in the posse. White had his reasons for suspecting Root now but, being a man of long experience in the subtleties of intrigue, he chose to watch developments rather than denounce Root immediately.

At five o'clock, when the heat of the dust of the streets was being swept away by a gusty wind out of the black-clouded horizon to the east, most of the riders of the posse were back in town. They mingled impatiently with the crowd, awaiting Root's promised speech. The street in front of the jail was impassable, crowded from walk to walk with a mass of grim, silent men — even those small ranchers who had until now taken side against Miles Root. Root, always showing a flair for drama, wasn't going to miss his opportunity this evening. During the afternoon he had ordered a platform built of foot-wide planks on barrel ends before the jail's entrance. Now, having secluded himself at the hotel all afternoon, he suddenly put in an appearance when the crowd was thickest.

A hoarse cheer from across the street welcomed his approach. A lane opened in the crowd, and he walked through it with his wide shoulders squared, a sober set to his rugged face that was plain indication of the seriousness of this affair. When he had

climbed to the platform, he held up a hand, commanding instant silence. Judge White stood directly below, in the front line of the men who crowded out into the street and filled the walks on either side of Root's crude rostrum.

"You all know why we're here," Root began, his voice deep throated and carrying clearly to the most distant of his listeners perched on the wooden awnings across the street. "Some time last night our good friend and sheriff, Ralph Fowler, was forcibly taken prisoner by two men who yesterday made themselves outlaws, Bill Peace and Al Sisson!" Root waited until the crowd's angry murmur had died, then he went on: "A message was found in Fowler's room at the hotel today . . . a message of warning, threatening the sheriff's life if we should make any attempt at capturing the outlaw who committed the crime. I'm here to ask you what you think we ought to do about it!"

This time the roar of protest that met his words took longer to wear itself out. Root made no attempt to stop the angry outburst. Knowing what was coming, he wanted to fan the smoldering tempers of the men to a white-hot flame. At length, across the utter stillness of the street, he spoke deliberately and solemnly: "Regardless of that warning,

I am for. . . ." His words ended as suddenly as they had begun, for his glance was attracted by the approach of a knot of fifteen or twenty riders coming into the far end of the street off the west trail. As he hesitated, a shout came from one of the riders down there, and the cavalcade lifted their horses out of their trot to a fast run.

In another five seconds, the shouts of those oncoming horsemen could be heard and understood. What they were shouting was: "We've got Peace!"

Instant pandemonium cut loose as the crowd surged along the thoroughfare to meet the riders. Those at the outer fringes of the mob ran. Those behind pushed their neighbors in a frantic attempt to see what was going on now.

Judge White let the mob break from around him before he stepped up onto the walk and ran as hard as he could to come up with the leaders of the crowd. A numbing premonition of what might happen set up a panic within him that mounted higher each instant. Soon he was close enough to see the leaders of the mob run in between the horses and up to the pony across whose saddle Bill Peace's limp frame was roped.

Someone grasped at the pony's reins, holding the frightened animal, while others

lifted Peace's inert bulk down. Judge White saw all that with a feeling of acute dread. Suddenly he was striding down off the walk, pushing his way through the gathering crowd to its center. As he came nearer, he reached into his coat pocket and pulled out the stubby Derringer he had thought to bring with him that afternoon. When he could force his way no further into the mob that now crowded in around the frightened horses of the posse, he lifted the Derringer high over his head, cocked it, and squeezed the trigger.

The blast ripped along the corridor of the street, attracting instant attention. Someone saw who had fired the shot and shouted: "Let the judge through!"

When White stood in front of the two men who were holding erect Bill Peace's loose figure, he held up a hand to command silence. It was a tribute to the regard these people held for him that those nearest backed away a step or two, recognizing his authority, and turned to silence those behind. The word went back through the packed crowd that Judge White was up front, taking things in charge. Everyone there knew that White had been at the cottonwood the day before. Now they remembered his outspoken hatred of Bill Peace

and decided that here was a good man to act as their leader at this time.

A few shouts of "Hooray for the judge!" and "Let White handle this!" went back through the crowd. And, in their eagerness, the leaders were calling: "Quiet down! Let's hear what he says!"

Someone helped White up into the saddle of the horse that had carried the unconscious Peace into town. From there, where he could look out across this sea of faces, White said in a loud, steady voice: "Here's what we wanted, men! Here's Bill Peace, alive, the best bait for a hang noose the law of this country ever had!"

A roar of grim satisfaction broke in on his words, falling away to a quick, restless silence as his upraised hand again commanded attention. When he spoke now, it was hurriedly, for he saw Miles Root making his way to the front of the crowd. "But I'm askin' you why we stop with the job half finished? Take Peace to jail and keep him there until he can talk! Then we'll make him lead us to where Al Sisson's hidin' our sheriff!"

The low, restless undertone of heated argument that broke loose was unreadable for long moments. Judge White tried to speak, couldn't make himself heard. Then Miles

Root stepped into the cleared space around the posse's horses, and White thought he had lost. As though to bear out his fears, Root threw up his hands and through the sheer force of his personality silenced those standing nearest.

What he said was: "Why wait? We'll take care of Peace now and Sisson later!"

A cold, relentless anger mounted up in Judge White. He looked down at the rancher. "What's the hurry, Miles? A play like that might spoil our chances of taking Al Sisson."

The crowd agreed, and shouted its approval. For once in his life Miles Root was faced by a greater will than his own. His face was white in anger as he realized it. Grudgingly, he gave in and made no protest as Peace was carried out through the crowd and taken to the jail. Root even made a pretense of helping clear the way. They threw Bill Peace onto the cot in one of the two iron-barred cells.

"Get Doc Baker," Judge White said to one of the men nearest. "The sooner Peace comes around, the quicker we'll finish the business." Then he looked out into the crowded jail corridors. "The rest of you clear out. We'll take care of him."

After the corridor was cleared of all but

a half dozen men, Miles Root among them, White said to the rancher: "Miles, I'll leave it up to you to throw a guard around the jail."

When Root was gone, the judge felt a great relief. But when Doc Baker came in, his concern returned. Baker was one of Twin Rivers' oldest citizens, an honest man, a friend of the judge's. Yet White wondered what the medico would say to the thing he had in mind.

Baker was efficient as he examined Peace. "Nothin' but a bump on the head," he finally said. "He'll be out of it soon."

White, standing alongside the medico, said softly, so that those in the corridor close by couldn't hear: "Send the rest out, Doc. There's something I have to say."

Baker looked surprised, puzzled, but he got up off his chair and looked out at the others. "White and I will see to Peace," he called gruffly. "The rest of you clear out. And open that window before you leave. This man has to have fresh air."

In another minute, White and the medico were alone with the prisoner.

"What's eatin' you, Judge?" Baker asked.

White gave him a level stare, deciding all at once to let this man in on his confidence. "Peace is innocent," he said. Then, before

120

Baker could recover from his amazement and interrupt him, the judge told the medico all he knew — of Miles Root, of Fowler's strange disappearance, of his doubts about the message Root claimed to have found. He finished by saying: "So it's up to you and me to see that Peace isn't in shape to be seen tonight. Or if he is, to keep these others, especially Root, out of here."

Bill Peace stirred faintly where he lay on the cot. Judge White leaned down over him just as he opened his eyes and stared around in bewilderment. The judge put his hand over Peace's mouth, said in a low voice: "You're goin' to be all right, Bill. Just don't try and talk." As he took his hand away, his voice droned on and on, Doc Baker nodding his approval at rare intervals. The bewilderment gradually went out of Bill Peace's intent stare.

Five minutes later, Doc Baker came out onto the walk in front of the jail. Miles Root was there, along with many others.

"You're all out of luck tonight, gents!" the medico announced to them. "Peace has a bad concussion. It's a cinch he won't recover consciousness tonight, maybe not for days. You'd all better go home and rest easy." He glanced down the street and out across the open sweep of range to the far

eastern horizon. Out there, black thunder-heads were banking high into the sky. What he saw made him chuckle. He added: "It's a poor evenin' for a hangin', anyway. Goin' to rain."

Miles Root was disappointed. Yet he accepted this unlooked-for development stoically. Immediately he asked himself how he could upset Judge White's plan of talking to Bill Peace when he recovered consciousness. Finally he knew what he would do. He started along the walk toward the livery barn at the far end of town. Half way down he met Joyce White face to face.

She had been at home all afternoon, her hopes shattered by Ralph Fowler's disappearance and Miles Root's discovery that so ominously explained it. Her father had been too uncertain of what he knew to tell her anything that would have revived her hopes earlier in the day. During the past hour he had been too busy. Only a minute ago one of their neighbors, returning home after the breaking up of the mob, had told her of Bill Peace's predicament. And that neighbor had mentioned hanging. Her oval face was pale, and her brown eyes flashed in anger as she found herself suddenly confronting the man she instinctively blamed for all Bill Peace's trouble.

Miles Root had barely time enough to greet her, "Evenin', Joyce," before she said bitingly: "You should be proud of yourself tonight, Miles! First you gather this mob, then you talk of hanging an innocent man!"

"But Peace is guilty, Joyce. Ralph Fowler was my friend. I'm doing a public duty."

"Bill Peace isn't guilty!" came her heated protest. "None of you knows what you're doing! The whole country has gone mad!"

All at once she caught the hint of amusement in Miles Root's glance that betrayed his sober set of countenance. At sight of it, she knew he was inwardly laughing at her, that she could look for no help from him. It sharpened her anger.

"I think you're really liking this, Miles. I'll remember it." With that she strode on past him, her glance holding nothing but an obvious scorn and loathing.

Root stood there a moment, watching her tall, proudly-erect figure as it disappeared into the crowd. He hadn't wanted this to happen and now cursed himself for a fool in speaking against Bill Peace. It would have been better to pretend sympathy for Peace, even after it was all over.

While he stood there, he felt a touch on his arm and turned to confront Peter Kennedy, owner of the bank. Kennedy said: "So

there's nothin' more doin' tonight?"

Root shook his head irritably. "They want to talk to Peace before they hang him."

"Which reminds me, Miles. When this is over, I'll have twenty sections of that land you've been wantin'. You figure to put in a bid on it?"

"At what price?"

"At your own price," Kennedy said. "We want to get our money out of it."

Here was something that made up a little to Root for his meeting with Joyce. He thanked the banker, told him he'd see him in a week or so, and then went on to the livery stable. Yet the more he thought about it, the more unsatisfactory it seemed to be. He was getting one thing without the other. He'd had high hopes, up until now, of making Joyce White mistress of one of the largest landholdings in this country. And, like a fool, he'd narrowed his chances a minute ago by one badly chosen run of words.

His temper running high and thin after getting his horse, he punished the bay unmercifully on the eight-mile ride that took him out to Wes Stanley's place. The makings of the storm behind suited his dark mood. He would pay Ed Trank well for what he would do tonight. He'd have Trank wait until late, until the town had quieted

down. Then the gunman could climb onto the roof of the saddle shop across the street from the jail. From there a man could look directly into the single window of the jail.

If Root remembered correctly, the cot in the cell Peace occupied would almost exactly center that window. A bullet couldn't miss a man who lay upon it. After Trank had finished that, he could head for the border on another errand. Miles Root had shrewdly guessed that Ralph Fowler was gone for good, and why he'd gone. *He'll head for old Mexico* was his judgment.

Al Sisson waited two hours for Peace to return. Then, more troubled than he cared to admit, the outlaw rode down to Wes Stanley's layout. It took some time for him to locate Peace's sign. From there on what he saw utterly mystified him. There was a splotch of dried, darkened blood smeared low down on the weathered boards of the barn, alongside the door. Higher up, a bullet hole showed. The full significance of what had happened didn't come to him until he noticed the newly dug grave near the corral. Then, frantically dreading what he was sure he'd find, Al Sisson performed the distasteful task of opening that grave.

Sobered by sight of the dead stranger's

face in the fading light of dusk yet relieved to find that it wasn't Bill Peace, he rode out from Stanley's burned cabin toward the gulch camp since to wait there would be the surest way of finding Peace. Something Peace had said that morning brought him added relief. *Like as not, he's gone in to see that girl,* he decided.

From a few hundred yards out along the faint line of the trail, Miles Root sighted Al Sisson riding away and recognized him barely in time to escape discovery. He let the outlaw get out of sight before he made a wide circle and followed. Well into the gulch, he warily climbed from the saddle, leading his bay far up one slope. There he rein-tied the animal to the gnarled trunk of a piñon and last of all drew his rifle from the boot under the saddle. He knew this gulch and his shrewd observation was: *Their hide-out is somewhere close.*

Less than an hour later, walking soundlessly through the darkness, careful of where he placed each foot as he went slowly forward, he sighted the winking light of Sisson's fire through the cobalt shadows up ahead. He circled to the left and, from above the camp, looked down over his rifle sights at Al Sisson's darkly outlined shape.

He squeezed the trigger. The brittle report of the gunshot slapped sharply up the gulch, and he saw Al Sisson double at the waist and fall forward in a loose sprawl. For a brief interval he watched Sisson's inert form lying there. Then, satisfied at what he had done, he made his way back to his bay horse and climbed into the saddle. He rode down the gulch, directly to Stanley's place. As he came within sight of the barn's dark shadow, a few pelting drops of rain fell out of the leaden sky.

He called loudly, "Ed!" and heard the echo of his voice slapped hollowly at him. Once more, "Ed!" and his only answer was that echo.

At length, as a gusty wind whipped the rain into a downpour, he reached around and untied his poncho from behind the cantle and put it on. He buckled it tightly against the stinging bite of the storm.

"So he high-tailed?" he muttered, half aloud. He had never been too sure of this Ed Trank, and the gunman's absence left him somehow unsurprised. At the worst all it could mean was that he himself would have to do the work he had intended for Trank. *And maybe it's better this way, too,* he mused, reaching down to caress the stock of the rifle.

As his hand touched the smoothly rounded heel-plate of the Winchester, a sudden thought slowed his pulse. He remembered the day, better than a week ago, when he had last used the Winchester. He had been on his north range and sighted a coyote at better than two hundred yards away. He had drawn the Winchester, raised the back sight, and killed that coyote at the first shot. But had he lowered the sight again?

Frantically he drew the .30-.30 from its scabbard and laid it across his lap. He looked at it, squinting his eyes against the wind-whipped rain. No, the sight was still raised, to the third notch. Did that mean that he had thrown his bullet high back there in the gulch — that it hadn't hit Sisson squarely in the chest?

"You're spooky!" he said aloud. Then he remembered another thing. He had been shooting downhill and hadn't aimed below his target to compensate for the natural tendency to shoot low while aiming downward. He had been in too much of a hurry to think of such things. *But he caved in like a pole-axed bull* was his final thought. Reassured then by the memory of Sisson's loose fall, he turned his attention back to Bill Peace.

From there on, on the long uncomfortable

ride to Twin Rivers, his desire to remove this last obstacle, Bill Peace, became a thing that twisted his mind to near madness. With Peace out of the way and those two small outfits along Snake River thrown in with his already far-ranging spread, nothing could keep him from becoming the biggest man in this country.

VIII

"WITNESS WANTED"

The storm struck Twin Rivers with a ferocity greater than most men could remember for a late-summer rain. With it came lightning that seemed to pick the town as its target. Time and again the bolts struck with deafening, prolonged blasts that shook the ground and left the few remaining saddle horses at the hitch rails terror-stricken and shaking with fright. At the height of the storm, when the water was streaming down in foggy sheets that made it impossible to see across the street, a jagged streamer of lightning hit the barn in the livery stable corral at the edge of town. And even for all the rain that poured upon its roof, its baled alfalfa and loft full of hay were soon a roaring mass of flame.

The word whipped through town: "Beck's barn is on fire! Get the horses out!"

The remnants of the crowd that had as-

sembled that afternoon now crowded the saloons, safely out of the storm. But many of these men had horses in the big corral alongside the barn. With the spreading of the news, the saloons emptied and every able-bodied man in town ran out into the rain and toward the corral to save the half a hundred head of terror-stricken broncs that might, even now, be trying to break down the corral-poles and be inadvertently plunging into the roaring inferno of the barn's blaze.

The guards at the jail were the last to leave. But, as the rain suddenly slacked off to a misty drizzle and with the livery barn's rosy flames mounting higher into the sky, one of the guards said: "To hell with this job. My blaze-face and my saddle are down there!" He set off at a run, and his leaving was a signal for the others.

Inside the jail, Bill Peace and Judge White had pulled a cot to the single window and were watching the blaze. As White saw the guards run off down the walk, his face took on a bitter smile.

"Their bad luck is our good luck, Bill!" he whispered. "The way's clear outside. I'll go get your guns."

He was gone from the cell room for a few seconds, and Peace heard him moving about

in the small cubicle up front by the door. Soon he was back with Peace's twin gun belts slung over his arm — the same guns Peace had taken from Ralph Fowler yesterday afternoon at the cottonwood.

"Strap 'em on, Bill. This is your chance for a getaway."

Reluctantly, Bill Peace took the belts. "What about you, Judge? They'll blame you for this."

As Peace uttered these words, Miles Root was turning his bay in to the hitching rail two doors above. He had just entered the street in time to see the guards lean their rifles against the jail's adobe wall and run down the walk toward the fire. He understood immediately what this meant. With the jail left unguarded, the rancher gave up his idea of climbing to the roof of the saddle shop opposite and waiting for his opportunity to send a bullet through the jail's window at Peace. Here was a sure way, a quicker one. He would walk straight into the place, finish with Peace, and be out of town before the gunshot had attracted the attention of those at the burning barn. He smiled.

He left the Winchester in its saddle scabbard. Instead, after he got down out of the

saddle, he paused to take his .38 from its shoulder holster and examine it to make doubly sure that five of its six chambers were loaded. Then, the weapon still in his hand, he came on down the walk and turned in at the jail door. He was just in time to hear Judge White's deep-toned voice say: "But you've got to, Bill! They can't do anything to me. I know enough about Miles Root to send a posse out after him. When we have him here, we'll get the truth out of him if we have to bend a gun barrel over his head! Now you get out of here!"

Root waited no longer. The light of a lantern shone through the door to the cell room, and now he stepped into that orange rectangle of light. The sound of his boot tread brought White and Peace wheeling around to face him. They stood in the corridor between the cells, the judge with the keys still in his hand, Peace with his twin .45s strapped to his thighs.

Peace's right hand made a short, quick stab toward his holster; but Root's upswinging .38 cut short that desperate motion. Slowly, Bill Peace's hands came up to the level of his wide shoulders.

"So you'll gun whip me, will you, Judge?" Root drawled, his stocky frame outlined by the door opening in which he stood.

White didn't answer for a moment. His hawkish, grizzled face drained of color. At length, he breathed, "Damn you, Root!"

The rancher's low chuckle was full of a strident menace. The weapon in his hand was held rock steady, his thumb on the hammer. Yet he was glorying in this moment, in seeing these two strong men so powerless in his grasp. Outside, the street was quiet except for the muffled crackle of the flames and the mutter of the crowd far out along it. There was plenty of time.

"How much do you know, Judge?" Root queried silkily. Then, when White made no answer, the rancher added: "Out of curiosity, I'd like to know."

It was Peace who supplied the answer, his drawl soft against the stillness of the room: "Plenty, Root! First, I didn't kill Stanley. You, or one of your men, did. Today I had to cut down a man at Stanley's place. I think he was one of your hired guns. Last night you were seen handing money to Ralph Fowler. Fowler was seen leaving town in a hurry, headed south."

"Much obliged," Root muttered. "I wasn't sure which way Ralph left. Now I'll know where to find him." His thumb drew back the .38's hammer, the click of its catch sounding loudly in the stillness. "So you

killed Ed Trank, eh? He's the one I hired to 'gulch Stanley."

That hammer-click worked a visible change in Judge White. He seemed to become a smaller man. The slack expression of his visage was plain evidence that he had lost all hope. "You can't do this, Miles," he intoned. "You won't live another day when they hear what I have to say."

"But you won't have anything to say. Dead men don't talk!" Root laughed harshly as he saw the sudden frenzy that took possession of the judge's glance. "You'll be found here, alongside Peace, one of his guns in your hand. It'll look like the two of you fought it out. They'll make a hero of you, Judge."

During the interval that followed, Bill Peace's hands edged slowly downward. "I'm goin' to make a try for you, Root!" he drawled.

"Sure, make one, Peace! I'll wait until your iron's free of leather. Then you'll get lead through your. . . ."

All at once his words broke off as the hard pound of boots sounded on the walk directly outside. A sudden indecision dilated Miles Root's black eyes. He stood transfixed by a sudden paralysis of fear for one instant. Then his glance swung around, and he

turned his head and looked back over his shoulder.

In that split-second Bill Peace's hands streaked downward and up. When Root's head jerked back again, Peace's guns were clearing leather.

"Root!"

The voice came from the outer doorway of the jail. It was Al Sisson's.

Root lunged sideways, clear of the doorway. His .38 blasted away the silence in an exploding burst of sound.

The thunder of his gun seemed to push Bill Peace backward, break the upward swing of his two hands. But before the concussion had died, his twin Colts were lancing flame in a pounding riot of sound that beat outward at the walls.

Judge White threw himself to one side, out of the way of those guns. He felt the air whip of Peace's bullets as they fanned past him.

Once more, Root's .38 exploded, its feeble roar deadened by the staccato blast of Bill Peace's .45s. That shot of Root's was his last, for already his Colt was slanted toward the floor. Twice his body quivered spasmodically at the hard impact of lead. His eyes stared wide and horrified at Peace, the hatred in them wiped suddenly away to

be replaced by one of utter bewilderment. Blood flecked his lips, until all at once a bullet made his mouth a misshapen, pulpy mass.

He tottered weakly out from the wall just as Al Sisson, six-gun in hand, appeared in the doorway. Then, slowly, the rancher's right knee gave way and his body swung to the right in a half turn. Some inner strength guided his hands, for even as he saw Sisson, his .38 raised a full two inches and his thumb had the power to draw back the weapon's hammer and let it fall.

But he was already dead, falling loosely, as the gun blasted the momentary silence. Its bullet ripped a channel down one of the floor planks. His fall tore loose the Colt from his grasp so that, when he finally lay spread-eagled on his back, his outstretched hand had the appearance of making a futile reach for the gun.

Judge White's fascinated, horrified gaze finally tore itself from Root. He looked at Bill Peace, saw the jagged circle of red smearing his shirt low on one side. "Bill, you're hit!"

"It can wait." Peace looked across at Al Sisson. "You drew it pretty fine, gettin' here when you did, Al. You saved our lives."

Sisson seemed not to have heard. His hard

stare regarded the prostrate form at his feet. "After all these years it had to be someone besides me that handed you your last poison!" he breathed. There was a thinly disguised regret in his tone. But all at once he looked up at Bill Peace and smiled. "Next to me, I don't know anyone I'd rather have seen do the job."

For the first time Peace saw that Sisson's shirt was torn at the shoulder, that the edges of the torn cloth were edged with red. "Who cut down on you, Al?" he queried.

The outlaw nodded toward the floor. "Our friend Root . . . out in the gulch. He tried a bushwhack but threw his shot too high. I played dead and, when he left, I followed him here."

From out on the street shouts echoed suddenly, the sound of boots pounding on the plank walk.

Hearing that, Judge White stepped around Peace and through the inner door, saying: "I'll have some fast talkin' to do."

The judge was partly right. But he had a helper out there in the person of Doc Baker. Between them they silenced the crowd that had heard the shots and run for the jail. They took turns telling the story, what they knew of it. Doc Baker made it his job to answer any objections from the crowd as to

what the judge had to say.

Later, when Baker had taken Peace and Sisson home to the office in his back room to bandage their flesh wounds and while the crowd was moving slowly down the street following the four men that carried what was left of Miles Root, Judge White came to the door of Baker's office. He looked in at Peace and said: "Bill, you've got a visitor out here."

Peace got up from the chair where he had been sitting, his move jerking the roll of bandage from the medico's hand. Peace didn't notice that, didn't hear the medico's half-amused oath. Beyond the door was Joyce White.

She stood tall and straight, her brown eyes shining with a light that meant a new world to Bill Peace. He took her in his arms. Judge White softly opened the front door and went out.

Afterward — it couldn't have been longer than two minutes — the front door opened once more and Judge White stepped in, a little breathless. He had a black book in his hand.

Joyce raised her head from Peace's shoulder and looked at her father and understood. A soft tide of color deepened the flush in her cheeks.

White glanced beyond them, into the medico's office, calling: "Doc, you and Sisson get out here! You're needed as witnesses."

"Long Gone" was one of the last Peter Dawson short stories to be published. It appeared under this title in the March, 1953 issue of *Zane Grey's Western Magazine.* Don Ward was editor of that digest-sized pulp magazine, and he subsequently selected this story to appear in the Western Writers of America story collection he edited titled BRANDED WEST (Houghton Mifflin, 1956). It was adapted for the screen by David Chantler and Daniel Ullman and filmed as FACE OF A FUGITIVE (Columbia, 1959) directed by Paul Wendkos and starring Fred MacMurray, Dorothy Green, and James Coburn. As so many scenes in Peter Dawson's Western fiction, much of the action in this story takes place at night, amid the yellow gleam of lamplight.

LONG GONE

The blast of the locomotive's whistle shrilled back over the rhythmic clanking of the gondola's trucks, and at once Ray Kindred stirred from a wary lethargy, shifting his long length to ease the prod of a .44 Colt against hipbone. When the whistle sounded again, he came to his knees and then slowly, with an infinite care, he raised up out of the creosote-stenched pocket among the butt ends of the ties until his pale gray eyes were staring outward. This was but the second time in over eleven hours he had risked a look anywhere but straight upward from his hiding place. And now he was weighing against a cool apprehension the friendly beckoning of a dusk-blurred pattern of nearby pine slopes.

He had caught this freight laboring slowly along a cañon grade in a bleaker, drier country early this morning, and he had sensed

no beckoning on taking that first outward look. Then, at midday, the train had been stopped at a way station and tank along the flats. There had been a prolonged interval of frozen uncertainty for him while a crewman slowly paced the length of the train toward his car. Kindred had waited, squatting on his heels, the .44 held idly in hand, until finally the man tapped the gondola's journal boxes and went on.

Two sobering possibilities had been in his thoughts constantly throughout the long day: one, that a man catwalking the cars could easily stumble on his hiding place, the other that the train might be stopped and searched at any time. Kindred had accepted these likelihoods stoically and with a customary fatality, though also with a measure of self-disdain, for he had made the concession of lying most of the time with the Colt drawn and his arm propped idly so that the weapon slanted in line with the upward edges of the ties.

Ignoring drowsiness and thirst had been hardest of all. The thirst he could endure. But each time he briefly dozed he was seeing the eyes again, a pair of blue, kindly eyes with a stare of death creeping into them. And the nightmare would invariably jerk him awake, cursing and with a raw temper.

He was trying to put that haunting vision of the eyes from his mind as a rearward glance showed him the caboose almost obscured by the settling darkness, the glow of its lanterns plainly visible. Some of the tautness was leaving his nerves then as he looked ahead. His back straightened in surprise at seeing the scattered lights of a town winking through the lodge poles, the locomotive already running past a gray-lined clutter of cattle pens at the settlement's outskirts.

An eager, gloating look at once shaped itself on his narrow face. He was thinking of the prospect of buying grub and a horse and saddle — or of stealing them — and then of losing himself in the high country to the north. Now was the moment for deciding whether to stay with the train or leave it. The choice wasn't difficult, and there was no hesitation in his reaching down for his wide gray hat, beating the dust and cinders from it, and then pulling it hard onto his blond head against the rush of smoke-tainted air. He pushed the .44 more snugly into the trough ahead of hipbone, a hard-fleshed pocket grown callused over the years of constant use. Then, hunching low, he lifted a leg over the gondola's swaying side.

The freight was slowing jerkily now, and as the first loading pen came abreast Ray

Kindred vaulted out and down. His boots hit the graveled embankment with a force that drove him to his knees, sent him skidding on in a smother of dust, and down into a weed patch. He came stiffly erect and took three deliberate steps in on the nearest corral. With his back against the poles he reached down and brushed the sand from his trousers, watching the caboose trundling in on him.

He saw the brakeman's silhouette in the cupola window, saw the man staring straight ahead. A down-lipped and disdainful smile patterned his narrow face. He brought up his right hand, its fingers outspread, and touched nose with thumb in a parting salute as the caboose lanterns went away.

For two full minutes after the rumble of the train had died against the stillness, he stood there hungrily breathing in the cool and pine-scented air, listening, his senses keening the evening, trying to judge it. He caught the yapping of a dog from the direction of town, and from somewhere above in the timber a cow's bell toned in a slow, unrhythmic note. A faint breeze whispered from the pine crests. The sounds were peaceful, as friendly as any could be to Ray Kindred. And finally, as he walked on along the corrals in the direction of town, his wary

instincts had passed a momentary affirmative judgment.

He found a windmill and log trough at the townward end of the pens, and there he drank his fill from the trickling feed pipe. Afterward, he sloshed water on his face and scrubbed away the grime. The feel of beard stubble along his hollow cheeks made him frown, for he was a vain man. And, thus reminded that he'd left all his possibles in the pouches of the saddle he'd hidden there in the cañon thicket this morning, he was feeling a strong disgust.

It had been a close thing, his jumping the freight, and in his hurry he'd thought only of the bundle of bank notes bulging the inside pocket of his coat. Looking back upon that crowded half minute, he knew he could easily have taken a few more seconds to get the razor and some other things. The disgust in him now was targeting an uneasy awareness that he'd been close to panic; and panic was a thing he couldn't abide, something he considered as deadly as a bullet to any man who lived so constantly with danger as he had these past years.

When he presently started on along the lane paralleling the tracks, he was thinking chiefly of a shave, of whether he should risk one in a barber shop or wait until later and

shave himself with the razor he intended buying along with the other things. He was pondering this minor detail as he followed a turning of the lane and came abruptly to its joining with a road that became the head of the street.

He passed some houses, built of log mostly and, by the time he reached a plank wall fronting the first few stores, he had decided that the town held no danger for him, provided he remained inconspicuous, made his purchases, and left. Just then he spotted the red and white pattern of a barber pole gleaming in front of a lighted window several buildings ahead. Its invitation instantly made him qualify the resolve to avoid giving anyone a close look at him. His pace quickened. Then the next moment a tall man turned toward him out of a lighted doorway to this side of the barber shop and came on at a slow walk, coat hanging open. And, just as the man was striding beyond the window's glow, a dull gleam of light was reflected from metal along his shirt front.

Ray Kindred caught that gleam and his stride almost broke. But then that same prideful arrogance that invariably froze out any trace of fear in him at moments of real danger carried him on at a casual, easy saunter.

As they passed, the man said pleasantly, "Evenin'."

Kindred drawled, "It's a good one," and walked straight on.

A chill rippled along his spine. He listened to the other's steady boot tread going away against the planks, listened for any break in it. There was none. Then shortly he came abreast the barber shop window. He looked in to see the barber alone, sitting in a chair by the wall reading a newspaper in the light of a coal-oil lamp hanging from the ornamental tin ceiling. He turned toward the door.

A deliberate glance back along the walk showed him the tall shape far up the street, still going away. He went on into the shop and let his breath go in a slow sigh of relief as he was closing the door.

The barber said, "How goes it?" and Kindred only nodded as he shrugged out of his coat.

He eased into the single barber chair and only then spoke: "Shave and a trim."

Most of Ray Kindred's remembered life had involved a crowding of his luck either by ignoring danger or fleeing from it. Tonight he was ignoring it, no longer fleeing. He was ignoring it even this moment, knowing the chance he took in having hung his

coat there so openly on the rack by the door with all that money in the pocket, knowing the .44 to be in plain sight at his belt.

The barber had been waiting by the chair, apron over arm. Now he reached over toward Kindred's waist, asking, "Lay it aside for you?"

"No."

That clipped, uncompromising word made the man draw his hand quickly away.

Kindred lay back in the chair and crossed his boots on the padded rest, scarcely noticing. He was lying there under the apron with a hot towel steaming the lather into his face before the barber spoke again.

"Rest of the boys come down with you to see the fun?"

"What boys?"

"From up the Buckhorn. From Miller's."

The man waited for a reply. When it didn't come, he went on, "You got the stink of that tie-camp in your clothes, stranger. Not that it ain't a right good smell. Clean like. Always did take to a good whiff of creosote now and then."

"Never hurt a man." Guardedly then, Kindred asked: "What's the fun you mention?"

"The dance. Down at the school, next to the Baptist meetin' house. Nesters and

homestead folk from Alder Valley mostly. Reed Williams aims to bust it up single-handed. Bill Shepley allows as how Reed had better keep clear."

"Haven't been around long enough for names to mean much." Kindred's scratchy voice was muffled by the towel. "This Reed now. Who's he?"

"Reed Williams. Runs the Brush brand. Alder Valley has been his private bailiwick up to now. Government land or no, he says, no one moves in there. The homesteaders have, right enough, and Reed's been layin' for 'em. Tonight he aims to pay off."

Kindred's interest was lagging, though he asked, "And who's Shepley?"

"Hell, you must have heard of young Bill Shepley even up on the Buckhorn. Sheriff. Was deputy before old Cromer passed on. Good man. But with Reed on the warpath he's liable not to be much of anything for long."

"Think he'll stand up to this Reed . . . ?"

"Williams, it is. That, Bill will! And a damn' shame, too. Might be the last of him. He runs cattle, and he's got a fine girl all set to marry if he'll only give up the law. She hates his wearin' the badge. But he's mule-stubborn. Says he's obliged to serve out the term as sheriff. And he won't quit

so long as Reed Williams crowds these grangers. Looks like real trouble."

"The usual."

Kindred spoke without any real interest, the warmth of the towel and not the strop-slap of the razor at the chair's side lulling him to a deep relaxation. He supposed it must be this Bill Shepley he'd met up the street. The man must be a fool, in the first place for not noticing strangers appearing in town around train time, secondly for backing a bunch of stray farmers against his own kind. *He was sure a fool not to give me the once-over* came Kindred's thought as the towel was taken away and his face wiped clean and then relathered. He felt almost safe now at this double assurance of the sheriff's poor abilities, so secure that he didn't even open his eyes at the touch of the razor along the side of his face.

The first strokes of the blade were long, unhesitating, and clean. Its touch felt good. Abruptly then the barber was saying, "Wasn't the usual that caught up with old Ben Sadler down to Burnt Springs this mornin'."

Kindred's eyes came wide open, that name sawing at his nerves. He warily searched the barber's face for any hint of a hidden emotion or double meaning. There

wasn't any he could see. The man was painstakingly watching his razor's upstroke along the underlip.

Kindred waited until the blade was being wiped before asking carefully, "Should I know this Ben Sadler?"

"Reckon not, since Burnt Springs is two hundred mile south." The razor was back again, working under the chin. As Kindred's awareness of it sharpened, he was once more being stared at by those gentle blue eyes, not the barber's but the ones that had haunted his fitful snatches of sleep throughout the day, the ones with the look of death creeping into them.

"Ben's an old-timer from these parts. Rode shotgun for Wells Fargo till he lost a leg in a smash-up when the Windrock road caved from under his coach. They gave him the Burnt Springs office soon as he could hobble 'round again. He's run it ever since. Or did. Got him a busted skull this morning when he come to open up the place."

Kindred waited for more, almost flinching now against the razor's keen touch. When the barber remained silent, he finally asked: "Why would he get a busted skull?"

"For the company money. Why else? They found him layin' along of his open safe, cash box cleaned. What men won't do

to lay hands on a dishonest dollar! Beat the bejesus out of a crippled old man! God A'mighty!"

There was something to be decided here, and Kindred considered it with the fingers of his right hand inching from the chair arm until they touched the handle of the Colt under the apron. There was a sudden dryness in his throat. He started to swallow. The razor left his neck with a jerk.

"Brother, you damn' near lost your Adam's apple that time! Get 'er swallowed."

Now Kindred did swallow, telling himself that if the man knew who he was the razor would already have struck deep. Nevertheless, as the silence dragged on and he felt the blade keening along his throat again, he was wishing he hadn't come here. He couldn't keep his hands from knotting, his long frame from holding rigid. It took a real effort to crowd back the urge to sweep aside the apron and run on out into the shielding darkness.

He realized suddenly that he was nearly panicked and for the second time this day. The thought brought with it a brittle anger. Gradually, it steadied him until his nerves were under control again.

Finally he was calm enough to drawl, "Maybe this Sadler asked for it. You don't

place a bet or even call if the deck's stacked against you."

The barber lifted the razor, frowned down at him. "Meanin' what?"

"The old boy could've got cashed in because he was scared. Because he ran or something when he should've just stood there and let it happen."

"Ben scared? When he's met up with . . . ?"

"Or there might have been a iron in the cash box he went for," Kindred cut in, telling himself — *He won't know he's hearing the truth!* — as he went on hurriedly: "These hardcases don't want to hurt no one nine times out of ten. If they do, it's because they're crowded into it. Like with old Sadler. He likely lost his head and made some fool try, and this bird had to clip him. Yeah, that's it. He lost his head, got in a panic."

"Who's to know?" The barber shrugged, wiped his blade clean, and then closed it. He tilted the chair up and rearranged the apron. "Anyway, a good man's gone, and the one that did it'll be dodgin' brimstone on into eternity. You say you want a trim?"

"Even it up all around." Kindred sat straighter, right hand resting idly on the

chair arm again. "Have they caught this hardcase yet?"

"Nope. Shepley got the word along about noon. To watch the railroad, that is. But they ain't at all sure the sidewinder come this way. Seems he'd rightly head off into the desert. There's a world of animals down there he could've stole."

Kindred considered this over quite an interval. Finally, in a tone utterly casual, he said, "Ought to be easy to close up the country. Mountains and all to this end, desert on the south."

"Oh, she's closed tight as a barrel bung a'ready. Ain't hardly a man between here and Alkali but what would gladly spend a week ridin' to square it for Ben if he's called on."

"What's Shepley done at this end?"

The scissors were clicking over Kindred's left ear, and he was breathing shallowly as the answer came: "Closed all the pass trails. Got a big crew stoppin' the trains up there. He'll be there hisself, come mornin'. If he's able, if he comes through this trouble with Reed Williams."

Kindred accepted the information stoically, with scarcely a ripple of inner excitement. He was weighing his chances coolly now, knowing them to be far slimmer than

he'd realized. But slim as they were, he would think of something to improve them. Meantime, he was wondering if there was anything more the barber could tell him.

All at once a startling notion made him chuckle softly. Then he was drawling, "Might be interestin' to take a couple days off and tag along with Shepley. Think he could use another man?"

"Sure thing. Want me to speak to him about it?"

"No, I'll look him up myself." As he spoke, Kindred was telling himself, *The joker might fall for it at that.*

His thinking was pretty much on dead center by the time he left the chair, paid, and pulled his coat on. The bulge at the right side of his coat put a friendly pressure against his stringy chest muscles as he closed the door. Once out on the walk again, his instinct sent him into the nearest shadows under the wooden awning fronting the ad-joining, darkened store. He was hungry with a real gnawing at his middle. But the risk of showing himself a second time as openly as he had at the barber shop would mean he was putting himself alongside the sheriff in being a fool.

Tobacco was the thing to dull his appetite, and now he took a sack of dust from his

pocket, rolled a smoke, and lit it with his face toward the store wall, killing the match quickly. His back was still turned to the street when a voice sounded from across the way: "Everything all set, Bill?"

"All set."

"You still don't want any help?"

"Not any, thanks."

Kindred faced slowly around, seeing a pair of figures idling at the opposite walk's edge, another coming on past them. He recognized the shape of Bill Shepley in the lone man and, thinking back on his conversation with the barber, a strong and sudden impulse carried him on out across the walk.

He was half way over the street and trying in his eagerness not to hurry when he called, "Sheriff?"

Shepley stopped, turned slightly to face him as he came on. "Yes?"

Kindred instantly recognized the wary stance the man had taken for exactly what it was, noncommittal at the moment but one that had nicely dispensed with any necessary preliminary move but the upsweep of hand for unlimbering the weapon along his thigh. Kindred enjoyed seeing that equally as much as he did the absolute certainty that his .44 could be lined at Shepley before the man's hand had lifted past holster. He

came on, his stride more deliberate now that he had Shepley's attention. Shortly he ducked under the tie-rail and stood within three strides of the man.

"You don't know me, Sheriff," he said. "But the barber across there tells me you're headed for the hills tonight and could use more help. If you can fix me up with a horse, you got yourself another man."

He felt Shepley's glance probing in at him and was thankful for the shadows. Abruptly the sheriff asked: "You wouldn't be a friend of Reed Williams, would you?"

"Who's Reed Williams?"

"If you are, now's the time to show your stuff," Shepley insisted.

"Man, you got me wrong. Whatever's botherin' you?"

Shepley took that in without any break in his impassive expression. "Where you hail from?"

"Miller's camp up on the Buckhorn." Moving his left arm slowly — so that his intention would be plainly understood — Kindred raised it and sniffed at the sleeve of his coat. He chuckled. "Can't you smell it on me?"

Shepley's square face lost its hard set. He smiled all at once, reminding Kindred of nothing so much as some care-free young

159

ranch hand. "All right," he drawled, "you're on. Hang around down by the school, and you can head out with me after I've finished one more chore. There's a chuck wagon up the pass, so never mind about grub."

He nodded and started on past Kindred. Then, as he came abreast, he halted abruptly and, almost within arm's reach now, leaned over and drew in a breath quite audibly. "That's creosote, right enough," he said. "See you later." And he turned and walked away.

Kindred laughed softly, delightedly at realizing how smoothly his bluff was working. But then he sobered. Shepley might be a fool, an overgrown kid beyond his depth in trying to deal with a situation beyond him, but he was nevertheless a likable fool. Kindred gave the man a grudging admiration for the positive word that they would be heading out together after he had finished his "one more chore" which must be his meeting with this Reed Williams. He hadn't betrayed by word or look any concern over the outcome of the meeting.

Yet the spot Shepley was in mattered little to Kindred now as he sauntered on after the younger man. Instead, he was thinking of the strangeness of the circumstances, of this being the first time in his life he had

ever depended on a lawman for anything but suspicion or hostility. The incongruity of Shepley's having become the means of his salvation filled him with smugness. Shepley would post him at some point along the pass he would be supposed to watch. His appearance with the sheriff would be his passport to the far side of the mountains. *By sunup they'll find me long gone,* he told himself.

"Long gone." He spoke aloud, smiling broadly, liking the sound of the words.

He had gone on a hundred yards past the spot where he had encountered Shepley before he caught the first faint strains of music sounding from far down the street. Shortly the lilt of the tune strengthened until he was walking in time with it. He passed a lighted saloon, aware of several loungers on the walk who scarcely noticed him; only when he was past a feed mill several doors farther on could he forget them. And now up ahead he made out the shadowed outline of a church with its spire thrust sharply against the stars. Beyond, lighted windows came into sight, silhouetting the headstones of a graveyard in front of the church.

The street rails by the lighted building were crowded with saddle horses and the teams of light rigs and wagons. The music

was coming from there. This must be the school, the dance.

A picket fence fronted the school lot, joining a head-high locust hedge separating it from the churchyard. Kindred walked in on that fence corner. From there he could see couples moving in the lighted room beyond the windows. He noticed one couple in particular, the man with head thrown back in silent laughter as he gyrated from sight whirling a girl whose dark curls swung outward with the turn.

Kindred was suddenly and powerfully longing for the feel of his arm about a woman's slender waist, any woman's and, in his rancor over the hopelessness of that longing, he tried to shut from his hearing the cordant strains of fiddle, concertina, guitar, and mouth-harp. He realized then that he was standing in plain sight, and he eased on down the line of locusts into the grassy graveyard. But he went only far enough to put himself in the deep shadows and out of sight of any passers-by. There he squatted on a mounded grave, his back to the high headstone, thus placing himself so that he could look through the thick lower branches of the bushes and keep an eye on the street.

Long gone. The phrase came back to him suddenly, out of nowhere and, as the min-

utes passed, he was idly trying to imagine what it would be like to be free again, free to come and go as he pleased, with money in his pocket, and for a time not to have to keep his eye and mind so everlastingly on his back trail. The voices from the other side of the hedge, a man's and a woman's, reached him only as a muted undertone at first. He wasn't quite sure of the first moment he became aware of them, and then he wasn't even curious enough to look toward the back of the lot and try to see who was speaking. He supposed it was a couple courting in the shadows. Then all at once the woman — her voice sounded like a young girl's — spoke in a choked outburst:

". . . thought it through! You aren't in your right mind!"

"But I am, Laura."

With the man's first plainly audible word, Kindred recognized him. It was Bill Shepley. The sheriff's tone was calm, unruffled, not even remotely the voice of a man afraid. His next words put emphasis to this quality in him as he added, "My head would hang the rest of my life if I stood aside and let Reed make this stick."

There was a moment's silence before the girl spoke again, lower than before, her words miserable, impassioned. "None of

163

this concerns you, Bill. None of it! You have the ranch. You have me. You'll have neither if Reed Williams kills you." Her words jarred Kindred, corded the muscles of his face as his jaw set hard. "Or even if you make an enemy of him."

"There's never been the day when I was afraid of Reed."

"Make him your enemy, and we have a burden to bear the rest of our lives," she went on, ignoring his positiveness. "And our children will have it to bear. Can't you look ahead and see what it all means, Bill?"

"That's what I am doing . . . looking ahead. If I back down to Reed now, it'll be to other things later. Alder's big enough for these people and Reed, and more. Let him boot 'em. . . ."

"Then get help, Bill! Call on some of your friends."

"They've offered, and I've turned 'em down. Reed Williams is just one man, isn't he?"

"Suppose he doesn't come alone?"

"He will."

Kindred waited out a longer silence now, one that kept him on edge, leaning forward, listening intently. And shortly the girl's voice came once more: "You were never intended

to be sheriff, Bill. Let the next sheriff do this after election."

"After Reed's sent all those people on their way, kicked 'em off land that's rightfully theirs? No, honey. No." Shepley's tone was gently ungiving. "It happens I'm the one to stop him. They'd laugh me out of the country if I backed down now."

"Then you're . . . you're lost, Bill. He'll kill you! As surely as. . . ."

The girl's words laid a shock through Kindred, one that for long seconds numbed him against understanding just why her voice had broken off so suddenly. Then, over his apprehension, he was hearing the echoes of hoof-falls along the street, imagined echoes of real sounds he had ignored some seconds ago in his concentration on catching what was being said.

His glance swung sharply streetward. He saw a pair of riders idly sitting their horses to this near side of the animals at the rails. They were in the light from the windows, looking this way, in the direction out of which Shepley's and the girl's voices had sounded.

At that moment came a cry that echoed Kindred's thought: "You see? He's not alone, Bill!"

"Never mind."

Those quiet words of Shepley's were overlaid with the sound of boots crunching against gravel beyond the hedge. Kindred saw a shadow moving past him on the far side, past him toward the street. And with a sudden foreboding he lunged erect and started on after Shepley.

He reached the fence corner, the cinder walk at the street's edge, and came around the end of the hedge. He saw Shepley standing there inside the fence not ten feet from him. The glances of the riders swung sharply from the sheriff to him. The light from the windows thinned the shadows here. He could plainly catch the hesitation of the pair at the street's edge now.

His sudden appearance had thrown them off balance. He wanted it that way. He asked: "Which one's Williams, Sheriff?"

"Keep clear of this, stranger." Surprise edged Shepley's tone.

"Which one is he?"

"I'm Williams." It was the stockier of the two, the nearest, who had spoken. He was heavy bodied, his full face wearing a stubborn, bulldog look as he asked abruptly: "You sidin' Shepley in this?"

"I am."

Kindred could plainly see the effect of his words. The far man, a hawk-faced oldster,

now glanced uneasily at Williams who came straighter in the saddle. Kindred told himself, *They're already licked,* pushing aside an uneasy awareness that neither man appeared particularly ready to drop this and ride away.

That unsettling awareness crowded into him saying, "So now we're even, gents. Who'd care to call the turn?"

Shepley said quickly, "Stranger, this is my. . . ."

"You're wastin' your wind, Sheriff."

Kindred spoke sharply, derisively, for Shepley's words were spoiling the play, weakening it to Reed Williams's advantage. There was still the chance that this pair would back down now that the odds were no longer in their favor. If it came to a shoot-out, Kindred was ready, confident. Whichever way it went, the all-important thing was to see that Shepley came through this with a whole skin. Never before had the life of another man even remotely mattered to Kindred. Shepley's did now.

He could see that Williams was about to speak. He didn't give the man the chance, saying in a taunting way, "Isn't what you planned on, is it? So now what? Do you play out the hand or fold?"

For several seconds Kindred thought that

his bluff had carried, thought Shepley safe. And over those seconds it was as though he stood apart, witnessing all this. Then suddenly from that onlooker's viewpoint he was struck by the absurdity of his being here at all, of his risking his neck for a man he didn't even know, didn't care about beyond the using of him.

He understood then that he, not Shepley, was the fool. He was making the same mistake old Ben Sadler had made this morning. He'd let himself be panicked into making a foolish move. He caught the sudden tightening of Reed Williams's face and instantly knew his bluff hadn't carried. A coolness flowed along his nerves as he sensed the violence about to erupt.

It came unexpectedly. Williams's partner simply lifted his off arm into sight, swinging up a two-barreled shotgun. Kindred's right hand slashed his coat aside. The moistness of his palm surprised him, for a split second slowed his draw. A voice inside him cried — *Hell, you're not scared!* — and afterward his draw came smoothly, fast.

He saw his bullet smash through the hawk-faced one's jumper. The man buckled at the waist, and his shotgun slanted downward. Both barrels thundered at the dirt ahead of Williams's horse.

Williams was moving now as his animal reared. His gun dropped into line uncertainly. At the same instant an explosion alongside made Kindred hesitate. Shepley had thrown his first shot. Too late he saw Williams untouched, saw the man's weapon settle its swing straight at him. He hurried the squeeze of trigger. He was staring into the rosy-blasting mouth of that other Colt as his own bucked sharply against his wrist.

A slamming weight hit his abdomen. He was thrown back off-balance into the hedge. He cried out hoarsely in triumph, seeing Williams sagging loosely in the saddle. Yet that fierce exultation at seeing his second kill was instantly dulled by stark terror. He was falling. He could see the stars wheel from overhead until he was looking straight at them. Their brightness faded. And then his staring eyes saw nothing.

As Williams's frightened animal bolted off into the darkness, Bill Shepley's glance left the two inert shapes sprawled at the street's edge, and he stared through the fence at the dead stranger. He heard Laura's quick step coming in behind him. Still, he stood looking down at Kindred.

"Bill! Bill!" He felt Laura's grip on his arm yet didn't look around at her. Then, in

a low, awed voice, she was asking, "Who was he?"

Shepley's head moved from side to side in a slow, baffled way. He sighed wearily, and only then thought to lift the gun hanging in his hand and drop it in its sheath.

"I'd decided he was the one that killed old Sadler," he said. "Now I'm just not sure who he was, Laura."

"Dark Riders of Doom" was Jon Glidden's second Western story, somewhat longer and more ambitious than the first. It was sent by his agent to Popular Publications where it was bought for *Big-Book Western* on May 12, 1936. The author was paid $126.00 (a penny a word). However, upon review and, notwithstanding one rather contrived and melodramatic episode, the story was considered too fine for that magazine, and instead it was published in the more prestigious *Star Western* in the August, 1936 issue. Already here Glidden was making capable use of the shifting points of view and the interactive characterizations which were to mark his Western fiction with a dimension of dramatic suspense absent from so many one-dimensional stories in which the protagonist's viewpoint is the only perspective provided a reader. This early story also makes an interesting contrast with "Long Gone," one of his last stories, indicating how much he had grown as a master of narrative and yet how many elements that characterize his best work were apparent from the beginning.

DARK RIDERS OF DOOM

I

"A SUMMONS IN THE NIGHT"

The smoke-fogged room wavered uncertainly before old Matt Weir's eyes as he looked momentarily beyond the tent of light in which he sat at the green-felted table. The quiet disinterest of his face was no betrayal of the inner uneasiness that told him he had been drinking too much. He blinked once, then focused his eyes back to the cards clutched narrowly fan-wise in his bony hand. Three queens and a pair of sevens.

"I'll call," he said thickly and spilled his last stack of chips into the pile at the table's center.

"Hell, I'm out of this!" the man who sat at his left growled and threw his cards across into the discard.

Matt took no notice but glanced up and met Crump Mundy's gaze of smug vacancy. Crump squinted one gray eye to ease the

smart of the smoke that curled up from a cigar clenched in yellow teeth. He eased his bulk forward and pointedly regarded the empty table-arc in front of Matt.

"That cleans you, Matt?" he asked, his voice flat and expressionless.

"Uh-huh. 'Til I've won this hand."

"Don't like it!" Crump growled. "You come into my place and throw away a year's work in dust. You ain't playin' your cards, Matt."

"The way I play poker's my own damn' business!" Matt flared.

"I know. But you've lost a two-thousand-dollar poke. You ain't goin' to like it when you sober up. You'll talk. Won't help my business any." Crump folded his cards and laid them face down before him.

The man on Matt's left smiled thinly and shot Crump the hint of a wink.

"I'm not beefin'," Matt said belligerently. "There's three hundred on the table there. I'm callin'. Show your tickets."

Crump shrugged and slowly turned his cards face up with his plump left hand. Four eights and a five of hearts.

Matt's eyes widened a trifle. "Four of a kind? Danged if I ever seen such ornery luck!" He tossed his cards onto the table face down, shrugged resignedly, and pushed

himself up out of the chair. He stood unsteadily, only the lower half of his spare frame caught by the circle of light. "Stake me to a drink?"

Crump jerked his pear-shaped head in the direction of the bar. "Tell George your drinks are on the house tonight. Sorry, Matt." Nothing but concern showed in his eyes.

He and the two others at the table watched Matt stagger to the bar and lean heavily against it.

"Nice dealin', Squire," Crump said, his glance still on Matt. "What did he have last hand?"

"Full house," answered the sallow-faced little man, sitting with his back to the wall. Matt's cards lay untouched where he had thrown them face down.

Crump's glance shuttled over the early-evening crowd. He nodded approval when he saw the four miners at the faro table. George, the bartender, leaned lazily across the bar, talking with two 'punchers, and the ring of their mellow laughter fit perfectly the half-empty bottle before them. Crump's eyes settled on the batwing doors, on the shadowy outline of the high-heeled, low-cut boots of a man who stood outside. Idly he watched the boots as the man stepped into

the room. A sudden quiet made him raise his glance to examine the newcomer. He stared squarely into the muzzle of a leveled Colt.

Crump stiffened and stayed that way. The tall, flat-hipped stranger stood carelessly alert, his face masked by a black bandanna that covered all but his shadowed eyes. He took one step aside to allow a second masked figure to take his place at the door. Then, disregarding the others, he walked toward Crump, nodding briefly in the direction of the back offices. Crump's pink face flushed with anger but, understanding what was meant, he got up and walked across the still room. As he opened the office door, the stranger said, "Hold on!"

Crump stepped to one side, and the man edged into the dark interior.

"You're against the light, Crump," the outlaw's soft drawl cautioned.

Crump entered warily and lighted the lamp.

"Shut the door," came the curt bidding. "Open your safe."

Crump, his nervousness leaving him, bent over the safe, saying, "Why the mask, Larry?"

"Who's Larry?" the outlaw countered, shifting his broad shoulders nervously. The

tumblerclick sounded as Crump spun the dial. "That's enough," he snapped. "I'll finish. Might be embarrassin' if you went for the iron in there."

Crump, always seeing ahead, sighed resignedly, and the expression on his face brought a mirthless chuckle from the other who bent down and deftly turned the dial until the door swung open. He raked out onto the floor a .45 Smith and Wesson, several bundles of paper, and a cash box that disgorged a great many silver dollars, a few gold coins, a bundle of greenbacks.

"Where's the gold?" asked the outlaw whose eyes had never strayed far from Crump.

"Gold?" Crump asked blandly. "There may be a couple of ounces in the cash drawers out front."

"I mean Matt's poke . . . what you stole from him this evening."

Crump flushed and straightened from his slouch. "Now see here, Larry . . . !"

"Get it!" rasped the other, cutting off the saloon owner's rising voice.

"Go to hell!" Crump shouted but checked himself as he caught the glint of the shadowed eyes beneath the gray Stetson.

The look made him move quickly to the wall. He swung outward on its hinges the

only picture in the room — a brightly painted thing showing a sternwheeler crawling away down a blue stream between clashing green banks. Crump reached into the cubicle behind the picture and brought out two heavy deerskin bags. Lamplight glinted brightly from the blued steel of a six-gun he had wisely chosen to leave undisturbed.

The man took the bags from him, threw them on the desk, and opened one. A quick glance satisfied him of the contents and, with a flick of his .38, he motioned Crump from the room. As the other passed out through the door, the outlaw holstered his gun, stuffed the bags into the pockets of his Levi's, and followed.

Old Matt was the only one at ease in the barroom. As the outlaw strode past him, he turned unsteadily from the bar, gazed fixedly at the man's retreating back. He jerked aloft a glass of whiskey in a secret toast and gulped it down. Abruptly his knee joints gave way and he slumped to the floor, sitting there with the bar for a backrest, his bearded chin on chest, snoring loudly.

Unexpectedly, on the heel of Matt's fall, the outlaw half turned, his hand dipped to his gun, and it came up in a thundering roar. The man alongside the Squire at the poker table jumped, shrieked once, and

clamped his hand to a shattered wrist as the gun he had drawn clattered to the floor.

Without a word the two masked men backed out through the doors. The quiet hush of the room held for long moments, to be broken at length by the soft cursing of the wounded man. Voices started a spasmodic hum of conversation that soon settled to a nervous undertone. Crump looked once at the wounded man, sneered with disgust, and walked over to stare belligerently at the sleeping prospector. With one nervous foot he pushed Matt sideways to the floor and glowered down at him.

"Another evening wasted! Squire, take him out and tie him to his burro. She'll head for his shack." Then he faced about and swept the room with a glance. If anyone had been smiling, Crump did not see it now.

Outside, in front of the Aces Wild, the two outlaws were joined by a third who emerged from the shadow of the awninged walk. Bandannas were pulled down, and the three hurried to the half light of the street where their horses stood haltered at a rail. But their exit down the street was unhurried and unnoticed. In two minutes they had passed the town limits of Whitewater and were trotting their horses up the night-shadowed cañon road.

"We sure picked the right time with the sheriff outta town. Did he kick up a ruckus, Larry?" one of the riders asked.

"No. Crump's waitin' for a sure thing," the leader answered. "You wait here, Quill, and see that Matt makes it home all right. They'll tie him onto Jinny's back and start her up the road. Leave the dust in his saddlebags."

Larry Scott reined in as he spoke and let Quill come abreast of him. The deerskin sacks changed hands. Larry and the third horseman rode on until Quill dropped out of sight in the blackness.

An hour later the two were threading their way over the boulder fields of Miller's Pass. The biting chill of the wind that swept down off Ermine Peak discouraged any conversation. Down the far slope the first belt of stunted cedar thrust up out of the gloom. They pushed the horses steadily, fast, anxious to get down into the warmer low country. The bluish disk of the rising moon pushed up above the far line of the foothills and brought out the jet folds of the cedar-covered slopes. Their way turned south, at right angles from the line of the mountains, dipped into a cañon to cut off the hint of light the moon had afforded.

A half mile farther on the walls fell away

around a sharp bend, and once again the moon showed in front. As they were crossing from the rocky cañon mouth to the tall cedars beyond, the screech of a night hawk brought them to a halt. Larry answered the call, wildly, accurately, and listened as the slap of the echo came back at him. He squinted to bring the dim shapes ahead into sharper outline, until he saw the moving bulk of a shadow come out of the trees. The oncoming form took on the shape of a rider. He came up quickly and reined in alongside.

"Soapy Wilson just rode in. Dave Martin wants to see you at the Box M tonight."

Larry jerked his slouched body erect. "Anything wrong?"

"Soapy couldn't say."

"Can't make it before midnight," Larry thought aloud. "Twenty miles. Can't Dave wait?"

"Soapy said he'd be expectin' you to ride over tonight . . . alone," the man repeated.

Larry looked ahead for a long moment upon that broad sweep of gently rolling land that lay south of the foothills. A silent night bird swooped across the silver pattern below and was gone. As he looked, it was as though he could pick out the buildings of the Box M from the misty distance.

From far away drifted up the wailing bark

of a coyote, and it seemed to him as he sat there in the stillness that the cry made more ominous the word his rider had just given him. So Dave Martin had finally sent for him. His pulse quickened and, now as he turned in the saddle to face his two riders, he had a foreboding that they were all heading into trouble. Yet when he spoke, his voice was calm and quiet.

"Soapy was wrong. We'll all go."

II

"OUTLAW'S BARGAIN"

"See anything yet?" Jake Rivers called out. He stood in the darkness of the wide porch of the Box M ranch house.

"Nothin', Boss," a voice drifted back from out front where cottonwoods arched a lane over the road leading from the building.

Jake, foreman of the Box M, sucked nervously at the pipe clenched between his teeth. "Reckon he ain't comin' tonight," he said, speaking to a man who stood near him, leaning against the adobe wall. His voice had scarcely broken off when he heard the scrape of a boot behind him. He turned quickly around and saw the outline of a man showing against the lighter adobe of the moonlit yard.

"That you, Frank?" he asked tersely.

"No," came the soft spoken answer. "It's Larry, Jake."

Jake's quick intake of breath betrayed his

astonishment. "Larry!" he said with a welcome ring in his deep voice. But when he spoke again, his tones were gruff and more controlled. "Dave's waitin' for you inside."

Larry did not move. Instead his brown eyes surveyed Jake's solid figure, finally settled on the mustached, wrinkled face he knew so well. It was too dark for him to catch any hint of an expression.

"No hurry, Jake," he said. "Seems you're proddy tonight. Comin' in I thought I saw a few of the boys planted. Their cutters loaded for me?"

"You'll have to get it from Dave, Larry," Jake answered tonelessly.

The man who had been standing near Jake stepped off the porch and walked across the yard in the direction of the bunkhouse. Only when he was fifty yards away did Larry motion Jake to lead the way. The two of them walked the half length of the porch to an open door that flooded a rectangle of yellow light onto the clay floor. Jake stood to one side.

Larry edged sideways into the little room that served as Dave Martin's office and stepped out of line with the door. A hasty glance showed him that Dave was dozing at his desk. Although Larry's entrance had

been noiseless, Dave stirred now and jerked wide awake.

"Larry!" came his hearty greeting.

"Howdy, Dave," Larry smiled warily. He stood leaning against the wall.

Dave noted his position and quickly understood, his sun-wrinkled face flushing in embarrassment. He moved over to close the door, waving toward a chair that stood in one corner. "Have a seat."

The two of them sat down. For a long moment Dave Martin studied the face of his former 'puncher, now turned outlaw. Something he saw in that sun-blackened, square-jawed face of the younger man brought a sigh from him.

"It's good to see you," he said finally.

"First time in two long years, Dave."

Dave coughed nervously and ran long fingers through his gray hair. He lifted his gaze to meet that of the younger man. "Larry, I've brought you here to bargain."

Larry frowned and raised his brows in silent question.

"It's about the stock I've been losin' . . . ," the rancher went on, then paused as though he expected an answer. Larry waited, saying nothing. The fingers of Dave's left hand drummed an uneven tattoo on the desk top, and for a space of moments

185

the two sat eyeing each other. "How much will you take to call your men off?" came Dave's blunt question.

A widening of the eyes was all that gave a hint of Larry's surprise. Then came a sudden understanding of the question, and a hot retort rose to his lips. He throttled it.

"So that's why you have the place guarded. Afraid I'd bring my wild bunch with me?" Larry queried accusingly. "Dave, not one of my men has ever run off a Box M steer."

"I'm losin' a hundred head a week lately!" Dave insisted.

"My boys are out of this," Larry said evenly. "You should know better, Dave."

"Larry Scott, you . . . are you runnin' a sandy on me?" Dave asked slowly, suspiciously.

"Have I ever lied to you, Dave?"

The rancher stared at him for a long moment then leaned back in his chair. "Never," he said gently. He raised a hand in bewildered protest. "But . . . look. It's. . . ." His voice faded to silence, and he waved a hand as if to dismiss what he said. His head sagged to his chest, and he stared moodily at the floor. Then he sighed. "Son, I'm licked."

"Licked?" Larry echoed.

"I thought it was your bunch. Thought I could make you pull your boys off 'til I was on my feet again. If it isn't you, who is it that's runnin' my herds into the hills?"

"I've known about it, Dave. You aren't the only one who figures it's me." Larry evaded a direct answer.

"They've started in on the Slash B herds now. Baxter lost two hundred head a week ago."

For the second time surprise showed on Larry's face. A dark look crossed his brow but was gone before Dave could define it "So Baxter's havin' his troubles, too? Queer!"

"Queer?" Dave raised his eyebrows.

"You'd think he could protect his stock with that bunch of hardcases he has ridin' for him."

"Oh, that," shrugged Dave. "I've tried guardin' my stuff, too, but it don't make any difference. The boys can't be in every pasture at the same time. It's always the one we leave unguarded that they raid." Dave sat pensively for a moment. "I didn't see how it could be you."

"You spoke of trouble?" Larry asked, frowning.

"Plenty. I was managin' fairly well until lately. Looked like we'd have a good roundup this year . . . like I'd be able to pay off my note to Baxter and have a little to run the place on besides. But now. . . ." Dave threw up his hands.

"I didn't know," Larry murmured. "Why didn't you send for me before?"

"You're an outlaw, Larry." Dave's blunt statement was not accusing.

"I see," nodded Larry. "Folks might not understand."

"Oh, hell!" Dave blurted out. "It wouldn't matter ordinarily. But I have to watch myself these days. Baxter would be on me in a minute if he knew I had any dealin's with you. You were my friend . . . always. I know that you didn't kill Ozzie Weir, and I'm stickin' by you. But the law says you did, and you chose to take to the owlhoot 'stead of standin' trial."

"I had my reasons. They'd have lynched me that night." Larry ruminated. He reached for his tobacco and papers and did not speak until he had made and lit a cigarette. "Dave, it means a lot to you to have this rustlin' stopped. It means somethin' to me, too, for everyone, includin' Sheriff Parsons, thinks I'm the one swingin' the sticky loop. They haven't a charge against me 'cept

that killin' of Ozzie Weir. I reckon I better see to it they don't pile anything on top of that."

"How about your raidin' Whitewater last winter? They have that against you."

"No. The Aces Wild is the only place we ever touched in town. Crump Mundy would never swear out a warrant against me. He's forked and knows that a word from me in the right place would put a noose around his neck. He'll let me alone . . . until he has a chance to drygulch me. I don't regret robbin' him. It kept my bunch from starvin' last winter."

"Not only your bunch but a lot of those nesters and prospectors up in the hills," added Dave. "People up that way say some mighty fine things about you, Larry."

Larry stared in thoughtful vacancy at Dave for two long seconds then abruptly sat forward in his chair. "I'm takin' a chance sayin' this, but I'll see to it you don't lose any more stock."

Dave was incredulous. "You mean, you know who's runnin' it off? Who is it?"

"I've got my reasons for not tellin' you, Dave," Larry countered. "One more thing," he went on, brushing off the crown of his hat with a nervous excitement. "About the money you owe Baxter. I . . . that is

. . . will he be too hard on you? He and Mona . . . ?"

Dave Martin got up slowly and looked fixedly at Larry. When he spoke, it was with an almost menacing tone. "Get this. Mona's marryin' Sid Baxter don't mean a damn' thing except that she loves him. If I thought she was doin' it for me, I'd lock her in the house to keep her from it. They've been in love since the first day he hit this country three years ago. Don't forget it!"

"No offense meant," Larry apologized. "I remember the day she met him. Since then there's been no one but Sid with her. But I heard they busted up after a while . . . right after I took to the timber."

"Didn't mean a thing," Dave informed him, softening in his manner. "Just a quarrel."

Larry turned to the door. "Well, Dave, I'll be high-tailin'. You know where to find me."

They walked out onto the porch and, after Dave had mumbled an awkward thanks to the man who had promised him so much, Larry disappeared in the direction of the barns.

III

"CROSSED TRAILS"

For weeks Mona Martin had each morning ridden the circle that brought her to the top of the bald ridge overlooking Fenton's Basin. Today, pausing there to blow the chestnut gelding she had named Dawn, she realized that for days she had been missing the freshness and mystery of the country below. Lush grass pastures climbed gently up to the darkly green, mist-shrouded carpet of the foothills while above them towered the jagged, snow capped peaks of the San Martinas.

An early morning breeze from the hills pressed to her slight figure the blue blouse that so well matched her eyes. The sun caught the burnished gold of her hair and shadowed her smoothly tanned face. She breathed deeply, relishing the crispness and fragrance of the chill air. Once again, she was glad to be alive. And this was partly

because of Larry's visit, his first to the Box M since he had taken to the owlhoot two years before to become an almost legendary figure in the country. It seemed strange to her that this boy who, under her father's guidance, had once roped and ridden and shot himself into the top cowhand of the whole range should now be riding the dark trails. But it was stranger still that he should come to them with an offer that meant her father's salvation . . . and hers.

Her impending marriage with Sid Baxter, owner of the Slash B, had lately become a symbol of her defeat and helplessness, but she was chained by necessity. Baxter had told her that the ten-thousand-dollar note he held against the Box M would be destroyed the day they were married and, notwithstanding the fact that Dave Martin would have lost his ranch rather than sacrifice her, she had consented. But if Larry went through with his promise, she would never go through with her marriage to the Slash B owner.

Once, long ago, she had believed that to marry dark, handsome, and gentlemanly Sid Baxter would bring happiness to any woman, but lately she had glimpsed his petty cruelties, his iron will, his arrogance, and she knew she could never grow to love

these things in him. More than that, she had come to fear him and his ways.

Her thoughts were interrupted as she caught sight of a moving speck below on the trail. As it approached, it took the form of a rider and, a few moments later, she saw it was Sid Baxter. He waved now, and she saw it was too late to run. As she waited for him, she could not repress a feeling of admiration for his horsemanship. Baxter was big and rangy. He sat his Steeldust as though he were part of the animal, his broad shoulders back, his solid body in perfect balance as his horse slogged up the rocky slope. As he reined up before her, he swept his Stetson off in mock courtesy, a half smile on his bland, dark face. His black eyes were mocking, arrogant.

"You're very beautiful, my dear," he greeted her.

Mona flushed at the intimacy of the words, but she checked herself. " 'Morning, Sid," she said quietly.

"You look mighty happy this morning," he continued.

"It's all this," she said, indicating with a wave of her arm the green and purple haze of the mountains. "Do you wonder?"

"It's just as it always is, far as I can see," Baxter replied, watching her curiously.

Then he added: "Maybe everything looks different to you this morning."

"Maybe," she said noncommittally, wondering at his quiet, shy smile.

"Couldn't be something that happened last night, could it?" he asked easily, avoiding her gaze as he rolled and lighted a cigarette. When he got no answer, he went on, "Understand Larry Scott paid the Box M a visit."

She could not hide her surprise. "How did you know?" she asked suddenly.

Baxter laughed shortly. "One of the boys."

"Spies, you mean?"

"Spies?" he echoed, his voice bland. "That's not a pretty thing to accuse your future husband of."

"Not yet, Sid," Mona said hotly. "You're not my husband yet! You forget the conditions of our bargain."

"Which were?"

"That it was purely a business deal. I was to marry you if you tore up that note. I could choose my own time."

"You still can," Sid said easily. "Only people are beginning to wonder. It's inevitable. Why not face it?"

"Sid," Mona said, suddenly serious. "How can you want a wife that wouldn't love you? You know I don't love you . . .

like a wife should love her husband."

"You will," Baxter replied confidently. "Just give me a chance. We might as well be married tomorrow. Waiting won't change things."

"Are you sure of that?" Mona asked quietly. "Larry Scott said last night he could stop the rustling and, if he does, Dad can pay you that note. There'd be no reason for our marrying, then, would there?"

"I reckon not. But Scott's making too much money with that running iron of his to throw it away because your dad asks him."

Mona flared up. "Larry's no rustler!"

"And a killer," Baxter added.

"That's not true!"

It was their old quarrel again, and Baxter rehearsed his points with cruel delight. "No? Why is he on the owlhoot? Everyone knows Ozzie Weir and Scott argued over something Larry wanted a secret. Ozzie was hunting these rustlers that are cleaning out your dad. Everyone but you knew Larry was swingin' a long rope while he was working for the Box M. And when Ozzie was found dead on the edge of the *malpais* with a thirty-eight slug in his back, everybody but you knew Larry did it. He's the only man in this country that carries that caliber six-gun, and he's

the only man in the country that had any reason for wanting Ozzie to keep out of the *malpais*. Do I have to tell you why?"

"No, you don't, but you probably will."

"I will," he corrected her. "It was because he was driving all his rustled stuff through there . . . stuff that he stole from your dad, from me, from four or five other spreads!"

"That's never been proven, Sid!"

Baxter sneered. "It has to everyone but you. Why do you think that mob tried to lynch him after Sheriff Parsons had locked him in jail?"

"I don't know, but a mob is always wrong!"

"To folks too blind to see the truth," Baxter added, with smiling insolence. "No, Mona. That tinhorn, gun-slick badman will never get you out of this for the simple reason that he's the one that got you in it."

"If he won't, nobody will!" Mona flared up. "Not even you, Sid. At least Dave Martin and his daughter will go down without having to bargain with you! I'm through . . . through for good!"

With that she wheeled the chestnut and left Baxter, riding down towards Fenton's Basin. Baxter leaned forward, his right forearm resting on the saddlehorn, and arranged the gaudy neckerchief he was wearing. The

expression on his face was smug and know-ing.

"You'll be back," he murmured. "You can't live on pride, my lady."

IV

"GUNS FLASH
IN THE MOONLIGHT"

Matt Weir's cabin topped a spruce-covered knoll that lay four miles up Jackrabbit Cañon from Whitewater. At the foot of the knoll a sun-splashed stream passed under the handrail bridge that brought the trail to Matt's side of the cañon. Matt was a solitary man and had chosen a solitary spot for his home. Back of the cabin the sheer rock wall climbed a hundred feet to the stellar blue of the sky. Half way up its precipitous side was the opening to Matt's mine. He was sitting at the mine entrance, smoking and resting his aching head, when he saw the rider coming up the trail.

He picked up his Winchester, let it hang in the crook of his right arm, and started down the path to the cabin, surveying the rider the while. He was in the cedars and hidden from view before the rider crossed the bridge. Matt quickened his pace, worked

around to a vantage point along the trail, and waited.

When the rider came up even with him, he said: "Howdy, you tinhorn badman!"

The rider was Larry Scott who turned abruptly in the saddle to face Matt.

"For a ranny that put away a quart of Crump's liquor last night, you're feelin' right smart," he retorted, swinging easily from the saddle to saunter over to where Matt was standing, leaning on his rifle. "Did Jinny get you home all right?"

"Sure thing. Had a little more than I could pack last night. First thing I knowed this mornin' was when that loco jackass tried to scrape me off alongside a cedar stump." Matt reached down to rub his bruised thigh. "Found my dust, too . . . in the saddle-bags."

"I promised you that you'd get it back," Larry said. "What did you find out?"

"Plenty!" Matt answered, his face suddenly gone pensive. "They raid the Box M tonight. Late. After midnight."

Larry looked up from the cigarette he was shaping in his long fingers. "Let's have it, Matt . . . from the beginnin'."

"Juan Mercado, that rib-stickin' Manuelo's kid brother, come foggin' up here yesterday mornin' and told me he

199

thought his big brother was gettin' ready to be away a few days with Crump's bunch of gunnies. I'd told Juan I'd pay him plenty to let me know when Manuelo started whettin' his knife and packin' his roll. So I showed up at the Aces Wild 'bout sunset, met Quill there, and sent him out to get the news to you, as you know. After that I starts flashin' my dust sacks and slackin' a godawful thirst. Wasn't long before they asked me into a game. From then on it was easy."

"How do you know it's tonight?" Larry asked impatiently.

"Crump," Matt answered and shrugged. "He's got the idea I can't take more'n a pint without losin' my senses. Soon as he thought I was too sozzled to keep my eyes open, he started talkin' to several of his quick-fingered *hombres* that came in. Told 'em to meet tonight at The Notch, up in the Box M east pasture about midnight. That was enough for me. I got so damn' drunk I can't remember much else, but I didn't care. I knew they was playin' marked cards ag'in' me, but then I remembered you said you'd get the dust back for me, so I just set back and watched the fireworks. Everything in the United States happened in that game! Four of a kind was only tol'able. They skinned me sudden."

"Will Crump ride with 'em tonight?" Larry asked.

"No. The Squire," Matt answered. "Crump's keepin' his back trail clear."

Larry flicked alight a match and touched it to his cigarette. He walked over to hunker down with his back against a cedar, frowning a long moment before he spoke. "Matt, I'm afraid the end's in sight."

"Afraid?" Matt queried.

"Yeah! Afraid." Larry's gaze was locked with Matt's now. "It's goin' to hurt someone I think a lot of."

"Mona?"

Larry nodded soberly.

"I know," said Matt, "but it's better to hurt her now than to let her marry the polecat and find it out later."

"If we can prove it's Baxter, I'll be a free man once more, Matt. I'll have to leave the country. Can't go back and face Mona."

"Hell, she'll get over losin' Baxter!" Matt insisted. "Maybe she knows already what a sidewinder he is. No one could be around him long without findin' it out." Matt hesitated, watching the hurt look in Larry's eyes. "You've taken enough for that girl, son! Tryin' to save her feelin's. The very day you took to the hills you knew Sid had killed Ozzie . . . killed him because he'd found

their hide-out. Don't forget . . . Ozzie'd told me about it, and I could have gone in and cleared up the whole works with lawman Parsons. I've waited two long years to see Baxter get what's due him. You forget Mona and her feelin's."

Larry sighed and rose to stamp out his cigarette. He walked over to where his big, shad-bellied roan stood ground-haltered.

"Maybe you're right, old-timer. Least-ways, I'm with you to the finish."

" 'Pears to me like the finish'll be when Baxter's got a rope 'round his neck, his feet swingin' clear of the ground."

After he left Matt's, Larry spent the rest of the day rounding up his men and making sure they knew their jobs in the coming showdown. For showdown it was, Larry knew, and all his distaste for facing it could not be put off.

The Notch was a place perfectly named. It was a V-shaped pass, the only way within miles of gaining the top of the rocky rim that right-angled south from the mountains to form the eastern boundary of the Box M. Further out onto the plain the rim fell away, its place taken by a fence that enclosed Box M lands all the way to the river, five miles south. The east pasture, bordered by the

rim, was a choice one, although at a great distance from the ranch buildings. Here Dave Martin kept a herd of yearlings and, because it was so remote, he had even now failed to put a heavy guard on the herd.

It was bright moonlight, shortly after midnight, when Larry, Quill, and Fay saw the little knot of horsemen that threaded their way through The Notch and into the Box M pasture.

"They'll drive back this way," Larry told them. "It's their shortest way through to the cañons. Quill, you and Fay cross over to the other side. Remember what I told you about the Squire. I want him."

Larry watched the two go afoot across the smooth, narrow opening to the other side and lose themselves in the rocks. In five minutes the moon-shadowed boulders looked deserted. It was a full hour before Larry heard the low rumble of the herd on the move. The sound increased in volume, and he knew that the Squire and his men were driving the herd fast for The Notch so that dawn would see them well into the cañon country.

Soon the moving shadow crept into view. Almost before Larry realized it, the point was close enough so that he could make him out. He waited minutes more until the

rider and two score of cattle had passed beneath him and into The Notch. Then he thumbed back the hammer of his Winchester. He had counted eight riders going into the pasture — more men than necessary to work the small herd — and knew that there would be keen eyes among them searching out signs of any moving thing. He saw now that only two men were riding the swing positions, so he lowered his rifle until the five drag riders came into full outline behind the bawling, tangled mass of animals.

The swing riders were passing below as he fired. The sharp crack of his .30-.30 seemed to knock sideways one of the five in the dust cloud of the drag. The rider had not yet fallen clear before the two guns across from him took up the echo on their own. Larry saw that Quinn, the best rifle shot of their trio, had shot the horse from under the smallest rider in the drag. That would be the Squire, for he was a small man, and it had been Quinn's job to take him alive.

In less than two minutes the shooting was abruptly over. Directly below, one of the swing riders lay where he had fallen among the rocks, his horse fast disappearing with the half-crazed animals of the herd that had stampeded back into the pasture. One

gunny had wisely wheeled his horse, when the shots spoke out, to streak back into the pasture again and disappear in the half darkness. Three drag riders lay a hundred yards out from The Notch, two instantly cut down by the rifles, a third trampled badly by the terror-stricken animals. The Squire had taken to cover, limping, and now the hollow snort of his Colt lanced flame from behind a huge outcropping of rock.

Larry, half nauseated by what he had just seen yet knowing the justice of his action, started working down the slope toward the Squire. He took advantage of all cover, crawling, running. Once he had to drop ten feet onto a narrow ledge directly in the Squire's vision, but he moved quickly and was well hidden before the gambler heard the falling gravel and sent a haphazard shot at the sound. In five minutes he was within twenty feet of the Squire, behind him.

"Reach, Squire!" his voice lashed out. The Squire straightened up tensely from where he had been crouching. Cautious always, he hesitated then slowly his fingers unclasped from the butt of his Colt, and he dropped it.

"Walk straight ahead, Squire," Larry ordered. "Remember, I don't like gamblers."

They had walked perhaps twenty steps

toward The Notch when Larry heard the faraway sound of pounding hoofs. This new sound was puzzling and unexpected, since the herd had wandered off out of earshot. Several riders were approaching, coming up fast.

"Behind the rocks!" Larry breathed and, when the two of them were crouched down, he thrust his .38 into the gambler's back, giving an unspoken warning that the Squire would not ignore if these were more of Crump's riders.

It was only seconds before they came into sight and swept on past. Larry recognized them as Box M riders, Dave Martin among them, yet he made no attempt to hail, hoping they would go on through The Notch without seeing the signs of the fight. But they spotted the bodies of the dead rustlers and slid their horses to a stop in a swirl of dust. Larry sighed and said, "Come on," and they walked up to the Box M crew. He told his story briefly while Martin listened, saying nothing.

"Take him to the house, boys," Dave ordered, as though it had become his affair.

"Dave, let me take him. I want to work this thing out my own way," Larry cut in, for the moment worried at what the gambler might tell if threatened by the Box M hands.

A thought of Mona was in the back of his mind, yet he at once sensed the futility of trying to keep his secret any longer. It was only delaying the eventual outcome, and he knew that could lead to only one thing — Baxter's exposure. So, with a shrug, he answered Dave's remonstrance and in five minutes the Box M men, with Larry and his men accompanying them, set out for the ranch house. In front rode the Squire, silent and unsmiling.

It was a grim crew the Squire confronted that night in the Box M office. This sallow, still-faced gambler had looked trouble in the face too often not to be able to estimate his chances but, when he was shoved in a chair, a strong light in his face, and looked over the men before him, he conceded his chance of facing this out was small. Still, he was a fighter, so he sneered.

"Squire, you've got your neck in a noose. You'd better talk."

Dave Martin's voice filled the small room as he intoned the words. He was sitting on the desk directly facing the Squire. Near the door stood Jake Rivers and Larry, the latter tense and watching for the Squire to show signs of weakening. For an hour Dave and Jake had been questioning the gambler who still sat unmoved, now holding a cigarette

in his tightly bound hands. Larry had not taken part in this, hoping disconsolately for some way out of the predicament. Now it came to him that he might maneuver the conversation in such a way that Baxter's character would suffer as little as possible.

"Squire," he spoke up, "there's something I haven't told Dave. Do you know how we knew you were raiding tonight?"

The Squire's habitual, expressionless mask changed imperceptibly as he shook his head.

"Crump Mundy tipped us off!"

The gambler's thin, sallow face turned a shade lighter, yet the expression did not change.

"It's a double-cross, Squire. Crump wanted you wiped out."

The Squire's eyes first betrayed his inner emotion. They smeared over in a dull hatred and seemed to focus on some far point beyond the walls of the room.

"If you talk, we'll see that you get a fair trial. If you don't" — Larry shrugged — "we won't be particular about turnin' you over to the boys. Crump says you're back of all this . . . that it's you who's swingin' the sticky loop. We're takin' his word for it . . . unless you've got proof."

"That whippoorwill!" the gambler mut-

tered, his voice low and sharp. "He wanted to cut down on me tonight. To get rid of me! I know too much. All right! I'll talk. The only thing I want is to see him swing before I do! Three years ago Crump started handlin' wet stuff. My back trail would be interestin' to a lot of people north of here, and Crump knew that. So he talked me in on his game. I waited to make my break 'cause cards is my game, and I don't much hanker usin' a vent iron. But Crump paid well, and soon I couldn't afford to leave. Wasn't long before we was runnin' plenty of stuff through the hills over to Pete Rango's place, the other side of Pemmican Buttes. You rannies never will find out how we worked through the hills." He chuckled mirthlessly. "I'm nothin' but an understrapper to that tub o' guts."

"So it's Crump Mundy?" asked Dave. "Baxter'll give a lot to hear that. He's been losin' plenty of. . . ."

The Squire's soft chuckle interrupted him. "Yeah! Baxter's herds have sprouted wings, too! You *hombres* think Crump's the big augur? Crump's called the turn, and I reckon I know who put him up to it. He's just another understrapper! What would you think if I told you. . . ."

Crash!

V

"BEHIND BARS"

The spang of a rifle blended with the sound of the breaking window. Glass splinters clattered to the floor. All except the Squire whirled to face the closed door. Larry's .38 was out as he turned back to flash a glance at the gambler. The Squire's lips were parted, his eyes wide and showing a slow horror. His tied hands raised up to feel his chest then came away bloody and sagged into his lap again as he looked at them. Abruptly his body relaxed, his head dropped forward.

Larry sprang toward the door and tore it open as the muffled beat of hoofs came from out front. He caught a glimpse of a shadow fleeing down the lane of trees that led to the road. Instinctively he knew that the range was too long for his revolver, so he turned back into the room.

They laid the Squire, still breathing, onto the floor.

"Ten seconds more, and we'd have had the answer," mumbled Dave, as he worked over the still figure, tearing the shirt away from the bloody chest.

"We had half the answer," replied Larry, knowing that the shot had given him a feeling of relief. "Crump Mundy."

"He said Crump was understrapper to someone higher up," Dave said and looked at Larry squarely. "Do you know who it is?"

"Give me another day, and I'll tell you," Larry replied, knowing that the time he was playing for would not save him the hurt in the end. "Right now, we'd better look after the Squire. He's our best witness."

Larry stayed with them until they had called in "Doc" Summers, a Box M puncher who once had worked for a vet and who looked the Squire over and ordered him taken into town at once.

"He may live," he said. "Get the spring wagon, Jake, and we'll put him on a mattress. It's goin' to take some careful drivin' to keep us from showin' up in Whitewater with a corpse."

All at once the confining space of the little office seemed to press in on Larry. He walked outside. The chill of the late night air seemed to revive him, to quiet something within him that was strangely disturbing.

211

Here there was nothing for him to do. He was walking off toward the corrals when Dave hailed him.

"We're takin' the Squire into town," Dave told him. "You leavin'?"

Larry nodded.

"We aim to call at the Aces Wild and smoke Crump out. Can I have Quill and Fay? We could stand two fast guns."

Days ago the prospect of seeing Crump Mundy brought to his reckoning would have fired Larry. Now it left him cold, disinterested. Dave, quick to sense that something beyond his understanding was happening, did not urge him to accompany them. Larry told him to take his two men.

After the other had gone back to the house, Larry went to the corral, whistled, and waited until his roan came toward him. He had put up the corral bars and was on the point of mounting when a voice stopped him.

"Larry!"

It was Mona. Facing about at her voice, he saw her coming from the house. The soft light of a waning moon made a playground of shadows on her face and made pale fire where the fine-spun hair framed her head. Her presence filled him with an excitement until he could not trust his voice to answer.

In a flash it came to him that she had changed from the girl he remembered to a woman. She was very different.

For a lingering moment she too seemed to catch the spell of this meeting. Then, excitedly, she said, "Larry, I saw him!"

"The Squire?" he asked, fearful that she might have been sickened by the sight of the wounded gambler.

"No, the man who shot him."

"Did you know him?" Larry blurted out and, on the heels of his question, he could have bitten his tongue out for asking it.

"Yes. It . . . it was Sid Baxter."

He hung his head. "I'm sorry about that." Then he looked at her. "No, I'm not either. Better you know it now than later."

"You knew about him, didn't you, Larry?" she asked softly.

"Yes."

"And you've kept it from me. Why?"

There was no answer he could make to this — none he had a right to make — so he remained silent.

Mona said: "I think I know. You thought I loved him and were afraid of hurting me."

He listened patiently, his face as impassive as he could make it.

"You shouldn't have done it, Larry." Her voice held something between a reprimand

and a caress. "Because I don't love him. I never did."

He listened blankly, tasting the excitement of those simple words, and then he reached out and grasped her arms. "Say that again, Mona," he said huskily.

"I don't love him. I never did."

"Oh, Lord," Larry groaned. "To think I could have stopped this long ago . . . if I'd only known."

"But why didn't you?"

He could speak now, and he did, simply, bluntly, honestly. "Because if you loved him and were happy with him, that's all I wanted."

Mona was silent a long moment, and then she said: "But why did you want my happiness, Larry? Did it mean anything to you?"

"Everything in the world. More than my own," he answered.

"You . . . you . . . how can I say it?" she asked gently. "Do you mean you love me, Larry?"

"Yes."

All at once, she was in his arms, pressed close to him, hugging his body to hers.

"Oh, Larry! What fools we've been. I love you, too. I always have."

He kissed her, but everything in his tired being rose up to deny his right to her until

he finished this. He moved her gently away from him. "Not that way, yet. There's still something left to be done."

And then he was gone. As his shadow passed into the misty distance, Mona's eyes glistened with tears of happiness.

The Slash B lay a hundred yards from the bank of the sluggish Rio Falto, deep in a cluster of high cottonwoods. There was a light, Larry saw as he dismounted on the low ridge to the north of the sprawling adobe ranch house. That light would be in the north wing. All the caution, all the stealth he had learned in these two years had been hard bought, but now he forgot them. Sid Baxter was in there, he thought, his rage quiet and consuming. All the guns that Sid Baxter ever owned could not bring him down now.

So he walked down the slope in the open, rubbing an open palm over each gun. Not a sound reached him as he paused beside the outside door of the room where the light was. He reached for the door knob, framing his challenge. The motion was not completed when he heard a sound behind him that made him whirl. As he turned, he bounded sideways and streaked both hands for his guns. A sudden, breath-slamming

impact, and he knew he had whirled into the man. He twisted his gun, still holstered, and shot, just as a crashing blow flooded his vision with white sheets of light and his knees buckled so that he felt himself falling, down, down. . . .

"Let's get him in jail before the boys run into a likely tree," was the next thing he heard over the throbbing drum in his head. He tried to move and couldn't. He opened one eye and, in that brief glimpse, he saw that several strange men were carrying him into a squat, sun-bathed adobe building beyond. Sheriff Parsons was one of them, and he knew the reference to a jail meant that he was in the hands of the lawman. Regardless of the pain, he opened his eyes and struggled with an effort that left him breathless.

"The ranny's showin' life," said a man with a beard. The others grunted, as they carried him through an office into a jail cell.

"It's my duty, Scott, to tell you that anything you say will be used . . . ," intoned Sheriff Parsons, once the ropes were off and he could sit up.

"Where's Baxter?" Larry cut in hollowly.

"Out after the rest of your wild bunch," Parsons told him.

"I want to see you alone, Sheriff."

The remark brought forth a derisive howl of laughter from the four men standing with the sheriff.

"You'll sure enough be alone . . . in here," one jeered. "C'mon. He wants solitude."

"Wait, Parsons!" he called as he saw the lawman turn to leave with the others.

Parsons was frowning as he sauntered back to the cell door. "Talk fast, badman. You gut-shot Jeff Lamb last night at the Slash B, and he was my friend. I'm a busy man. If I don't round up some deputies, you'll be lynched within two hours."

"I was at the Box M last night," Larry told him. "Helped Dave Martin round up some rustlers who were workin' a herd of his east toward the cañons. Dave's likely in town, now. Get him and. . . ."

"Save your wind, youngster!" Parsons sneered.

Larry only then remembered that Dave Martin was one man Parsons hated above all others. It was an old feud, one that had smoldered for years. Once Parsons had been a Box M hand. Dave had fired him for habitual drunkenness. The years had not lessened their dislike for each other nor had they lessened Parsons's liking for liquor. Even now Larry caught the pungent smell

of it about the sheriff and knew that there would be no reasoning with the man in his present condition.

"Send for Dave?" Parsons jeered. Then the smile faded and his lower lip protruded in an ugly grimace. "You're seein' nobody. For two years you've been curlin' your tail, swingin' a wide loop that damned near cleaned every ranch in the county. You're poison, and I don't hanker to give none of your friends the chance to get you out of here. I aim to see you brought to trial. After that, I'm goin' to be the one to arrange your necktie-party."

Some inner caution stopped Larry as he was about to tell Parsons what he knew of Baxter. For Baxter had thrown his political influence to help elect Parsons more than two years ago, and he recognized that the sheriff would turn a deaf ear to anything said against his patron.

When the door leading to the office had slammed shut behind the sheriff's burly figure, Larry knew that he meant what he said. Tomorrow there would be a trial — unless a lynching removed the possibility — and there would be many wanting to rush things through to a quick conclusion. A remembrance of Mona Martin suddenly quieted his wrought-up feelings and for delicious

seconds he was re-living his moments with her of the previous night. Few words had passed between them, yet Larry knew for a certainty that their lives were pledged to each other. For two years he had fought, planned, and prayed that he might bring her happiness. Now it was in his power to give it to her.

Then he abruptly realized that fate was robbing him of the finest thing that had ever come into his life. There was faint hope that anyone or anything could influence Baxter or Parsons to give him the chance of proving his innocence. Himself guilty of rustling and the murder of Ozzie Weir, Baxter would see to it that all possibility of help reaching Larry Scott was removed. Parsons, biased by his hatred for Dave Martin, would be putty in Baxter's hands. The trial would prove the outlaw guilty. Larry had seen enough of Whitewater justice to know that no time would be lost in taking him to the cottonwood at the cemetery gates. All would be gone . . . Dave, Mona, Matt, and those reckless, fearless men who had for two years lived a hunted existence with him on the owlhoot.

There came the conviction that all this could not be. All at once there returned that reckless, high-born courage that had

brought him through so many tight places. Twenty-four hours to live! Between him and freedom stood the three-foot-thick walls of an adobe jail and the will of two stubborn men. Larry's face creased into its old smile as he realized that a lot can happen in twenty-four hours.

VI

"DOOMED TO DIE"

The sun-scorched adobes of Whitewater reflected a dazzling glare as Mona rode down the one main street and turned in at Jepson's livery stable. Her horse, Dawn, was almost foundered for he had made the ride of his life in those early morning hours. For a long while after Larry had left, she had leaned against the corral in the dark, numb with happiness. Then, slowly, it had come to her where Larry had gone.

With a strangled cry she ran for the office, where her father was overseeing the handling of the Squire. In a torrent of words she had told him about seeing Sid Baxter, and of what Larry had said. She was sure that Larry was riding for the Slash B to square accounts with Baxter.

Dave Martin knew the truth when he heard it, and he was a man of action. He left Mona standing there, while he called all

hands together. In another moment, before Mona could reach the corral, they had thundered out of the yard. She saddled Dawn and followed, only to learn when she got to the Slash B that Baxter had captured Larry and taken him to Whitewater with the Box M men hot on their trail. Sheriff Parsons had been there and gone with Baxter. Ling, the Chinese cook, told her this and assured her the Box M couldn't possibly overtake Larry and his captors.

She followed doggedly. Three hours of hard riding. Now as she turned Dawn over to the stable boy, she knew she and her father had lost. Whitewater in all its history had never seen such activity on a weekday morning. Dust hung like a pall in the still air over the false front stores, churned up by dozens of buckboards, spring wagons, and horses that moved continually up and down its street. She didn't need anyone to tell her that the news of Larry's capture had spread like seeds in the wind.

"Miss Mona!" a voice called, and she turned to see Jake Rivers towering above the crowd on the sidewalk. He pushed toward her and was soon at her side. "You shouldn't be here," he said.

"Jake, where's Dad?"

"He's up at the courthouse trying to see

Judge Wallace. I'm just takin' him the news that the judge won't be in town 'til tomorrow."

"What are we going to do, Jake?" she asked, finding it hard to keep an even voice.

"Come out here," Jake answered mysteriously, leading her out into the street, away from the crowd. "There's too many back there would like to hear what I got to say."

"Can we get him out?" Mona asked and then regretted her question because she already knew the answer.

"No. But we're doin' the best we can. Dave says to lay low until the trial tomorrow. He's sent some of the boys out to bring in Luke McVickers, Rod Halloway, Wes Fenton, and a lot of others who'll help us get Larry a fair trial. Don't you worry, Miss Mona. He'll be all right."

"If Dad brings them, it'll mean guns, Jake."

Jake shook his head dubiously. "We're not breathin' a word about Baxter until the trial. When we do, we'll have guns to back it up."

"Why doesn't Dad go to the sheriff and tell him about Sid?"

"Parsons was out at the Slash B when Larry come bustin' in. He and Baxter is too thick, and you know what he thinks of your

dad. He wouldn't listen. Baxter's got his gunnies in town, keepin' an eye on things. They're honin' for gun play and, if Larry was busted out of jail, they'd start somethin' we couldn't finish."

Mona rested a hand on Jake's arm and looked him squarely in the eyes. "Tell me the truth, Jake. Has Larry a chance?"

Jake's glance wavered and fell before hers. He muttered something that Mona did not understand. It was enough. She turned away and left him, made miserable by her frustration.

Old Matt Weir had come down from the hills to attend the trial of his son's killer. He was using this evening as an occasion on which to drown his sorrows. Just now he had propped his spare frame against the familiar bar of the Aces Wild. Crump Mundy was not to be seen, and Matt vaguely wondered at his absence.

Never had Matt seen so many free drinks. Never had he been the center of such interest. It was early evening, and the place was crowded. Ten minutes ago Sid Baxter had come in to shake his hand and promise him that Larry Scott would hang for Ozzie's murder no later than the afternoon of the following day.

"I'll be there to tie the knot, Sid," he had said ominously. "I can build a knot that's slow torture. May Larry Scott's soul rot in hell!"

That had been his toast, cheered by many in the room who had drunk it with him. Matt smashed his glass against the bar and turned to call for another drink, smiling inwardly at the look on Baxter's face.

A little later he left the place to walk unsteadily along the crowded street to the hotel, followed by a few of his more boisterous fellow drinkers. Sober-minded citizens had gone to bed, so those Matt now met were out for the same pleasures he was finding, and he was greeted everywhere as something of a hero. They laughed at him and with him, glad to see that he was enjoying his one, brief moment as a popular idol.

"Turnin' in, Matt?" one of the hangers-on called as he entered the hotel.

"Just bookin' a room," Matt answered, thickly. "Be back in a minute."

The elderly night clerk scowled at Matt as he came up. Without any formality Matt reached over, pulled the register to him, and scanned the recent entries. He ignored the still-scowling clerk as he turned from the desk and made his way up the stairs. Once

the clerk opened his mouth to say something to this intruder, but a glance out front showed him that Matt's friends were waiting, so he wisely decided to let events shape themselves.

When Matt reached the upstairs hall, his legs lost their unsteadiness. He walked quickly the length of the hall to room 34 and knocked softly upon the panel. The door opened, and Mona Martin stood framed in the lamplight that flooded out. Matt spoke softly, the door opened wider, and he was admitted.

Five minutes later he joined his friends below.

Shortly after midnight Matt looked through slitted eyes at the men in the smoke-filled saloon. There was not one sober man among them. At least if there was, Matt had overlooked something. With a satisfied sigh he turned to the bartender.

"Ralph, fetch me three quarts of Old Crow. I'm makin' the rounds."

Ralph tendered three unopened bottles, caught the gold piece that Matt flipped to him, and stood there to watch the old prospector weave through the batwing doors. One of the drunks yelled to Matt, asking where he was going, but Matt merely waved an arm carelessly, not looking back.

Four doors down was the jail. Matt's steps became more wobbly as he approached it. Out front were three guards, lean, flat-hipped, serious-eyed men who scowled until they recognized him then grinned.

"Howdy, old rooster!" greeted Lefty Craig. These were all Slash B men, Matt knew, posted by Parsons and Baxter to guard the jail. Three in front and two out behind. Matt had ascertained that, having walked around the place earlier in the evening.

"Howdy, yourself," Matt answered. "Ain't you boys thirsty?" and he held up a bottle by the neck.

"Naw," answered Lefty, licking his lips.

"Lay aside your cutters, boys." Matt spoke loud enough so that those at the rear could hear. "Ozzie Weir's dad wants to treat you to a drink. Go out back and get the others, Lefty."

"Can't do that, old-timer," said Lefty, suddenly serious. "Sid would raise hell."

It was then that Matt saw Harmless Ogden. Harmless, the frail, stoop-shouldered little man whose guns had snuffed out many lives, was one of the three in front. He had not left his station at the jail door to come and talk to Matt as had Lefty and the other. An uncertainty crept into the back of Matt's

liquor-jumbled mind and stayed there like a slow threat.

"Right!" he said, answering Lefty, "it's you boys' duty to guard this place. I'll gun whip your whole outfit if you let that murderin' polecat outta there before his trial."

Matt's threat brought roars of laughter. Even Harmless chuckled. The two guards out back heard and came to stand at one corner, looking on. Matt set two of the bottles on the ground by the wall, opened one, and passed it. When Lefty handed it back to him, it was a third empty.

"Lefty!" one of the guards out back called, "don't we get none of that?"

"Hell, let 'em wait!" growled Matt, tipping the bottle to his lips. It went around again and came back less than half full.

"Damn it, Lefty, send that bottle back here!" came another call. Matt pretended not to hear. He wandered over to Harmless, held out the bottle to the little gunny.

"Drink?"

"Uh-huh."

"Drink to the coals of hell roastin' Larry Scott," insisted Matt. "He beefed my boy."

"Nope." Harmless's voice held finality. "You and the rest have your fun. I'm stickin' here."

Matt gave a careless shrug and walked

back to the others. "I reckon Scott can't claw his way around the building to the back."

"Stay here," Lefty ordered the man with him who was following after Matt.

"I want more of that belly-wash," this man answered defiantly. "That's Old Crow, and it ain't often I get a chance at good whiskey. He can't break jail. Let Harmless take care of him."

The two argued until a call came from Matt at the back where they could see him with the bottle tilted up to his lips. A quick glance up the street told Lefty the town was nearly deserted. He tossed the keys to Harmless without a word, nodded toward Matt, and led the way back.

Twenty minutes later the second bottle was nearly gone. Matt heaved himself to his feet from where he had been sitting against the adobe wall of the jail. Lefty, through his stupor, saw the serious look on his face. " 'S matter, Matt?"

Matt pushed his hat back and scratched his head with one long, bony finger. "I want t'see th' pris'ner."

Lefty shook his head solemnly. "Can't do it. No one's t'see th' pris'ner."

Matt passed him the bottle and watched him take a long pull.

"Pris'ner beefed my son. Gotta see 'im."

"Harmless has the keys," volunteered Pete Bassett, the man sitting next to Lefty.

"Don't need keys," answered Matt thickly. "Talk through the window. Here, gi' me a hoist."

"No!" Lefty growled.

"You ornery cow nurse!" Matt bellowed. "I'm Ozzie Weir's old man an' the pris'ner beefed my son. Now, I reckon there ain't no one got a better right to talk to th' pris'ner than me. Gi' me a hoist, or I'll blow th' hell out of th' rest of that likker." Matt drew his .45 and took unsteady aim at the bottle in Lefty's hand.

"Here! Y'old fool! Put up that hog-leg!" Lefty ducked the bottle behind him. "Pete, lift Wild Bill up to thet window, or we'll all be lyin' in our own blood."

Lefty abruptly lost all interest in Matt and focused his attention on the bottle once again. He took a long drink, sighed, and then his head sank onto his chest and his lips parted in a long, slow snore.

Pete made an ineffectual attempt to lift Matt up to the window. It sent them both sprawling. Pete laughed, and Matt cursed, waving his .45. "There ain't no sense in a man lettin' likker get the best of him," he said as he staggered back to Pete again.

"Brace yo'self, Pete! You ain't drunk."

"Goddlemighty, what am I then?" Pete moaned, now on all fours under the window.

"Let's get this over with and go after s'more rot gut, Pete. Stay set right where you're at! I'm comin'." So saying, Matt steadied himself and climbed onto Pete's back. The .45 Colt was still in his grasp as he reached and pulled himself up to the window.

"Larry!" he whispered, then aloud: "Scott, drag your mangy carcass over here! I got things to say." Inside he saw the vague outline of Larry's head and shoulders.

"Matt!" came Larry's answer.

"Take this!" Matt growled in an undertone. "Look in the empty chamber. Watch out for Harmless Ogden. He wouldn't drink." And before the other could reply, the old prospector had launched into a tirade. "You're the crawlin' sidewinder that got Ozzie. I'm comin' to see your necktie party tomorrow, *zopilote* and, after you've quit kickin', I'm hopin' they fill your carcass with hot lead an' sink your head down in the ground. You ain't . . . ," his words abruptly cut off as Pete flattened. The two of them piled up against the wall, Pete laughing quietly. After they had picked

231

themselves up, Matt said, "Let's go up the street for 'nother snort."

They tried to rouse Lefty and the other two, but three quarts of Old Crow had done their duty. So Matt and Pete staggered their uncertain way up the street, this time to the far end. Matt, as he walked away, cast one glance to where Harmless was sitting on the steps of the jail office. He shook his head sorrowfully.

When they were standing at the bar, he sighed: "Now I c'n get sozzled."

VII

"JAIL BREAK"

Watch out for Harmless Ogden! Those five words hammered at Larry's brain as Matt and Pete went around the corner of the building and out of his sight. Their voices faded into the still air, and the quiet held. Idly he fondled the Colt Matt had thrust at him through the bars, thinking of Harmless. He could remember the lazy drawl, the gray eyes, the boyish face of the Slash B gunnie, and knew him to be the deadliest killer of all that wild crew Baxter had gathered around him.

Strangely enough, he found no trace of fear when he thought of meeting Harmless. He groped for an idea that would show him a way of escape. Several came, but he discarded each one, knowing the man who was against him.

Watch out for Harmless Ogden, Matt had said. *He wouldn't drink.*

Now the words were full of meaning. Harmless would be clear headed, alert, and naturally suspicious of anything his prisoner might do or say. He could not be taken in by an ordinary ruse. Abruptly Larry recalled Matt's reference to the empty chamber in the Colt and decided there might be something there to help him. He spun the cylinder, pushed the ejector, and forced out through the loading gate a tightly rolled slip of paper. It was pitch dark in the cell, but his eyes, accustomed to it, made out the writing:

Larry:
If Im luckey ther wont be anybody garding the jail when Im gone. Walk right out. Mona has steaked a horse out in the arroyo behind the cort house. Head for the hills. Squire is going to live. Hes in bed at Doc Roberts house. The boys will get Baxter. The Squire has agreed to tell Parsons all he noes. Gud luck.

Larry crumpled the note, his mind racing over the implications of Matt's message. If Baxter discovered that the Squire still lived, he would make another attempt at killing him. Parsons might even help him to hunt

down the Squire. It was certain that he wouldn't take the Squire's story against the word of Baxter.

No, there were two things Larry could do. He could break jail and hightail it, letting Baxter get the Squire out of the way and remain the big augur of this country. It would mean that Larry Scott was on the owlhoot forever. Or he could break jail, get the Squire and Parsons together, and make the sheriff believe the story. It was his only chance for freedom and happiness — with Mona.

He stepped over to the window and could see the three sleeping gunnies below. They were out of the way. Out in front would be that gun-slick, sober killer, Harmless Ogden. Between them was the office. Every moment he lingered, he knew Harmless would be getting more suspicious about the silence of the other guards.

He stepped to the cell door and brought the Colt up, held its blunt snout within two inches of the lock. The bellowing roar of the shot seemed to rend the walls apart. He fired once more, pointblank, then sent his weight crashing against the bars. The door gave way, and he half way fell through it as it swung open. He caught himself and leaped for the office door, tearing it open,

sidestepping. The deafening thunder of a gun blast greeted him, seemed to throw him back as he felt the air rush of a bullet fan his cheek. He stepped swiftly out. Harmless fired again, and Larry caught the slug in his left upper arm. His own .45 bucked in his hand, waist high, at the purple flame lance that came from Harmless's gun. Two, three times he squeezed the trigger then threw the empty gun at the place where Harmless should be. With a bound he was in the office and away from the door.

It was then he heard the thick, pulpy cough and knew his bullets had found their target. He stood unmoving for many seconds. Abruptly a piece of furniture scraped, crashed hollowly to the floor and there followed a thud that could have been nothing but a man's body falling. He waited seconds more. He yanked his own guns from the hook on the wall and left.

At the rear of the jail yard he struck an alley and ran down it toward the edge of town, hesitated, then went on to the next alley. He cut into the street, yet stopped as he came to the front of a house. There he crouched and waited, wondering if he had come too late.

He did not have long to wait. From inside the sound of someone moving about served

to quiet his fears. Suddenly the door swung open, flooded a brief rectangle of light into the night, and closed behind the figure of a man. It was Sheriff Parsons who stood there, looking up the street, swinging about his burly waist a belt, weighted down by two holstered, ivory-handled Colts.

Parsons took two quick steps toward the street before he felt the gun jab into his back. He froze in his tracks, speechless, while swift hands flipped his guns from their holsters.

"Quiet, Parsons! Put your hands down and step lively. We're callin' on Doc Roberts."

Parsons moved, turned up the street, and they walked farther toward the edge of town.

"You'll hang for this, Scott!" the sheriff said huskily when he had picked up the courage to speak.

"The second time you've mentioned that. Save your wind!"

Behind them from the jail came the excited sound of voices. Once Larry told Parsons to hurry as he heard the sound of horses moving up the street. But the riders went the other way, and then they were turning in at the doctor's house. A voice from out of the shadows of the porch stopped them.

"That's far enough. What'll you have?"

"Let us in, Quill," answered Larry, knowing the voice. The other didn't answer, but Larry caught the quick surprised intake of breath. Before they entered, Larry said to Quill, "I want to know where Baxter is. When you find out, come back and let me know."

Dave Martin was inside with the doctor. His face was lined and drawn, but as soon as he saw Larry a smile erased the look.

"Matt told me you'd be here," he said, causing Larry to wonder how Matt had been able to guess what his actions would be.

Dave's glance took in Larry's bloody sleeve, and he came over to look at the wounded arm.

"Never mind that, Dave. Take us in to the Squire."

The sheriff had not moved since he entered the room. Now, at Larry's words, he fidgeted nervously, sensing in them something ominous. Dave indicated a door at the rear, and Larry motioned the sheriff toward it. In a plainly furnished room they found the Squire. He smiled wanly as he saw who it was that came in. His face was pale, and Larry had an indefinable regret at what he knew the little gambler would be facing once he was well enough to leave his bed.

"Can you talk, Squire?" he asked.

The Squire nodded.

"Then tell Parsons who it was killed Ozzie Weir."

The Squire gave Parsons a long look then said simply, "Baxter!"

The words struck Parsons like a whiplash. He gulped and swallowed thickly.

"You knew it, didn't you?" Larry asked, suddenly convinced that more than surprise showed in the sheriff's face.

"Me?" Parsons queried, hoarsely. "If I'd have known. . . ."

"Cut it!" snapped Larry. "Go ahead, Squire. Tell Parsons why Ozzie was beefed."

"He knows," the Squire told them. "Ozzie had Baxter's hide-out spotted . . . knew where he was runnin' the herds he lifted. Baxter's the one, lawman. Stretch his neck and this county's beef will stay in home pasture."

The sheriff mumbled an oath, trying to pick up his courage. "Scott, if I'd known. . . ."

"What would you have done?" Dave cut in, his level gaze fixed on the blubbering lawman.

"He'd been arrested long ago," said Parsons with a show of bravado.

"We're askin' you to do that now!"

Dave intoned the words.

Parsons started to speak, then his jaw clamped shut as some inner emotion guided him. His bearing of confidence gave way and before those who watched him he seemed to shrink into himself.

"Baxter's in town," Dave put in, and the words put a trace of fear in Parsons's eyes.

"I can't go after him tonight," the sheriff said lamely, groping for a way out. "Every ranny he's hired is in town tonight."

"They're mostly drunk," said Larry. "No trouble there."

"There's Harmless Ogden. . . ."

"Dead!"

The one word went unquestioned, yet every man in the room connected it with the dull roar of gunshots they had heard minutes ago. Parsons thought for long moments, until the quiet of the room oppressed them all with a sense of indefinable embarrassment.

"You're yellow, Parsons!"

It was the Squire who spoke quietly, accusingly. Parsons whirled on the gambler, glad of someone on whom to vent his wrath.

"Yellow! By all that's holy, you low-lived. . . ."

"Parsons!" Larry's single word stopped

the sheriff like a blow in his face. "I'm goin' after Baxter."

Parsons was not the only one who stared at Larry. Dave, too, looked at him as though he had not heard right.

"You can't, Larry! You'll be one against twenty."

Quill entered the room at that moment, walked over to Larry, and spoke in an undertone. Larry nodded, looked once more toward Parsons, and said: "I'm leavin', Parsons. Don't interfere!"

He was out of the room before Dave, helpless in the face of this recklessness, could utter a word to stop him. Hardly had the door closed behind Larry when Dave reached for his Colt, raised it from the holster, and leveled it at Parsons.

"You and me are goin' to stop this killin'," he said.

VIII

"GUNMAN'S LAST DRAW"

"Crump Mundy's ridin' point for the border," Quill told Larry as the two walked toward the lights that winked up the street. It was an hour before dawn, yet the town was alive with people who would not seek their beds again this night.

"Anyone tailin' him?" asked Larry, only half way interested.

"He cut out alone . . . on a high lonesome."

Larry accepted the news, not caring. Crump's luck would give out on him one day, and death would take him, probably at the hands of one of his victims. Below the border they knew his breed.

For the first time Larry noticed his arm. It was when the blood had run down and onto his hand that he realized he must be losing a lot of it. He stopped, asked Quill to tie up the arm above the wound. Then

they went on again, neither of them speaking. The arm was starting to throb.

A little further on Quill said, "I sent Fay to round up the Box M crew."

"I can do this alone, Quill."

"Huh-uh! You're crowdin' your luck too much."

He did not answer, admitting to himself that it mattered little how many guns faced him or were in back of him in this encounter. He would meet Baxter and that was all he wanted. For a moment a thought of Mona crowded in on him, and there was a pang of regret at what he was going into, a regret intense and painful.

"Better take to the walk," Quill's voice interrupted his thoughts. They were nearing the jail. Larry nodded, for on the walk they would have only one flank exposed. "Baxter sent most of his gunnies out scrubbin' the brush for you."

The news should have been reassuring, but again Larry did not care. The edge was wearing off the nervous excitement he had felt for the last hour, and he knew he was tired, weary to exhaustion. He cursed softly, trying to summon that quick energy he knew he should feel at this moment, but it would not come.

Along the street they passed groups of

men who were discussing the jail break, others who voiced their wonder at Parsons's disappearance. So intent were they in hearing and telling of the events of the night in the murky darkness that Larry and Quill passed by unnoticed.

As they came abreast the Aces Wild, Larry thumbed loose the butts of the two .38s and made for the doors. He edged through, and Quill came directly behind. The quiet in the room warned him something unusual was taking place. His eyes shuttled quickly over the crowd until they found Baxter. The Slash B owner was standing at the bar, one arm extended, and with that arm was clutching Matt Weir by the shoulder. As Larry looked, Baxter shook the old prospector easily, as though it were no effort. It was plain to see that Matt was not pretending this time. He was dead drunk. Baxter's voice broke through the silence.

"Here's the man who helped Scott escape!" He slapped Matt alongside the face so hard that all could hear the click of Matt's teeth. "You're a pack of sneakin' coyotes if you let this man live 'til sunup."

Baxter looked up then, his dark face twisted and ugly, and by chance his glance rested directly on Larry. His expression broke, changed, and he pushed those on

either side of him away. Matt, free now from Baxter's grasp, reeled and pitched to the floor.

Baxter's next action was instinctive. He shot a quick glance around the room to see how many of his men were there. The glance reassured him, for he took two steps forward, planted his feet apart, and sighed aloud: "Scott!"

Others looked now, and there were those who knew Larry and told the others. Then all of them, seeing what was coming, backed out of line of the expected bullets.

"Fill your hand, Baxter!" Larry said quietly, and something within him hardened his nerve until he gloried in this moment.

"You looked for it, Scott. You'll get it! Save the county the expense of a trial." Baxter's words cut through the hush of the room.

Larry waited, knowing the futility of words, sensing that the other's talk signified an uncertainty. There was nothing, no warning whatever, that gave away Baxter's sudden move! All Larry knew was that his start for his own draw was a split-second behind Baxter's. Yet his confidence was supreme, his movement one lightning-smooth flow of muscle. His down-hanging hand flicked upwards, and no man there would see the

smooth play of motion that flashed the .38 hip high, crashing out! Baxter lurched from the impact of the bullet even before his own Colt cut loose, yet it was not enough to spoil completely his aim. A blow smacked Larry's thigh, high up, throwing him backwards. He steadied himself, firing again, and saw the blood gushing from the hole in Baxter's throat. The man was falling, but the five slugs that tore into him kept him erect — until the hammer click told Larry his gun was empty. Baxter sank to his knees, tottered there an instant, then sprawled full length in his own blood.

"Hold it!"

It was Quill who shouted, catching a Slash B man in the act of drawing. He covered the man with his Colt. Steps sounded on the board walk outside, and Larry shifted sideways, bringing the door within his vision. His other .38 was in his hand as Dave Martin burst through the doors, six-gun in hand. Parsons followed after him, stopped dead in his tracks, and stared, bewildered.

It was then that the familiar faces of several Box M hands detached themselves from the group and stepped forward. Eight men with leveled, menacing guns stood lined up alongside Dave Martin when the room began to spin before Larry's eyes. He blinked

wearily, tried to hold objects in focus, and then blackness settled down.

It was as though he had waked from a deep, restful sleep. Above him the *vigas* of the room slanted away to a whitewashed adobe wall. There was no pain — nothing but a sense of peace. Then, slowly, his mind was crowded with the blast of guns and the smell of powder smoke. He tried to move, but the effort was too great, so he lay there slowly letting the torment subside.

He felt a touch on his arm. He turned his head and saw Mona. She had been sitting there, watching him. The perfect oval of her face was outlined against a window where geraniums grew. The blue of her eyes was deep and sparkling like the color of the sky above mountains at dusk. He drank in the vision of her loveliness, and then she bent toward him. Her kiss told him what he had to live for.

In 1940 Dodd, Mead & Company co-sponsored a competition with Street & Smith's *Western Story* for a first Western novel. The winning novel would be awarded a prize of $2,000. It would be serialized in *Western Story* and published in book form by Dodd, Mead. Although Jon Glidden's first stories were published in 1936 and numbered over sixty in all by the middle of 1940, he had yet to write a story longer than 40,000 words. Jon set to work with his customary industry on a novel he titled THE CRIMSON HONDO. It combined, as would many of his subsequent novels, a mystery within a Western setting. Jon's submission was awarded the prize. Its title was changed to "The Crimson Horseshoe" when it ran serially in seven installments in *Western Story* (11/16/40 - 12/28/40). Dodd, Mead published the book version under the same title in 1941. "Lost Homestead" was written shortly after this first novel was completed. It was submitted to Jon's agent on September 9, 1940 and was purchased by *Western Story* for $270 on December 1, 1940 even as his first novel was being showcased in that magazine's pages. It was published in the issue dated April 5, 1941. Henceforth, the name Peter Dawson, either as the author of four more novels serialized in installments

or of stories of varying lengths, became a staple in *Western Story*. "Lost Homestead" was later selected for reprinting in Street & Smith's *Western Story Annual* for 1943.

LOST HOMESTEAD

I

"GUN-BLOCKADED WATER"

Late afternoon of that still, hot day saw dust hanging lazily at almost the exact center of Los Alamos Basin. Down out of the north, from a jagged line of peaks, wound a stream's silvery ribbon. It was marked by a broad green line of trees and lush grass. Half way across the basin, having followed its eastern edge along a maze of drab, torn badlands, the stream swung west past the town of Tres Piedras. Beyond, it bisected the grassy lowlands for close to twenty-five miles. A low notch in the heights to the west marked the place where it left the basin and coursed downward to the desert's hazy floor.

The tail-like streamer following the dust cloud deep in the basin pointed east, in the general direction of a trail that would eventually have a man back across Navajo country and into upper New Mexico. For many

days now the center of that dust haze had crawled west along the trail, almost from its beginning at Santa F. Ten miles a day, occasionally twelve, at rare intervals fifteen, the progress of the four-hundred longhorns whose hoofs churned up that visible sign had been a relentless, onward surging. This afternoon the herd had slowed for the first time in over sixty days. The reason: its goal lay in sight.

Red Knight, owner of the herd, was riding drag, a bandanna tied half way up on his lean face against the dust when Clem Reynolds, his aging *segundo*, appeared through the haze to call sharply above the thirsty bawling of the cattle: "Fence ahead, Red! Only way to the river is down a damned lane! Do I go 'round it?"

Red cuffed back his Stetson to send a sifting line of dust down off the hat's back brim onto his wide shoulders. He scrubbed his forehead with his hand, and his gray eyes narrowed in speculation as he listened to the bawling of the herd. His answer was: "Go down it, Clem!"

That reply only hastened a happening that, either way, would have been inevitable. Red's two wing riders pressed in on the flanks and presently, after a perceptible slowing, the thirsty animals were hemmed

in on either side by the stout lines of a four-wire fence. Red held his roan back until the dust had settled somewhat then put him on at a walk between fields of new corn, ankle-high wheat, and bright green patches of chili. A low 'dobe appeared out of the dust, an overalled figure standing in its shaded yard, leaning on a hoe. Red lifted a hand in greeting, got no answer, and rode on, puzzled by the show of unfriendliness that had met his first wordless interchange with a man of this country.

But he had little time to dwell on this puzzle, for the next moment he heard shouting ahead and the drag slowed, the long-horns impatiently milling and bawling. Then Clem Reynolds appeared once more out of the dust fog, quirting his brown gelding, bellowing at a steer that blocked his path. His pony rammed the steer's flank and came on, shying from flying hoofs. Clem, face flushed angrily, pulled rein.

"We're stopped!" he said in a grating voice. "Right at the river! Bunch of jaspers loaded down with artillery! They say we can't go on!"

A rock-hard gravity took Red Knight's ordinarily good-humored face. He eyed his foreman as though wanting to make sure no joke lay behind his words. Then: "Let's go

have a look." He started ahead, retracing Clem's route along the crowded fence to the left. A swing rider appeared out of the fog close at hand, and Red called: "Get back and hold 'em, Ed. Send Tex up front!"

The roan, wise to his business, nicely avoided the arcing horns and the angered rushes of the saltier bulls going along the crowded lane. The smell of water was strong in the air, and the herd, thirst crazy, pressed vainly against the leaders. Red finally rode clear of that dusty welter of packed animals to find two of his men, Jim Rhodes and Frank Phelan, holding the lead steers at the mouth of the lane that emptied down onto the sands along the river bank. Gathered below, along the rush of the clear-water stream, were twelve riders headed by a massively built man mounted on a black stallion. This individual sat with a Winchester sloped across the horn of his saddle. There were more rifles behind him. Not a man of the dozen lacked a thigh holster. A few wore two.

"Keep 'em there!" Red called to Phelan and put the roan down toward the men who blocked the way.

He was keenly aware of his empty thigh. This morning, on breaking camp, he had ordered all guns checked in with the cook

who had driven his chuck wagon on ahead and now had obviously also been stopped at the river. Red's motive in taking the guns from his men had been distinctly honorable. It didn't seem friendly to come riding into strange country wearing weapons.

He stopped ten feet above the man on the black. "What's the trouble?" he inquired mildly.

"You don't go across," was the prompt answer. The speaker appeared to be close to Red's age, crowding thirty. He was handsome in a blunt way, his square, good-featured face darkly bronzed. Tall, he lacked an inch or two of Red's height, which was six two. But he was heavier and, in contrast to Red's dusty outfit of worn boots and faded denims, his whipcords, fancy-stitched boots, and blue-and-white checked shirt were glaringly immaculate. One thing completed the contrast. His hair was black, Red's a bright sorrel.

"How come?" was Red's steady query.

The man lifted massive shoulders in a shrug. "We say so."

"You're sheriff?"

The man laughed, shook his head. "Just plain Duke Clanton."

There was a touch of arrogance to Clanton's looks that galled Red. But he didn't

255

give any outward sign of that as he drawled: "These critters haven't tasted water for three days, Clanton. That's about as far as they can go without it."

"Tough," Clanton said with mock-sorrowful expression. He let it go at that.

There was something here Red couldn't understand. He tried to find his answers by saying: "I'm Knight, from Texas. I was in last fall filin' on graze across there." He lifted a hand to indicate the low westward hills. "Had a man on it all winter, workin' on a tank and stringin' wire. Now I'm bringin' in stuff to. . . ."

"You ain't," drawled Clanton. "And Spence left here in March."

At Red's elbow Clem Reynolds asked sharply: "Why would Ned do that?" Clem counted Spence, the man Red had left on the homestead, his best friend.

"Climate wasn't right for his health," was Clanton's answer.

"Let's get this straight." Red held down his anger. "I'm on my way across the river. I'll water and keep straight on, if that's what's worryin' you."

"Was I worryin'?" came Clanton's smooth drawl. "We say you don't cross the river. You don't even water here."

It was bluntly put, a challenge Red had

no way of answering. Once again he was aware of his empty thigh. He was also aware of the bawling, crowding herd behind, of his tired crew.

"You can't deny a man water," was the only reply he could think to give Clanton. "These critters can't go back. They wouldn't live to do it! What law . . . ?"

Again that coarse laugh of Clanton's rang out. "What about the law? We make our own! Brother, you got a few things to learn! First off, we don't want cattle north of the river. Stay over here with the nesters, if you want, but don't set foot across there." He jerked his head toward the narrow stream's opposite shore.

"We can settle that later," Red said. "Right now you can let me through to water. I'll keep my stuff on this side."

"Damned right you will! All the way. We shoot the first critter that dips snout in this creek!" Clanton's rifle nosed up.

But for the thing that happened then, Red Knight might have led his crew to a disastrous end. A steer broke through the two point riders and charged toward the stream. Lazily almost, Clanton lifted the Winchester to his shoulder, following the animal's loping charge. The steer waded into the stream, and his head dropped to drink. Clanton's

rifle spoke sharply. The steer stiffened, lunged a step, and fell over on his side, his blood darkly clouding the clear water. Clanton's bullet had smashed his heart.

Then, as Red's boots were swinging out to gouge the roan into a charge at Clanton, a voice called from behind: "Hold it! Knight, come across here!"

Turning, Red caught the nod of a man in bib overalls leaning on the corner post of the nearest fence. The man added: "Don't commit suicide!"

Red gave Clanton a long level glance which also showed him several drawn six-guns in the rank of men behind. He lifted reins and brought the roan wheeling around to the fence.

"My handle's Jennifer," the man in overalls announced. "Toad Jennifer. I own this farm." With a gesture he included what lay behind the fence he leaned on. He looked up squint-eyed at Red. "Better go easy with Clanton. He's boss on the Circle D."

Red remembered having heard of the outfit. "Tom Dennis's?"

Jennifer nodded. "Was Tom's. But the old man died this last fall, leavin' his daughter owner. Clanton rods for her. Sheepman!" His last word was added scornfully.

"Sheep?" Red's glance went to Clanton

258

again. "I thought Dennis was a big name in cattle."

"It was. But Clanton talked the girl into stockin' the layout with woollies. Ain't you winded the stink yet?"

Red heard someone approaching and turned to see Clanton coming up on them. Clanton eyed Jennifer sourly. "Don't get any ideas, Toad," he drawled. Then, to Red: "And don't pay him to let you water stuff inside his line. That won't work, either."

Jennifer flared: "I guess I got a right to. . . ."

"To do exactly as we say." Clanton slapped the oiled stock of the rifle. "Knight, turn around and go back! We don't want any more ten-cow outfits in this country!"

Clem Reynolds rode up, saying: "Red, we can't hold them much longer!" He looked at Clanton, his old face apoplectic. "Shuck them guns and step down, and I'll beat your liver white, mister!"

"Easy, Clem!" Red said quickly. "Better start pushin' 'em back." He saw that his old foreman was on the verge of causing serious trouble. Clem glared a last time at Clanton then rode back to the head of the lane to give orders to the crew.

"That's showin' sense," Clanton observed suavely.

"I'll repeat that invitation," Red drawled, openly running his hand along his weaponless thigh.

"Another time." Clanton rode back to join his men.

"Callin' that gent a skunk is abusin' the name of a noble animal!" Jennifer muttered. "Well, I tried. Was only goin' to charge you a nickel a head to let you water inside my fence."

"Thanks," was all Red could think of to say. He was about to join Clem and the others when a thought made him say: "We'll be camped out on the flats tonight, Jennifer. I'd appreciate knowin' more about this. The food ain't so fancy, but I'd like to buy you your supper."

"I'll be there," was Jennifer's answer.

II

"ADVICE FROM A BASIN MAN"

The lights of Tres Piedras pinpointed the night off to the northwest, seeming feebly to mirror the star-sprinkled and vast reach of cobalt sky that was crystal clear except for a long belt of thin clouds in the west. The chuck wagon was a faint grayish blob below the redly glowing fire. The night's stillness was ridden with the plaintive bawling of the thirsty herd. Red, a generous supper under his belt, listened to the off-key chant of a night rider and wondered if those clouds off there meant that it sometimes rained in this dry country. He glanced at Clem then at Toad Jennifer.

"So we really are licked," he mused. "I thought I'd find a way around it."

Jennifer shook his near-bald head. The three of them had had the fire to themselves these last twenty minutes. The others had either gone back to riding circle around the

herd or to their blankets for all were worn out by the trying three-hour battle of pushing the stubborn longhorns back up the narrow lane and out across the flats to this spot, three miles from the creek.

"There ain't any way around it," declared Jennifer. "This Clanton has guns to back him. He's got all them outfits north of the creek to raisin' sheep. They're makin' money, and they'll fight."

"But this Dennis girl," Red insisted. "Her old man was half longhorn, if what you say is true. Where's her pride?"

"Burned out, same as old Tom's was. He took a lickin' two years runnin' on a bad drought. It whittled down the outfit some. He left the girl with a loan at the bank and half his range burned out. It must've been easy for Clanton to swing her over. Add to that his courtin' her and her likin' same and you have your answers. There ain't an oversupply of men hereabouts that could fill Duke Clanton's boots."

"Where's your law?" Clem asked, his voice sounding tired and dried up.

Jennifer chuckled softly. "Where it's been for the past ten years. Tom Dennis put Harvey Jenkins in office, and Clanton's bunch will keep him there. Anything the Circle D does is right by Harv. Same as it

was before Dennis cashed in. Someone swung a powerful big sticky loop in here last year. Seemed partial to Circle D stuff. When Dennis blamed us small outfits, Jenkins backed him. That's another thing."

"What is?" Red asked when the basin man hesitated.

"This rustlin'. Dennis's guess was way wide of the mark. I know my neighbors. They're honest. They didn't have to steal to make a livin'. All the same, we got blamed. It's just one more reason why Gail Dennis let Clanton sell her on sheep. Now she thinks she's gettin' even. They've made the creek a boundary. No cattle north of it. Rammin' it down our throats, so to speak."

The silence ran out, broken only occasionally now by the bawling of a thirsty, wakeful animal. Red's tanned face was a mask of gravity as he stared into the coals of the fire. Finally he drawled: "And I'm stuck with four hundred critters that'll be four hundred carcasses unless they get water within the next two days, three at the outside. Well, I won't sit here and take it!"

"I've been thinkin'," Jennifer said. "There ain't but two parties in the valley that could help you any. One's Doc Masker, owner of the saloon in town. He might buy up your critters and take a chance on turnin' some

money resellin' 'em. He'll drive a hard bargain."

"Who's the other?" Red queried.

"Gail Dennis."

Red sat straighter. He laughed, a laugh that sent Toad Jennifer's eyes down to the gun at his hip. Toad had noticed that the whole crew now wore guns and was privately thankful they hadn't when meeting Clanton's bunch, which outnumbered them.

"That's a hot one!" drawled Red.

Jennifer cocked his head speculatively. "She might buy. I can't get it out of my craw that she don't know how you was treated today. She ain't hardhearted enough to deny a man water for his animals when they're near dead from thirst. It's an idea, Knight. You might try and see her."

"How would I go about it?"

"See Doc Masker first. Then go to the girl. Get 'em to biddin' against each other."

"But whichever way it goes, I lose."

Jennifer nodded reluctantly. "Seems like you do."

Red came erect, thumbing alight a match and holding it to a newly rolled cigarette. "Clem," he drawled, "we're takin' a slight *pasear* around."

"Where to?"

"Down to the river."

Jennifer shook his head. "Not a chance. Clanton's men are ridin' the creek. Poke your head in there and you'll run into the same trouble you did this afternoon. Only more of it."

"That's what I'm after tonight. Trouble!"

"Suit yourself." Jennifer shrugged. Then he looked up at Red. "How come you ain't inquired after Spence?" he asked.

"Too many other things to think about," Red admitted guiltily. Strangely enough, he'd almost forgotten Spence, the man he'd left on the homestead last fall. "What do you know about him?"

"Only that the last time he was seen was in town, at Doc Masker's place. Duke Clanton and four or five of his men cleaned him down to his boots and underwear in a stud game. Next mornin' he'd disappeared. The day after his jughead was found down on the desert, draggin' the hull under his belly. That was three months ago. No one ever found him."

"Dead?" Clem asked in a hollow voice.

Again Jennifer shrugged. This time he added no word to that gesture.

Clem stood up, looking at Red. "What're we waitin' on?" he said acidly. "I got to do somethin' to keep from goin' loco!"

As they walked out of the dim circle of

firelight, Jennifer called after them: "Mind if I wait here till you get back? I'd sort of like to know how you come out."

"Help yourself to blankets," Red said, waving in the general direction of the chuck wagon. Then, as they went to the rope corral and got their ponies, he forgot about Jennifer, too preoccupied with his other troubles to give the man another thought.

III

"THE WOMAN IN THE HOTEL"

The town of Tres Piedras, so named for the three rocky buttes that rose half a mile to the south of the creek behind it, seemed only half alive as Red and Clem rode its street at nine-thirty.

"Some dump! Walks rolled up already," Clem observed sourly, as they came between the rows of false fronted stores. He nodded ahead. "Would that be Masker's joint?"

"Looks like it." Red swung across, and they put their ponies in at the saloon's tie-rail. A barely discernible painted sign on the face of the broad wooden walk awning read **Rosebud Bar** and below it **R. J. Masker, Prop.**

"Funny," Clem observed, as they ducked under the tie-rail and crossed the walk, "but I hadn't expected ever to hit a town as dry as this and want a drink less."

Red made no reply but shouldered in through the batwing doors, his eyes squinted against the rude glare of overhead lamps that cut the thin smoke fog of a barn-like room. The Rosebud was unpretentious, even for so small a town as Tres Piedras. Wider than it was deep, the bar and a door-way occupied the back wall. To the right were faro and blackjack layouts, to the left two poker tables. Half a dozen men were at the bar, four more seated around one poker layout. Red's glance went to the latter and remained there.

Duke Clanton was one of the four, sitting with his back to the saloon's side wall. As the doors swung shut behind Clem, Clanton's glance lifted and met Red's, and a slow smile broke across his wide face. Seeing that smile, the others turned and also looked toward the doors.

Sudden decision started Red across there. Under his breath, he warned: "Stay set, Clem!" He stopped close to the nearest chair at the table, looking at Clanton and drawling: "This is luck!" He was at ease, feeling better than he had any time during the last six hours. Here was his chance to even the score with Clanton. Clem had his back covered, and a cool nervelessness was settling through him. No one at the table

made a reply, yet wariness touched the eyes of all four.

"Go for your iron, Clanton!" Red said abruptly, deciding not to waste more words.

Clanton's left hand folded his cards and then lay on the table. "No dice," he said. "I ain't lookin' for trouble, Knight."

"I am! All you've got!"

"Don't let him ride you, boys!" Clanton said none too steadily.

Here, sitting calmly before Red, refusing to fight, was the man who was costing him his future in this country. He heard Clem drawl behind him: "Keep your hands in sight, apron!" and was aware of the barkeep raising his hands.

Then, still sure of himself, Red hooked a boot over the rung of the nearest Clanton man's tilted chair and pulled. The chair skidded from under its occupant, and the man went down heavily. Yet, instead of taking offense, he scrambled to his feet.

"You can't make me mad, brother!" he said quickly.

Once again Red thrust sharply with his boot, this time against the table edge. The table caught Duke Clanton in the stomach and tilted sideways away from him, spilling chips, money, and cards onto the floor with

a rattling thud that made the planking tremble.

Still Duke Clanton made no move. His smile returned, and he drawled: "We could talk this over, Knight!"

Just then a voice that Red recognized as his foreman's gave a painful grunt. Then Clem was swearing saltily and another voice was saying: "Lift 'em, stranger!"

Red didn't turn until the wary tightness of Clanton's smile relaxed, and the Circle D man said blandly: "You've got a gun lined at your spine, Knight!"

Facing about, Red was brought face to face with a man standing close behind him. In one hand the man held a gun lined at him. In the other hung Clem's horn-handled .45. Clem, off to one side now, was pale and holding his right wrist. It was obvious to Red that his foreman had been surprised by the entrance of Clanton's man through the doors behind him.

A chair scraped. Red faced Clanton again. The Circle D foreman pushed the overturned table aside and came in close to Red. "I ought to fix you for a set of store teeth, Knight," he drawled. "Instead, I'm makin' you a proposition."

Red stood there silently, trying to judge where he could hit Clanton to make the

most of the one blow he felt was all he'd be able to throw before getting a bullet in the back.

"You'll like it, too," Clanton said. "I want to buy your herd. Or rather Miss Dennis does."

Red shook his head. "No deal."

Clanton's bushy black brows raised slightly in surprise. "Thinkin' of Doc Masker?" he queried. "Because if you are, you're fresh out of luck. Doc's away. He'll be gone a week."

"It's still no deal."

"Isn't Gail Dennis's money as good as Masker's? I can offer you spot cash within an hour. Within ten minutes, if you'll wait while I go across to the hotel and see if she's available."

"What the devil, boss?" said one of the trio, a dark-faced half-breed who'd been at the table with Clanton. "She's. . . ."

"Shut up, Pete!" Clanton snapped in the first show of outright anger Red had seen him display. "Want to see her, Knight?" he queried pressingly.

Reason was beginning to dissipate Red's anger. Clanton was offering him the only way out of this predicament. It galled him to give in to the man, but after a moment he nodded his answer.

"I'll be right back," Clanton said and stepped around Red and across through the doors which swung shut sharply behind him.

Red looked back at Clem and, ignoring the others, said: "How about that drink, partner?"

They stepped unchallenged across to the bar. As the barkeep set the bottle before them, he said in a hoarse whisper: "Stranger, you better make tracks while you got the chance!" He nodded toward the alley door nearby.

Red smiled wryly, poured their drinks, and emptied his glass at a gulp. Ordinarily he felt no need for whiskey. But the warmth of the liquor seemed to steady his nerves and, Clem's glass also empty, he poured another. He knew that Duke Clanton had level-headedly put aside a personal grudge for some obscure reason. His long acquaintance with trouble and the ways of men in trouble told him that something unexpected was going to happen, something so important that it made Clanton willing to ignore an insult.

He was draining the last drop of that second drink when Clanton reappeared at the doors. The Circle D foreman said briefly: "She'll see you. Across the street."

"Come along, Clem," Red said and went out the doors.

Following Clanton across the street, Red was aware that Clanton's men were coming along behind him. Clanton made no pretense at friendliness but walked up the broad steps of the hotel verandah and into the lobby. He nodded to a door in the right corner of the lobby, saying briefly: "She's in there. Go ahead."

The room Red entered was small, furnished with cheap deal chairs and tables, a writing room. A woman sat behind one of the tables near a window, and Red's first glimpse of her made him halt in surprise a moment before he came on into the room.

He had expected something different, a woman with more looks, refinement. This woman had a coarse appearance; her face, rouged and powdered, might once have been pretty but now showed age.

"Miss Dennis," Clanton said, "this is Knight."

The woman nodded. "Sit down," she invited.

Red took a chair, annoyed at the familiarity of the smile that accompanied her words. Clanton came over, carrying another chair, calling back to the door: "It's all right, boys. We don't need company." He gave

273

Clem, who stood leaning against the wall alongside Red, a scowl and sat down. "Better let him have it straight out, Gail," he said.

The woman nodded. "That's the way I do business. Take it or leave it!"

Her manner irritated Red. His opinion of the late Tom Dennis suffered some revision. His opinion of Toad Jennifer changed somewhat, too, for the homesteader had spoken respectfully of Gail Dennis.

"Take what?" he inquired.

"Her offer." Clanton gave the woman a look. "Tell him."

"Twenty-five hundred," she said flatly. "And that's every damn' cent you'll get!"

Profanity from the mouth of a woman was something Red had rarely heard outside the walls of a saloon. But he overlooked it as his mind took in the shock of her words. Twenty-five hundred dollars for his herd!

"That's barely six dollars a head," he drawled. "These critters of mine are fat, even if they are thirsty. No old crowbaits, either, most of 'em three-year-olds! They'd bring thirty dollars on the open market."

"This isn't the open market," Clanton reminded him.

In the following silence a fly buzzed at the hot chimney of the lamp and fell wing-

burned to the table top. Streetward sounded the clop-clop-clop of a fast-walking horse. Clem shifted his position, his shirt sleeve rubbing audibly against the wallpaper. Red looked up at him.

"Take that or nothin'!" Clanton put in.

"What'll you do with the herd?" Red asked the woman.

She shrugged, and her look was undecided. Her hand went up to smooth down a lock of her lusterless mouse-colored hair.

Clanton put in quickly: "Get it on its feet and drive south to Tucson. Make money."

"While I take my lickin'."

Clanton nodded. Red looked at Clem. A barely perceptible lift of the shoulders told him that Clem was as much at a loss as he was himself.

Abruptly, Red said: "You spoke of payin' cash."

Clanton gave the woman a meaningful glance. She reached down under the table, and her hand came up and tossed a tight roll of paper money across the ink-spattered table. "Count it!"

"And give us a bill of sale," Clanton drawled.

Red counted the bills. Twenty-five hundred dollars. He hunched sideward toward

Duke Clanton as he pushed the roll deeply into a pocket of his Levi's.

Suddenly, his shoulder close to Clanton's, he threw his body to the side and up in a swift lunge. His shoulder caught Clanton on the jaw, throwing him off balance as he tried to dodge. Then Red was on his feet.

Braced that way, he put all the drive of his tall frame behind the swing of his right fist. The woman screamed. Clanton's hand dipped toward his thigh. His big fist was closing on gun butt as Red's knuckles slammed his jaw. The blow lifted Clanton's heavy frame half up out of the chair. His body went loose, his eyes rolled to the whites, and he sagged down and sprawled at full length on the floor. Before he had straightened out, Red had stooped to snatch his heavy .45 from holster.

Red pivoted toward the door in time to catch a Clanton man coming through it. The woman, on her feet and cringing back to the wall, screamed again as the .45 in Red's hand exploded. The man in the doorway choked out a startled groan, and his right arm hung limply. He lunged back out of the door, colliding with a second man as Red sent another bullet after him.

"The window, Clem!" Red said. Picking up the chair he'd been sitting on, he hurled

it through the lower sash of the nearby window.

Clem climbed through the jagged opening. Red followed feet first, pausing astride the sill to shoot again into the lobby. Then he jumped, his legs took up the drive of his six-foot fall, and the two of them ran down the passageway between the hotel and the adjoining building. Coming onto the street two buildings below and across from the saloon, they chose a pair of horses at the nearest tie-rail and pounded out of town before the first shouts announcing their flight echoed along the street.

A mile from town Clem drew close to Red's pony to say: "Did you bust his neck?"

Red grinned broadly at his foreman. "He'll live." Then he asked, shouting above the pound of their ponies' hoofs: "Did Jennifer say what color Gail Dennis's hair was?"

Clem looked puzzled. "No. Why?"

"Want to make me a bet?"

"Depends."

"That the woman back there was not Gail Dennis!"

"I'll be hornswoggled!" was all Clem Reynolds could think to answer.

Twenty minutes later, when they had wakened Toad Jennifer out of a sound sleep at the cow camp, Red was asking: "What

does Gail Dennis look like, Toad? What color's her hair?"

Toad frowned, muttering under his breath at the rough handling the last few seconds had given him. "Who in tarnation cares? It's light, corn-colored."

"And this woman could have been mated to a mouse." Red laughed long and loud.

"What woman? What's so funny?" demanded Jennifer.

"Tell you later. Right now we've got to move."

"Where to?" Jennifer was reaching for his hat.

"Anywhere but here. We're movin' the herd. On west. I've got an idea."

"It'd better be good!" drawled Clem, leaving to rout the four sleeping members of the crew from their blankets.

Red was looking toward the west where what looked like a high bank of hills now blotted out the stars. Those dark masses, backing the hills that edged the desert, hadn't been there an hour ago. They were clouds. Red Knight was gambling on them.

IV

"RED'S GAMBLE"

"Clem, get the herd movin'," Red told his old foreman as soon as the crew was gathered at the now nearly dead fire. "Push west, fast as you can. Nels," he spoke to the cook, "hitch your team. I'm going with you. Tex, your job's the horses. Every man take a rifle. If you're stopped. . . ." He hesitated a moment then added: "But you won't be. It'll take 'em a while to find the camp. By then we'll be gone."

"What's all this addin' up to?" Clem asked.

"Water," was Red's cryptic answer. "When you get out a ways turn those two horses loose. The ones we came out on."

"How about me?" Jennifer asked. "Ain't you got another job?"

Red's glance went to the basin man gratefully. "I want to move the herd five miles, better seven," he explained. "Is there a wash

off there you're sure will run water if it rains?"

"Why sure, Red," Jennifer said, "they all run . . . if it rains. But it ain't goin' to. Those clouds don't mean a thing."

"Maybe not. But you ride the chuck wagon with Nels and me. And if your back's strong enough to heave some dirt, you can help us throw an earth dam across a wash and catch the run, if there's rain."

"You're doin' this for nothin', Red," was Clem's gloomy reminder. "You sold those critters."

"Clanton can't produce a bill of sale," Red said.

"But there's still the sheriff," Jennifer reminded him.

"And there's Gail Dennis," was Red's reply.

"What about her?" This from Clem.

"I don't know yet. But I do know I won't let these critters dry up and blow away. Get goin'! If the law stops us, we've tried anyway."

The next hour seemed interminable to Red Knight. Sitting the jolting, swaying seat of the chuck wagon between Nels Hansen and Toad Jennifer, he studied the dark cloud bank to the west until his eyes ached. He vainly tried to catch the taint of rain

riding the cool night air, but only the tang of dust and the smell of horses and harness leather blended with its freshness.

"It never rains this late in the spring," Jennifer said once.

"But it's going to tonight."

After that they sat in silence, the cook following Jennifer's brief instructions. The miles fell behind. They climbed to more broken country where the hills were bare and treeless under the starlight.

Finally Jennifer said, "This ought to do," as they brought the dark gash of a deep wash in sight. "This thing'll run water if she rains a drop south of the creek."

Red swung around from a wheel hub as the team came to a stand. "Drag out the shovels, Nels," he ordered. "Then take a horse and go find Tex and have him bring his bunch across here." The cook would have little difficulty in finding the wrangler, for they had come directly west since leaving the camp ground.

Work was the only thing that seemed to ease Red's mind, and work he did, bending over a shovel at the bottom of the high-banked wash. He channeled out a shallow trough across the bed of the arroyo, marking the line of a dam to be thrown up. Jennifer also began to work. For an hour and a half

they shoveled in silence. Red paused only twice and both times climbed the far bank to stand on the wash's rim and peer upward at the sky. The last time he saw the clouds advancing darkly, their upper reaches almost directly overhead.

"Want to lay money on it, Jennifer?" he called. But the only reply that came to him was a solid grunt as the basin man strained against the weight of his shovel.

Shortly after that Nels Hansen slid down the bank and spelled Jennifer. In ten more minutes Tex Olds was there with another shovel from the chuck wagon. No one spoke.

They heard the herd moving up out of the east a long time later. By then the bank of dirt and gravel running across the wash had risen knee high. And only then did Red surrender his shovel.

"Keep at it!" he called, climbing the east bank.

Weariness was cutting him bone deep. His shirt clung to his back wetly, and his curly red hair was sweat plastered as he took off his Stetson to blot his forehead. In the saddle of Tex's pony, swinging out from the chuck wagon in the direction of the sound made by the herd, he felt a splashing drop of rain strike his left hand. He reined in

quickly. A fitful gust of wind whipped another drop in at his face, then another struck his right shoulder with a weighty drive.

All the weariness went out of him as he touched Tex's gray with a light spur. He felt like shouting, singing, riding fast to feel the whip of the now strengthening breeze cut his face, but he took his time, his thankfulness a sobering thing. Then, gradually, his elation was wiped away by the knowledge that he'd gained only a temporary victory. The pressing bulge of the money roll in his right pants pocket was a grim reminder of things to come.

When he had found the herd and his old foreman, Clem said: "You must've brought along one of them crystal balls to gaze into, fella. What do we do?" They both wore ponchos now against the gusty flurries of rain.

Red took him on ahead, pointing out the wash at a place where it widened and the bank sloped less steeply. "Hold 'em here till it runs, Clem, then let 'em work down. Not too far or they'll tramp down the dam. Send a man to help us throw up more dirt when you've got 'em settled."

The rain was coming in fitful, wind-driven squalls when Red got back to the chuck wagon. He slid down the bank to take Jen-

nifer's shovel and worked with a new strength, ignoring a broken blister on his hand. Frank Phelan appeared to announce that the herd was being held in the wash. Frank got to work with a shovel, and from then on the earthwork dam grew fast.

Red was thankful that lightning and thunder didn't come as the storm hit. A driving, straight-down rain settled in at last. He stood up, leaned on his shovel, and called: "That's all! Now all we have to do is wait."

He looked with satisfaction at the four-foot slanting wall of earth that crossed the wash. There was no trickle of water yet, for the hungry soil in the uplands was soaking in the rain as fast as it fell. But soon now there would come a trickle then a rush of water. If the herd was placed right, if the dam held half an hour, better forty minutes, the animals would be watered and safe on the unstaked graze of this open country.

As they wearily climbed the bank of the wash, they saw a glow shining through the gray curtain of the rain. Coming up on it, Red saw that the cook had built a cedar fire under the wagon. A piece of sheet iron wired below the wooden bed protected the dry planking.

"Got a head on his shoulders, that grub slinger," Jennifer commented admiringly as

they lined up to take steaming hot tin cups of coffee.

The wash began running after the rain had stopped, as the first hint of the false dawn was graying the far horizon. They were all there to see the herd moved slowly down. Up the wash sounded a low roar. Then, around a bend above, came a foot-high and foaming wall of water rushing slowly down, filling the wash from bank to bank.

"Hold 'em," Red called and spurred his pony down the four hundred yards to the dam. There he worked feverishly with a shovel for five minutes, gouging a notch into the dam. Minutes later, when the foaming, debris-strewn water dropped slowly into sight, his effort was rewarded. The water hit the dam, filled in behind it quickly and would have overflowed and washed it away but for the notch that let the overflow escape. Even with the notch, a pool some sixty feet broad was gradually filling in behind.

Clem and his men let the herd drift down to the pool. Soon they stood heads down to the muddy water. Presently, Red saw the flow slackening and used his shovel again and filled in the notch. The water rose slowly and in another hour, when the sun's disk edged over the eastern flats, the pool

was full to within a foot of the top of the dam.

Jennifer, who had stood on the bank above, called suddenly: "Trouble comin', Red!" There was an edge to his voice that made Red climb quickly up the bank to stand beside him.

Jennifer pointed valleyward. Red saw a knot of riders topping a rise three miles away in the direction of the town.

"Clanton and the sheriff, I reckon," Jennifer commented.

"You'd better hit for home and stay clear of this, Jennifer," Red said hurriedly. "Thanks for all you've done. I'll drop around the first chance I get."

Then he was off at a run for the chuck wagon where a black gelding was tied. "Clem, get up here!" he called sharply. He was swinging into the saddle when Clem rode up over the bank. Red pointed at the oncoming horsemen. "Better tell the boys not to get proddy," he said. "If Clanton wants the herd, let him have it. If he's got a warrant for me, tell him anything you want. Tell him I've started south for Tucson. Remember, we don't know a thing about those two jugheads someone stole in town last night."

"Where you goin' if it ain't to Tucson?"

"Across to pay a call on Gail Dennis."

Clem whistled. "Askin' for trouble, ain't you?"

"Clanton's crew will be with him. That means I shouldn't have any trouble getting in to see her."

"When you see her, then what?"

"I don't know." Red turned the black away toward the nearest rise that would conceal him from the advancing posse. Then he paused to add: "Better get yourself some extra tobacco, Clem. You're liable to run short in jail."

"Hey," Clem called as he went away. "You can't let 'em lock me up!" But as Red skirted the rise and rode out of sight, a wide smile broke the severe planes of the old man's mustached face. "Like Hades he don't know what he's doin'!" He turned to the cook. "Nels, you got any extra makin's?"

V

"QUICK SALE"

Red crossed the river west of Tres Piedras, close in to the low hills that edged the desert. Once beyond the stream the look of the country changed indefinably, although it had the same rolling, grassy, tree-dotted outline as that to the south. All at once Red realized what it was that was different. Bunches of sheep grazed in the distance. The white cones of herders' tents showed here and there. Occasionally Red glimpsed a herder and his dog. It was strange not to see cattle grazing a vast, rich stretch of country like this. Something seemed to be lacking, and an impotent anger gradually took Red. Cattle-bred, he couldn't admire a man — or a woman! — who would sell out a range like this to sheep.

With two things to judge by, her foreman and her business, Red could feel little respect for Gail Dennis. The fact that she had

let Clanton talk her into forsaking cattle for sheep convinced him that the girl must be weak willed at best. He was convinced, too, that this errand would be a fruitless one. He tried to think why he had left the chuck wagon, left Clem to the mercy of the posse, and couldn't. He had acted on impulse alone, curious about the girl.

It didn't dawn on him that there was little point in seeing Tom Dennis's daughter, until he had already asked a herder the way to the Circle D. Then, because he would have had to ride ten miles back to the chuck wagon but only three more to the ranch, he went on.

Circle D's headquarters bore the unmistakable signs of good living as Red first looked down on it from half a mile's distance. The house was built of rock, slate-roofed, shaped like a crude U. A quadrangle line of cottonwoods bordered a grassy yard. Outbuildings lay at a generous distance below the house which crested a long slope.

Red came in along a lane between whitewashed pasture fences. A big buckskin stallion was the lone occupant of a small meadow on his right. Across the land, two fine mares and their foals raised their heads to watch him pass. Once again he had a moment of strange anger. Fine horses and

sheep didn't seem to go together.

Closer in, the layout had a deserted look. Red came in warily. Not until he'd left the head of the lane and was passing the biggest of the corrals did he see anyone. The man was evidently the cook, for he came out of a small 'dobe hut and emptied a bucket into a shallow ditch nearby. He paused a moment to look at Red then disappeared through the door. Red's appearance seemed to have caused no more than casual interest.

Climbing the slope from the outbuildings to the house, Red rode a graveled path to the tie-rail outside a picket fence that enclosed a patio. He sat the saddle stiffly a moment, wondering if he was being observed. Then he swung aground and went through the gate and up to the broad, white painted door that was shaded by a wide portal.

His knock went unanswered a long moment. Then the door swung open on a broadly smiling Chinese who tilted his head graciously and waited for Red to speak.

"Miss Dennis in?" Red asked.

"I see. You come in?"

"I'll wait here."

The door swung shut. Red sauntered over and leaned against a roof post. He built a smoke, feeling the tautness of nerve strain

ease out of him. It was pleasant here, cool, the fragrance of flowers filling the air. He revised his opinion of Gail Dennis somewhat. Every sheepman he had known had lived in near squalor, close to his pens, his outfit pervaded by the stench all cattlemen recognized as part of the business. The contrast between what he now found and what he'd expected brought a slow smile to Red's bronzed face.

The door opened abruptly again and the girl who appeared in it caught a trace of that smile. Later, Red was to be thankful for that good beginning, for Gail Dennis in turn smiled and her "Good morning," was as pleasant as though she were speaking to an old acquaintance.

His " 'Mornin', ma'am," was a trifle slow in coming. This girl had a freshness and a look of vivaciousness so foreign to his expectation that he stood a moment in awe of her.

Tall, her figure willowy and with a trace of boyish angularity, Gail Dennis's laughing blue eyes seemed to mock all his former certainties of her. She wore a light blue percale dress, tight waisted, sprigged with a yellow daisy pattern. And her hair was a golden blond, not corn-colored. It was brushed back in a sweeping pompadour

gathered in a knot at the nape of her slender neck.

Red's first impression was of a beautiful face. Then he decided that there was more character than beauty in it. The girl's generous mouth lacked the shallow rosebud quality of surface prettiness, and the sun had tanned her skin a deeper olive than he knew was considered fashionable.

As he hesitated, a slight flush rose into her face. "You wanted to see me?" Her voice had a lilting musical quality that made him eager to hear it again.

"I was told you were the person to see about a certain matter. Fact is, I'm new here and not acquainted with the rules. It's about. . . ."

"You must be Knight, the man who took out the homestead north of here," she said, as he stumbled for an explanation.

Red nodded, puzzled by her continued cordiality.

She went on: "Duke . . . Mister Clanton, my foreman . . . mentioned you."

"He did?" Red's puzzlement was mounting. "Tell you anything in particular?"

"Only that he'd persuaded you not to bring your herd across the river. I suppose that's why you're here, to discuss the sale."

Sheer astonishment held Red speechless

a longer moment than was necessary. There was something he wanted to know, and his next question sought that answer: "What if I've decided not to sell?"

The girl's head tilted gravely as she met his glance. "In that case there's nothing I can do about it. But we'd hoped to keep the river a boundary between the sheep and the cattle. Mister Clanton says they don't mix."

Red stifled his amusement. Clanton obviously omitted details in telling Gail Dennis of their meeting. "So they say," he drawled. "I've been wonderin', ma'am, just why you gave up your father's business."

Her laugh rippled pleasantly. "Wasn't his a rather old-fashioned theory? There's more money in sheep. Dad tried for years to lift his debts by raising cattle. I'm giving sheep a trial."

Red digested her explanation in the sudden knowledge that Clanton was playing a game of his own. He felt the urge to mention exactly what had happened but ruled that out for a selfish reason. Clanton had evidently been ordered to make the attempt to buy up Red's herd rather than let the newcomer take up his homestead. Red intended now to find out what kind of a deal Clanton had been ordered to make.

"I might sell," he said slowly, "but I have a crew to take care of and. . . ."

"I'll be fair with you," the girl put in quickly. "What's your price?"

"Twenty a head. Let's see," — Red made a mental calculation — "that comes to an even eight thousand. You'll be able to sell for thirty a head this fall, providin' you graze 'em right."

Gail Dennis smiled, and a small sigh escaped her. "I was afraid you'd ask more." Abruptly she held out her hand. "It's a bargain, then! Eight thousand. Would you rather see Mister Clanton again or will my check do?"

Red swallowed with difficulty and met the firm clasp of her hand. He got out: "Your check's good, ma'am. If you've got pen and ink, I'll write out a bill of sale."

At that moment she looked beyond him, out the lane and the trail that led southward toward Tres Piedras. "Here comes Duke now," she announced.

Red turned, saw a line of riders in the distance. He did some quick thinking that made him say: "Might be a good joke on Clanton to have everything signed, sealed, and delivered before he gets here. I'll leave without him seein' me, and you can have it as sort of a surprise."

The girl frowned. Red added quickly: "You might as well know the truth, ma'am. Clanton's offer last night was lower than yours by a good bit."

He had guessed shrewdly. This time the color that mounted to the girl's face was brought on by anger. A bright emotion Red couldn't fathom was mirrored in her eyes.

"Sometimes I don't quite know Duke," she murmured then gave Red a look of guilt, as though she'd spoken out of turn.

"You can't blame him for tryin', can you?" he said. "Nor me for turnin' down his offer. Shall we sign the papers now?" He didn't want Clanton to interrupt the completion of this transaction.

The girl turned and went in the door. She was gone less than a minute, returning with a pen and ink, a box of letter paper, and a checkbook. They sat down at a table alongside a broad window. Red wrote out his bill of sale, she a check for eight thousand dollars on the Tres Piedras Bank.

Folding the check, Red thought of something else. "There's a story goin' the rounds that you're on the outs with your neighbors across the river," he said. "It isn't any of my business, but I wondered why."

"When Dad was alive, he had enemies," the girl told him willingly enough. "He

claimed that the ranchers across there stole cattle from him. But that's all over now. Duke has persuaded the ones who hated Dad to bury the hatchet."

With this added proof that Duke Clanton was nicely concealing his dealings with the small ranchers from the girl, Red said good bye, went out to the tie-rail, and untied the black. Swinging out from the picket fence, he called: "I'm headin' out the back way so Clanton won't see me."

Gail Dennis laughed and waved to him.

VI

"CLANTON BACK TRACKS"

An hour and a half later Red was riding the main street in Tres Piedras. He turned into the walk awning that fronted the bank. Crossing the walk, he saw a man wearing a pearl-gray Stetson, whose dark face was vaguely familiar, straighten from his slouch against an awning post and turn to hurry away down the walk. Sure that he had been recognized, Red went in the bank and presented Gail Dennis's check to the cashier. The man examined the check with a frown, said, "Excuse me a moment," and walked over to go in a door with a frosted glass panel lettered **PRESIDENT**.

He reappeared in a few moments with a banded sheaf of paper money. "I didn't have this much on hand," he explained. He counted out eight thousand dollars and pushed the bills through his wicket.

Red said, "Thanks," and went to the en-

trance. He glanced down along the walk. Far down he sighted the man with the light Stetson who had reacted so strangely to his appearance. Accompanying this individual was another from whose shirt front metal glinted brightly in the sunlight.

"Better make tracks, fella!" Red mused aloud but thought of something else. He stepped past his gelding into the street and continued obliquely on across to the hotel. Short of the steps he turned aside to the passageway he and Clem had used in escaping last night.

As he'd expected, the broken window was unrepaired. He looked through it into the empty room. Voices came from the lobby beyond the door. The chair he had thrown through the window last night leaned brokenly against the near wall. The table was pushed out from the wall. Near its outside edge stood a wastebasket Clanton had somehow missed overturning in his fall.

Red took from his pocket the rolled bills Clanton's woman friend had given him last night. He tossed the money in through the window. It struck the edge of the wastebasket, hung there a moment, and fell down out of sight inside.

Recrossing the street, he was lifting a boot to stirrup a quarter minute later when a

gruff voice from behind on the walk called: "You, Knight!"

Red turned. The man who had spotted him less than five minutes ago stood closest, his dark half-breed's face set in a sneer. Beyond him was a spare old man, grizzled, hawkish of face and with pale-blue eyes now stony of look but giving a hint of shiftiness. This one wore a sheriff's silver star.

As Red turned, the lawman stepped slowly forward. "I'll handle this!" he said flatly to his companion. Then: "Goin' someplace, Knight?"

"I thought I was," Red drawled.

"You are. Only it ain't where you think. You're under arrest."

"What for?"

"Robbery, horse stealin', attempted murder!" The sheriff's gun rocked suddenly up at Red. "Get his hogleg, Pete!"

The half-breed eased around Red and took his gun. Then he planted his hand in the middle of Red's back and roughly pushed him toward the walk.

Red caught himself, stiffened, and was wheeling on the man when the sheriff said sharply: "Hold it! No rough stuff, *amigo!* There's Duke down at the office. Come along, Knight."

Red gave the half-breed a brief, unread-

able look before he stepped onto the walk. The sheriff seemed momentarily puzzled over his docile acceptance of his arrest and growled a warning as they started on, side by side: "We're goin' to make this stick, Knight."

Red shrugged, more interested in Pete who flanked him on the other side, walking even with him. The half-breed swaggered, his manner arrogant after his rough handling of the prisoner. Their passage along the walk occasioned some interest. Passing the saddle shop, they had to walk close together to edge through a group that eyed them curiously. Red suddenly slowed his stride. Then, too quickly for Pete to anticipate it, he thrust his leg out and tripped the man with a hard blow at his swinging knee.

Pete stumbled and fell. Red's hand flashed down and recovered his gun thrust through the half-breed's belt. He swung on the sheriff to catch him flat-footed, his hand barely raising toward his now-holstered gun.

Red dropped his own .45 into leather and drawled, "You two go on ahead!" as Pete, his face black with anger, picked himself up off the planking.

For a brief moment, all three stood without moving. "Want to make a try for it?" Red invited.

All the lawman said was: "Don't be so doggone proddy, Pete!" And to Red: "You comin' or ain't you?"

"Think I will," Red said. "But after you."

Laughs came from the group nearby as Sheriff Harvey Jenkins turned and, with the Clanton man, preceded his prisoner. In them Red had his first hint of the lawman's unpopularity. It brought him a little relief to think that thus the odds against his getting out of this spot were lessened.

Before the sheriff's office, a plain board shack built onto the near end of a substantial stone jail, Red saw Duke Clanton's sleek black stallion standing hip shot at the hitch rail. He smiled faintly as Jenkins opened the screen door and called: "No sidesteppin', gents!" His warning made the half-breed, following Jenkins in through the door, wince visibly.

Duke Clanton's big frame was slouched in a swivel chair behind the small room's rolltop desk.

"Where the devil you been, Harv?" he said querulously. Then, seeing Red coming through the door, he stiffened.

Without preliminary Red said: "Tell him why I'm not under arrest, Clanton!"

Duke Clanton's broad face took on an angry color as his eyes fastened on Red's

301

holstered gun. He gave the lawman, then Pete, a questioning look.

"Had some trouble with him," Jenkins muttered.

Clanton's manner abruptly changed. He smiled openly. "Now don't get us wrong, Knight," he began suavely.

"He's trumped up some charges against me." Red nodded to the sheriff, having noticed the swollen lump on Clanton's jaw where his fist had connected last night. "Supposin' you explain 'em."

"You'll admit we could make those charges stick," Clanton said.

"How? When did I steal a horse? And what's this about robbery?"

"You headed out last night with twenty-five hundred bucks of my . . . of that lady's money," Clanton corrected himself quickly. "You swiped a couple of jugheads to make your getaway. You. . . ."

"Didn't you find the money?" Red asked blandly. "I tossed it into the wastebasket. Or maybe you weren't seein' much right then." The taunting remark brought instant anger to the Circle D man's face. "As for the two horses, you didn't find 'em at our camp this mornin', did you?"

"Then how the devil did you get out of town?" Jenkins flared.

302

"We could've walked. You can't prove we didn't. We weren't in possession of those horses this morning."

"Turned 'em loose, that's what you did!" the sheriff grumbled.

"Pete, go look for that money in the wastebasket in the hotel writin' room," Clanton said tersely. "If it's there, I want it all. Understand?"

Red leaned against the wall by the door as the half-breed went out. "Now how about this attempted murder?" he said.

Jenkins started to say something when Clanton waved him to silence. "Skip it, Harv! We're too late. He's seen Gail Dennis." There was a hint of grudging admiration in the glance he fixed on Red. "Well, what happens now, Knight? You leavin'?"

"I may, or I may hang around. I'd sort of like to know what happened to Spence."

He was watching Clanton closely as he mentioned the man he'd left on the homestead last fall. He could not be sure of Clanton's reaction, except that one moment the man's glance was open and unguarded and the next inscrutable with wariness.

"Spence?" Clanton's expression went pious. "Tough luck about him. He was a good man."

"You said yesterday the climate didn't agree with him."

Clanton shrugged. "I was talkin' through my hat. Don't know what happened to him."

"You can forget I mentioned it. Only I won't." Red eased out from the wall as the door opened and Pete reentered the room.

The half-breed handed Clanton the roll of bills. Clanton counted it and thrust it in his pocket. "Withdraw the charges, Harv," he told the sheriff. "It was a misunderstandin' all around." He gave Red a shrewd look. "You played it smooth, Knight. How much did you tell her?"

"Enough." The eagerness Red detected in Clanton's casually put question convinced him that Gail Dennis had given her foreman some uneasy moments out at the Circle D.

Clanton shrugged. "Let that old duffer out of there, Harv," he said.

Puzzled, Red watched the sheriff reach for a bunch of keys and unlock the padlock on the solid steel-paneled jail door. The lawman opened the door and disappeared into the half-lit interior of the jail. In there unoiled hinges squeaked, and the sheriff's voice sounded in some unintelligible remark.

Then Clem Reynolds's querulous tones

shuttled out to Red: "Maybe I've been in a worse jail, but I'll be hanged if I know where!" He came out the door, blinking against the stronger light. Then he saw Red, and his old seamed face took on a broad grin. "You didn't forget me after all?" When he spotted Clanton, the smile vanished. "How come you're shinin' up to this polecat?" he asked Red.

"We've been talkin' over a few things. Among them, Ned Spence."

"What about Ned?" Clem barked.

"Clanton can't seem to make up his mind."

The old lawman wheeled on Clanton so abruptly that the Circle D ramrod edged back toward the wall. "Your bunch was the last to see Spence alive," he drawled tonelessly. "What happened to him?"

"I wouldn't know," Clanton's face even bore a trace of regret, "except that we saw him ride away that night."

"The devil you don't!" Clem scoffed.

"Easy, Clem," Red cut in. "We'll find out sooner or later." He nodded to the sheriff. "Give him his gun."

At a nod from Clanton, Jenkins reached to a shelf over his desk to take down and hand across Clem's full-looped shell belt and holstered gun.

"Let's be goin'," Red said.

The ramrod took his time cinching the gun about his flat waist, all the while eyeing Clanton darkly. Before he followed Red out the door, he drawled: "Somethin' tells me I'm one day havin' to even things with you for Ned, Clanton! When that day comes, you'd better have your joints oiled for some sudden shootin'!"

VII

"THE SKY'S THE LIMIT"

Outside, on the walk, Clem asked Red: "Get anything out of Clanton?"

"Not much. What happened this mornin'?"

"Clanton took the herd. The boys were headed for Jennifer's the last I saw of 'em."

They walked on, Red acquainting his foreman with developments since their parting at dawn. When he mentioned Gail Dennis's buying the herd, and the price she'd paid for it, Clem gave an astonished whistle. "Not bad!" he conceded, then went on to post Red on what had happened with the arrival of the posse. "Clanton was cocked for trouble, ravin' mad when he found you'd hightailed! Madder when he saw our critters had had water. Threatened us with everything from a bull whip to hangin'. But I took it and let 'em put the handcuffs on me and told 'em to take the herd. That got

307

Clanton's goat. They brought me in and locked me up. Wouldn't even buy me any breakfast. I'd give a month's pay for a big steak right now!"

"Let's get one," Red suggested, and they turned toward a restaurant.

Finished with a good meal, Red asked: "What happened to the horses we left here last night?"

"Feed barn. I'll take 'em out to Toad's directly."

Red reached into his pocket and brought out his money. He thumbed four hundred dollars from the roll of bills and gave it to Clem. "Here's enough to last you and the others until tonight," he said. "I'll be back by dark."

"Where you goin'?"

"To the homestead. Maybe I can run on to something that'll tell us what happened to Ned."

Clem looked at the bills, a slow smile breaking across his face. "We're liable to give this town's tail a mighty good twist with this much to go on."

"Twist it all you want," Red grinned. "You're due a good bust."

They parted at the entrance to the Rosebud, Clem saying: "I'm goin' to have one before I go out after the boys."

"Only one, though," Red warned him good naturedly, as he left.

He was to remember his remark later. He would have found it even more significant had he noticed the man who stood nearby along the walk and witnessed the exchange of money and overheard what he said. That individual hurried down to the jail where he spent some moments in earnest conversation with Duke Clanton. Presently he was back again, shouldering his way into the Rosebud.

Clem found Toad Jennifer bellied up to the saloon's bar. Relief was plain in the basin man's glance when he saw the other.

"Am I seein' right?" he demanded. "It ain't you, packin' an iron, free as the breeze! What happened?"

Clem ordered whiskey. Over three drinks he posted Jennifer on what had happened since early morning.

"Reckon we ought to go out and collect your side-kicks to start the celebratin'?" Jennifer said finally.

Clem never answered that question. For at that moment a lanky, range-outfitted 'puncher sauntered up to the bar and called loudly for whiskey, adding just as loudly: ". . . to get the stink of sheep out of my craw! Who's the two-legged polecat that

sold out this country? My last trip it was run by white men!"

"Which sentiments are mine exactly!" drawled Clem, pushing away from the counter and thrusting out a gnarled hand. "Shake, partner! We're drinkin' for the same reason."

The stranger shook. Presently, after the proper introductions and much talk, the stranger, whose name was Reese, said: "How about me buyin' this round?"

He bought. Clem bought, then it was Toad's turn. Two more congenial souls joined the trio, both agreeing readily to the now belligerent belittling of the business engaged in by all outfits north of the creek. After Clem's sixth drink, when talk got around to the merits of stud as against draw poker, Reese's suggestion that they settle the argument by a friendly small-stakes game met with complete agreement.

The barkeep accordingly lit the lamp over the nearest table, broke out a new deck of cards and a rack of not-so-clean chips, and all five men took chairs. The game started at a two-bit limit. Clem won. The limit was raised to a dollar. Then, finally, as Toad began to win his share, and Clem's luck was holding, Reese plunked a fat wad of bills on the felt and drawled: "The devil with

this penny-ante stuff! Any reason why the sky ain't the limit?"

Clem smacked his roll down alongside his hefty stacks of chips. "No reason at all!"

So the limit was forgotten. Also forgotten was Clem's luck. It didn't desert him swiftly; but as the afternoon dragged on his chip stacks dwindled. To counterbalance this, Toad Jennifer's luck started running high along about dark. Once he leaned over and whispered to Clem: "Don't let this bother you. I'll make it good if you'll stick and help me make a cleanin'!"

So Clem's conscience, badly troubled, eased somewhat. He told himself that he'd get the rest of his pay from Red and easily pay the crew. Besides, he'd owned two dozen head of the herd Red had sold this morning.

They sent a swamper out for sandwiches at supper time, ordered another quart, and kept the game going. At nine Toad Jennifer was amazed to find that he'd won slightly more than two thousand dollars. At that point Reese and the other pair tossed in their cards, and Reese expressed the sentiments of all three when he said: "Fun's fun, gents, but it's got to stop sometime, and mine stops before I have to throw in my

boots to cover a bet. That agreeable with you, Jennifer?"

"Sure is." Toad let out a long, relieved sigh.

Reese rose and stretched and yawned, noting the empty table in front of Clem. "About busted you, didn't it, old-timer?"

"Just about." Clem was cashing in thirty-four dollars in chips, all that remained of his four hundred. He said ruefully: "Let's be travelin', Toad."

They all had a last drink and left. Clem parted company with Toad, whose horse was at the livery corral. They agreed to meet on the way out of town. Down the street Clem was about to climb into the saddle when Reese came along and called: "How about a night cap, partner? Got a bottle in m' room 'cross at the hotel."

"Uhn-huh!" Clem shook his head. "Got to be gettin' out to meet Toad."

"Wha's matter?" Reese's tongue was thick after his day-long bout with the bottle. "Ain' my liquor good 'nuff?"

"Sure. But. . . ."

"No buts 'bout it!" Reese threw an arm about Clem's shoulders. "Drown our sorrows, that's what we will! We're sure a couple pikers to let that dang sheepman clean us out."

"Toad ain't a sheepman!" Clem protested.

On their way across to the hotel, he carefully explained just who Jennifer was. Presently, with a couple more drinks, he forgot all about meeting Toad. He was in the hotel forty minutes. Those forty minutes were all that were necessary to decide a certain something the Clanton man wanted to make sure of. Toad Jennifer started home alone.

VIII

"SHOTS IN THE NIGHT"

Fourteen miles across the valley was the shack Ned Spence had lived in the past winter. Going through it for some hint as to Spence's disappearance and then calling on the nearest neighbor, a sheepman, took Red until dark. He couldn't turn down the sheepman's invitation to stay for supper, and it was eight before he started back to town, expecting to find Clem and the crew well on the way to a memorial celebration after sixty days on the drive.

But the more he thought about it, the less he wanted to join in the fun tonight. He was dog-tired. He was uncertain of the future, and he wanted to be alone to think things out. Should he break his unworded bargain with Gail Dennis and buy another bunch of cattle and stock the homestead? Or should he forget it entirely, homestead in another part of the country, and take his

crew with him? After all, he'd promised them jobs.

He chose to wrestle with his knotty problem rather than join the crew in town, swung off the town trail, and headed for the river, intending to find where Jennifer lived and spend the night there. In the bright starlight he studied the dark horizon and tried to strike the creek at the point the herd had yesterday, at Jennifer's fence. He rode slowly, enjoying the night's peaceful stillness and the crisp, bracing air. In the next hour the only foreign sound to break the stillness was what seemed like a faint, far off shot. He forgot it a moment after he heard it.

Red felt a small regret over the decision he finally reached — to leave the basin. The past years of footloose wandering made him yearn to settle down somewhere, that had been his reason for coming here. In only two days he'd grown to like the country. Yet, common sense told him that this pleasant hill-bordered valley wasn't to become his home. Sooner or later he'd have another run-in with Duke Clanton. Sooner or later he'd follow the impulse to see more of Gail Dennis, to get to know her.

This girl had attracted him strangely. There weren't many like her, he reflected, then bitterly remembered Jennifer's state-

ment that Gail Dennis and Duke Clanton would one day be married. It galled him to realize that Clanton was deceiving the girl. Yet it wasn't his place to inform her of her foreman's deceit. That would be someone else's task. She probably wouldn't know the real Clanton until it was too late and then would begin years of bitter disillusionment for her.

Well, he'd had his share of trouble here and enough luck to counterbalance it. He'd met a girl he liked uncommonly well. He'd forget her. He'd made some money. If he didn't waste time, he could put a second herd on another range before the end of summer.

He rode his roan across the creek toward a high sandy spur he thought close to the place where the herd had tried to cross yesterday. Once on the other side, though, the look of the night-shadowed land was unfamiliar. There was no lane where the lane should have been. Irritated, Red rode south, knowing he'd come to the road running toward town. At the road he made his guess on which way Jennifer's place lay and turned east, riding leisurely, glad that this star-studded, bracing night was one that would cleanse a man's thinking.

All at once Red heard a sound close

ahead, one he couldn't identify. He was riding the line of a fence and decided it might be the gentle swing of a loose wire against a post. But suddenly an elongated shadow showed on the trail ahead. Instantly he recognized it as the outstretched figure of a man.

He vaulted from the saddle, dropping the roan's reins. As he was kneeling alongside the man, the sound came again. It was the racking, indrawing of breath into choked lungs. Turning the man over, Red looked down into the face of Toad Jennifer. Blood made a glistening line at one corner of the basin man's mouth. Toad's eyes were closed. In this new position, his breathing came easier. Tearing open his shirt, Red saw the small dark blotch of a wound high on the left side of his chest.

"All right, Toad?" he asked when Jennifer's eyes opened briefly. His answer was a vacant stare. Jennifer was still unconscious.

Tying his bandanna over the wound, Red was thinking of getting Jennifer quickly into town when the muted hoof thud of a trotting pony shuttled down along the trail. He stiffened, came erect, and drew his gun. His glance went quickly to a stunted piñon that grew close to the trail. Quickly he led the

roan behind the tree. There he stood, wariness high in him, for he knew now that someone had tried to murder Toad Jennifer tonight.

The sound of the oncoming pony strengthened quickly. Then came something else, a high thin voice crooning the strains of "Red River Valley." Red knew that voice. It was Clem Reynolds's! Instantly he was reassured and stepped out from the concealment of the tree.

Clem was drunk, not roaring drunk but pleasingly so. He was within ten feet of Red before he saw him and even then found nothing strange in a lone dismounted rider blocking the trail, for he called heartily: "Evenin', stranger. Got a drink handy?"

"It's me, Clem. Better get down and help."

Somewhat sobered by the flat tones of Red's voice, Clem obeyed quickly. "Who's that with you?" he asked as he came up.

"Toad."

Clem chuckled. "Passed out, eh?"

"No. He's been shot."

"Shot!" Clem was really sober now. He stared down helplessly at Jennifer, trying to explain: "Him and me met up with some regular gents and had the best game. . . ."

"Tell me about it later," Red cut in, trying

to keep down his anger. He knew that somehow Clem had failed to keep his promise
of the morning. "The thing now is to get
Toad to a doctor. He's hurt bad. Here, give
me a hand."

As gently as they could, they lifted Jennifer's loose bulk so that he straddled the
roan's withers. Red, in the saddle behind
him, held him erect.

"You go on ahead and be sure there's a
doctor ready," he ordered Clem. "I'll stop
at the first house and get a rig to carry him
in. Hurry!"

Clem went up into the saddle and was
wheeling the pony around when Red felt a
light blow strike his left cheek. An instant
later the sharp *crack!* of a rifle cut across
the stillness, and he knew that the blow on
his face had been the air impact of a passing
bullet. Instinctively, he put spurs to the
roan, calling: "Ride, Clem!"

The roan's lunge carried him on past the
other man. Suddenly, creekward, sounded
the explosions of two more guns. Red swung
away from them, hearing the pound of
Clem's pony behind. With the roan at a run
it was hard steadying Jennifer's loose bulk.
He covered a hundred yards before more
shots sounded, this time the lower-toned
blasting of a .45 fired four more times. And

now he couldn't any longer hear Clem's horse. He looked back over his shoulder to see Clem's dim shape streaking along the line of the trail from which he had been angling. Far behind Clem the red stab of powder flame cut the night's blackness, and Red made out vague hurrying shapes back there. Clem, realizing the predicament of Red's roan caught carrying a double load, had evidently decided to decoy the killers away. He would make out all right. He'd had a good start on his pursuers.

Red swung even more sharply away from the trail, riding the abrupt-sloping bottom of a deep gully for a good half mile. He had circled, starting back this way, intending to take Jennifer to his farm. Then suddenly he reasoned that whoever had tried to kill the basin man would doubtless be watching the layout. That thought brought him up out of the gully to strike a straight line to the river. Crossing it twenty minutes ago he'd seen a light a mile or so away on the north side. He should be nearly on a line with that place now. It was important to get help for Jennifer.

He thought once that Jennifer's spare frame straightened under his hold. That was shortly after the roan crossed the stream and headed out across the flats beyond, going

toward the light, now in sight. But when he spoke to Jennifer, there was no answer, and the man's weight was as limp as it had been before.

The light shone from a shack, a sheepman's. Below the shack was a roofless barn, a corral, pens, and a windmill whose spidery bulk towered blackly against the heavens. Red drew his Colt and held it in his rein hand as he walked the roan in across the barn lot. Then a dog barked savagely and dashed out of the nearest pen, snarling at the roan's heels.

The roan shied and narrowly missed unseating him. Red was swinging his gun around to shoot so as to frighten off the dog when a voice called sharply from the direction of the windmill: "Down, Mike!" Immediately the dog quieted and slunk away in the darkness. "Lift 'em, stranger!" came the voice again, its note ominous.

Red tossed his gun to the ground but didn't lift his hands, since he had to hold Jennifer erect. "Can't," he drawled. "He'd fall off if I did."

"Who you got there?" came the voice again, and now Red could see the speaker standing a few feet from the windmill's nearest leg.

"Toad Jennifer."

The man breathed an oath of surprise. "Toad! What's wrong with him? What was all that shootin' across the creek?" He advanced toward Red slowly.

"It was meant for us. I got away with Toad. He's shot."

"The devil he is! Why didn't you say so? Here, let me lift him down!"

The man rocked his rifle down from the crook of his arm, laid it on the ground, and reached up to catch Jennifer's weight as Red let him go. Red came aground. The man called sharply, "Jim, open up!" The shack door opened on a boy's slender figure, a feeble wash of lamplight coming out across the littered yard.

The man looked at Red and gave a visible start. "You're Knight, ain't you?" he queried.

Red nodded and said: "Let's get Toad in a bed."

The shack was a single room, poorly furnished, lacking any feminine touch. Double bunks ranged one wall, a stove and packing-box cupboards the one opposite. There were a table, two chairs and a crude plain chest. Nothing else.

"Get a fire goin', Jim," the man said, as he and Red laid Jennifer on the lower bunk. He pulled Jennifer's shirt aside, saw the bul-

let hole, and looked questioningly at Red. Red told him briefly what had happened.

"I'm Sewell. This is my kid, Jim." The sheepman nodded to the gangling youth laying a fire in the stove. The hint of a smile broke the gravity of his long face. "Maybe you've heard of me?"

Red shook his head.

"Toad and me is friends, even if I do live the wrong side of the line," Sewell explained. "I was at Masker's place last night when you called Clanton's bluff. Your talk sure did me good. That highbinder needed takin' down!"

"Hadn't one of us better get to town for the doctor?" Red put in impatiently.

Sewell looked down at Jennifer. He shook his head. "No can do. The sawbones left for the Wells today to help a woman with a baby. Won't be back till toward mornin'."

"But we can't let Jennifer die!" Red flared. "He's bad hurt. There must be someone else."

Sewell's look was thoughtful. He turned to his son. "Jim, get a bridle on Bessie! You're goin' for help."

"Where?" the boy asked, already on the way to the door.

"Tell you later," Sewell said. As the door swung shut on the youngster, he turned to

323

Red again. "You wouldn't like what I'm doin', so I'll keep it to myself. Now what about that scrap across the river?"

Red told him of his sale of the herd, of leaving Clem in town this morning. Sewell interrupted at that point to say: "I can tell you part of what happened. Three of Clanton's men were in a poker game with your side-kick and Jennifer at supper time tonight. Toad's luck was goin' strong. Your man's was not."

In a few more moments, as Red finished, Sewell said: "You'll want to go back, won't you, and see what happened to Reynolds? Go ahead. The boy'll bring help, and I'll look after Toad." When Red hesitated, he added: "Don't think I'd give Toad away. I hate Duke Clanton's guts as much as I like the girl he works for."

In these few words Sewell did much to ease Red's worry over leaving Jennifer in unfriendly hands. Sewell was to be trusted. He had also hinted that Clanton was responsible for the ambush across the river.

Red went out into the yard, found his .45, and mounted the roan again. Leaving, he saw the boy lead a hackamored mare up to the shack and stand talking to his father. Before the darkness hid them, the boy had climbed onto the mare and was headed out

in the direction opposite the one Red was taking, riding fast.

Back across the river, Red was undecided what to do. Finally he turned upstream again, this time following the creek bank, determined to find Jennifer's layout and see if his men were still there. He came to Jennifer's lane, followed the fence in, and found a gate. Beyond it, a faintly marked trail led in through a dense cottonwood grove then climbed steeply to a knoll on which stood a pole cabin, barn, and corrals. The gray outline of his chuck wagon showing in the deeper shadow of the barn convinced him that this was Jennifer's place. There was no light in the cabin. Red approached warily, keeping to the cover of the small trees.

He was within fifty yards of the cabin when a gruff voice, off to his left, said mildly: "That you, Red?"

"Nels?" Red answered, recognizing the cook's voice. He reined the roan off there and saw the cook's heavy shape come out of a nearby tree's dense shadow. "How come you're roamin' around out here?"

"Trouble, boss," Nels told him. "Bad trouble! A while ago we heard shootin' off toward town. We'd been in Toad's kitchen, tryin' to work up some fever over a stud game, waitin' for Toad to come home. That

shootin' sounded suspicious, so the boys went out to saddle up and go see what the ruckus was about. They was all crowded in the corral when half a dozen jaspers rode out of the trees and threw down on 'em. Caught 'em cold! I was still in the kitchen and managed to duck out the front door and get away."

"What happened to the others?"

"Gone!" was the cook's ominous answer. "They lined 'em up and headed out the road. I heard one jasper say they'd have a hard time findin' enough cots in the jail to go around."

IX

"LYNCH FEVER"

Red's astonishment prevented his immediately taking in the full significance of Hansen's words. "Jail!" he echoed.

"That's what he said. It don't make sense, unless they're tryin' to even it up with all of us for the rumpus you and Clem raised in town last night."

Red's thinking was coming a little clearer now. "That isn't it," he said and sat considering a long moment, having to make a choice between two decisions. He wasn't quite sure any more that Toad Jennifer was in safe hands and was already blaming himself for having left the basin man. Then there was the crew. And Clem! He didn't know what luck Clem had had in getting away. Nor what Clanton hoped to accomplish by having the crew jailed. He wanted to get to town and find some answer to this mysterious and unexpected development.

He had a thought that made him ask: "Has anyone had a good look at you, Nels? Any of Clanton's bunch, I mean? You weren't there yesterday when they stopped the herd. How about this mornin'?"

Nels frowned thoughtfully. "I was at the wagon the whole time," he answered. "They wasn't close enough to see me."

"And they didn't get a look at you tonight?"

The cook shook his head.

"Then get a hull on a horse and head for town. Go straight on in and see if you can pick up anything on Clem or the rest. They'll. . . ."

"Clem?" Nels cut in. "What about him? Ain't he in jail?"

"No. Tell you about it later. Right now I need information. You're the only one who can get it. I'm meeting Jennifer across the river in a few minutes." To save time Red was going to wait and tell Nels about Jennifer and Clem later. He glanced up at the wheeling stars. "It's close to eleven now. At midnight I'll be waiting for you half a mile this side of town near that old barn with the caved-in roof. You can't miss it."

"There's an awful lot here I don't understand, Boss!" Nels protested. "Why . . . ?"

"Later, Nels!" Red interrupted. "We've

got a whale of a lot of work to do. See you in an hour." He reined the roan around and went back down toward the river through the trees.

A quarter hour later he was riding in on Sewell's place. The dog again barked savagely but seemed to remember the roan and, after a few last half-hearted yips, stopped worrying the animal. The shack door opened as Red dismounted close to the small, roofed stoop. Sewell stood in the doorway, and beyond him his son crossed the room carrying a steaming basin of water.

"How is he?" Red's query was urgent.

"Doin' all right." The sheepman stepped aside to let him enter.

The light of the unshaded lamp, sitting on the table alongside the bunk where Jennifer lay, blinded Red for a moment. Then, as his eyes became accustomed to the glare, he made out a figure kneeling by the bunk beyond the table.

At the instant he knew who it was. Gail Dennis turned and looked at him. The lamplight edged her head with spun gold. Her prettiness was breath-taking; color heightened the olive hue of her cheeks. In spite of her clothes, a pair of waist overalls and a dark red cotton shirt open at the

throat, and her wind-blown hair, she was still utterly feminine.

"He's going to be all right," she said softly, and her smile was a reminder of this morning's meeting.

Red knew now why Sewell hadn't warned him of whom he was to find. It was natural that the sheepman would believe his antagonism toward Circle D's foreman would carry over to its owner. As evidence of this, Sewell said questioningly: "You ain't sore, Knight?"

Red shook his head in a brief negative. He crossed the room to stand at the head of the bunk, looking down at Jennifer. Toad now lay propped up on folded blankets and a pillow. Gone from his face was the deathly pallor of an hour ago. His breathing was even.

"He's asleep," Gail Dennis said in a hushed voice. She nodded to a bottle of whiskey on the table. "He took a good drink of that. It'll keep him quiet, stop the chance of a hemorrhage. If he rests, he has a good chance." She gave Red a look of near pleading. "Sewell's told me some things I didn't know. About Duke. I . . . I didn't realize what kind of a man he was. He did this to Jennifer, didn't he?"

Red was uncertain, half embarrassed.

"Let's wait until we find out," was all he could think to say.

"You don't have to try to cover up for Duke!" Gail told him. "I can see things now I couldn't before. Perhaps you were kind not to tell me. Is there anything I can do to help?"

"Not a thing except to look after Toad. We're pullin' out as soon as we can," Red lied. "I reckon when we leave, things will go back to normal."

The girl's glance clung to him, seeming to see beneath his mask of indifference. "I want you to know I'm sorry . . . very sorry for the way this has turned out," she said finally. "You should be taking up your homestead. I shouldn't be running sheep." She shrugged restlessly. "You have my promise that things will be different from now on. I'm having it out with Duke."

"Better go easy with him. You wouldn't want trouble."

Gail's smile was enigmatic, somehow lacking in amusement. "I still have a few friends I can call on," she said.

Red held out his hand. "I'll be leavin'."

The pressure of her fingers tried to make up for the things she was leaving unsaid. She breathed, "Good bye," and then he left her.

Sewell followed him out into the yard. "I couldn't help tellin' her, Knight. Someone maybe ought to take a hefty kick at the seat of my pants, but I'm glad I did it."

"That doesn't matter now. What does matter is that she has some friends to count on."

"Don't think she ain't! Maybe we're makin money at this stinkin' business but, for me, I'll take cattle and starve if I have to. There's a few besides me thinkin' the same way. We all knew old Tom Dennis, and we'll stick by his girl."

"Well, here's wishin' you luck."

Red went astride the roan and out into the night. Once again weariness settled upon him, but it was a different feeling now. His wind was played out, and a heavy depression was settling on him. He had said farewell to the one girl who, in contrast to all others he had known, had prompted in him a feeling deeper than reverence. He was riding out of her life because he saw no possible way of their ever becoming more to each other than they were now, mere casual acquaintances. Perhaps she hated him for having exposed the man of her choice. It had seemed inevitable since their meeting that this should happen, inevitable because all Red's hopes in coming to this country had

been blasted in the space of two days.

He forcibly put her from his mind, looking ahead to his meeting with Nels Hansen. His lean face sobered to a stern, rock-like gravity as he grimly faced the solution to tonight's dilemma. There would be more trouble. He was almost glad to be riding into it.

"They've got the whole dang bunch locked up!" were Hansen's first words after meeting Red. "You didn't tell me they let Clem go this mornin'. He got tangled up with three Clanton men in a no-limit game at the saloon an' they took him to the cleaner's while Toad was the heavy winner. Now they're sayin' that Clem shot Toad for his winnin's. Claim they found Toad's money in Clem's pocket after they'd shot Clem's horse out from under him in that fight down the road tonight. They're makin' lynch talk, and they've got a reward out for you! You're supposed to have got away with Toad's carcass." Hansen paused, out of breath, having put together more words in one piece than Red had ever thought possible for the ordinarily untalkative man.

"What about the crew?" Red asked. "Why are they holdin' them?"

"Rustlin'!" Nels said harshly. "They tried to run off the herd tonight, accordin' to the

story. And I dang well know they weren't within ten miles of where Clanton was holdin' those critters!"

"It's beginnin' to make sense now," Red breathed.

"What is?" Nels demanded testily. "Clanton's taken over the saloon, set up a second bar. Does that make sense? Drinks are sellin' at half price, for nothin' to them that can't buy! The town's wild! If they don't bend a good cottonwood limb with Clem at the end of a rope before mornin', I'm a coal-black Swede!"

"We'd better get in and see what we can do." Red's tall body was erect in the saddle as he stared off toward the winking lights of the town.

"What good'll it do us? We're two against half a thousand! And that bunch of drunks ain't foolin'!"

Red shrugged. "We'll see. How about the jail?"

"Guarded front and back. What really happened to Toad?" Nels had almost forgotten the basin man.

Red told him, then: "We'll work down along the alley across the street from the jail."

It wasn't difficult to reach the dark alley. The few men they met had indulged too

heavily of Clanton's free liquor and were probably on the way home to sleep it off, for they paid no attention to Red and Nels. But at the head of a narrow passageway between two stores, as Red looked out onto the street, he saw that Clanton's whiskey was having a different effect on nine-tenths of the town, most of whose citizens seemed to have forgotten their beds for the duration of the night.

Two crowds were massed along the street's broad length. One was centered in front of the Rosebud. The other, the biggest, completely filled the street in front of the jail. This last was the most noisome and ominous looking. The walk and the hitch rail in front of the sheriff's office were clear, being paced by two deputies armed with sawed-off shotguns. They ignored the taunting jeers and mocking laughter of the onlookers. But it didn't take much imagination for Red to see that the mob, restless and still undecided, would in the end take the chance on rushing the jail to lay hands on a man they considered a murderer, Clem Reynolds. And, unless Red's hunch was wrong, the deputies would offer little resistance.

He and Nels stood for minutes in the shadowed entryway to the passage, watching

the traffic that moved along under the walk awnings. Red was trying to think of a way to get Clem and the others out of the jail. He recognized the sobering fact that nothing less than dynamite would clear the street or sway the crowd from its grim purpose.

Nels finally broke the silence, voicing Red's worry. "We ain't got a Chinaman's chance, Boss! I once heard of a cashier firin' a house at the edge of a town to draw away a mob makin' a run on his bank. But even that wouldn't work here. These jaspers got their hearts in their work. And don't figure to stick your neck out by walkin' across there with a gun. You wouldn't live to pull a trigger twice!"

"Not a chance," Red agreed, and in that moment hope nearly left him.

Clanton's reason for this iron-bound frame-up was obscure. But Red had no doubts that this was Clanton's doing. The fact remained that the Circle D foreman had laid the groundwork for a revenge that was out of all proportion to Red's having come off best in the sale of the herd. Clanton evidently took Red's small success as a personal affront. He'd framed Clem with murder and come close to taking Jennifer's life. He had saddled Red's crew with a charge of rustling that would be almost im-

possible to prove false. Lastly, he had put out a reward on Red to make sure that he couldn't help his men.

There weren't any loopholes for Red to work through. He was outlawed. Clem would probably die at the end of a rope, even though Jennifer lived to tell his story, for the truth would come too late. Red considered for a moment the possibility of forcibly taking several townsmen out to see Jennifer on the possibility that the wounded man might have regained consciousness. But there was no assurance that Jennifer could talk, that he wasn't dead by now. And even if Jennifer could speak, Red couldn't be sure of getting back to town to rescue Clem before the hangman got him.

Sheer desperation turned his mind to another possibility. "Nels," he said gravely, "we've got only one chance. Here it is." And he stepped back into the passageway and spoke to his crewman earnestly for long moments.

When he had put his last question, Nels's answer came on the heels of a long-drawn gusty sigh. "I reckon it's better than standin' here watchin' it happen. Sure I'll help. But we may be too late."

His words added to Red's urgency as they rode out the alley to the west limits of town.

Red pushed the roan hard along the trail, irritated at having to hold the animal in so that Nels, on a slower horse, could keep abreast. The three-mile ride that brought them within sight of a redly glowing light in the distance seemed to take an eternity. But at last they were close enough to make out that light as a big camp fire, the dark sprawling shadow of bunched cattle beyond it telling Red he had guessed correctly on this being Clanton's cow camp.

"Remember, we ride straight in." He added a last warning word to Nels. They were close enough now to see a man's shape momentarily outlined against the big blaze. The man's walk was uncertain, and Red thought he saw a bottle in his hand. He drew his Colt and held it in his free hand, cushioned in his lap behind the generous swell of his saddle. Nels, seeing his move, did likewise. They were within a hundred yards of the fire, Red going on with the roan at a trot. Here, close at hand, was his one chance of saving his men, the one wild gamble left him.

Thinking that, he rode boldly in. He and Nels were well within the range of the fire's broad circle of light before they were hailed by one of the three men lying or sitting on blankets close to the blaze. The man who

gruffly called to them merely rolled over onto his elbow and looked in their direction, his shout more a greeting than a challenge. His voice was thickened by whiskey, his words hardly intelligible.

Red answered that hail with "Who's got a drink?" and kept coming on.

He had now spotted the fourth man, the one he'd seen cross before the blaze a moment ago. This one was now approaching the fire from the far side with an armload of dead cedar.

"Tarnation, it ain't . . . ," began one man as he recognized Red.

His hand stabbed toward the gun at his thigh a full second too late. For Red cocked his weapon up from his lap, drawling: "No . . . it ain't!" His .45 arced around then in time to catch the man on the other side of the fire as he dropped his armload of wood to draw.

Nels, alongside Red, said flatly: "Go ahead! Make a try for it!" His hard-set face and the .45 in his hand were compelling enough to make the trio on the blankets lift their hands.

Red swung to the ground and sauntered over there to relieve the three of their weapons. One wore a pair of .38s, making the count of surrendered pistols four. Two rifles

lay against a saddle nearby. Red took them. Then he went around the far side of the fire and took from the fourth Clanton man a pair of silver-mounted .44s.

"Where'd you pick these up . . . at a circus?" Red drawled as he thrust the weapons with the others through his belt. A growl of impotent rage was his only answer. Red motioned his prisoner across with the others. "Hunt up some rope," he told Nels.

The cook, gone a brief moment beyond the wide circle of the blaze's light, reappeared with three coiled riatas.

"There's a buckboard off there," he told Red. "We could tie 'em to the wheels."

Less than five minutes later the four Clanton men, gagged with their own bandannas, sat each at the foot of a wheel, arms extended and roped to spokes, legs tightly wound with many turnings of the manila.

Red gave them a last inspecting glance, told them: "Someone'll be out in the mornin' to cut you loose." Nodding to Nels, they both hurried back to their horses. There, Red handed Nels the half-dozen six-guns and the rifles.

There was no need for them to speak as they set about their work. They rode out to the margin of the herd and circled it to the point farthest from the fire. Outflanking the

last bald-faced steer, Red cautioned Nels only once, saying: "Not too fast!" Then both of them shouted, spurring their mounts at the nearest sleeping animals.

Wakefulness ran through the herd. Downed animals lunged to their feet; those standing shied away from the pair of riders and drifted off into the night. A lead bull shook his shaggy long-horned head and plodded straight for the lights of Tres Piedras. The animals nearest him followed in a long thick line. Soon the others, urged from behind, got into motion. Within five minutes the whole herd was on the move.

"Easy!" Red cautioned once as Nels's horse swung suddenly aside to cut back a steer that broke from line. "Let the salty ones go. We don't need 'em."

"What happens when we get close in, Red? How're we goin' to put 'em where we want 'em?"

"Fences," Red answered. "It was fences that helped Clanton make his play yesterday, and they'll help us make ours tonight. All that land this side of town is under wire."

"Ought to be a cinch." Nels's momentary skepticism was forgotten.

"If we work it right," was Red's reservation.

X

"CATTLE DRIVE DOWN MAIN STREET"

Duke Clanton had just finished a long talk with Tres Piedras' mayor, Tom Higgins. Several minutes ago he'd taken the mayor, full of dubious misgivings, into Doc Masker's office. Over a drink and much persuasion, he'd convinced Higgins that the course the mob was taking tonight was the right one. This stranger, Clem Reynolds, had killed one of the basin's most upstanding citizens. Furthermore, Knight's crew had had the gall to try and steal the herd Knight had this morning sold to Gail Dennis. It was obvious that the normal workings of the law weren't fast enough to take care of a situation like this.

"To blazes with the courts!" Clanton had finally worked up the boldness to say. "In the old days they didn't wait on the courts to condemn a killer, did they, Tom? We ain't waitin' tonight!"

Higgins was convinced in the end. So convinced that just now he stood on a chair under the big chandelier at the center of the Rosebud's main room, addressing the crowd. He was a trifle drunk, but his words came loud and clear. Instead of constraining the mob, his speech was to do more than any one thing so far to spur it on. He was privately a little concerned over having sent a man out to the Circle D an hour ago to inform Gail Dennis of the treachery of her foreman, for Clanton's maneuvers now seemed honest and above board. Higgins was trying to make up for his lack of faith in Clanton who last year had helped vote him into office.

As his stentorian voice rolled on, holding the attention of the crowd, a brief inscrutable smile played across Duke Clanton's face. He saw Pete Hernandez on the edge of the crowd and sauntered over behind the half-breed, touched him lightly on the shoulder, and just as casually sauntered back to his place at the office door again. Presently Pete was standing beside him.

"Go tell Jenkins to get ready." Clanton's voice was barely audible over the bellow of the mayor's. "It's comin' any minute now. Tell him he's to throw up his hands and give in. We don't want no one hurt."

Pete's head tilted down in a brief affirmative. He left Clanton's side, working his way inconspicuously toward the swing doors up front. Out on the walk he unobtrusively pushed his way through the crowd listening to the mayor's harangue. When he was in the clear, his stride lengthened, and he started for the jail.

He had taken only a dozen steps when he saw a rider break through the outskirts of the crowd in front of the jail and come streaking down the street, recklessly threatening to overrun anyone who got in his way. Pete recognized the rider as a Clanton man and hailed him.

"Find the boss quick!" the rider said breathlessly, as he drew his nervous pony to a stand beside the half-breed. "Hell's busted loose! It's the herd!"

"Forget the herd," Pete drawled. "We got somethin' else to think. . . ."

"Forget 'em! When they're headed down the street? There!" He raised a hand and pointed. Pete, looking toward the jail, saw the crowd beginning to break into a wild flight. Beyond, in a dark oncoming mass topped by rocking, glistening horns, the street was jammed, walk to walk, with cattle whose lumbering gait seemed like the onrush of a tremendous slow flood

along a dry riverbed.

Pete turned and ran. Behind him shouts and curses and cries of terror struck over the undertone of low-thundering hoofs. Far down the street, beyond the mass of cattle, a six-gun exploded. The lead steers broke into clumsy lope. Pete tried to claw his way into the crowd in front of the Rosebud, but others were doing the same thing.

Red Knight had a moment ago lifted his Colt and fired it over his head in a blasting crescendo of sound that struck terror through the herd lined down the street. Luck had been with him and Nels. The fenced pastures out beyond the street's far limit had formed a perfect aisle down which to drive the four hundred animals. Now, in full flight along the main street, the herd was like a ramrod thrust down the choked barrel of a muddied shotgun. Up ahead the two separate crowds were fast melting off the street. Saddle horses and teams, terrified, lunged and broke out from the tie-rails, threatening to run down pedestrians.

The crowd caught first, in front of the jail, was in the greatest danger. For along those two rows of facing buildings nearest them there were no passageways and few inset doors offering shelter. Tres Piedras' citizens, ranchers and sheepmen alike,

turned and ran for their lives. Through the dust Red made out Nels Hansen's blocky shape. He reined over there, close to his cook, and shouted: "Make it fast, Nels!"

Nels needed no urging. As Red reloaded his Colt, the cook was already spurring his horse in through the animals of the drag, pushing on up deeply into the main body of the herd. He was risking being thrown and trampled, but he rode solidly, the bullets in his gun belt and his buckles glistening dully in the reflected light of a store window he passed, a rifle cradled across the swell of his saddle. He struck out viciously with rein ends to prod animals out of his way and shot once or twice when some unruly steer jammed his horse against another.

All at once, Red looked up the street to see it clear ahead of the leaders of the herd. Miraculously, the crowd in front of the Rosebud had melted in through the doors. The alley out behind the saloon must be jammed. The jail crowd had somehow managed to find cover, too. There wasn't a man in sight ahead of the long line of the charging cattle, now loping in terror-stricken flight down the long straight aisle between the buildings.

Red saw Nels, up ahead, charge in before the front door to the sheriff's office. An

instant later the cook was out of the saddle, kicking in the flimsy screen door, his horse left to his own devices. Seeing the cook safe, Red sighed in keen relief. As the first muted blast of gunfire sounded from inside the jail, he set about accomplishing his own job. Nels would have Clem and crew out of their lock-blown cells in another thirty seconds. It was Red's turn to push up into the herd, past the scattered animals of the drag. No prodding was needed now to keep the steers on the run. They had stampeded and would run until in the clear beyond the far limits of the town.

He used his gun twice, reloading each time. The roan worked tirelessly, nimbly, as a good cutting horse will when in danger of being pushed off his feet. Once he would have gone down but for Red's lifting his head so that he could find his footing again. Red shot and killed the steer blocking the way, and the roan jumped the falling carcass and was clear of the death-slashing hoofs the next instant.

Slowly, the roan crowded his way towards the street's south walk. Under firm rein, he lunged up onto the walk and in under the awning. Ahead and opposite a steer crashed into an awning post, broke it, and a thirty-foot stretch of awning sagged down and was

splintered to kindling as the herd hit it. Red, riding the other walk, felt the hackles rise along his back at the thought that he might be caught under a similar obstruction.

The saloon windows lit the backs of the animals twenty yards ahead. The roan had nearly stopped. Cattle jammed the walk where the wall of the building beyond the Rosebud jutted out to make an impassable pocket. Red lifted his Colt, aimed at the up-curving horn of a steer caught in the pocket, and squeezed the trigger. The steer's head tossed violently. Then with a bellow of pain and rage, the animal charged out from the wall. The ones packed behind charged also. The jam melted away, and Red rode in toward the light of the Rosebud's doors. Thirty feet short of them he stood in the stirrups and reached above to catch a hold on an awning joist. The roan went on, pushed from behind by the relentless surge of the herd. Red swung up until he lay flat across the joist, his body in the shallow opening made by that joist and the smaller up-slanting roof support that gave the awning its slope. He wormed his way across and on to the next and lay there so that one joist supported this thighs, the other his chest. There, gun in hand, looking down and in through the small rectangle

over the saloon's swing doors, he waited while the frenzied cattle lunged past below him.

He could see a narrow wedge of the Rosebud's room packed with men's bodies clear to the doors. Below him the last animals moved past and up ahead. The thunderous volley of their hoofs striking the thick walk planks gradually faded as the street and walks cleared of animals. Red tensed, watching the saloon doors.

From up-street came the sound of voices, the slam of a screen door. Red leaned down and looked back and out to see a group of shadows moving across from the jail toward him along the hoof-churned dust. Except for the slurring sound of boots, an ominous silence seemed to follow in the wake of the herd's receding tumult. Those men would be his crew: Nels, Clem, Ed, Tex, Frank and Jim. Counting himself, they were seven against whatever guns the Rosebud would shortly disgorge.

Lying there across the awning joists, Red thought back over his plan. He had risked much in this attempt at freeing his crew from jail. Now he was risking even more in stepping into a shoot-out with Clanton and his men. His hunch had been that the men responsible for tonight's mob violence

would be the first to set foot on the street again after the herd's passage. He was gambling on that hunch and on the presence of his own men on the street as a surprise.

Still he was confronted with the responsibility for the lives of his men. Here he was, leading them into danger when he, and they, could have ridden straight out of the country and had satisfaction in looking back on having got the best of Clanton. But in this moment Red knew that neither he nor his men would turn tail to run from what they now faced. Clanton had thrown down the gauntlet of a challenge. Not one of his men would have wanted to let pass this chance.

"Spread out!"

That hushed word, drifting across the street's gathering silence, was uttered by Clem Reynolds. Red heard it, and the touch of sheer confidence in it did more to wipe out his doubts than anything. Hardly had that group of shadows fanned out to cover a fifty foot wedge of the street's width, before another voice, this one from the saloon, spoke out sharply:

"Ben, Sid, Pete! All of you! Get up here!"

It was Clanton who gave that curt order. Looking down over the doors, Red saw men shifting aside, others taking their places. As he had foreseen, Clanton was accepting the

responsibility of making the first appearance on the street.

Someone said: "Duke, there was shots across at the jail."

"I know," Clanton snapped. "It's Knight tryin' to break his bunch out. Pete!"

He was having trouble marshaling his men, but the big man threw the doors wide in a solid thrust. Before the doors had swung shut again, he was through them, a six-gun in each hand, stepping warily aside and out of the lamp glow that flushed across the walk and into the street.

It must have taken Clanton a few seconds to see into the darkness, for in the following brief interval no word was spoken. Then suddenly his voice grated out: "Who's that? Sing out or we shoot!"

He was standing less than ten feet from the spot below which Red lay. Red sensed immediately that his men were in plain sight and in danger of being cut down, so he drawled flatly: "Up here, Clanton!" It would give his men the time they needed to meet this threat.

On the heels of his words a man on the opposite side of the doors fired suddenly. Two shots of his .45 had blasted the stillness when a gun from the street answered. Its lone reply brought the Clanton man pitch-

ing outward and sprawling in a broken fall to the walk. Clanton, who had a moment ago looked upward, wheeled quickly away and out of line. His gun lifted. It's lancing flame licked upward in the direction of Red's voice.

Red had had his Colt lined down on Clanton, the hammer thumbed back, trigger finger tightening. But all at once, even with the odds against him, shooting Clanton cold-bloodedly seemed like murder. He had an advantage up here, having chosen it to get clear of the herd more than for the reason of surprising the Circle D crew. As he was thinking this, Clanton put the line of a joist between himself and Red's gun, and Red had lost his edge.

Once again Clanton's gun exploded aimed upward, his bullet flickering a splinter from the roof that gouged Red's forehead. Red was suddenly impatient at being robbed of a target as other guns cut loose. He reached out, lifted his legs off the joist, and swung down. Letting go his hold, he hit the walk in a crouch. Clanton, seeing his shape suddenly appear out of the shadows, whirled and threw three thought-quick shots at him. The first bullet took Red in the left shoulder. It spun him halfway around, put his side to Clanton's gun. The next tore the left sleeve

of his shirt. The third went wide of its mark for, as Red's body turned, his gun arced down at Clanton. His gun beat Clanton's last shot. He saw the big man's stooped body straighten rigidly as his gun fired. A man behind Clanton went down, stopping a slug from the street. Another behind him staggered drunkenly to the side to grasp the support of an awning post. Yet another ran in through the doors, two more down the walk. Red thought he heard the pound of hoofs down the street blended with the guns. The acrid stench of powder smoke was strong in the air as his men blasted home their small advantage of surprise.

Clanton's stiffening was brief. The next moment he was again crouching, right arm limp at his side, left hand blurring up. Red thumbed the hammer of his weapon again. It exploded in unison with Clanton's. Red went down to his knees under the numbing wrench of a blow at his right thigh. Clanton, as though caught in the stomach by the hoof of a kicking bronc, bent double and fell face downward on the walk.

Some mighty inexhaustible force seemed to possess the Circle D man. He straightened his bent body, lifted head and gun arm, and laid his sights on Red again. Red slumped sideward, and Clanton's bullet

stirred a breath past his head. He fired then, taking time to look across his sights. Before his gun had bucked up out of line, he saw the hole that dead-centered Clanton's forehead and brought the big man's frame flat to the planking in sure death.

It was over then, over but for the snap shots from the street that lent speed to the heels of the last three Clanton men left standing. As the boot pound of their hurried flight faded into the after-echo of the guns, two things happened almost simultaneously.

Harvey Jenkins, the sheriff, called loudly from behind the saloon doors: "Duke, are you there?" As he spoke two riders appeared out of the obscurity on the far side of the street. The leader of this pair, small of body, reined in suddenly as Clem's voice called: "Lift your hands, you two! Who are you?"

"Gail Dennis. Is Red Knight with you?"

Red felt weakness go through him as the girl spoke. His shoulder stabbed with pain as he pushed himself up on an elbow, trying to stand. His bad leg buckled under him, and he fell again, trying to call out to her.

Weariness and loss of blood dulled his mind as he lay back on the walk. He was vaguely aware of the crowd spilling from the saloon and gathering about him. Dimly, too, his eyes made out Gail Dennis's face, look-

ing down into his. That was the last he remembered as he struggled to try and find the strength to speak to her.

The room was airy, light, and it hurt Red's eyes to open them. For long minutes he stared upward at the whitewashed ceiling. Then, curious, he turned his head and looked toward the wall with the window in it. The wall was clean and light, too. Near the window was a small steel table covered with a white cloth. Bottles and an enameled basin sat on it.

"Hospital!" he breathed. The feebleness of his voice made him smile.

"Yes, Red," came a voice that made him turn quickly. It was Gail.

She was wearing the dress she'd worn that first day at the ranch, the blue one. Her hair was done the same way, too, only more loosely now than then. And, looking into her face, he was instantly worried at the tiredness he saw there.

"You've been very sick, Red," she said. "Try not to talk."

"Then you'd better," he said, and she smiled.

"Don't worry. Clem and the others are all right. Jim Rhodes came out of it with a broken arm. It's mending nicely. You see,"

she added, "you've been here three days now."

"How about Toad?"

"The doctor doesn't know why, but Toad's going to live." Gravity touched her glance. "Toad remembers. Duke Clanton shot him then left him lying in the road, while he waited for Clem. And something else about Duke. Pete Hernández, one of his men, talked before he died that night. Duke had hired him to steal cattle from Dad two years ago. It was Pete who hunted down Ned Spence and turned his horse loose on the desert. At the end, Pete said something about Duke's wanting to marry me and afterward take over the whole basin." She tried to smile again, but the expression was lost against the soberness in her eyes.

He lay looking up at her, not wanting anything to change. For the moment there was nothing more he desired. Gail was looking down at him with a tenderness that could mean only one thing. He loved this girl, and she might one day love him.

There was something more she had to say. "I . . . I've had your men take the herd across the river and put it on my graze." She hesitated, as though making up her mind to something. "I don't know how you'll take this, Red, but I've offered them

jobs until you're on your feet again. I want to offer you one, too."

Red did his best to nod. He wanted to say something but was afraid to.

Gail's glance didn't meet his now. Then she was saying: "I need a foreman and a crew that knows cattle. All Dad's men quit when I brought in the sheep. Now I want to go back to cattle. Could you stay on and . . . and would you help me get started again, started the right way?"

Then she was looking at him, a pleading in her eyes. Red lifted his hand and held it out to her. Sudden thankfulness brought her smile back again. Her hand met his.

"We'll get along, Red!" she murmured.

About the Author

Peter Dawson is the *nom de plume* used by Jonathan Hurff Glidden. He was born in Kewanee, Illinois, and was graduated from the University of Illinois with a degree in English literature. In his career as a Western writer he published sixteen Western novels and wrote over 120 Western short novels and short stories for the magazine market. From the beginning he was a dedicated craftsman who revised and polished his fiction until it shone as a fine gem. His Peter Dawson novels are noted for their adept plotting, interesting and well-developed characters, their authentically researched historical backgrounds, and his stylistic flair. During the Second World War, Glidden served with the U. S. Strategic and Tactical Air Force in the United Kingdom. Later in 1950 he served for a time as Assistant to Chief of Station in Germany. After the war,

his novels were frequently serialized in *The Saturday Evening Post*. Peter Dawson titles such as HIGH COUNTRY, GUNSMOKE GRAZE, and ROYAL GORGE are generally conceded to be among his best titles, although he was an extremely consistent writer and virtually all his fiction has retained its classic stature among readers of all generations. One of Jon Glidden's finest techniques was his ability, after the fashion of Dickens and Tolstoy, to tell his stories via a series of dramatic vignettes which focus on a wide assortment of different characters, all tending to develop their own lives, situations, and predicaments, while at the same time propelling the general plot of the story toward a suspenseful conclusion. He was no less gifted as a master of the short novel and short story.

We hope you have enjoyed this Large Print book. Other Thorndike Press or Chivers Press Large Print books are available at your library or directly from the publishers.

For more information about current and upcoming titles, please call or write, without obligation, to:

Thorndike Press
P.O. Box 159
Thorndike, Maine 04986 USA
Tel. (800) 223-2336

OR

Chivers Press Limited
Windsor Bridge Road
Bath BA2 3AX
England
Tel. (0225) 335336

All our Large Print titles are designed for easy reading, and all our books are made to last.

chair, and I never wanted any metal in my leg – I wanted to stay home, it's all shit, everything is shit . . . !' By this time he was yelling as if he'd gone out of his mind.

The nurse returned with a syringe.

'Give me a hand,' she said to the orderly, who was standing, silent and stupid, beside my bed.

The nurse looked at the temperature chart. 'Grolius,' she said in a low voice, 'do try and be reasonable. You're in pain, aren't you? I . . .'

'. . . An injection!' he yelled. 'What else, an injection! But . . .' he suddenly groaned, 'don't think I'm going to keel over with joy just because you're gracious enough to give me an injection . . . give the Führer an injection!'

You could have heard a pin drop. A voice said: 'For God's sake, give that arsehole an injection!'

No one spoke, and the nurse murmured: 'He's beside himself . . . really, he's beside himself . . .'

'Shit,' murmured the wounded man, and once more he whispered: 'Shit . . .' I leaned down and saw that he'd fallen asleep. His slack mouth looked bitter and almost black in the reddish stubble of his beard.

'There now!' the nurse said brightly. 'Now we'll have supper!'

She began handing round cocoa and sandwiches. The portion for the thigh casualty was placed on the one-armed man's chair. The cocoa was really good, and the sandwiches were spread with tinned fish.

After taking care of everyone, the nurse stood in the doorway holding the empty tray. 'Anyone else need anything . . . anything urgent?' she asked.

'Pills!' shouted someone from the far end of the car. 'Pills! I can't stand the pain!'

'What?' said the nurse. 'No, not now, in half an hour

you'll all be getting pills for the night anyway.'

'Nurse dear,' asked Hubert, 'where are we here?'

'We're in Nagykaroky,' she replied.

'Shit!' Hubert cried. 'Oh, goddamn shit!'

'What's matter?' I asked.

'Because we'll only be going as far as Debrecen after all. Half a night more at the most. Then there'll be another fucking hospital where we won't be allowed out.'

'But I thought we were going to Vienna, that's what I heard,' said the one-armed man. 'Aren't we?'

'Balls,' someone shouted. 'The train's going to Dresden.'

'Nonsense . . . Vienna Woods . . .'

'You'll see, Debrecen's the end of the line.'

'Really?' I asked.

'Are you sure?' I asked.

'Yes,' he said gloomily. 'Here, have a drink, I'm quite sure.'

But I didn't want a drink on top of the cocoa, I didn't want to destroy that wonderful sense of well-being. I smoked a cigarette, lay back carefully on my pillows and looked out into the night. I had tucked the blackout curtain slightly to one side and could look into the soft, dark grey night passing by. The train was moving again, everything was quiet except for the groans of the sleeping thigh casualty. Let's hope he sleeps all the way to Debrecen, I thought, let's hope the one-armed fellow keeps his mouth shut about his gold badge and his bloody sarge . . . and let's hope no one at either end of the car starts yelling and screaming 'shit'; and when the nurse comes I'll ask her to take my pulse so I can feel her gentle hand, and if she has some pills for me I'll let her put them into my mouth, like yesterday, and for a tenth of a second I'll feel her warm, white fingers on my lips.

But after the orderly had collected the dishes, they started playing gramophone records, Beethoven, and that made me cry, simply made me cry, because it reminded me of my mother.

Hell, I thought, never mind, no one's going to see. It was almost dark in the compartment, and we were being rocked from side to side, and I was crying . . . I would soon be nineteen, and I'd already been wounded three times, was already a hero, and I was crying because I was reminded of my mother.

In my mind's eye I clearly saw our home in Severin-Strasse, the way it had been before any bombs had fallen. A comfortable living room, very snug and warm and cheerful, and the street full of people, but no one knew who they were or why they were there. My mother was holding my arm, and we were silent, it was a summer evening and we were coming out of a concert . . . and my mother said nothing when I suddenly lit a cigarette, although I was only fifteen. There were soldiers in the street too, since it was war and yet not war. We weren't in the least hungry and not at all tired, and when we got home we might even drink a bottle of wine that Alfred had brought from France. I was fifteen and I would never have to be a soldier. And everything about Severin-Strasse felt so good. Beethoven, what a treat a Beethoven concert was.

I could see it all quite clearly. We had passed St Georg's, and a few whores had been standing there in the dark beside the urinal. Now we were passing the charming little square facing St Johann's, the small Romanesque church . . .

The street narrowed. We had to walk in the road and sometimes step aside for the tram; then we passed Tietz's, and finally the street widened out: there stood the great bulk of St Severin's tower. I could see everything so clearly: the shops with their displays – cigarettes, chocolate, kitchen spoons and leather soles. I could see it all as clear as day.

It was the nurse's gentle hand that startled me.

'Here we are,' came her voice, 'here's the Novalgin Quinine for your fever, and there,' she said as she handed me the thermometer, 'let's have your temperature!'

The mild fever gave me a feeling of contentment. It brought the goo on my back to the boil again, and now I was a hero again, four years older than before, wounded three times, and now an authentic, official hero. Even the sergeant in the Reserve wouldn't be able to touch me, for by the time I was back there again I would have the silver badge, so how could they possibly get at me . . . ?

By now I really did have a fever: 38.6, and the nurse entered a blue stroke on the curve of my chart that made it look quite alarming.

I had a fever, and from Debrecen it wasn't that far to Vienna, and from Vienna . . .

Maybe the front would collapse again at some corner, and there would be a big push, and we would all be moved to the rear, the way I'd heard it told so often – and like a shot we'd be in Vienna or Dresden, and from Dresden . . .

'Are you asleep, young fellow?' Hubert asked, 'or would you like another drink?'

'No,' I said, 'I'm asleep, asleep . . .'

'Okay, then. Goodnight.'

'Goodnight.'

But sleep was still a long way off. Somewhere towards the front of the car a man started screaming his head off. Lights were switched on . . . people shouted, ran, the nurse arrived and the doctor . . . and then all was quiet again.

The thigh casualty groaned and snored softly in his sleep . . .

Outside the night was once more totally dark, no longer grey; it was blue-black and silent, and I found I could no longer think of Severin-Strasse. I could think only of Debrecen . . . strange, I thought, when we did Hungary in geography you so often put your finger on Debrecen; it lay in the middle of a green patch, but not far away the colour turned to brown, then to very dark brown, that was the Carpathians, and who would ever have thought that one day you'd be swaying so quickly and quietly on your way to Debrecen, in the middle of the night. I tried to imagine the town.

Perhaps there would be some fine cafés there, and lots of things to buy, with *pengö* in your pocket. I glanced across at Hubert, but he had fallen asleep.

It was very quiet, and I longed for the tears to come again, but the image of my mother and of Severin-Strasse was completely wiped out.

The Cage

A man stood beside the fence looking pensively through the barbed-wire thicket. He was searching for something human, but all he saw was this tangle, this horribly systematic tangle of wires – then some scarecrow figures staggering through the heat towards the latrines, bare ground and tents, more wire, more scarecrow figures, bare ground and tents stretching away to infinity. At some point there was said to be no more wire, but he couldn't believe it. Equally inhuman was the immaculate, burning, impassive face of the blanched blue sky, where somewhere the sun floated just as pitilessly. The whole world was reduced to motionless scorching heat, held in like the breath of an animal under the spell of noon. The heat weighed on him like some appalling tower of naked fire that seemed to grow and grow and grow . . .

His eyes met nothing human; and behind him – he could see it even more clearly, without turning round – was sheer horror. There they lay, those others, round the inviolable football field, packed side by side like rotting fish; next came the meticulously clean latrines, and somewhere a long way behind him was also paradise: the shady, empty tents, guarded by well-fed policemen . . .

How quiet it was, how hot!

He suddenly lowered his head, as if his neck were breaking under the fiery hammer-blow, and he saw something that delighted him: the delicate shadows of the barbed wire on the bare ground. They were like the fine tracery of intertwining branches, frail and beautiful, and it seemed to him that they must be infinitely cool, those delicate tracings,

108

all linked with each other; yes, they seemed to be smiling, quietly and soothingly.

He bent down and carefully reached between the wires to pick one of the pretty branches; holding it up to his face he smiled, as if a fan had been gently waved in front of him. Then he reached out with both hands to gather up those sweet shadows. He looked left and right into the thicket, and the quiet happiness in his eyes faded: a wild surge of desire flared up, for there he saw innumerable little tracings which when gathered up must offer a precious, cool eternity of shadow. His pupils dilated as if about to burst out of the prison of his eyeballs: with a shrill cry he plunged into the thicket, and the more he became entangled in the pitiless little barbs the more wildly he flailed, like a fly in a spider's web, while with his hands he tried to grasp the exquisite shadow branches. His flailings were already stilled by the time the well-fed policemen arrived to free him with their wire-cutters.

I Can't Forget Her

I can't forget her; whenever I emerge even for a moment from the vortex of everyday life which with its constant pressure tries to keep me beneath the surface of human reality; whenever I can even for a second turn my back on the ceaseless bustle of the crass pomposity they call life, and pause where their inane shouting cannot reach me: then her image appears before me, as close and distinct and ravishingly beautiful as I saw her years ago, when she was wearing a collarless coat that revealed all of her delicate neck.

At the time they had given up hope for me. The captain had said we were to make a counter-attack, and the lieutenant had made a counter-attack with us. But there was nothing to attack. We ran blindly up a wooded hill one spring evening, but on the expected battleground there was complete silence. We paused on the hill, looked away into the distance, and could see nothing. Then we ran down into the valley, up another hill, and paused again. There was not an enemy in sight. Here and there behind bushes were abandoned holes, half-finished positions of our troops in which the meaningless junk of war had been hastily left behind. It was still quiet; an uncanny silence lay heavily under the great vault of the spring sky that was slowly covering itself with the darker veils of twilight. It was so quiet that the lieutenant's voice startled us: 'Carry on!' he ordered. But as we were about to proceed the sky suddenly roared down upon us, and the earth burst open.

The others had quickly dropped to the ground or flung themselves into the abandoned holes; I just caught sight of

110

the sergeant's pipe falling from his mouth, and then it felt as though they had knocked my legs from under my body . . .

Five men ran away after the first load had come down. Only the lieutenant and two men stayed behind; they hastily picked me up and ran down the slope with me while up above, where we had been lying, a fresh load came roaring down.

It was only much later, when all was quiet again and they laid me on the forest floor, that I felt any pain. The lieutenant wiped the sweat off his face and looked at me, but I could clearly see that he was not looking at the place where my legs must be. 'Don't worry,' he said, 'we'll get you back all right.'

The lieutenant placed a lighted cigarette between my lips, and I can still remember: while the pain increased again I still felt that life was beautiful. I was lying at the bottom of the valley on a forest path beside a little stream; up above, between the tall fir trees, only a narrow strip of sky was visible, a strip that was now silvery, almost white. The birds were singing, and an indescribably soothing silence reigned. I blew the cigarette smoke upward in long blue threads and felt that life was beautiful, and tears came to my eyes . . .

'It's all right,' said the lieutenant.

They carried me away. But it was a long way, almost two kilometres to the point where the captain had retreated, and I was heavy. I believe all wounded are heavy. The lieutenant carried the front end of the stretcher, and the other two walked behind. We slowly came out of the forest, across meadows and fields, and through another forest, and they had to set me down and wipe off their sweat, while the evening sank lower and lower. When we reached the village, everything was still quiet. They took me into a room

111

where the captain now was. On both sides, school desks had been piled up against the walls, and the teacher's desk was covered with hand grenades. As I was being carried in, they were busy distributing the hand grenades. The captain was shouting into a telephone, threatening someone that he would have him shot. Then he let out a curse and hung up. They set me down behind the teacher's desk, where some other wounded were also lying. One of them was sitting there with his hand shot to pieces; he looked very contented.

The lieutenant gave a report on the counter-attack to the captain, and the captain yelled at the lieutenant that he would have him shot, and the lieutenant said, 'Yessir.' That made the captain yell even more, and the lieutenant again said, 'Yessir,' and the captain stopped yelling. They stuck big torches in flowerpots and lit them. By now it was dark, and there seemed to be no electric current. After the hand grenades had been distributed, the room emptied. All that was left were two sergeants, a clerk, the lieutenant and the captain. The captain said to the lieutenant: 'See that security sentries are placed all round the village; we'll try to get a few hours' sleep. Tomorrow we'll be starting out early.'

'To the rear?' asked the lieutenant quietly.

'Get out!' yelled the captain; the lieutenant left. After he had gone, I looked for the first time at my legs and saw that they were covered with blood, and I couldn't feel them, I felt only pain where normally I would have felt my legs. I was shivering now. Beside me lay a man who must have been shot in the stomach; he was very quiet and pale and scarcely moved; from time to time he merely stroked his hand, very quietly and carefully, across the blanket that covered his stomach. No one paid any attention to us. I imagine the medic had been among the five who had run away.

Suddenly the pain reached my stomach and crept higher very quickly; it flowed up like molten lead as far as my heart, and I believe I began to scream and then fainted . . .

I woke up and first heard music. I was lying on my side, looking into the face of the fellow with the stomach wound and saw that he was dead. His blanket was all black with congealed blood. And I could hear music, somewhere they must have found a radio. They were playing something quite modern, it must have been a foreign station; then the music was wiped out as if by a wet rag, and they played military marches, then came something classical, and they let that music go on. Then a voice above me said very softly, 'Mozart,' and I looked up and saw her face and realized at the same moment that it couldn't be Mozart, and I said to that face: 'No, it's not Mozart.'

She bent over me, and now I saw that she was a doctor or a medical student, she looked so young, but she was holding a stethoscope. Now all I could see was her loose, soft crown of brown hair, for she was bending over my legs, lifting the blanket so that I couldn't see anything. Then she raised her head, looked at me, and said: 'It *is* Mozart.' She pushed up my sleeve, and I said softly: 'No, it can't possibly be Mozart.'

The music went on playing, and now I was quite sure that it could never be Mozart. Some of it sounded like real Mozart, but there were other passages that couldn't possibly be Mozart.

My arm was all white. With gentle fingers she felt my pulse, then came a sudden needle prick, and she injected something into my arm.

As she did so, her head came quite close, and I whispered: 'Give me a kiss.' She blushed deeply, withdrew the needle, and at that moment a voice on the radio said:

'Dittersdorf.' Suddenly she smiled, and I smiled too, for now I could get a proper look at her because the only torch that was still burning was behind her. 'Quick,' I said in a louder voice, 'give me a kiss.' She blushed again and looked even more beautiful; the light from the torch shone on the ceiling and spread in wavering red circles round the walls. She gave a quick glance over her shoulder, then bent over me and kissed me, and at that instant I saw her closed eyelids from very near and felt those soft lips while the torch flung its restless light round the room and the captain's voice bellowed into the telephone again and now some different music was being spewed out of the speaker. Then a voice called out an order, someone picked me up and carried me out into the night and placed me in a cold van, and I had a last glimpse of her standing there, her eyes following me in the torchlight, right among all the school desks that were piled up like the absurd rubble of a collapsing world.

As far as I know, they are all back now in their proper jobs: the captain is an athletics instructor, the lieutenant is dead, and there's nothing I can tell you about the others – after all, I knew them only for a few hours. No doubt the school desks are back in their proper places, the electric light is working again, and torches are lit only on very romantic occasions; and instead of bellowing 'I'll have you shot!' the captain is now shouting something harmless such as perhaps: 'Idiot!' or 'Coward!', when someone can't do a grand circle on the crossbar. My legs have healed up, and I can walk quite well, and they tell me at the Veterans Affairs office that I should be working. But I have a different, much more important occupation: I am looking for her. I can't forget her. People tell me I'm crazy because I make no effort to do a grand circle in the air and land smartly on my feet like a good citizen and then, eager and thirsting for praise, step back in line.

Fortunately they are obliged to give me a pension, and I can afford to wait and search, for I know that I shall find her . . .

Green are the Meadows

The tram was crossing a street whose name – white on blue at the corner under the street-lamp – suddenly seemed familiar to him. He blushed, pulled out his notebook, and found the name of the street, circled in red, on a scribbled page: Bülow-Strasse. He now realized he had always passed over this page, although at heart he hadn't forgotten the name for so much as a single day . . .

The tram slowly rounded a curve and stopped. He heard music from a bar, saw gas lamps burning in the dusk; from somewhere beyond a garden fence came the laughter of young girls, and he got off. The suburb was like all the suburbs: pockmarked, dirty, dotted with little gardens and somehow appealing: it had the smell, the sound, the colour and the quite indescribable atmosphere of vulnerability . . .

The man heard the tram screeching off and set down his bundle. Although he knew the number by heart, he put his hand into his pocket and once more leafed through his notebook: 14 Bülow-Strasse. Now there was no way of avoiding it. He realized why he had always refused the job of picking up the cigarettes in this particular town. Of course there was many a Bülow-Strasse, every decent town had its Bülow-Strasse, but only in this town was there this house, number 14, where a woman by the name of Gärtner was living, a woman for whom he had a message about something that had happened four years ago and that he should have told her about four years ago . . .

The gas lamps lit up the high fence of a lumber yard, and

painted on the fence were huge white letters. Through the gaps he saw the light-coloured piles of trim boards, and he wearily deciphered the inscription on the fence: SCHUSTER BROTHERS: then he took a step backwards because the lettering on the fence was so big that his eyes had trouble following it, and much farther along, lit up by another gas lamp, he read: OLDEST LUMBER YARD IN TOWN. At the spot where he could read the final N of this display of integrity there was a large black house in which a few windows shone with a yellow light. The windows were open, he saw lamplight, heard radio music, and somewhere he heard again the girls' bright laughter. Someone was playing a guitar, and a few boys' voices were gently singing, 'We lay by the camp fire, Conchita and I . . .', other voices joined in, and a second guitar was struck up; the girls' laughter had died away.

The man walked slowly along beside the fence as far as the second gas lamp, which stood exactly between the T and the O. The shining tram rails continued on into a narrow street with closely packed buildings whose façades were almost dead, dark and frightening; the buildings seemed to have been burned out.

The dusk had grown thicker; he now saw those dead façades lit up by a tall, gently swaying lamp, and at the far corner there was another group of young fellows; the tips of their cigarettes glowed in the dusk. That must be the entrance to Bülow-Strasse . . .

He was still standing between the T and the O. It was quiet, with only the low, plaintive sounds of the two guitars and the soft voices coming to the end of the song. On the other side of the street were allotment gardens. Just then, a man standing in the dark lit his pipe, and he saw the match light up a fisherman's cap and a pudgy, heavy face, its lips puckered to blow out the match with one puff of smoke. Then all was swallowed up again in the silent darkness. He strolled slowly on, and at the end of the lumber yard's long fence the silence was suddenly broken; from the open doors of a bar came loud male laughter and in the background a frantic male voice yelling from a radio. The first cross-street seemed almost undamaged: loud laughter reached him and shouts and the murmuring conversation of people sitting on chairs outside their doors . . .

While walking past this scene as if he were passing an open, crowded living room, he was thinking: I can still go back. I don't have to be in this Bülow-Strasse. But he went on, as if under some compulsion, towards the traffic lights, and he had soon reached the group of young fellows at the street corner. There was some noise coming from Bülow-Strasse, too, but as he quickly turned the corner he saw that these façades also showed great black gaps, and for a moment he wished that number 14 might also have been destroyed. That would solve everything.

At the corner he hesitated. Once I enter the street, there's no going back, he thought. They will recognize me as a stranger, ply me with questions, and I'll have to tell them everything. He made a quick turn to the left and pushed his way through the group of youngsters into the bar. 'Evening all,' he said, sitting down at the table nearest the door. The landlord behind the counter, tall, thin, dark-complexioned, nodded and called out: 'Beer?'

'Yes,' said the man.

On a table to his right lay the crutches of an amputee. Beside the fat amputee, who had pushed his hat to the back of his head, sat a man and a woman with troubled expressions, their hands clasped wearily round their beer glasses. Over in a corner some men were playing cards, and

118

on the radio a woman was now singing, 'Mamma says it's wrong to kiss, Mamma says it isn't done . . .' The landlord brought the beer, and the man said, 'Thanks.' He put his bundle down on the chair beside him and fumbled in his breast pocket for a crumpled cigarette.

So this is it, he thought, this is the bar. This is where he sang his 'Rosemarie' and his 'Green are the Meadows'; where he cursed yet proudly showed off his decorations, where he bought cigarettes and stood singing at the counter.

Then all he could see was the man, whose name had been Gärtner, being shot to death by a sergeant called Stevenson. That little, red-haired Stevenson with the cheeky face had shot him right in the stomach with his machine pistol, four shots one above the other, and he had never seen a mouth that had once sung 'Rosemarie' so distorted with pain. They had dragged him round the corner of a building, taken off his tunic and ripped open his trousers; a mass of blood and faeces had welled out of his stomach, and the mouth that had once sung 'Rosemarie' and 'Green are the Meadows' in this very bar had been silenced by pain. They had heard no more shooting, they had taken his paybook from his pocket, and he had jotted down: Gärtner, 14 Bülow-Strasse, with the idea of telling the wife if he should ever find himself in this town. Gärtner hadn't said another word, that horrible mass of blood and faeces came slowly welling out of his stomach, and they – the other man and himself – could only look on helplessly until suddenly a voice behind them shouted 'Hands up!' and they discovered that this red-haired sergeant was called Stevenson. The next moment twelve trembling Americans were standing round them, and he had never seen men tremble like that; they trembled so much that he could hear the light tinkling of their machine pistols, and one of the Americans said: 'That's one gone, Stevenson . . .'

Stevenson made a swift, discarding gesture; he and the other man understood and threw their weapons behind them. The other man – he had never found out his name, they had only known each other for half an hour – had been carrying a machine gun like a big black cat under his arm; now he flung the machine gun behind him into a broad puddle of wet ordure. He heard it splash, just as in the old days their swimming instructor had demonstrated a dive, and in his mind's eye he could still see the bald, yellow globe of the gas lamp. He only came to when one of the Americans in his excitement fired a shot right past his nose, and they saw that Gärtner was dead and heard tanks rumbling towards them . . .

He looked at his beer and noticed a little vase of flowers next to his glass – a twig with yellow, plump, but fading pussy-willow, and he realized that spring had come round again, just as it had done so long ago. It must be exactly four years since Stevenson had shot Gärtner in the stomach until blood and faeces poured out. The amputee gave a brutal shrug, and the expressions of the man and woman became still more troubled. The youths outside the door must now have been joined by the girls: he could hear the girls' high laughter, and then they all began to sing, and the man and woman sitting with the fat amputee, their hands still miserably clasping their beer glasses, now looked through the open door and listened to the singing. 'Max!' the amputee called out to the landlord. 'Bring us three more beers, will you?'

The man could hear that the couple sitting with the amputee were trying to whisper their objections. Outside the young people were singing songs whose words he couldn't make out, soft, soothing, sentimental tunes.

The landlord came past his table, picked up the empty glass, and asked: 'Same again?'

'Yes.'

The man glanced at the cigarettes he had wrapped in a pair of blue work trousers. Outside the laughing, singing voices of the boys and girls gradually moved away. From the radio now came a talk, and the landlord twiddled the knobs doggedly until music came on again.

'I'd like to pay!' the man called out.

The landlord came over. While putting down the money he asked in a low voice: 'Gärtner – didn't Gärtner use to come here quite often?'

'That's right,' the landlord said at once, smoothing out the note the man had given him. 'Did you know him? Willi Gärtner?'

'Yes. Is he still alive?'

'No, he got killed in the war.'

'When?'

'Oh, I don't know – quite late, I think, towards the end. Where did you meet him?'

'We worked together.'

'At Plattke's?'

'Yes, at Plattke's . . . and his wife, what's she doing?'

The landlord looked at him in surprise: 'But she's at Plattke's now! Aren't you there any more?'

'No, I'm not . . .'

'I see,' said the landlord indifferently. He picked up the empty glass and called out to another customer: 'Just a moment – I'm coming!'

The man got up, quietly said, 'Goodnight,' and, without looking back, left the bar.

Here and there in the unlit, open windows he could see

the glow of cigarettes, and he could hear the distant wail of radio sets. The building next door to the bar was number 28. It was a grocery. In the dim half-light he could see the cardboard signs for Maggi and Persil, and in the gloom beyond the shop window a basket of eggs, a pile of cereal packages, and a big glass jar with sour pickles and onions floating around in it. It was like looking through the glass of a neglected aquarium. The objects seemed to float and sway, mollusc-like, slimy creatures carrying on their lecherous existence in the dim half-dark.

So this is it, he thought. This is where his wife bought her vinegar and soup packets and cigarettes, and somewhere round here there'll also be a butcher and a baker . . . a stomach like that must, after all, be nourished for a long time before it can be shot up so expertly that blood and faeces come pouring out in a viscous stream. Everything must be done in its proper order. For at least eighteen years a stomach like that must be regularly filled with all those things to be bought for a week's wages from the butcher, the baker and the grocer; and sometimes that stomach must also drink beer and sing, and the mouth belonging to that stomach is also allowed to smoke cigarettes, everything in its proper order . . .

The people sitting outside their doors have no idea that somewhere in the world there is an American who shot up their Willi – right through the stomach – flutch . . . flutch . . . flutch . . . flutch . . . he would never forget that sound, the demonic mildness, that gentle flopping which had riddled Gärtner's stomach.

The people didn't seem to notice him. He was just someone going home with a pair of blue work trousers under his arm. He stopped and fumbled in his breast pocket for another crumpled cigarette. The crumpled ones were his, that had been agreed. As he stood there he glanced at the next front door and saw that it was number 18. Then came a gap, so the next house must be number 14. He saw lighted windows there and some chairs outside the door.

Glowing ashes had been scattered all over the bomb site, and here and there the remains of briquets were smouldering and there was a smell of rags and potato peelings that had caught fire. In a lighted window he had a fleeting glimpse of a heavy, stout fellow with a cigar in his mouth, and behind his back a woman standing at a stove in front of a smoking frying pan.

Four years ago it had also been spring, it had also been April, everything had turned green again after a terrible winter. They had been aware of that in the chill nights when they had crouched futilely in their holes, guarding bridges over rivers that in many thousands of places could be waded across: they had been aware of it: it was spring. And when the grey dawn came they retreated, attacked and were attacked. The troop units were torn apart, patched together again. Whole regiments cleared out or went over to the enemy; many of the men were caught again at street corners and rounded up, and there was always some officer there to take command. They were posted at street corners or shoved at night into holes just so they could be well and truly shot to pieces. As a result one found oneself with new comrades every day. He had known Gärtner for only half an hour. A lieutenant had arrived and said, 'Come with me!' and had stationed him at the intersection beside Gärtner and the man with the machine gun. Gärtner had given him a cigarette, which at that time was worth more than all the decorations put together. Grenades had burst somewhere, tanks had rumbled, there had been some shooting, and suddenly those bullets had flopped into Gärtner's stomach . . .

He was still staring at the glowing piles of ashes, breathing in the repulsive stench of scorched rags. Outside number 14 two women were sitting on chairs, dark, stoutish figures in whispered conversation. In the doorway itself stood a young fellow, smoking; he walked towards the youth and said: 'Could I have a light, please?'

In silence the fellow casually held his glowing butt against the cigarette, and while the kitchen odours that permeated the youth's clothing rose into the man's nostrils together with the smell of cheap soap, he looked beyond his cigarette into the open, unlit corridor, and then – in that half-second he needed for lighting his cigarette – he heard a couple embracing in there in the dark; he heard those indescribable sounds of wordless tenderness, that gentle groaning that was like suppressed pain; he felt the blood mounting, hot and tormenting, to his head. He hurriedly thanked the youth and walked quickly, very quickly, back, past the glowing ash heaps, past the un-damaged houses, the gaps and the grocery. By the time he reached the corner he was almost running because he could hear the tram screeching towards him from behind; and when he glanced over his shoulder and saw its dim yellow lights approaching in the gentle, spring darkness, he broke into a run.

He was so afraid of missing the tram that before reaching the tram stop, where he paused for a moment, he caught only snatches of the young people's singing: the group now seemed to be standing somewhere near the allotment gardens. Now they were singing 'Green are the Meadows' so earnestly and meltingly that no more laughter was to be heard between the verses.

The tram came to a stop and he was glad to be able to get on. He wiped away his sweat, had one more passing glimpse of the lumber yard's neatly lettered fence, and wished that the tram could have continued on and on, forever . . .

The Rain Gutter

For a long time they lay awake smoking while the wind swept through the house, loosening tiles and tumbling bricks; pieces of plaster sailed down with a crash from the upper floors, shattering below and spreading into rubble.

He saw only a dim sheen of her, a warm, reddish hue when they drew on their cigarettes: the soft outlines of her breasts under her nightgown and her calm profile. The sight of the narrow, firmly closed crease between her lips, that little valley in her face, filled him with tenderness. They tucked the covers in firmly at the sides, nestled close together, and knew that they would keep warm all night long. The shutters rattled, and the wind whistled through the jagged holes in the window panes; above them it howled in the remains of the attic, and somewhere there was the sound of an object slapping noisily and steadily against a wall, something hard, metallic, and she whispered: 'That's the gutter, it's been broken for a long time.'

She was silent for a moment, then took his hand and softly went on: 'The war hadn't started yet, and I was already living here, and whenever I came home I'd see the piece of gutter hanging there, and I'd think: they *must* have it repaired; but they never did. It hung crooked, one of the clamps had come loose, and it always seemed about to fall at any moment. I always heard it when there was a wind, every night when there was a storm and I was lying here. And when the war started it was still hanging there. On the grey house wall you could clearly see where the water had flowed sideways into the wall after every rain: a white path, with a grey border leading down past the window, and on either side there were big round patches with white centres surrounded by darker grey rings. Later on I went far away, I was put to work in Thuringia and Berlin, and when the war was over I came back here, and the gutter was still hanging there: half the building had collapsed – I'd been far away, far, far away, and I'd seen so much pain, death and blood, they had shot at me with machine guns from airplanes, and I'd been scared, so scared – and all that time that piece of galvanized iron had been hanging here, sending the rain into empty space because the wall below was almost completely gone. Roof tiles had fallen off, trees had been toppled, plaster had come crumbling down, bombs had fallen, so many bombs, but that piece of galvanized iron had continued to hang from that one clamp, it had never been hit, its crooked slant had never given way to the blasts.'

Her voice became even lower, almost a chant, and she pressed his hand. 'So much rain came raining down,' she said, 'in those six years, so many deaths were died, cathedrals destroyed, but the gutter was still hanging there when I came back. Once again I heard it clattering at night whenever there was a wind. Can you believe that I was happy?'

'I can,' he said.

The wind had subsided, it was quiet now, and the cold crept closer. They pulled up the covers and hid their hands inside. In the darkness he could no longer distinguish anything, he couldn't even see her profile, although she was lying so close that he could feel her breath, her calm, regular breathing warm against his skin, and he thought she had fallen asleep. But suddenly he could no longer hear her breathing and he groped for her hands. She moved her hand down and grasped his and held onto it, and he knew

127

they would be warm and he wouldn't have to shiver all night long.

Suddenly he became aware that she was crying. There was nothing to be heard, he just knew from the movements of the bed that she was wiping her face with her left hand. Even that wasn't certain, but he knew she was crying. He sat up, bent over her and felt her breath again: it seemed to spread over his face like a current gently flowing past him. Even when his nose touched her cold cheek, he still could see nothing.

'Lie down,' she whispered, 'you'll catch cold.'

He remained leaning over her, he wanted to see her, but he saw nothing until she suddenly opened her eyes: then he saw the glint of her eyes in the darkness, the shimmering tears.

She cried for a long time. He took her hand, held it, and firmly tucked in the covers again. He held her hand for a long time, until her grip relaxed and her hand slowly slipped out of his – he put his arm round her shoulder, drew her close, and then he too fell asleep, and as they slept their breathing alternated like caresses . . .

Autumn Loneliness

How long we spent standing there at the corner I can't tell you. I was filled with a sense of anticipation that was really quite unjustified. It was now autumn, and each time a tram stopped at the corner people came streaming towards us, their footsteps rustling in the dead leaves, and in their steps was joy, the joy of people going home.

We must have stood there for a long time. It had been still quite light when suddenly, without a word, we had stopped, as if to mount guard over the deepening melancholy of autumn, a mood caught in the tops of the plane trees as they slowly shed their leaves.

There was no real reason for it, but each time the tram rang its bell at the corner and people came streaming into the avenue towards us and the tram drove on ringing its bell – each time I was convinced that someone was about to come, someone who knew us, who would ask us to join him, whose homeward steps would force our own weary, aimless footsteps to keep up with the tempo of his happy excitement.

The first ones always came singly and walked very fast; then came the groups, in twos or even threes in animated conversation, and finally another trickle of weary individuals passing us with their heavy burdens before dispersing into the houses scattered among gardens and avenues.

It was a constant suspense that held me spellbound, for after the last person had passed by there was only a brief respite before we heard the distant ping-pinging of the next tram at the previous stop – clanking and screeching its way to the corner.

We stood under the branches of an elderberry tree that reached out over the street far beyond the fence of a neglected garden. Rigid with tension, he had his face turned in the direction of the people approaching through the rustling leaves – the face which, mute and set, had been accompanying me for two months, which I had loved, and also hated, for two months . . .

During the time it took four trams to arrive, the tension and anticipation felt wonderful as we stood there in the steadily deepening melancholy of dusk, in the soft, exquisite, damp decay of autumn; but all of a sudden I knew that no one to whom I might belong would ever come . . .

'I'm leaving,' I said huskily, for I had been standing there much too long as if rooted to the bottom of some swampy bowl that was about to close imperceptibly over me with a velvety, relentless force.

'Go ahead,' he said without looking at me, and for the first time in two months he forgot to add: 'I'll come with you.'

His eyes narrowed to slits; without moving, he kept his hard, metallic gaze fixed on the deserted avenue where now only a few single leaves were slowly circling to the ground.

All right, I thought, and at that moment something happened to me, something was released, and I felt my face collapsing, felt sharp, bitter lines forming round my mouth. It was almost as if my inner tension had been tightly wound up and was now being released as if by a blow: uncoiling inside me with incredible speed, leaving nothing behind but that hollow, mournful void that had been there two months ago. For at that moment it dawned on me: he was standing here waiting for something quite specific; this spot, this street corner under the spreading branches of the elderberry tree, was his objective, the goal of an arduous

130

flight, of a journey lasting two months, while for me it was just another street corner, one of many thousand.

I watched him for a long time, which I could do undisturbed as he had ceased to notice me. Perhaps he thought I had already left. In his watchful gaze was something resembling hate, while his shallow, rapid breathing shook him like the prelude to an explosion . . .

If only he would remember, I sighed to myself, to give me one of the two cigarettes and my share of the bread. I was afraid to ask, for now the tram was stopping again at the corner. Then I saw, very briefly, the first and last smile on his face before he rushed forward with a smothered cry. From among a cluster of people, some of whom he had thrust aside, I heard a woman's gasp breaking the melancholy silence of the autumnal evening, and something like a shadow fell across the astonished void of my heart, for now I knew that I would have to go on inexorably alone, that I would also have to accept the loss of the cigarette and the bread and of the two months of shared danger and shared hunger . . .

I turned away, dipped my tired feet into the golden waves of dead leaves and walked out of the town, once again towards that Somewhere. The freshness of the falling light was still permeated by the spicy smell of burning potato plants, the smell of childhood and of longing. The sky was starless and drained of colour. Only the grinning face of the moon hung over the horizon, watching me mockingly as I plodded on under the weight of the darkness, towards that Somewhere . . .

Beside the River

To tell the truth, I'd never known the meaning of despair. But then, a few days ago, I found out. All of a sudden the whole world seemed grey and wretched; nothing, nothing mattered any more, and I had a bitter lump in my throat, and I thought there was no way out for me, no escape and no help. For I had lost all our ration cards, and at the ration office they would never believe me, they wouldn't replace them, and we had no more money for the black market, and stealing – I really didn't like to steal, and anyway I couldn't steal enough for that many people. For Mother and Father, for Karl and Grete, and for myself, and for our youngest, the baby. And the special mother's card was gone, and Father's manual worker's card – everything, everything was gone, the whole briefcase. I suddenly realized it in the tram, and I didn't bother to look or even ask. It's useless, I thought – who's going to hand over ration cards, and so many, and the mother's card and Father's manual worker's card . . .

At that moment I knew the meaning of despair. I got off the tram much earlier and walked straight down to the Rhine; I'll drown myself, I thought. But when I reached the bare, cold avenue and saw the calm, wide, grey river it came to me that it's not so easy to drown oneself; still, I wanted to do it. It must take a long time to die, I thought, and I would have liked a quick, sudden death. Obviously I couldn't go home any more. Mother would simply throw up her hands, and Father would give me a good hiding and say it was a disgrace: a big lout like that, almost seventeen, who's no good for anything anyway, not even for the black market – a big lout like that goes and loses all the ration cards when he's sent out to queue up for the fat rations! And I didn't even get the fat. It was all gone after I had been queuing for about three hours. Still, that might not have lasted too long, that trouble with Father and Mother. But we would have nothing to eat, no one would give us anything. At the ration office they would laugh in our faces because once before we had lost a few coupons; and as for selling or flogging something, we had long ago run out of things, and stealing – you can't steal for so many.

No, I had to drown myself, since I didn't have the nerve to throw myself under some big fat American car. There were many cars driving beside the Rhine, but there wasn't a soul in the avenue. It was bare and cold, and a damp, icy wind blew from the grey, swift-flowing water. I kept walking straight ahead and eventually was surprised at how fast I reached the end of the avenue. The trees seemed to fall away on either side of me, keeling over like poles and disappearing, and I didn't dare look back. So I very quickly reached the end of the avenue where the Rhine widens out a bit and there is a launching ramp for kayaks and a little farther on the ruined bridge. There wasn't a soul there either, only over by the launching ramp an American sat staring into the water. It was odd, the way he was crouching there, sitting on his heels; it was probably too cold to sit on the stones, so there he squatted, throwing precious cigarette butts into the water. Each butt, I thought, is almost half a loaf of bread. Perhaps he isn't smoking at all, but all the Americans just smoke a quarter of a cigarette and throw the rest away. I know it for a fact. He's lucky, I thought, he's not hungry and hasn't lost any coupons, and with every butt he throws three marks and seventy-five pfennigs into the cold grey Rhine. If I were he, I thought, I'd sit down by the stove with a cup of coffee instead of squatting here by the cold Rhine and staring into the dirty water . . .

I ran on; yes, I believe I did run. My thoughts about the American had been very brief and fleeting; I had envied him no end, it was terrible how I envied him. So I walked on or ran, I forget now, all the way to the ruined bridge, thinking: if you jump off from up there it's all over, all over in no time. I once read that it is hard to drown yourself by going into the water slowly. You have to plunge in from high up, that's the best way. So I ran towards the ruined bridge. There were no workmen there. Maybe they were on strike, or it's impossible to work out there on the bridges in cold weather. I saw nothing more of the American, I never once looked back.

No, I thought, there's no help and no hope, and no one will replace our ration cards, there are too many of us, Father and Mother, my brother and sister, the baby and I, plus the special mother's card and Father's manual worker's card. It's hopeless, drown yourself, then at least there'll be one less mouth to feed. It was very, very cold, there in the avenue beside the Rhine; the wind whistled, and bare branches fell from the trees that in summertime are so beautiful.

It was difficult to climb onto the ruined bridge; they had knocked out what remained of the paving, and there was only the skeleton left, and along it ran a kind of little railway, probably for hauling away the rubble.

I climbed very carefully, and I was terribly cold and very much afraid of falling off. I can well remember thinking: how stupid to be scared of falling since you want to drown yourself! If you fall off here, onto the street or onto the rubble, you'll also be dead, and that'll be all right, that's what you want. But it's quite a different thing, I can't explain it. What I wanted was to throw myself into the water and not smash onto the ground, and I thought of all the pain one might suffer and maybe not even be dead. And I didn't want to suffer. So I climbed very carefully over the bare bridge right to the end, the very end where the rails stick out in the air. There I stood, looking into the grey, grey murmuring water, there I stood close to the very end. I felt no fear, only despair, and suddenly I knew that despair is beautiful, it is sweet and nothing, it is nothing, and nothing matters any more.

The Rhine was fairly high, and grey and cold, and for a long time I stared into its face. I also saw the American squatting there, and really did see him throw a precious butt into the water. I was surprised to find him so near, much nearer than I had thought. I looked once again along the whole length of the bare avenue, and then suddenly looked down into the Rhine again, and I became terribly dizzy, and then I fell! All I remember is that my last thought was of Mother, and that it might after all be worse for me to be dead than to have lost the ration cards, the whole lot . . . Father's and Mother's and my brother's and sister's and the baby's, plus the special mother's card and Father's manual worker's card, and . . . yes, yes, my card too, although I'm a useless mouth, no good even for the black market . . .

I guess I must have sat there for an hour beside the murky Rhine, staring into the water. All I could think of was that blonde broad, Gertrud, who was driving me nuts. Hell, I thought, spitting my cigarette into the Rhine: throw yourself in, into that grey brew, and let it carry you down to – to Holland, yes, and still farther, say into the Channel, right down to the bottom of the sea! There wasn't a soul around, and the water was driving me nuts. I know for sure it was the water, and my thinking all the time of that good-looking broad who wouldn't have me. Nope, she wouldn't have me, and I knew for sure that I'd never, never get anywhere with her. And the water wouldn't let go of me, the water was driving me nuts. Hell, I thought, throw yourself in and those goddamn women won't bother you any more, throw yourself in . . .

And then I heard someone running along the avenue like a maniac. I've never seen anyone run like that. He's in trouble, I thought, and stared at the water again, but the footsteps in the deserted avenue above made me look up again, and I saw the kid running toward the wrecked bridge, and I thought, I'll bet they're after him and I hope he gets away, never mind if he's been stealing or whatever. A thin, lanky kid, running like a maniac. Again I looked at the water – throw yourself in, a voice kept whispering . . . You'll never get her, never, throw yourself in and let the grey brew carry you to Holland, goddammit, and I spat the third cigarette into the water.

For God's sake, I thought, what are you doing here in this country, in this crazy country, where every living soul can think of nothing but cigarettes? In this crazy country where the bridges are all gone and there's no colour, no colour anywhere, dammit, only grey. And everyone chasing after God knows what. And that girl, that crazy, long-legged broad, will never be yours, not for a million cigarettes will she be yours, damn it to hell.

But just then I heard that crazy kid crawling around up there on the bridge. The iron skeleton rang hollow under his boots, and the crazy kid climbed right out to the far end, and there he stood, for the longest time, also looking into the dirty grey water, and all of a sudden I knew that no one was chasing him, but that he . . . Goddammit, I thought, he wants to throw himself into the water! And I got a real shock and couldn't take my eyes off the spot where that crazy kid was standing, not moving, not making a sound, up there in the gap of the ruined bridge, and he seemed to sway a little . . .

I automatically spat the fourth cigarette into the Rhine and I couldn't take my eyes off that figure up there. I turned cold all over, I was terrified. That boy, that young kid, what kind of troubles can he have, I thought? Girl trouble, and I laughed – at least I think I laughed, I can't be sure. Can this young kid already have girl trouble, I thought? The water said nothing, and it was so quiet that I thought I could hear that kid's breathing as he went on standing there, motionless, silent, in the gap of the ruined bridge. Goddammit, I thought, it mustn't happen, and I was just going to call out when I thought, you'll scare him and then he'll fall for sure. The silence was weird, and we two were all alone in the world with this dirty grey water.

And then, for God's sake, he looked at me, really looked at me, and I was still sitting there, not moving a muscle and Splash! the crazy kid was actually down there in the water!

That really woke me up, and in no time I'd thrown off my jacket and cap. I dived into the cold water and started swimming. It was hard work, but luckily the current carried him toward me. Then suddenly he was gone, gone under, dammit, and my shoes were full of water, they felt like lead on my feet, my shirt was like lead too, and it was cold, icy cold, and not a sign of the kid anywhere . . . I paddled on, then trod water for a bit and shouted, yes shouted . . . and dammit if the kid didn't come up again, he was already a bit downstream, and I hadn't thought the current was that fast. Now my body seemed to warm up a bit, with panic, at the sight of that lifeless bundle being swept off in that grey dirty water, and me after it, and when I was less than two yards away – I could actually see the blond hair – he was gone again, just gone, dammit . . . but I was after him, head down, and Christ Almighty! I'd grabbed hold of him.

Nobody in the world can know how relieved I was when I'd grabbed hold of him. In the middle of the Rhine, and there was only grey, cold, dirty water, and I was as heavy and cold as lead, and yet I felt relieved. It's just that I had no more fear, that's what it must have been . . . and I swam slowly across the current with him to the shore and was surprised at how close the shore was.

Jesus, I had no time to shiver or moan, although I'd had a lousy time of it. I'd swallowed a whole lot of water, and the dirty stuff made me feel sick as a dog, but I rested till I got my breath back, then I grabbed his arms and pumped them up and down, up and down, up and down, just like they tell you to, and I got pretty damn hot over it . . . There wasn't a living soul up there on the river bank, and no one heard it or saw it. Then the kid opened his eyes, a pair of bright blue child's eyes, for God's sake, and he sicked up water, kept sicking it up . . . Dammit, I thought, the kid's got nothing but water in his stomach, and nothing but water came up, and then he felt he had to smile, the kid actually smiled at me . . .

By that time I was as cold as hell in those wet things, and I thought, you'll catch your death, and he was shaking like a leaf too.

Then I pulled him up and said: 'Go on, boy . . . run!' and I just grabbed him by the arm and ran up the ramp with him, he was as limp as a rag doll in my arm, then he stopped again and sicked up some more grey water, dirty grey Rhine water, that was all, then he could run better.

Goddamn, I thought, he has to get warm and you have to get warm, and in the end we ran pretty good, right up to the avenue and then a bit along the avenue. I began to feel quite warm and I sure was panting, but the kid was still shaking like a leaf. Dammit, I thought, he needs to get indoors and then into a bed, but there were no houses there, just a few piles of rubble and some rails, and it was already getting dark. But then one of our vehicles turned up, a Jeep, and I dashed out onto the street and waved my arms. First it drove on, there was a black driving it, but I yelled at the top of my voice: 'Hey there, bud . . .' and he must have heard from my voice that I was an American – you see, I wasn't wearing a jacket or a cap. So he stopped, and I hauled the kid over, and the black shook his head and said: 'Poor kid – almost drowned, did he?'

'Yes,' I answered, 'let's go, and step on it!' I told him where my billet was.

The boy sat next to me and gave me another of those pathetic smiles, enough to make me feel pretty weird, and I felt his pulse a bit, it seemed okay.

'Hurry!' I shouted to the black. He turned around and grinned and really did speed up, and all the time I was saying: 'Make a left, now right, right again,' and so on till we actually stopped at my billet.

Pat and Freddie were standing in the hallway and laughed when they saw me coming: 'Boy oh boy, is that your charming Gertrud?' But I told them: 'Don't laugh, fellows, help me, I've just fished this kid here out of the Rhine.' They helped me 'carry him upstairs to our room, Pat's and my room, and I told Freddie: 'Make us some coffee.' Then I threw him down on the bed, pulled off his wet things, and rubbed him for a long time with my towel. God, how skinny the kid was, how terribly skinny . . . he looked like . . . like, hell, like a long, limp, white noodle.

'Pat,' I said, for Pat was standing there watching me, 'you go on rubbing, I have to get out of these wet things.' I was as

139

wet as a drowned rat, too, and scared to death of getting the flu. Then Pat handed me the towel, for the lanky kid on the bed was now red all over like a baby, and he smiled again . . . and Pat felt his pulse and said: 'Okay, Johnny, he's going to be all right, I guess.'

The boys were damn good about it; Freddie brought us some coffee, and Pat scrounged some underwear for the kid, who lay on the bed drinking coffee and smiling, and Pat and I sat on the chairs, and Freddie went off, I guess he went off to the girls again.

Jesus, I thought, what a scramble, but it turned out okay, thank God!

Pat stuck a cigarette between the kid's lips, and you should've seen how he smoked! These Germans, I thought, they all smoke like crazy, they suck on those things as if they contained life itself, their faces go all queer. And then I remembered that my jacket was still lying down there by the water, with the photo, and my cap too, but shit, I thought, why would I still need that photo . . .

It was real peaceful and quiet, and the kid was happily chewing away, for Pat had given him some more bread and a can of corned beef and kept refilling his mug with coffee.

'Pat,' I said after a while as I lit up too. 'Pat, d'you suppose it's all right to ask him why he tried to drown himself?'

'Sure,' Pat replied, and asked him.

The lad gave us a wild look and said something to me, and I looked at Pat and Pat shrugged his shoulders. 'He's saying something about food, but there's one word I can't understand, I just don't get it . . .'

'What word?' I asked.

'*Marken*,' Pat said.

'*Marken*?' I asked the boy.

He nodded and said another word, and Pat said: 'He's lost them – those things, those *Marken* . . .'

'What's that, *Marken*?' I asked Pat. But Pat didn't know.

'*Marken*,' I said to the boy. '*Was ist das*?' – that being one phrase I could say properly in German, and I could say *Liebe* too, that's all. That goddamn broad had taught me . . .

The boy looked baffled; then with his thin fingers he drew a funny kind of square on the top of the bedside table and said: '*Papier*.'

I can understand *Papier* too, and I thought I knew now what he was trying to say.

'Ah,' I said, 'pass, you've lost your pass!'

He shook his head: '*Marken*.'

'Damn it all, Pat,' I said, 'this *Marken* is driving me nuts. It must be something pretty special to make him want to drown himself.'

Pat refilled our mugs, but that damned *Marken* kept nagging at me. My God, hadn't I seen that youngster standing up there, not moving, not making a sound, in the gap of the ruined bridge, and Splash! goddammit?

'Pat,' I said, 'look it up, you've got a dictionary.'

'Sure,' said Pat, jumping up and bringing the dictionary from his locker.

Meanwhile I nodded at the boy and gave him another cigarette, he'd eaten the whole can of corned beef and all the bread, and the coffee must've done him a power of good. And Jesus, the way these guys smoke, it's crazy, they smoke the way we sometimes used to smoke in the war when things got tough. They always smoke as if it was war-time, these Germans.

'Here we are!' Pat cried. 'Got it!', and he jumped up, took a letter out of his locker, and showed the kid the stamp on it, but the boy just shook his head and even smiled a bit.

'*Nee,*' he said, and he repeated that crazy word that had made him try and drown himself, and I'd never heard it.

'Hold it,' Pat said, 'I've got it, it's a word that means "ration cards",' and he quickly turned over the pages of his dictionary.

'Still hungry?' I gestured to the kid. But he shook his head and poured himself another cup of coffee. Jesus, the way they can put away coffee, by the bucket, I thought . . .

'Damn it all,' Pat cried, 'these dictionaries, these crappy dictionaries, these goddamn fucking dictionaries – a kid like that tries to drown himself for some reason or other, and you can't even find it in the dictionary.'

'Look,' I said to the boy, in English of course, 'just tell us what it is, take your time, we're all human, we must be able to understand each other. Tell him, tell Pat,' and I pointed to Pat, 'just tell this guy.' And Pat laughed, but he listened very carefully and the boy told him slowly, very slowly, the poor kid was all embarrassed, taking his time about it, and I understood some of it, and Pat's expression turned very serious.

'I'll be damned!' Pat exclaimed. 'How can we be so dumb! They get their food on ration cards, right? They have ration cards, get it? Goddammit, we never thought of it, and that's what he's lost, and that's why he jumped into the Rhine.'

'I'll be damned,' I muttered. 'A kid like that jumps into the river, and we don't know why, can't imagine . . .'

We should at least be able to imagine it, I thought, at the very least, even if we can't actually experience it, we should at least be able to imagine it . . .

'Pat,' I said, 'if he's lost them, they'll have to give him

some new ones. It's just paper, and they can print them, they simply have to give him some new paper – it's not money, after all. It can happen to anyone, you know, losing them, surely there must be plenty of that printed stuff around . . .'

'Balls,' Pat replied, 'they'll never do it. Because there's some people who just *say* they've lost them, and they sell them or eat twice as much, and the authorities get fed up. Christ, it's like in the war, when you've lost your rifle and suddenly there's a guy coming at you, and you simply can't shoot because you haven't got a rifle. It's just a goddamn war they're carrying on with their paper, that's what it is.'

Okay, I thought, but that's terrible, then these folks end up having nothing to eat, nothing, nothing at all, and there's not a thing to be done about it, and that's why he ran like a maniac and threw himself into the Rhine . . .

'Yes,' Pat said, as if answering my thoughts, 'and he's lost them all, the whole lot, for – I believe it's six people, and some other cards too, I just don't get what he means – for a whole month . . .'

Jesus, I thought, what are they going to do if that's how it is! They can't do a thing, that kid goes and loses all the ration cards, and I thought to myself I'd drown myself too if I was him. But I still couldn't imagine it . . . no, I guess nobody can imagine it.

I stood up, went over to my locker and got two packs of cigarettes for the kid but then I really had a shock, the way he looked at me. He sure gave me a weird look, he's going to go out of his mind on us, I thought, clear out of his mind, that's the kind of face the kid was making.

'Pat,' I shouted – yes, I guess I shouted. 'Do me a favour and take that boy away, take him away,' I shouted. 'I can't stand it, that face, those grateful eyes, all for two packs of

143

cigarettes, I can't stand it – I tell you, it's as if I'd given him the whole world. Pat,' I shouted, 'take him away, and make him a parcel of everything we've got here, pack it all up and give it to him!'

Jesus, was I glad when Pat left with the kid. Pat'll make him a nice big parcel, I thought; and there you sat beside the dirty grey water, chatting a bit with the river all because of some skinny girl's face and thinking: throw yourself in, throw yourself in, let yourself be carried all the way to . . . ha, Holland, for Christ's sake! But that child threw himself in, splash! threw himself in because of a few scraps of paper that were worth maybe less than a dollar.

The Green Silk Shirt

I did exactly as I had been told: without knocking I pushed open the door and walked in. But then it was a shock suddenly to find myself confronting a tall, stout woman whose face had something strange about it, a fantastic complexion: it was healthy, it positively shone with health, calm and confident.

The expression in her eyes was cold; she was standing at the table cleaning vegetables. Beside her was a plate with the remains of a pancake which a big fat cat was sniffing at. The room was cramped and low-ceilinged, the air stale and greasy. A sharp, choking bitterness caught at my throat while my shy gaze roamed restlessly between pancake, cat and the woman's healthy face.

'What d'you want?' she asked without looking up.

With trembling hands I undid the clasp of my briefcase, hitting my head against the low doorframe; finally I brought the object to light: a shirt.

'A shirt,' I said huskily, 'I thought . . . perhaps . . . a shirt.'

'My husband has enough shirts for ten years!' But then she raised her eyes as if by chance, and her gaze fastened on the soft, rustling, green shirt. When I saw an ungovernable craving flare up in her eyes, I was sure the battle was won. Without wiping her fingers, she grabbed the shirt, holding it up by the shoulders; she turned it round, examined every seam, then muttered something indistinguishable. Impatient and anxious, I watched her go back to her cabbage, cross to the stove, and lift the lid of a sizzling saucepan. The aroma of hot, good-quality fat spread through the room.

145

Meanwhile the cat had been sniffing at the pancake, apparently not finding it good or fresh enough. With a lazy, graceful leap, the cat jumped onto the chair, from the chair onto the floor, and slipped past me through the door.

The fat bubbled, and I thought I could hear the crackling bits of bacon hopping about under the saucepan lid, for by this time some ancient memory had told me that it was bacon, bacon in that saucepan. The woman went on scrubbing her cabbage. Somewhere outside a cow was lowing softly, a cart creaked, and still I stood there at the door while my shirt dangled from a dirty chairback, my beloved, soft, green silk shirt, for whose softness I had been longing for seven years . . .

I felt as if I were standing on a red-hot grill while the silence oppressed me unutterably. By now the pancake was covered by a black cloud of sluggish flies: hunger and revulsion, a dreadful revulsion, combined in an acrid bitterness that closed my throat; I began to sweat.

At last I reached out hesitantly for the shirt. 'You,' I said, my voice even huskier than before, 'you . . . don't want it?'

'What d'you want for it?' she asked coldly, without looking up. Her quick, deft fingers had finished cleaning the cabbage; she placed the leaves in a colander, ran water over them, stirred them all under the water, then again lifted the lid of the saucepan where the bacon was sizzling. She slid the leaves into the saucepan, and the delicious hiss again revived old memories: memories of a time that might have lain a thousand years in the past, yet I am only twenty-eight . . .

'Well, what d'you want for it?' she asked somewhat impatiently.

But I'm no good at bargaining, no, although I have visited every black market between Cap Gris Nez and Krasnodar.

146

I stammered: 'Bacon . . . bread . . . maybe some flour, I thought . . .'

Now for the first time she raised her cold blue eyes and looked at me coolly, and at that moment I knew I was done for . . . never, never again in this life would I know the taste of bacon, bacon would forever remain no more than a wave of painful aromatic memory. Nothing mattered any more, her gaze had struck me, transfixed me, and now my whole self was draining out . . .

She laughed. 'Shirts!' she cried scornfully. 'I can have shirts for a few bread ration coupons.'

I snatched the shirt from the chair, knotted it round the neck of this virago and strung her up like a drowned cat on the nail beneath the big crucifix that hung black and threatening on the yellow wall above her face . . . but I did this only in my imagination. In reality I grabbed my shirt, bundled it up, and stuffed it back into the briefcase, then turned to the door.

The cat was crouching in the hallway over a saucer of milk, greedily lapping it up. As I passed, it lifted its head and nodded as if wanting to acknowledge and comfort me, and in its green, veiled eyes there was something human, something unutterably human . . .

But because I had been advised to be patient, too, I felt obliged to try again. If only to escape the oppressive brilliance of the sky, I made my way under crippled apple trees, among cowpats and busily pecking chickens, towards a somewhat larger farmhouse situated to one side under the solid shade of some ancient linden trees. The bitterness must have blurred my vision, for it was only at the last moment that I noticed a brawny young farm lad sitting on a bench in front of the house and calling out endearments to two grazing horses. When he saw me he laughed, and called through an open window into the house: 'Number eighteen's coming, Ma!' Then he slapped his thigh with glee and began to fill a pipe; his laughter was answered indoors by a throaty chuckle, and the shiny, crimson face of a woman appeared for a second in the window like a dripping pancake. I turned on my heel and ran like a madman, my briefcase tucked tightly under my arm. I didn't slow up until I reached the village street again and walked down the hill that I had climbed half an hour earlier.

I breathed a sigh of relief when I saw the friendly, grey snake of the highway below me, bordered with gentle trees. My pulse slowed down, the bitterness subsided, while I rested at the crossing where the cobbled, neglected, fetid village street emerged into the freedom of the highway.

I was dripping with sweat.

Suddenly I smiled, lit my pipe, pulled off my old, sticky, soiled shirt, and slipped into the cool, soft silk; it flowed gently down my body and right through me, and all my bitterness melted away, all of it, to a mere nothing; and as I walked back along the highway towards the railway station I felt welling up inside me a yearning for the poor, abject face of the city, behind whose contorted features I had so often seen the humanity bred by misery.

The Waiting-Room

At first when I woke up I couldn't believe it – no, it couldn't
be true. Once more I stuck my hand out from under the
blanket and took it back again. Was I still dreaming? It
couldn't be true; could the cold really have broken overnight? It was warm . . . and mild; but oh, was I suspicious! I
don't know whether you were also born in 1917 – we are a
very suspicious lot, the survivors of that generation, as rare
as cigarettes among so-called honest folk. Well, in the end I
had to trust my senses: I got up. Yes, it really was mild, the
sunshine was warm and gentle, the windows were entirely
free of ice . . . they shimmered moistly, like the eyes of
young girls who still believe in love.

My heart felt so light while I was dressing – what a relief
that the cruel, murderous cold had broken. I looked out of
the window: surely people were striding out more freely
and happily, although the street was wet, but with a benign
wetness, and from between grey clouds shone a moist
sun . . . and yes, I could almost believe that the trees were
turning green! What arrant nonsense, in the middle of
January. But you see how little one can trust one's senses
and how right I was to be suspicious; oh, careful, careful!
You will find it ridiculous, but after walking only a few
hundred yards I felt myself sweating . . . I really was. You
will think: 1917, born during one war and cracked up during
another . . . No, no, it's really true, I was sweating . . .

And I felt so light, the mild air and the sun and the
dreamlike certainty that the cold seemed really to have
broken made me reckless; at the corner I bought a good
cigarette with almost the last of my money, pumped it

voluptuously through my lungs, and blew the thin, grey smoke into the springlike air. I responded with a regretful smile to a pretty, red-haired girl who offered me bread-ration coupons and the next moment I had jumped onto a tram passing at full speed. Wasn't there, in spite of all the misery, a gleam of relief in people's eyes that the cruel cold had been conquered by a 'warm air front'?

Didn't the sweet, tender air vibrate with sighs of relief? I even found a valid tram ticket in the depths of my coat lining, which meant that I could keep the fifty-pfennig piece intact in my pocket.

I smoked the entire cigarette without pinching it out. That hadn't happened for a long time – how reckless! I calculated in a kind of daze: since April 1945 . . . that meant for almost two years, since my first days as a prisoner of war, I hadn't smoked an entire cigarette without pinching it out. Was some fundamental change taking place in me? I spat the butt, which was almost burning my lips, out into the street. The conductress called out cheerfully: 'Main station!' I got off deep in thought . . .

What bliss, to submerge oneself in the bustle of the huge waiting-room! You will say, or at least think: how can a man who was a soldier for many years, who has had to wait to the point of stupefaction for so many trains in all the waiting-rooms of Europe – how can a man like that enjoy sitting in a waiting-room? Oh, you don't understand. In this swarm of harried, weighed-down fellow creatures who, in the aftermath of war, are travelling – must travel – to somewhere from somewhere – in the midst of this bustle I pursue the secrets of solitude, of that blissful solitude which I was never allowed to find . . . Here I can be truly alone, truly, truly alone and dream, dream to my heart's content. Silence is not for us . . . silence scares us; with cruel fingers silence rips off the frail blanket of stoicism that we have spread over our memories and thrusts straight into the teeming, bloodied darkness of our brief, pain-fraught life. Silence . . . silence is like a great snow-white screen onto which we project the joyless film of our lives. Silence can offer us no rest . . .

But here, in this impersonal hum, the ebb and flow of outlandish images, in the midst of sounds I do not hear, of apparitions I do not see . . . here there is a kind of peace, that's right, some kind of peace: here I can abandon myself to my dreams.

You will find this very foolish; but I have meanwhile discovered that there is nothing more pleasant than foolishness. Unfortunately we were never given enough time to be foolish . . . that was the trouble. We were too young when the horror broke over us, and now we are too old to 'learn'. Or would you care to tell me what I am supposed to learn? With that mild, warm air, hadn't hope reawakened in those grey, pathetic faces of the homeless?

I idly jingled my fifty-pfennig piece against a bunch of safety pins I carried in my pocket, a habit I had picked up in the army – I always have to carry some safety pins in case buttons are ripped off or fabric gets torn; a cheap little quirk, you must admit, not an expensive indulgence.

I drank my beer straight down; today the insipid stuff tasted marvellous – I was really thirsty; but what had happened to my appetite? I sat down on a chair that had just been vacated and wondered about my appetite, which seemed to have vanished with the cold . . . or had the cigarette absorbed it? I was profoundly shocked; where was my hunger, that faithful companion of so many years, that many-headed creature, often searing and vicious, sometimes just gently growling or amiably prompting: that mysterious monster that was second nature to me, fluctuating between wolfish greed and pitiful pleading?

One day, by the grace of God, I shall write a poem, a poem about my hunger. I became very uneasy.

Not only because of my hunger, not only because of this unexpected spring, not only because of my faraway, phantom beloved, perhaps unborn, or perished in the ghastly embrace of the war, for whom I sometimes waited here with a quaking heart . . . no, no, I was also here for a purely practical reason. I was waiting for Edi. Edi was to tell me whether the deal would come off; if so, I would be the richer by three hundred marks – if not, well, I wouldn't be. But if it did come off I could buy a violin, which I craved . . . it would make me happy, even happier, even freer . . . oh, a violin! I love music almost more than I do that faraway, phantom beloved, who, I often believe, will appear any moment in the door of the waiting-room, so that I look tensely and with a trembling heart in that direction . . . breathless and intoxicated by the thought that she has now become flesh and blood and will walk towards me with a smile.

So I was waiting for Edi. You may sometimes have wondered what people in waiting-rooms are waiting for! You probably believe that they are all waiting for arriving and departing trains. If you only knew the kind of things a person can wait for. One can wait for anything that exists between Nothing and God. Yes, there are even people waiting for Nothing.

My hair is now considerably thinner; illnesses, usually found only among the aged, plague me according to the season; and if I – please don't be alarmed! – take off my shirt, you can see some scars that might affect you like a painting by Goya; and the scars you could look at if I . . . but since you are a lady I will say no more. You won't believe that I finished school ten years ago, by the skin of my teeth incidentally, and that during those ten years I have never been out of uniform, except for the last five months, since my return from P.O.W. camp – and I have never hated anything in my life so totally and profoundly as that uniform! I didn't know what occupation to enter on my release papers. High-school student? High-school graduate? Oh, if only I could have said, with a clear conscience: labourer. But with thinning hair and at almost thirty . . . high-school graduate? It didn't seem funny to me – at that moment my eyes were opened . . .

It was the biggest mistake of my life to listen, against my better judgment, to the advice of so-called sensible older people who told me to 'volunteer': because it was inevitable, 'then you'll have it over with!' and so on. And the same people give me all kinds of advice today: learn a trade, go to university. Perhaps you will understand that today I am very suspicious of these so-called sensible older people who, after all – I should have thought of that! – are also the voters of those earlier days.

Waiting-room! By the grace of God I may one day write a wonderful poem about you. Not a sonnet. Some formless, ardent, passionate creation, as irrational as love . . . O waiting-room, thou art the wellspring of my wisdom, thou art my oasis . . . and I have found many a decent cigarette butt in thy depths when my heart was heavy.

I find the relative freedom of a civilian to be extremely pleasant and amusing; it is a glorious thing to be truly free, as free as a person can be without money. With money, of course, this freedom would have an even more golden face.

Don't talk to me about careers! I'll get by . . . tramp, you think, gypsy? So what? Do you find that very anti-social? So what? . . . I won't go under that easily.

Even in the waiting-room the air was – yes, lighter, I'd say. Hadn't the burden of those terrible hours of waiting been lightened for the travellers now that the icy cold had disappeared overnight as if by magic? And yet there was this waiting, waiting . . .

There are even some people who await something – note the difference between waiting and awaiting. Waiting is the condition of a certain impatient hopelessness; awaiting is an expectant certainty: slack sails are filled with the intoxicating breath of hope.

But Edi didn't turn up. I became impatient, restless. Oh, if only I hadn't involved myself in this deal! Time and again I regretted it, and time and again I fell for it; you sell all your freedom when you begin to make deals. Involuntarily, you think of some stupid 'compensation', as they call it . . . it bores its way, deeper and deeper, gnawing like a worm at the precious peace of dreams and freedom. Always that net you have to slip through. I made up my mind never to get involved in such things again. Why not simply take up begging? How wonderful to be able to rattle off some phrase or other that would yield a modicum of bread and cash.

Of course Edi didn't turn up. Not that he is unreliable: I know him well – we spent many a dark Russian night together in cold and heat, in the dark womb of the earth which is the infantry's element. Edi is quite a smart fellow, although he has been laughing at me for as long as we've known each other, and although he is just a shade too dressy for my taste. But he's loyal. He found me a place when I returned from P.O.W. camp, and he kept my head above water for those first few weeks. And he is reliable. If he doesn't turn up, there must be some good reason . . .

perhaps they had caught him – who knows? – he's probably involved in all sorts of murky deals I know nothing about; his hands often tremble so strangely, he seems so jittery. And how calm he always used to be! Nothing could faze him or frighten him. But this strange peace in which we children of the war find ourselves has utterly corrupted Edi; he is sinking, I can feel it; he's gradually going under . . . the temptation to become unscrupulous is so great that scarcely anyone can resist it. Oh, Edi . . . I shall tell him, in a calm and friendly manner, that I won't make any more deals with him, not even the so-called legitimate ones.

Ah, my beloved . . . my faraway, faraway darling dove . . . if only you were here! Once again I plunged into that beautiful daydream, I cast everything away and went towards her . . . that faraway, nameless one, the only one . . . towards her, my only true home about whom, by the grace of God, I will some day write one last poem.

Suddenly I felt a rough punch on my right arm and I turned round, startled and annoyed. I looked into the face of an elderly woman who had apparently prodded me on purpose: I awoke to so-called reality, and the 'true' face of the waiting-room loomed before me: grimy, musty . . . wretched, ugly . . . worn-down, worn-out figures, loitering, squatting on bundles that looked as if they couldn't possibly contain objects worth keeping. But the old woman plucked impatiently at my sleeve. 'Hey . . . young man!' she said. I looked at her squarely; she was sitting on a chair beside me. Grey hair, a coarse, plain face . . . a farmer's wife, I thought. A grey-blue kerchief, a wrinkled face, swollen, work-worn hands. I looked up at her expectantly. 'Yes?'

She seemed to hesitate a moment, then pointed to the brown hat lying on my right knee: 'Wouldn't you like to trade it? I could use it, for my son!'

155

I was not surprised. When you spend half a day sitting around in waiting-rooms, you get to know the secrets of our so-called modern economy, based on the secret cigarette currency and carried on in the form of barter. I laughed.

'No, I need it myself – it's about the only thing I possess, and after all it's still January.'

The old woman shook her head with an exasperating calm. 'January!' she said scornfully. 'Can't you see that spring has come?' She pointed to the ceiling of the waiting-room as if spring were to be seen there in the flesh.

I looked up involuntarily; the woman had turned away and was digging into some piece of luggage lying half under her chair; in doing so she bumped a youth who was sleeping with his elbows on the table; he opened his eyes in annoyance, swore under his breath, then laid his head down on the table. A young girl sitting opposite me and reading a book glanced up; with a frown she looked at the woman and me and went on reading. The old woman had finally dug out what she was looking for, and her coarse fists placed a big round loaf of bread, brown bread, between us on the table.

'I'd give you that for it,' she said stolidly. I have no doubt the look I gave the bread sealed the fate of my hat. I'm no good at bargaining. I know – I should have pretended to be stand-offish, should have ignored the bread, but I'm no good at bargaining, as I told you before. And besides – at the sight of the crusty brown bread my hunger was back again. In less than no time there it suddenly was beside me, this time wagging its tail and barking with pleasure, like a puppy whimpering expectantly as it sniffs at the house-wife's apron; with one astonishing bound it had come back from some distant place where it had gone off for a wàlk. All that was no doubt to be read in my eyes. The woman knew

156

even before I did that she would get the hat . . . oh, that farmer's wife could write a psychology of hunger. How many hungry eyes have hung around her front door!

But I resisted. 'No, no . . .' I said fervently, and involuntarily grabbed my hat as if to protect it. 'No – for a loaf of bread?' My eyes flickered between the bread, my hat, and the woman's cold face. 'No,' I repeated, trying to give my voice firmness. 'Not for a loaf of bread!' The woman seemed somewhat surprised. 'Aren't you hungry, then?' What an infamous way to try and snatch my hat from me! For a split second I wondered whether I shouldn't grab the loaf, put on my hat, and make a run for it. But then I would never again be able to enter that waiting-room in a calm frame of mind.

I shook my head vehemently. The woman gave a little smile, a bit more lenient, it seemed to me; then without a word she leaned down and fished out a second loaf from the depths under her chair. 'Well?' she asked triumphantly. The light of victory was plain to see in her eyes. The thought that I had only to say the one little word 'yes' to gain possession of two fragrant loaves of bread intoxicated me. But had the Devil in the shape of a barterer's soul taken possession of me? 'You must . . . give me some . . . money, too,' I stammered, blushing. 'You . . . I'm unemployed . . .' The woman suddenly looked quite angry. 'Unemployed?' she repeated, dragging out the word incredulously.

I merely nodded, blushing ever more deeply, for the girl opposite me had once again looked up disapprovingly. 'Twenty marks,' I said bravely, staking everything on one card, and as if the Devil were really driving me I playfully spun my nice brown hat on one finger . . . for all the world like some careless youth. Oh, I knew it was a sort of farewell caress. The woman poked round in an old leather purse, grumpily picked out a few notes, and placed them beside the loaves. 'That's it!' she said sternly. Thus I was unwittingly thrust into the role of the person who is to blame for the deal, and the woman looked at me as if I were the most despicable swindler she had ever laid eyes on. Twelve marks I had counted with bated breath . . . two loaves and twelve marks, what riches! And how quickly I could calculate: four German or three Belgian cigarettes . . . two American ones! I stuffed the notes into my pocket, drew the loaves towards me, and quickly gave the woman my hat. She turned it round and examined it, her expression indicating that it was absolute rubbish, before it disappeared under the chair into that invisible container. I felt as if I were the lowest of criminals. Then my hunger took a wild leap over everything. I broke off a big chunk from one of the loaves and ordered another glass of beer from the waiter as he rushed past.

After my hunger had been fed its chunk, I was quickly alone again. In fact I even forgot that I had money for cigarettes in my pocket. The sweet grey veil of my dreams had been pulled across again. Ah, wasn't this a day when the beloved might arrive? Wasn't she on her way to me with her golden hair and black eyes, and with a smile that knew everything, everything . . . she was coming closer . . . closer and closer! Surely she was hungry! Oh, my beloved must be hungry, but I would not face her empty-handed; no doubt she was cold too, but oh, I would wrap her up in the warmth of this springlike day. If she was suffering fear and pain, my heart was open to her. I would give her my room, my bed, and I would sleep on the hard bare floor.

It was dusk outside and getting cold again; there was an icy draught round my feet and head. I looked desperately for my hat . . . oh, my hat! You won't believe it, but there was no regret in me, only distress . . . no, I did not regret having traded my hat, but it hurt me that it was gone. The cold was cruel, and it was a long way to my room with the bed where I could hide.

How infinitely rich I was in possessing a bed I could crawl into to escape the cruel cold. I would simply stay in bed; nothing and nobody could force me to get up. Mind you, there was silence there. But better to be exposed to silence than to the cold. Believe me, the worst thing is the cold. It crept towards me, across the stone floor and through the ceiling. What a nasty trick, to put on the mild, kindly garment of dusk just to pounce upon me again! I hurried . . . hurried out of the station, waited desperately for a few minutes for the tram, and finally walked home.

It was as if my head were gradually freezing solid, as if it were being showered with invisible ice. I had the horrible feeling that it was shrinking, leaving nothing but a tiny button in which a frantic pain was concentrating. What a fool I was to think that spring was here . . . it was January, bitter, stark January. All I could feel was that grinding pain in my head, but then it spread like some crazy turmoil throughout my skull . . . spreading, shrinking, taking possession of everything. In the end my whole head consisted only of pain and was growing tinier and tinier . . . a glowing, frightful needle-point drilling away at my consciousness, my reason, my whole being.

I believe I was feverish when (I don't know how) I reached home . . . I was feverish, haunted by dreams; my beloved was with me, but she was not smiling: instead tears were streaming from her black eyes.

And corpses were piled up round me like ramparts . . . ragged, mutilated corpses, some fat, some wizened.

When I woke again to so-called reality, I found myself lying in hospital . . .

Several times a day I would see round me those grave faces of the doctors who seemed to know all the secrets of life and death.

I had the dreadful notion that I might have woken up from my dreams wearing a uniform again. What was the difference between this hospital and a field hospital? No, there would be no more fever charts and grey-and-white-striped pyjamas for me. I am sure the urge for freedom made me recover so quickly that the doctors could congratulate themselves. I was well on my way back to health . . .

The day soon came when I could say goodbye to the nurse and shake her hand gratefully. I felt compelled to hurry, hurry, as if my beloved had now, at this very moment, arrived and was standing in the entrance to the big waiting-room. I had to hurry . . . but the nurse called me back. 'Good heavens,' she said, shaking her head, 'you can't go out in this cold without a hat!' And with a smile she handed me a hat, a blue one, nearly new, that fitted me perfectly . . . oh, I have quite a normal head.

Didn't it seem as if Someone were holding a protective hand over my head? Do you understand . . . ?

An Optimistic Story

Numerous requests to write a truly optimistic story gave me the idea of relating the fate of my friend Franz, a story that is true yet at the same time strange and almost too optimistic, with the result that one has a hard time believing it.

One day my friend Franz was fired from his job as a cub reporter on account of inordinate and insurmountable shyness, and he found himself out on the street almost penniless, hungry, and young enough to be desperate – all this on a sunny spring morning. I hope that the people wanting optimistic stories have no objection to a sunny spring morning, but for the time being, on account of his unemployed condition, I am forced to begin the story on a rather gloomy note. Franz was left with only fifty pfennigs. He gave much thought to what he should do with this. His most fundamental wish was for something to eat, for at all hours of the day and night he felt hungry, and his depression over being fired increased his appetite. Experience, however, had taught him that, to the very hungry, an incomplete meal was worse than no meal at all. Merely to stimulate the taste buds without satisfying them meant – as Franz well knew – worse torment than plain ordinary hunger. He toyed with the idea of appeasing his appetite by smoking, by inducing a kind of mild stupor, but then it occurred to him that smoking in his present condition would probably lead only to nausea.

Brooding over his dilemma, therefore, he walked past the displays in the shop windows. In a chemist's window he saw a display of indigestion pills, fifty pfennigs a package; Franz's digestion was in perfect order: he had none to speak of, in fact couldn't have, since these things do require some physical basis, and for many days Franz had been eating minimal quantities which had been totally consumed in his innards. Franz offered the chemist a mental apology, quickened his pace past a butcher's shop and a bakery, found himself, somewhat calmer, outside a greengrocer's, and wondered whether he shouldn't buy ten pounds of potatoes, boil them, and eat them with their skins. Ten pounds of potatoes in their jackets would certainly not give a mere illusion of satisfied hunger: they would actually satisfy it. But to boil potatoes he needed either wood or coal, as well as matches to light the stove; and since no one had yet thought of selling matches singly (here I permit myself to lay my finger on a sore point in the otherwise blessed and sophisticated state of our economy), the purchase of a box of matches would have meant sacrificing two pounds of potatoes, quite apart from the fact that he possessed neither wood nor coal.

There is really no need to list in detail the number of shops Franz walked past while a plan was taking shape in his head to buy a whole loaf of bread and eat it up on the spot; but a loaf costs fifty-eight pfennigs.

Franz remembered that he still had a tram ticket good for three more trips, with a face value of sixty pfennigs and a resale value of at least thirty. With eighty pfennigs he could easily eat his fill and buy two cigarettes. He therefore decided to make a clean break with his shyness and sell the tram ticket. Luckily he had just reached a tram stop. Studying the waiting passengers, he tried to read from their expressions how they would react to his unusual offer. Then he approached a man with a briefcase and a cigar, braced himself, and said: 'Excuse me . . .'

'I beg your pardon?' said the man.

'Here,' said Franz, presenting his tram ticket. 'Unusual circumstances, a temporary embarrassment, oblige me to dispose of this ticket. Could you perhaps . . . would you . . . ?'

'No,' said the man suspiciously, and with such finality that Franz immediately desisted. Blushing, he left the tram stop, crossed the street, and found himself in front of a newspaper kiosk. Here he stopped and started to read without taking anything in. He made vain efforts to tear himself away from the kiosk, and when the woman inside asked him: 'Yes, sir?' he knew he was done for, and with the last vestiges of good sense he named the fattest newspaper he knew, saying huskily and with an unhappy sigh: *'World Echo.'* He handed the fifty-pfennig note into the kiosk and received a forty-page packet of paper and printer's ink.

Aware of having committed one of the greatest follies of his life, he decided to go into the park in order at least to read the newspaper. The sun shone very mildly, and it was spring. He asked a passer-by the time and was told it was ten o'clock.

Seated in the park were pensioners, a few young mothers with children, and some unemployed. Noisy children were fighting over places in the sandbox; dogs were scuffling over bits of discarded greasy paper; the young mothers threatened and called out in the general hubbub. Franz sat down, opened his newspaper with a flourish, and read a bold headline: BRILLIANT POLICE!, followed by: 'Our police must recently have perfected some brilliant investigatory methods. They have succeeded in arresting a butcher for black-market activities. In view of the well-known rectitude of this trade . . .'

With an angry gesture Franz closed the newspaper and got up, and at that moment an idea came to him of such ingenuity that it may be regarded as the turning point towards the

163

optimistic part of our story. He neatly folded the news-paper, suddenly raised his hitherto shy voice, and called out quite loudly: '*World Echo*! World's Last Echo!'

He was surprised at his own courage and went on shouting, amazed that people took so little notice of him; even more amazed when someone asked him: 'How much for the paper?'

Franz replied: 'Fifty pfennigs,' looked into a disappointed face, and now had enough presence of mind to say: 'The latest edition – make it thirty, if you like. Forty pages, an excellent paper . . .'

He accepted the tiny ten-pfennig notes and, puffed up with pride, left the park convinced that everything would turn out all right. After briskly crossing a few streets he hopped onto a moving tram and remained surprisingly cool-headed when the conductor came round asking: 'Any more fares, please?'

After two stops he got out and walked to the station. Here he bought a cigarette for ten pfennigs, threw ten pfennigs into a beggar's hat, and with his last ten pfennigs bought a platform ticket. Smoking cheerfully, he passed through the barrier and fastened his attention on the Arrivals board. On discovering that a train from Frankfurt was due in one minute, he hurried to that platform. A voice over the loudspeaker said, 'Stand back!', and already the train was approaching. And when the train had come to a stop he suddenly had a new idea. Allowing his cigarette to dangle casually from one corner of his mouth, he ran alongside the train shouting: 'Hella! Hella dearest! Hella darling!' al-though he knew nobody of that name. He shouted implor-ingly, desperately, like a hopeless lover, and eventually, having run all the way from the engine to the tail end of the train, he abandoned his shouting and running with an air of deep resignation. He assured himself of a good exit by wending his way, heavy-hearted and defeated, among the parting couples and grumpy porters. He walked back down the stairs and finally spat out the cigarette butt that had been threatening his lower lip.

Like all shy people who suddenly discover their own courage, he had the feeling that the world was his oyster. From the Arrivals board he took in at a glance that the next train wasn't due for twenty minutes, coming from Dortmund. He decided to go into the station buffet.

Franz wrote me all this in great detail. These days he has plenty of leisure: somewhere in a foreign country he is living with an adorable wife in his own villa. But I must condense his story; I have been charged with writing a brief, optimistic story, for people no longer trust long-winded optimism, so I cannot describe the minutest nuances of every single emotional reaction, the way Franz did.

Let us hurry on, then. He entered the station buffet, buttonholed a waiter, and said hastily, like someone whose time is of inestimable value: 'I'm Dr Windheimer. Has Dr Hella Schneekluth been asking for me?' The waiter looked at him sceptically, shook his head, pushed up his glasses, and, disconcerted by the anything-but-shy eyes of my friend, said: 'No, sir, I'm sorry.'

'Terrible,' said Franz, and 'Thanks.' He sighed, groaned, sat down at a table, pulled out his notebook, which contained nothing, put it back in his pocket, pulled it out again and began to draw girls' profiles in it, until he was interrupted by the waiter saying: 'Can I get you anything, sir?'

'No, thanks,' Franz calmly replied, 'not today. I don't feel like anything today.'

The waiter looked at him again over the top of his spectacles and went off with his tray of empty beer glasses. At the next table Franz now spied a peasant woman with a little girl who, with admirable persistence, were eating their way through a basketful of thick sandwiches as if driven by a stubborn, proud, indescribably ennobling sense of duty to fulfil some loathsome task. They had not ordered anything to drink – thrifty folk.

At that moment Franz's hunger announced its presence with such vehemence that he couldn't help laughing, so loudly that everybody turned towards him – the woman, the child (both of them with a chunk of white bread in their half-open mouths), the waiter, and all the rest. Franz looked at a page in his notebook as if he had discovered something outlandishly amusing there. Then he got up, approached the waiter again, and said in a loud voice: 'If anyone should ask for me – Dr Windheimer – I'll be back in ten minutes,' and left.

Outside he studied the Arrivals board again and discovered to his horror that he had overlooked an arrival from Ostend printed in red. He raced over to the platform in question, saw the long, luxurious train standing there, was already opening his mouth, about to call out, when he remembered that he must use a foreign name, and he called out – no, he shouted: 'Mabel! Mabel dearest! Mabel darling,' and the result was what justifies me in describing this story as optimistic: in the very last carriage, in the very last compartment, at the last window before the pessimistically snorting engine, the head of a sweet-looking, fair-haired girl looked out, and she cried: 'Yes!' (in English, of course). Franz stopped in his tracks, looked her in the face, and said: 'Yes, you're the one,' and I must assume that she too, despite his empty pockets, found him to be the right one; for he ended his really disgustingly detailed letter with: 'We understand each other perfectly. Mabel is adorable. Do you need any money?'

I replied by telegram with the one word: 'Yes.'

I'm not a Communist

The bus always stops at the same spot. The driver has to be very careful, the street is narrow, and the bay where the bus has to stop is cramped. Each time there is a jolt that wakes me up. I look to my left out of the window and always see the same sign: LADDERS ANY SIZE – THREE MARKS TWENTY PER RUNG. There is no point in looking at my watch to see the time: it is exactly four minutes to six, and if my watch says six or even later, I know my watch is fast. The bus keeps better time than my watch! I look up and see the sign: LADDERS ANY SIZE – THREE MARKS TWENTY PER RUNG; the sign is above the window of a hardware shop, and in the window among the bottling jars, coffee mills, mangles and china a small, three-rung ladder is displayed. At the present time, there are mostly garden chairs in the window, and garden loungers. On one of these a woman reclines, a life-size woman made of papier mâché or wax – I don't know what kind of stuff they use to make mannequins. The mannequin is wearing sunglasses and reading a novel called *A Holiday from Myself*. I can't make out the name of the author, my eyes aren't good enough for that. I look at the mannequin, and the mannequin depresses me, makes me even more depressed than I already am – I ask myself whether such mannequins really have a right to exist. Mannequins made of wax or papier mâché and reading novels called *A Holiday from Myself*. It is all so depressing – to the left of this shop window is a pile of rubble on which mounds of garbage and ashes lie smouldering in the sun. It depresses me to see the mannequin right next to them.

168

But what interests me most is the ladders. We really should have a ladder. In the cellar we have shelves for our preserves, and the shelves are very high because the cellar is narrow and we have to make the best use of the space. The shelves are poorly made. I nailed them together out of some boards and fastened the whole thing with a piece of thick rope to the gas pipes that run through our cellar. If they were not firmly fastened, I am sure they would collapse under the weight of the jars.

My wife does a lot of bottling. In summer there is a constant smell of freshly boiled cucumbers, cherries, plums and rhubarb. For days on end the smell of hot vinegar permeates our home – it almost makes me ill, but I do see that we need the preserves. The shelves are very high, and on the top shelf are the cherries and peaches we eat on Sundays in winter. On Saturdays my wife always has to climb up there, and she usually stands on an old wooden crate. Last spring my wife fell through a crate like that and had a miscarriage. I wasn't there, of course, and she lay in the cellar bleeding and calling for help until someone found her and took her to hospital.

On Saturday afternoon I went to the hospital and took my wife some flowers: we just looked at each other, and my wife cried – she cried for a long time. It would have been our third, and we had always talked about how we would manage with three children in two rooms. It is bad enough having to live in two rooms with only two children. I know there are worse things – there are people living six or eight to a room. But it is also hard to manage with two children in two rooms on the same floor as three other parties who have no children. That's hard. I don't want to complain – I'm not a Communist, for heaven's sake, but it's really hard.

169

I'm tired when I come home and I'd like to have half an hour's peace and quiet, only half an hour to eat my supper, but just when I get there they're not quiet and then I smack them – and later, when they're in bed, I feel sorry. Then I sometimes stand beside their bed and look at them, and at such moments I am sometimes a Communist . . . Don't tell anyone – it's only for a few moments, you see.

Every evening, when the bus stops, I feel a jolt and look to my left: the suntanned face of the mannequin in the swimsuit is half hidden by the sunglasses, but the title of the book is clearly visible: *A Holiday from Myself*. Maybe one day I'll get off and look for the name of the author. And above the shop window hangs a sign: LADDERS ANY SIZE – THREE MARKS TWENTY PER RUNG. Our ladder would have to have three rungs, that would be nine marks sixty. No matter how much I juggle the figures I can't come up with nine marks sixty. Now it's summer anyway, and it'll be November before my wife begins climbing onto the crate again on Saturdays to bring down a jar of peaches or cherries for Sunday – not till November. So there's plenty of time.

But my wife is expecting again. Don't tell any of our relatives, and please don't tell the people on our floor. There'll be trouble, and I don't want any trouble. All I want is half an hour's peace and quiet a day. The relatives will be angry when they hear that my wife's expecting – and the people on our floor will be even angrier, and I'll start smacking the children again – and then I'll feel sorry again, and at night when they're asleep I'll stand beside their bed and for a few moments be a Communist. It's all so pointless – I'll try not to think about it again till November. I'll look at the mannequin reclining on the lounger

reading a novel called *A Holiday from Myself* – that mannequin right beside the pile of rubble and the mounds of ashes
from which a dirty yellow stream flows into the gutter
whenever it rains.

Contacts

Not long ago my wife met the mother of a young girl who cuts the nails of a cabinet minister's daughter. The toenails. There is now great excitement in our family. Formerly we had no contacts whatever, but now we have contacts, contacts that are not to be underestimated. My wife takes this girl's mother flowers and chocolates. The flowers and the chocolates are accepted with thanks although also with some reserve. Since knowing this woman we have been feverishly wondering what position we should propose for me when we reach the point of meeting the girl herself. So far we have never seen her; she is rarely at home, moves of course only in government circles, and has a charming flat in Bonn: two rooms, kitchen, bath, balcony. But nevertheless there is talk that she will soon be available. I am very curious about her and, needless to say, will behave with due humility, though also with determination. It is my belief that in government circles humble determination is appreciated, and it is said that the only people who stand a chance are those who are convinced of their own ability. I am trying to be convinced of my abilities, and I soon will be. Still, wait and see.

To begin with, our credit has improved since it has become known that we have contacts in government circles. The other day I heard a woman in the street say to another: 'Here comes Mr B, he has contacts with A.' She said it very quietly but so that I should and could hear it, and as I walked past the ladies they smiled sweetly. I nodded condescendingly. Our grocer, who until now had reluctantly allowed us very limited credit and, with a suspicious expression, watched margarine, grey bread and cigarette tobacco disappear into my wife's shopping bag, now smiles when we arrive and offers us delicacies the taste of which we had forgotten: butter, cheese and real coffee. He says: 'Now wouldn't you like some of this magnificent Cheddar?' And when my wife hesitates, he says: 'Do take some!', then lowers his eyes and grins discreetly. My wife takes some. But yesterday my wife heard him whisper to another woman: 'The Bs are related to A!' It's uncanny the way rumours get round. In any event, we eat butter and cheese on our bread – no longer grey bread – and drink real coffee while waiting somewhat tensely for the appearance of the girl who cuts the nails of the cabinet minister's daughter. The toenails. The girl has not turned up yet, and my wife is growing uneasy, although the girl's mother, who meanwhile appears to have developed a fondness for my wife, reassures her and says: 'Just be patient.' But our patience is wearing thin since we have been making ample use of that tacit credit which has recently been granted us.

The daughter whose toenails our young lady cuts is the minister's favourite daughter. She is studying history of art and is said to be extremely talented. I can believe it. I can believe anything, yet I tremble because the young pedicurist from Bonn still hasn't turned up. We look up encyclopedias and all available biological textbooks in order to gather information on the natural growth rate of toenails, and we discover that it is minimal. So this minister's daughter cannot be the only one. Our young pedicurist probably grasps one toe of Bonn society after another in her adorable hands and removes the burden of dead cells that can pose a threat to nylon stockings and ministerial socks.

I hope her scissors don't slip. I tremble at the thought that she might hurt the minister's daughter. Female art historians have terribly sensitive toenails (I once was in love with an art historian and, on throwing myself at her feet, accidentally leaned my elbow on her toes, without dreaming they could be so sensitive; all was over, and since that day I have known how sensitive are the toes of female art historians). The young girl must be careful; the influence of the daughter on the minister and of the pedicurist on the daughter (who is suspected of social ambitions) is said to be extraordinarily great; and the pedicurist's mother had hinted (everything is hinted) that her daughter has already managed to secure a position for a young man of her acquaintance as clerk in the outer office of a departmental head. 'Departmental head' were the magic words for me. The very thing.

Meanwhile the mother of the young lady continues to accept flowers and chocolates with the same kindly smile: we are glad to make this sacrifice on the altar of high society, while we tremble: our credit keeps rising, and people are whispering that I am an illegitimate son of A's.

We have advanced from butter and cheese to pâté and goose-liver sausage; we no longer roll our own but smoke only the better brands. And we are informed: the young lady from Bonn is coming! She actually arrives! She arrives in the car of a secretary of state whose toes she is said to have rid of a whole colony of sinister corns. So be prepared: she is about to appear!

We spent three days in a state of extreme nervousness, and instead of ten-pfennig cigarettes we now smoke fifteen-pfennig cigarettes, since they do a better job of calming our nerves. I shave twice a day, whereas I used to shave twice a week as befits any normal unemployed person. But I have long ceased to be a normal unemployed person. We copy testimonials, over and over again, each one neater and more cogent than the last, type out *curricula vitae* (eighteen copies to be on the safe side), and rush off to have them notarized: a whole stack of paper will supply information on the tremendous capabilities that predestine me for the position of clerk in the outer office of a department head.

Friday and Saturday go by while we consume (on credit, of course) a quarter of a pound of coffee and a package of fifty fifteen-pfennig cigarettes a day. We try to converse in a jargon that might conceivably correspond to government circles. My wife says: 'I'm really so down, dahling,' and I reply: 'Sorry, dahling, must stick it out.' And we actually do stick it out until the following Sunday. Sunday afternoon we are invited for tea with the young lady (a reciprocal gesture for those twelve bouquets and five boxes of chocolates). Her mother has assured us that I would spend at least eight minutes alone with her. Eight minutes. I buy two dozen plump pink carnations – three for each minute: magnificent specimens of carnations, so plump and pink they seem about to burst. They look like the essence of rococo ladies. I also buy a delightful box of chocolates and ask my friend to drive us there in his car. We drive to the house, honk like mad, and my wife, who is pale with excitement, keeps whispering: 'I'm really so down, dahling, so down.'

The young lady looks delightful, slender and self-assured, quite the government pedicurist, yet she is gracious and charming, although a little reserved. She sits enthroned at the head of the table, fussed over by her mother, and I am dismayed to count seven persons at the table: three young scoundrels with their wives and an elderly gentleman who is kind enough audibly to admire my flowers – but our chocolate box is really delightful, it is made of smooth gold cardboard, has a lovely pink pompon on top, and altogether looks more like an exquisite powder box than a box of chocolates: this box, too, is audibly admired by the elderly gentleman (I am deeply grateful to him for this), and during the introductions I notice that the mother says to her daughter: 'Mr B and wife,' then after a pause, with more emphasis: 'Mr B.' The young lady throws me a meaningful glance, nods and smiles, and I can feel myself turning pale: I feel that I am the favourite and now accept the presence of those three young scoundrels and their wives with a smile.

The tea party progresses somewhat stiffly: first we discuss the enormous advances in the chocolate industry since the currency reform, a conversation prompted by a chocolate box that seems to have caught the fancy of the elderly gentleman. I have a dark suspicion that he has been invited to the tea party by the mother for tactical reasons. But for my taste the old fellow is too blatant about it, too undiplomatic, and the other three scoundrels, whose chocolate boxes remain ignored, give a bitter-sweet smile and the tea party progresses stiffly until the young lady takes out a cigarette: a ten-pfennig one, and embarks on some delicate government gossip. We spring to our feet, all five of us, to offer her a light, but she accepts only mine. I can feel my chest swelling and begin to have visions of my office in Bonn: red leather armchairs, cinnamon-coloured curtains, fabulous filing cabinets and, as my superior, a retired colonel who for sheer compassion can hardly see straight . . .

Suddenly the young lady has vanished, and for a while I fail to notice the signals of her mother who is trying to convey to me that I should leave the room, until my wife nudges me and whispers: 'Idiot – out!'

Breathing heavily, I go out of the room. My conversation with the young lady is carried on in a completely down-to-earth, businesslike manner. She receives me in the drawing-room, looks with a sigh at her watch, and I realize that some of the eight minutes have already passed – probably half of them. As a result, my speech, which I cautiously begin with 'Sorry,' turns out to be somewhat confused, but she smiles in spite of it all, accepts my gift of three English pound notes, and finally says: 'Please don't overestimate my influence – I'm willing to try simply because I'm convinced of your abilities. You will receive an answer in about three months.' A glance she casts at her watch tells me that it is time for me to leave. I toy briefly with the notion of kissing her hand, but refrain, whisper my most humble thanks, and stagger out. Three months. Incidentally, she was pretty.

I return to the tea party and on the faces of the three young scoundrels, whose chocolates were almost totally ignored, I discern poisonous envy. Soon there is an impatient honking outside, and the young lady's mother announces that her daughter has been summoned back to Bonn by telegraph in order to relieve the cabinet minister of his calluses; his golf game was to begin at nine tomorrow morning and it was already five o'clock, and with those calluses he would not be able to play. We look out into the street to see the minister's car; it is powerful but not particularly elegant. The young lady leaves the house with a charming little leather case and a briefcase. The tea party breaks up.

When we get home my wife, who has taken careful note of everything, tells me that I was the only one to be alone with 'her'. The question as to what 'she' is like, I answer with: 'Charming, my dear, quite charming.'

I do not tell my wife about the three-month waiting period. Instead I discuss with her what further courtesies we can show 'her'. My idea of offering 'her' three months' salary is rejected by my wife as an appalling lack of good taste. We finally agree on a motor scooter to be delivered to her anonymously but in such a way that she will know who sent it. Surely she would find it practical if she were motorized and would be able to ride from house to house with her charming little leather case. If she succeeds in treating the cabinet minister successfully (the fellow seems to have an advanced case of fallen arches), perhaps my intolerable waiting period of three months will be curtailed. Three months is more than I can manage, our credit is not all that great – I hope that the motor scooter, which I shall buy on instalments, will tip the balance, and that after only one month I will be sitting in those red leather armchairs. For the time being we both – my wife and I – feel completely down, and we sincerely regret that there is no such thing as an eighteen-pfennig cigarette – that would now be the very thing for our nerves . . .

At the Border

At the time, when I declared my desire to join the Customs service, the whole family was indignant. Only Uncle Jochen was sensible: 'Go ahead,' he said, 'go ahead and join it.'

One must make allowances for a certain degree of indignation: I had completed high school, taken a few terms of philosophy, was an ensign first-class in the Reserve – and now merely wished to become a Customs officer.

I have an excellent figure, am healthy and intelligent; moreover, I have always been obedient, so my career was off to a good start. A sense of duty was coupled in me with what I would almost like to call a calm broadmindedness.

By the time I had completed my training period and gone home for a few days' leave, with three shirts, three pairs of underpants, three pairs of socks, a nice uniform and the title 'Customs Probationer', the family's indignation had somewhat subsided. My father unbuttoned a bit and was to be heard saying publicly: 'My son, you know, the one who was an ensign first-class – my son is now with the Customs.'

My first day on duty I guarded the barrier at Bellkerke. It was hot and completely quiet – an afternoon; nothing was happening and, although I was tired and moody, numerous thoughts crossed my mind. After being relieved, I sat down, put those thoughts into some useful order and wrote a short treatise: 'Possible Border Incidents During Border Duty', a completely theoretical essay, I must admit, but one which as a modest tract aroused the attention of my superiors. In addition, the essay led to my promotion (out of turn) to Customs Assistant. This proves that my studies in philosophy had not been altogether in vain. I was transferred to the internal Customs service.

By the time I next went on leave, the family was already completely reconciled. In my free time I pondered on a short treatise for which I had as yet no title. In bold moments I almost considered 'The Frontier of Philosophy' but, while I was still uncertain as to the title, the work progressed well. I submitted it for publication in *The Customs Service News Letter*, where, under the title of 'The Philosophy of the Frontier', it reinforced my reputation as an analytical Customs officer and resulted in my appointment to full clerk.

Meanwhile I expanded my practical experience and planned to add to my essay an appendix entitled 'The Burdens of a Functionary'. I had high hopes of this work: it was to show the complexity of our existence at the border as well as in the internal service, and to demonstrate that a uniform does not impair the free flow of thought. I wear the smart green uniform with pride.

Needless to say there is no dearth of envious colleagues, most of whom come from the raw ranks of the mere practitioners, crude types to whom the beauty of the written word cannot be conveyed. There are actually those among them of whom I know for a fact that they have never yet read the literary supplement of a newspaper. Not without a strong inner hesitation I have meanwhile started on a third essay: 'Safety of the Frontier, or The Frontier of Safety?' Into this essay, in order to stop the mouths of the envious, I intend to weave much practical knowledge: above all, my experience that it is almost always the diplomats and the riffraff who get away with it, and I have found that the riffraff smuggle so diplomatically and the diplomats so riffraffishly that I will take the liberty of closing my essay with the words: Germans, stay at home and make an honest living! Actually I cannot see why – except in wartime! – one should bother to visit countries other than one's own. French morals and English perfidy infiltrate our country, nothing else.

Under the influence of certain intimate occurrences, my appendix, 'The Burdens of a Functionary', became so copious that it almost threatened to turn into a little book of its own. But I persisted and continued my polishing efforts.

My promotion to inspector was made conditional upon demonstration of my practical qualities, and I did not hesitate to report immediately to the front line: I posed as a coffee buyer at a large West German railway station, penetrated the very heart of a gang of which I became a member, and gradually let the current of this gang carry me onward and upward. I slept in extremely dubious dumps, was obliged to consort – in the service of the state – with women as seductive as they were dangerous, drank with thieves, ate with sinners, smoked with criminals and played cards with hardboiled villains. Stubbornly, patiently, I soldiered on, towards the top, and one day – oh bliss of mission accomplished! – I could give the agreed signal: seventeen men, eleven women, were arrested, and among those captured was the head of the gang.

Although the security of commerce was not completely restored, it was now raised to a higher level. I was given special leave; none of the envious now dared to accuse me of inadequate practical experience. When shortly afterwards I submitted my just completed essay, my triumph was complete: I was promoted to chief inspector and am presumably justified in regarding my career as secure. Moral: let no one be prevented from following the career of his choice!

The Surfer

After travelling thirty-six hours the young man arrived dead tired in Cologne; it was a hot Sunday afternoon in summer. The station square was crowded; large posters and decorative banners proclaimed a pharmacists' convention. The young man plodded from hotel to hotel, moving farther and farther away from the station, and finally found accommodation at the edge of the old part of the city. The hotel clerk told him he could share a room with another gentleman who had offered to give up the second bed in his room.

The young man climbed up the hot, narrow stairs carrying his only luggage: a briefcase and a bottle of lemonade he had asked for downstairs. On hearing a grumpy 'Come in,' he opened the door; the first thing he saw was a small white table on which lay many little pieces of paper and a pile of loose, dark-brown tobacco. The room faced the street. The windows were open, the shutters pushed out, and in the wan light the tobacco took on a purplish look. Opposite the door was a mirror; the washbasin had a long, black, yellow-edged crack in it, and in an open wardrobe he first saw only musty darkness but then distinguished a crumpled raincoat and a shabby briefcase from which a leg of some underpants protruded. To the left of the door was an iron bedstead with a white counterpane on which lay a black jacket. He finally made out his roommate lying on the second bed in the shadows of the farthest corner: a stout, unshaven fellow, his blue and white striped shirt arching tautly over his belly. The young man took him for one of the many pharmacists who were filling up all the hotels.

He approached the stout, motionless figure, who from time to time puffed out clouds of smoke, and quietly introduced himself: 'My name's Wenk.' Without looking up or stirring, the man on the bed mumbled something that sounded like 'Welter' and 'That's okay,' and continued to drowse.

Wenk turned on the tap, placed his briefcase on the bed, hung the man's jacket over a chair and his own over the brass knob of the bedpost, and took off his shirt. He washed slowly and thoroughly, cleaned his teeth and shaved. Welter neither moved nor spoke. His only movement consisted of occasionally opening his thick, swollen-looking lips and puffing out clouds of smoke. On either side of the projecting shutters, the smoke rose into the white triangles of sky.

Wenk felt much refreshed after his wash, lit a cigarette, then lay down on his bed and fell asleep. When he awoke, he found the other man had got up and was shaving. The air had cooled off, and a light breeze gently swayed the shutters. Outside the street was still quiet; somewhere in one of the neighbouring houses a girl was practising an étude, appropriately enough for a Sunday afternoon. She played badly, with many wrong notes, and at one place where the young man expected a cluster of semi-quavers she invariably stumbled or stopped.

Welter was standing in front of the mirror, vigorously swishing his foam-tipped shaving brush around on his face. He still had his pipe clenched between his teeth, but it seemed to have gone out. His shirt sleeves were rolled up, and the movements of his hairy, powerful arms were brisk. Wenk got up, relit his cigarette, and stood by the window. The street was empty, grey and quiet; in the house across the street, a slight, deeply tanned man in a singlet was leaning on the window-sill smoking a black cigar. Farther back in the room he saw a woman in a red petticoat powdering under her arms. The girl at the piano was now playing a folk tune, but that too she played badly, although softly and almost shyly.

'I envy you,' Welter said suddenly in a warm, attractive voice, 'being able to sleep in this heat.'

'When you've been travelling for thirty-six hours . . .' said Wenk, turning to Welter, who was just wiping the lather from his razor.

'Pharmacist?' asked Welter.

'No,' laughed the young man, 'I thought you . . .'

'For heaven's sake!' Now Welter was laughing. 'Although I've nothing against pharmacists, in fact I wish I were a pharmacist . . . By the way,' he continued, lighting his pipe, 'I've also been travelling thirty-six hours, yet I couldn't sleep – I wish to heaven I were a pharmacist!'

After so many hints Wenk felt obliged to ask, out of politeness: 'You mean your job's such a terrible one?'

But Welter was busy rinsing the lather from his face and cleaning his brush. Outside in the street it was growing noisier and, leaning out, Wenk saw what seemed to be a victorious football team in yellow jerseys, surrounded by a crowd of fans, pass by below. Across the street the woman was now leaning out beside the man. She was plump and young, and both she and the man looked bored. Welter had finished now; he was just putting on his tie and asked casually: 'Which route did you take?'

'Munich–Hamburg, Hamburg–Cologne.' Wenk had meanwhile removed his jacket from the bedpost.

'Good idea. Let's go for a bite to eat, shall we? I hope I'm not intruding . . .' Welter asked.

The two men spent the whole evening together; they

seemed to take to each other. They sat, drank some wine, strolled along the Rhine, and Wenk even persuaded Welter at one point to have an ice cream sundae. But he did not find out about Welter's occupation until later, after they had returned to the hotel. The wind had subsided, and beyond the shutters there was now a heavy, oppressive heat. They were both lying on their beds smoking. From the street came a mild jumble of voices and the sounds of turned-down radios. For a long time they were silent. Wenk smoked his cigarettes quickly one after another, hastily, greedily, until they almost stuck to his lips; then he would toss them across the room into the wash basin. The glow of Welter's pipe swelled from time to time in the dark, then contracted again, covered by ash.

'And why,' Welter finally said quietly, 'why have you been travelling such a long way?'

Wenk hesitated for a moment, then said: 'I've been following a woman . . .'

'Is she beautiful at least?'

'I think so, yes.'

They fell silent again and continued to smoke. From the hot streets and the scorching pavements, the heat rose in oppressive clouds.

'Ah yes,' Welter sighed. 'You see, I'd say you were twenty-eight years old, fair hair, about six feet tall. What would you do if you had five thousand marks?'

Wenk was silent, but the silence was suddenly different. 'Yes,' Welter sighed again. 'What would you do? The thing is, I'm looking for someone who's about six feet tall, twenty-eight years old, with fair hair. My boss relies on my intuition. "Welter," he said, "go and look for him. We must have him. Your intuition will help you." Oh,' he gave a scornful laugh, 'my own intuition makes me sick. In this heat everything makes me sick. But tell me, what would you do?'

Wenk remained silent for a while. When he began to speak, his voice was subdued, tired, slightly ironic. In the darkness he had flushed and was smiling. From outside still came that gentle, impersonal hum, and Wenk lit another cigarette. He said: 'I think I would do as they do in movies. Become a surfer or some such thing . . . Riviera . . . Florida . . . surfing. D'you know about surfing?' Welter didn't answer. Only the glow of his pipe swelled in the dark and subsided again.

'Just for once, to have no worries for three weeks or three hours,' Wenk continued, 'or three minutes, three seconds, like those rich whores with their johns who go surfing. Can you understand that?'

'Oh yes,' Welter said softly.

Again they were silent for a while as they smoked. Then Welter asked suddenly: 'You wouldn't take the girl along, the one you've been following?'

Wenk burst out laughing. In the dark he groped for his jacket, threw it across to Welter's bed, and said: 'You win, it's been in my breast pocket the whole time – it's all there . . .'

Welter did not stir or make any move to pick up or search the jacket. After a minute he merely asked: 'Do you think you'll be able to sleep?'

'No,' said Wenk.

'Then we might as well get started.'

In Friedenstadt

By the time I reached Friedenstadt, it was too late to phone Sperling. The station was surrounded by darkness, the little square filled with the kind of silence that even in small towns doesn't begin to descend until around eleven. Once again I had miscalculated, just as, while gambling that afternoon, I hadn't won, as I'd expected to, but had lost everything. To look up Sperling at eleven at night would have meant the permanent loss of his favour. That big hunk of a man, almost six foot six, slept at this hour as if pole-axed, while his brutish snoring filled the heavily curtained bedroom.

During the two minutes I stood hesitating on the topmost step outside the station, the few people who had got off the train with me had disappeared. I walked slowly back into the musty, semi-dark hall and looked round for somebody, but there was no one there except the man at the barrier, who seemed to be lost in thought as he stared out at the platform. His shiny cap gave him an air of solidity. I approached him; he raised a peevish face to me.

'Excuse me, sir,' I stammered, 'I find myself in a predicament. I wonder if you . . .'

He interrupted me, coolly waved his ticket punch past my nose, and said in a bored tone of voice: 'You're wasting your time – you can take my word for it. I haven't a penny in my pocket.' The expression in the fellow's eyes was icy.

'But . . .' I tried again.

'You're wasting your time, I tell you. I don't lend money to strangers – even if I had any. Besides . . .'

'The fact is . . .'

'Besides,' he went on imperturbably, pronouncing each syllable like a veritable lead weight, 'besides, even if – and you can take my word for it – even if I was a millionaire, I wouldn't give you anything, because . . .'

'Good heavens . . .'

'. . . because you've cheated me. No, don't go away!' I turned back and watched him take the used tickets out of his pocket and carefully search through them, as if counting the little bits of pasteboard like money.

'Here,' he said, holding up a pale blue object, 'a platform ticket, and it came from you.'

'Sir!'

'And it came from you! You should be grateful I'm not having you arrested, but instead . . . instead you're trying to cadge money from me. Don't go away!' he shouted at me, since I was trying again to sneak off in the dark. 'Do you deny it?' he asked in a cold, insistent voice.

'No,' I said . . .

He put his hand on my shoulder and took off his cap, and now I saw that his face, thank God, wasn't all that brand new.

'Young man,' he said, 'tell me frankly – what do you live on?'

'On life,' I answered.

He looked at me: 'Hm. Can one live on that?'

'Certainly,' I said, 'but it's difficult, there is so little life.'

The man put on his cap again, glanced round, then looked down into the black, empty tunnel leading to the platforms. The entire little station was dead. Then he looked at me again, pulled out his tin of tobacco, and asked: 'Roll or fill?'

'Roll,' I said.

He offered me the open tin and filled his pipe with his broad thumb, while I deftly rolled myself a cigarette.

188

I sat down at his feet on the floor of the little booth where he usually sits, and we smoked in silence while the clock hand over our heads moved quietly on. The soft sound came to me almost like the purring of a cat . . . 'Well,' he said suddenly, 'if you don't mind waiting for the eleven-thirty, you're welcome to sleep at my place. Where are you going anyway?'

'To Sperling.'

'Who's that?'

'A man who sometimes gives me money to buy life.'

'For nothing?'

'No,' I said, 'I sell him a piece of my life, and he prints it in his newspaper.'

'Oh,' he cried, 'he has a newspaper?'

'Yes,' I said.

'In that case,' he said, '. . . in that case,' and he pensively spat out the juice of his pipe, barely missing my head, '. . . in that case . . .'

We were silent again in that semi-dark, musty station hall where the only sound was the gentle, steady purring of the clock hand, until the eleven-thirty arrived. An old woman and a pair of lovers passed through the barrier, then the man closed the iron grille, plucked my sleeve, and helped me up.

By the time we reached his little house, Friedenstadt was enveloped in darkness, and I knew: Sperling's brutish snoring had now reached its climax: it would be roaring through the house, making the windowpanes and the house plants tremble, but I still had a whole night ahead of me . . .